ADVANCE PRAISE FOR *HOLD MY GIRL*

"An unforgettable story about two strong women thrown into an impossible situation. Carr, a compelling storyteller at the top of her game, begins with a narrative that could come straight from the news and effortlessly mixes in aspects of race, culture, class, and mental health to add irresistible tension and complexity. I found myself both moved by the characters and spurred to examine my own assumptions and biases, as the story moves gracefully toward its surprising yet inevitable conclusion."

—Barbara Josselsohn, bestselling author of
The Lilac House and *The Cranberry Inn*

"A compelling and thought-provoking read. In *Hold My Girl*, Charlene Carr dares to ask, 'What if?' when there are no easy answers. This is a page-turner of a story that explores motherhood, vulnerability, and colorism in the age of assisted fertility. Congratulations to Charlene on turning a real-life thought into a fictional scenario to such great effect!"

—Charmaine Wilkerson, bestselling author of *Black Cake*

"In *Hold My Girl*, Carr does a remarkable job exploring an emotionally fraught topic in a way that is both deeply thought-provoking while also relatable. In the vein of Jodi Picoult, she weaves a tale where there is empathy for both sides of the story, forcing the reader to put themselves in the characters' shoes and ask the question: What would I do? A poignant look at motherhood, identity, and what it means to be a family, *Hold My Girl* will linger with you long after you close the pages."

—Kalyn Fogarty, author of *What We Carry*

"A tense, captivating book that will both set your heart racing and wrench it apart."

—Ronali Collings, author of *Love & Other Dramas*

"For fans of Ashley Audrain's *The Push* and Celeste Ng's *Little Fires Everywhere*, this breathtakingly taut story will pin you to your seat. Charlene Carr plumbs the deepest secrets of motherhood with an unflinching eye, while delivering a poignant exploration of how much our hearts can carry. Sure to inspire engrossing book-club discussions, this novel will stay with you long after you read the last word."

—Marissa Stapley, *New York Times* bestselling author of *Lucky*

"*Hold My Girl* deftly explores the tribulations of motherhood through a compelling narrative that portrays both sides of a headline-making controversy about biology, motherhood, and race. Thoughtful, tense, and affecting, Charlene Carr has skillfully crafted a page-turning story with compassion at its center."

—Ashley Audrain, *New York Times* bestselling author of *The Push*

"What would you do if the child you birthed is not biologically yours and the other mother wants her back? *Hold My Girl* poses that very question in this breathtaking gut-wrencher of a page-turner. Charlene Carr deftly crafts this story of motherhood, identity, and family ties with unflinching honesty. With every twist and turn that unfolds, you'll be left emotionally invested in and sympathizing with both Katherine and Tess, two flawed characters as real as the rest of us. This is a story that'll stick with you long after you finish reading."

—Kerry Lonsdale, *Wall Street Journal* bestselling author of *Everything We Keep*

"*Hold My Girl* is a pulsating page-turner of a novel that will forever change how you think about motherhood, biology, and family. I tore through the pages of this gorgeous, gripping story of who gets to be a mother, and how instinct, love, and longing will either break us or transform us. An incredible book!"

—Christy Ann Conlin, author of *Heave,*
Watermark, and *The Speed of Mercy*

"Charlene Carr pulls off an extraordinary emotional tightrope walk with these imperfect characters and the impossible situation they're thrust into. Each fresh twist had me shifting my sympathies until the very end. *Hold My Girl* is a beautiful, unflinching examination of what it means to be a mother."

—Shelby Van Pelt, *New York Times* bestselling
author of *Remarkably Bright Creatures*

"In *Hold My Girl,* Charlene Carr unflinchingly pulls the reader into the broken hearts and spiraling minds of two mothers who are thrust into an unimaginable situation. With poignant insight and—at times—unsettling accuracy, Carr has crafted not only a compelling, intensely propulsive page-turner but a deeply emotional exploration into the very essence of what it means to be a mother. I was spellbound from start to finish."

—Heather Marshall, author of the #1
international bestseller *Looking for Jane*

"*Hold My Girl* is an emotionally complex, absolute triumph of a novel that raises thought-provoking questions about what it means to be a mother, a wife, and a friend. Charlene Carr writes fearlessly and brilliantly from the heart about motherly love, loss, and difficult moral choices. Her characters are so real, you ache for them as they struggle to do the right thing in impossible circumstances. I was riveted from the first page and couldn't stop reading. I needed to know how this beautiful, heart-wrenching book would end. It's an absolute must-read."

—Julianne MacLean, *USA Today* bestselling author of *A Curve in the Road*

"*Hold My Girl* is a deeply resonant story of loss, infertility, and the complexities of motherhood. Filled with the ache of longing familiar to those who have hoped for a child, *Hold My Girl* captures the painful experience of infertility and the lengths many of us go to become mothers. For those who have experienced the loss of a baby or those who have endured the trials of IVF, you will see yourself reflected in both Katherine and Tess. For readers who haven't, you will find renewed compassion and empathy for those in your life who have. I've been waiting for a book like this to land on my nightstand, and I am grateful it finally exists. I couldn't have loved it more."

—Joanne Gallant, author of *A Womb in the Shape of a Heart*

"Charlene Carr's poignant novel, *Hold My Girl*, holds nothing back in the story of two mothers and one daughter. [In] a story that is both every mother's dream and every mother's nightmare, Carr bares the souls of her characters in ways few writers can as she exposes their darkest secrets and desires. An emotional and thought-provoking read I will not soon forget."

—Barbara Conrey, *USA Today* bestselling author of *Nowhere Near Goodbye*

"A tender exploration of secrets, loss, and motherhood, and the lengths the heart will go to protect what it has found."

—Lọlá Ákínmádé Åkerström, international bestselling author of *In Every Mirror She's Black*

ALSO BY CHARLENE CARR

A New Start Series

When Comes the Joy

Where There Is Life

By What We Love

Forever in My Heart

Whispers of Hope

Behind Our Lives Trilogy

Behind Our Lives

What We See

The Stories We Tell

Stand-alones

Beneath the Silence

Before I Knew You: A Novella

HOLD MY GIRL

HOLD MY GIRL

MY

GIRL

A Novel

CHARLENE CARR

sourcebooks
landmark

Copyright © 2023 by Charlene Carr
Cover and internal design © 2023 by Sourcebooks
Cover design © Holly Ovenden
Internal design by Laura Boren/Sourcebooks

Sourcebooks and the colophon are registered trademarks of Sourcebooks.

Published by Sourcebooks Landmark, an imprint of Sourcebooks
P.O. Box 4410, Naperville, Illinois 60567-4410
(630) 961-3900
sourcebooks.com

Cataloging-in-Publication Data is on file with the Library of Congress.

Printed and bound in the United States of America.
MA 10 9 8 7 6 5 4 3 2 1

For Z:
My inspiration.
My daughter.
My love.

This book contains sensitive material relating to infertility, pregnancy loss, and other topics that may be triggering for some readers. Please be kind to yourself as you read. Set the book aside or speak with someone you trust if you need time or help to process your emotions. For a more thorough list of possibly triggering topics, please visit charlenecarr.com/contentwarnings.

1

KATHERINE

S HE COULDN'T THINK ABOUT THE VOICEMAIL. KATHERINE INHALED sharply. The muscles in her neck clenched. She took another deep breath, willing herself to relax. She wouldn't think about it. Not today. Instead, she thought of Patrick. Patrick, who managed to get to work on time, who kept perfect records for his clients, who never forgot a friend's birthday, but could not, no matter how much she emphasized the importance of it, put the keys in the bowl by the front door.

They needed a second set. They'd had a second set, of course, but Patrick had lost it.

Katherine wrenched the couch cushions to the floor and swiped her hand along the crevice. This was exactly why it did matter to vacuum everywhere, despite Patrick and her mother calling it anal. No nasty crumbs or sticky residue were on her hands.

Also, no keys.

Katherine stood, exhaled, and replaced the cushions, pushing them tight so the edges lay flush. She propped her hands on her hips and surveyed the room. This exquisite room in this stunning house Patrick had provided for her.

Mostly provided.

She hadn't worked full-time in over two years, and he'd been fine with it. Better than fine. She hadn't worked at all since Rose was born—almost a year now of putting her interior design business on hold. When she'd brought it up, asked if he thought it was time to start working again, Patrick, with his kind eyes, told her she worked plenty. She took care of him, Rose, the house. It was enough.

So maybe Patrick forgetting to put the keys in a practical place wasn't such a big deal. Maybe she should stop mentally lecturing him, preparing the argument—sharp enough to make an impression, but not so sharp to create an uncomfortable distance between them—for when he came home that night.

But he was making her late, and Katherine Matheson was never late.

"Mama!"

"Just a minute, sweetie."

"Mama!"

Katherine scanned the living room again. Everything was where it should be, as it always was. She walked through to the kitchen. Scanned. Everything here, too, was where it should be…which was Patrick's argument. Everything was always where it should be, so how hard would it be to see the keys if he left them on the counter, or the coffee table, or his dresser? She'd find them.

"Mama!"

Katherine clenched her jaw, fighting to not let frustration get the best of her. She'd told Saadia she'd be at the party fifteen minutes early to help set up, which was five minutes ago. And now, if she wasn't in the car in precisely four minutes, she'd be late for the start, even if she caught every green light. Which meant she was already late, because how likely was that?

Katherine picked up her phone and clicked on Patrick's picture. She paused. If she talked to him, asked where the keys were, he'd ask how her day was going, and what would she say? She'd received a phone call from the fertility clinic. A strange message, "a rather serious issue regarding your IVF procedure," and she hadn't called back.

Telling him would put voice to the fear she'd lived with for almost a year—that Rose wasn't hers. Katherine was light-skinned for a Black woman, even a mixed-race one, but Rose, as a newborn, had been so white she made Patrick's cream-colored skin look tan. Her hair was fine and straight and almost blond. Her eyes were a bluish-green, which was possible. Patrick had blue eyes, and Katherine's aunt on her mother's side had a hint of green.

They'd joked about it in the beginning, Katherine forcing a smile. To her, it had never been a joke.

Katherine closed her eyes, swallowed. The call, whatever the doctor had to say, would be nothing, of course. A formality. Maybe someone's life was about to irrevocably change, but it wouldn't be hers.

"Mamaaaa!"

Katherine spun. A laugh burst out at the sight of her baby on the floor, the little miracle she'd nearly given up hope of having. Rose's sweet chubby legs splayed in front of her, a grin on her face, and the keys held high in her hand, as she shook them like a rattle. "You little scamp!"

Katherine dropped the phone in her bag, then stepped toward her daughter. She scooped Rose and the keys into her arms and smothered the girl with kisses, her stress easing at the sound of Rose's laughter. She wouldn't be early, but if she were lucky, she wouldn't be drastically late.

Katherine pulled into the last spot at Natural Ways Wellness Centre, the site of her first job when she'd branched out on her own, starting KM

Interior Designs. Ten minutes late. It was fine. The five red lights and construction holdup weren't the end of the world.

Still, she'd wanted to be early. Saadia was Katherine's most loyal client. Each time Saadia expanded to another section of the building, growing the center from a two-room fertility-focused naturopathy operation to one that could accommodate a second acupuncturist, an osteopath, two massage therapists, and a pelvic floor physiotherapist, she'd called Katherine for the redesign, and Katherine had come.

Today was a chance for Saadia to celebrate ten years in business, to show the world, and her family, all she'd accomplished. The media would be there. Past and potential clients would be there. Saadia's father, who'd written Saadia off as nothing more than a snake-oil salesman, would be there.

Although her demeanor and outlook on life were a little more New Age than Katherine expected of a serious business person, Saadia Medina was exceptional at her job. Katherine, who not too long ago would have nodded her head along with Mr. Medina's dismissal of a career in holistic health, was now a believer. After charting her basal body temperature, tracking her cervical mucus, multiple IUIs, and two rounds of IVF, with all the accompanying drugs and injections, it wasn't until Katherine finally stopped interacting with Saadia only as her client and became her patient that, on her third round of IVF, she'd gotten pregnant with Rose.

So, for Saadia, Katherine wanted this day to be perfect. She sighed as she turned off the car and unbuckled her seat belt. Even if the day wasn't perfect, *it'd be perfect enough*. Those words were Patrick's, a phrase he hauled out when overwhelm flooded Katherine—fear that something would not go exactly as she'd planned. A phrase Saadia would echo.

Katherine glanced into the rearview mirror, adjusting her curls and checking for any smudges of mascara, then stepped out of the car. She lowered her shoulders and relaxed her jaw. A smile played across her lips as she unfastened Rose's car seat, took in her girl's pink cheeks and bright eyes. Saadia wouldn't be stressed. The most easygoing person Katherine knew wouldn't be worried or annoyed, either. She'd laugh about Patrick forgetting to put the keys in the bowl yet again, place her hand on Katherine's arm, and say, with that calming voice and smile, "Katherine, he's not you."

Katherine pulled Rose into her arms and turned toward the center, determined to have a good time…if only she could stop thinking about that voicemail.

2

TESS

TESS WIPED HER BROW AND STARED AT THE VIALS BEFORE HER, making sure the labels were perfect, checking and double-checking her work. In her first weeks at Enviro Lab, labeling was all she did, with a dozen machines ticking and whirring around her, sweat pouring down her back, desperate to remove the gloves that stuck to her like a second skin, the goggles that made her observe the world as if through a fishbowl.

Now, at least, she had moved up the ranks enough to be a cookbook scientist—or so the higher-ups joked—following "recipes" created by people who knew more, had done better with their lives. Yet still there was the nausea that came from being stuck in this windowless space with its oppressive heat, the constant whir vibrating her bones, the acrid stench of chemicals burning her nostrils. The ache from standing, hour after hour, on hard linoleum. She'd sprung for high-end shoes with amazing support. They helped, but not enough. Tess pressed her hands into the small of her back, arching through the pain, her rigid muscles barely allowing a stretch. Last night's outing made it all the worse. She pushed the pain away, wishing she'd thought to take some acetaminophen, then did a mental assessment of her morning's work. She verified that assessment by one last glance at the protocol. She ensured her workstation was clean and organized, ready to continue where she'd left off at the start of her next shift.

Satisfied, she peeled off her gloves, goggles, and lab coat, then headed to her locker, nervousness flowing through her. She leaned against the wall to take off those high-end, worth-every-penny shoes and slip into her bargain-store sneakers.

"Can't handle the rigor of a full day's work, eh?"

Tess placed an equally cocksure smile on her face, wishing Tim would piss off, grow bored of making her—the one university dropout on the floor—the butt of his jokes. "Yeah, that must be it. Explains why I'm coming back tonight, then working a shift and a half tomorrow." Tess straightened. "When's the last time you worked beyond your cozy eight to four?"

"Don't need to." Tim leaned against the lockers across the room. "You wouldn't, either, if you applied yourself." He grinned. "Come out to dinner. I'll tutor you. Help you get that degree."

Tess slammed her locker closed. "If I wanted the degree, I'd get it." She walked past Tim, avoiding his gaze, wishing it were just that easy, wishing she had the nerve to say what she wanted to—that while she'd heard around the proverbial watercooler that Tim had barely gotten his degree, struggling to maintain Cs and the occasional B throughout his schooling, Tess's GPA, in the full three and half years she'd studied, had never dropped below a 4.0.

Outside, Tess squinted against the sun, resisting the urge to do a pit check, regretting that in her rush she'd forgotten to bring a change of clothes or deodorant at least. She'd gone heavy the previous night: too many drinks, leaving the club at two in the morning with a one-syllable-name man. She'd crawled out of Rob's or Bob's bed at half past three, making it to her apartment in time for two hours of sleep before needing to wake for her shift.

If she had a car, she could race home, freshen up, change into something other than the plain T-shirt and torn jeans she'd worn under her lab clothes. Tess hesitated, debating whether she should head home anyway, skip the center. When she'd received the invite—in the mail, not an Evite— she'd tossed it on the table. An event sure to be filled with oodles of formerly infertile women? No thanks. But then she'd thought of Saadia—her kind eyes, her reassuring voice, how she never made Tess feel crazy or desperate or weak. How when Tess had rushed into the center—without an appointment—her face aglow, excitement coursing through her because her baby had made it past twelve weeks, the only one to make it that long, Saadia had stopped what she was doing, shared Tess's joy, *ooh*ed and *aah*ed over the blurry black-and-white image Tess held in her hand.

So Tess had picked the invite back up. She'd booked the time off work. She'd written to Saadia, telling her she'd come. As sad as it was, Saadia, her acupuncturist, was the closest thing Tess had to a friend, and except for her evening excursions, Tess hadn't done anything social in months.

Besides, she didn't want to miss the babies. The thought of seeing them terrified Tess, but if someone allowed her to hold one, breathe in its perfect scent, feel the air rising and falling within its living lungs, that'd be something. Not enough, but something.

Tess slowed her pace, the better to let the breeze cool her off, make her look half-presentable, even if that meant she'd be a few minutes late. As she approached Natural Ways Wellness Centre, Tess slowed her pace even more. Half a dozen cars were already in the lot, women exiting the vehicles, waving with smiles, balancing car seats and diaper bags and toddlers on their hips.

Tess's phone buzzed. She pulled it from her back pocket to see the screen lit with the word *UNKNOWN*. That word hadn't flashed in over a year; back then, the letters ignited fear or excitement—usually both. Now, though, it would mean a telemarketer or scam caller. She was done with the fertility clinic, which meant they were done with her.

Tess set her phone to silent and slid it back into her pocket. She stood tall, lifted her chin, and opened the door, her eyes searching for Saadia, who stood across the room with three women around her. Her hand was on the shoulder of one of them, an earnest, comforting expression on her face. Tess continued to scan, looking for someone, anyone who would ease this urge to bolt.

These were lovely women, Tess knew. Women who, like her, had been desperate to start a family. From the looks of it—the children weaving through the crowd, the laughter, the round bellies and glistening ring fingers—the majority of them had gotten it: a baby, or babies; a husband who stayed.

Once, Tess had been active in the Facebook group Saadia ran. Once, she had been blinded by hope and possibility. Tess had been wary when Saadia invited her to the group—a place to discuss what fertility diets they were trying, the herbs and supplements they were taking, whether this drug or that had better success rates, and most important, to share their stresses and fears, successes, and losses. It seemed hokey. And it was, a bit. But it had gotten her through. A place where she could talk without shame.

Until her shame was too large to speak of. Until she knew, no matter how she wished it, she could never be one of them. Tess shuffled past the tables and chairs, past women who either didn't recognize her or decided not to, fearful of what to say.

She shouldn't have come. She would say hello to Saadia as soon as she got the chance, then she'd flee.

3

KATHERINE

THE INSTANT KATHERINE STEPPED THROUGH THE DOORS OF THE wellness center, a layer of the weight she'd been carrying slipped off her shoulders. She'd chosen mystic lake gray for the walls, with the slightest hint of green. Large canvases of woods, waterfalls, and icebergs hung strategically, drawing the eye. Plush seats lined the lobby, the fabric dyed a Baltic Sea green, several shades darker than the paint. Katherine had designed every aspect to feel comforting, relaxing, safe. And it was. People lounged in the chairs, chatted in corners, stood around tables laden with food, contentment plastered across their faces.

Seeing Saadia busy with her guests, Katherine scanned the room for Tracey, Saadia's half sister and one of the few genuine mom friends Katherine had. They'd met through one of Saadia's fertility meetups a few months before Katherine started her final IVF protocol. "My sister's been through it," Saadia had said, making the introductions. "Another IVF warrior. You two will align."

They had. One-on-one coffee dates throughout Katherine's pregnancy and half a dozen playdates since Rose was born. Late-night texts and phone calls when Rose had been cluster feeding and Katherine was at her wit's end, in a dazed exhaustion, terrified she was doing something wrong.

With no Tracey in sight, Katherine scanned the room again, this time registering all the familiar faces. In Halifax, a coastal city of more than three hundred thousand, full of families who had been there for generations, it was typical to find someone you knew at any large event, but today was like a reunion. Most of the faces, even ones she'd never seen in person, she recognized from the fertility Facebook group. It was odd, seeing people in person she'd shared such intimacies with through the safety of a screen.

Katherine's phone buzzed, jolting her back to the voicemail, making her wonder if anyone else had received a message about "a serious issue," whether serious could be as devastating as Katherine feared. She slipped it out of her pocket, saw it was Patrick, decided to call back later. She turned to Rose, who crawled to an end table and pulled herself to standing. Pride thrummed through her girl, green eyes sparkling.

A woman smelling of lavender and peanut butter sidled up to Katherine, a twin tugging at each leg. "She's so big." Tiffany grinned, her youngest child in a wrap, sucking hungrily at her breast. "Almost a year now?"

"That's right." Almost a year. *So why now? Why would the clinic call now?*

"These devils will be three next month."

Katherine glanced at the boys. "They must be a handful." She brought her gaze back to Tiffany, hoping to see a hint of the exhaustion Katherine had been fighting for months. But Tiffany seemed more relaxed as a mother than anyone Katherine knew, utterly content, and utterly and unabashedly unconcerned with what anyone thought of her.

Despite barely knowing Tiffany at the time, Katherine had been notable enough to receive an invitation to Tiffany's youngest's birthday party. When Katherine had walked into Tiffany's house, the first mother to arrive, she'd walked into chaos. Tiffany's crew ran up and down the hall and through the rooms like wild animals, climbing the furniture and tumbling over each other. Crumbs littered the floor, dog fur rolled across the laminate like tumbleweed in the breeze, jellied fingerprints spread through the house, reminiscent of ancient cave paintings. And Tiffany hadn't seemed to care.

Even now, Tiffany shrugged. "Mostly they keep to themselves. Not today, apparently"—she laughed—"but mostly. Some days they're so wrapped up in their own lives, they hardly seem to remember I exist."

Katherine smiled and looked at Rose. Perhaps they should have tried for twins. Rose was in no way wrapped up in her own life. At home she clung to Katherine, followed her around, screamed if they were separated too long. Patrick blamed it on Katherine, for being too clingy herself: so afraid of something harming Rose, she'd manufactured an unhealthy attachment.

In those first months after Rose's birth, Katherine let her house fall to shambles, neglecting baseboards, inside the oven, windowsills—everything most people ignored. Things she imagined Tiffany didn't even consider. Once Katherine had risen out of the haze of adjusting to life with a newborn, shell-shocked, with eyes bleary, she'd gone right back to it. The thought of living in a house like Tiffany's made her sweat, made her feel as if she'd be failing everyone, Rose most of all.

Maybe that was the difference—conceiving naturally, as Tiffany had, no need to worry about your legitimacy as a mother. In those long years of trying, in her lowest moments—when Katherine had felt as if she were the only woman going through it—she'd often wondered if she'd been meant to have a child. Her body, it seemed, wasn't made for it. It was only a trick, a miracle of science, that had allowed Rose's existence.

Katherine's throat tightened once again. The threat of moisture tingled behind her eyes. Probably it wasn't the difference of conceiving naturally. Probably it was just Tiffany. And just Katherine. Nothing to do with scientific intervention, with babies conceived in petri dishes or not.

"Oh, there's Joanna!" Tiffany's face became awash with pleasure. "Enjoy yourself." A friendly squeeze of Katherine's arm and Tiffany was off, rubbing Joanna's round and perky belly, leaning in for a one-armed hug over the bump. Katherine pulled her gaze from the two women. It landed on Tess.

Katherine's smile wavered. Her stomach sank. Tess, who should have been here with her own child. Their egg retrievals had been on the same day, but unlike Katherine, Tess hadn't had her embryos frozen due to ovarian hyperstimulation syndrome. She hadn't had swollen ovaries leaking fluid, bloating her abdomen and thighs, the pain tight, terrifying, putting her life at risk. She hadn't had to wait three months for her body to fully heal from the condition, then another two preparing for frozen embryo transfer. So Tess's child would have been older than Rose. Fourteen months by now.

Compassion twisted through Katherine, with a thread of guilt. It always did upon seeing the women who didn't get their happily-ever-after, no simple reason why Katherine and not them had been so lucky.

Tess stood in the corner. Alone. Furtive. Her green eyes, always so piercing, cast to the floor. She looked fragile. Though she was only four years younger than Katherine, the phrase "a wisp of a girl" came to mind, as if the trials of life could blow her right over.

But they hadn't. She was here among all these women, all these babies, with a stomach as flat as could be. She was brave. Katherine crouched to pick up Rose then walked over.

"Tess." Katherine hoped her smile was bright, friendly, without showing pity. It was hard not to feel it—the poor woman looked terrified someone was talking to her. Katherine had suspected the transfer didn't go well when Tess disappeared from the online chats, but Katherine had been so consumed with her own recovery, then her own pregnancy, she'd hardly thought of it. She only knew because Patrick talked to Tess's brother, who'd said she lost the baby.

"Katherine. Hi." Tess tucked a strand of hair behind her ear, her cheeks flushing, looking like she wanted to sink through the floor. She bit her lower lip, then released it, as if someone had told her, or she'd read some-where, that she shouldn't do that.

"You're looking lovely." Katherine gestured to her. "New hairstyle?"

"Oh, uh, yeah." Tess tucked her hair back again, though it hadn't shifted.

Almost two years had passed since they'd run into each other in the waiting room before their egg retrievals. Now, Katherine had her child, here, in her arms, while Tess had lost everything, and all Katherine could think to say was "New hairstyle?"

She could smack herself. She was smarter than this. But what was there to say? It wasn't as if she could ask, her hand on Tess's shoulder, amid all these smiling women, *Why are you here? Why are you putting yourself through this?*

"You too?" Tess looked away. She clasped one hand over her wrist. Her lower lip twitched.

Her too, what? Of course, the hairstyle. Katherine touched a hand to her curls. "Yes. Decided to go natural." She reached out and touched Tess's arm. Tess flinched, but Katherine held it there, waiting for Tess to make eye contact. "I was so sorry to hear about your loss. Patrick, he told me about—"

"Yeah. Um." Tess pushed out a smile. She shrugged, awkward, like a nervous teenager. "Life. Right?"

14

Pulling away from Katherine's touch, Tess gestured toward Rose. "Your daughter is beautiful."

"Thank you." Katherine adjusted Rose on her hip as she cuddled into her, the weight of her girl settling against her shoulder like something always meant to be. Faulty reproductive organs or no, Katherine *was* made for this.

Rose raised her head and smiled, her glance as furtive as the one Tess had worn earlier.

Katherine shifted Rose so she was facing Tess. "Rose, can you say hi?"

Rose's smile flickered, coyness and mischief behind her green eyes.

"This is Mommy's friend. Tess."

"Hi, Rose." Tess's smile beamed, but her eyes pinched. "What a pretty little top you have there. Do you like bunnies?"

Rose nodded, her smile growing.

"Katherine."

Katherine felt a hand on her shoulder and turned to see Mandy, Saadia's assistant. Anxiety contorted her features. "I hate to bother you," said Mandy. "But I don't want to bother Saadia." She gestured to Saadia, standing in a group of women, her arms around one of them, comforting as always. "There's some mix-up with the caterer. He's on the phone, upset, and…well…I know it's not your job, but could you talk to him? He's on hold in the office."

Katherine suppressed a sigh. Saadia had mentioned that Mandy wasn't the most capable hire, but that all people needed a chance. "I have my daughter here. I'm sure you can handle—"

"He's so angry." Mandy pouted her lips.

"I'll take her." Katherine turned to Tess, who looked like she couldn't believe she'd spoken. "It'd be no trouble."

"Perfect." Relief flooded Mandy as her shoulders relaxed comically. "So, you'll come?"

Katherine let out a sound of surrender. Tess put out her arms, and Rose leaned into them without a whimper.

Minutes later, Katherine opened the office door and reentered the party, the satisfaction at diverting a mini catastrophe thrumming through her veins. But where chatting and laughter had filled the space, a tense hush now permeated the air. The guests huddled around the reception desk. Silent. Listening. Katherine crossed the room, a lump in her throat.

Katherine looked at the swiveled screen, the words seeming to come at her in slow motion: "VitaNova Fertility Centre's only comment at this time is that any families involved will be contacted privately for testing. It is unclear how many families were affected or whether this was an isolated incident. The nurse accused of the crime is in police custody…"

The camera panned away from the reporter in front of VitaNova to an image of a woman. Irene. Katherine's nurse, Irene, head down, being led into Halifax Provincial Court.

"What's going on?" Katherine whispered as she sidled over to Tess, accepting Rose back into her arms.

Tess stared at the computer screen, mouth slightly agape, wordless, as the images flickered by.

"There was a switch." Tracey put her hand on Katherine's shoulder. "At the clinic. With the eggs. There was a switch."

$$4$$

TESS

A SWITCH.

The women had pressed in around her, their eyes on the screen, the words that had been their greatest fear clustering them in. The weight of Tess's phone seemed to triple, the pressure of that small object against her backside throbbing as her mind pulsed with the knowledge of that unknown call. And still she couldn't reach for her phone.

Her legs itching to dart, Tess had thrust Rose into Katherine's arms, then weaved her way out of the crowd of shell-shocked women. She stood outside the center's doors, her heart pounding as she shuffled out of the way of a woman with a rounded belly pushing past her. Tess pulled out her phone. Not only a missed call, but a message. She clicked the screen to call her voicemail: "Hello, this is Samantha from VitaNova Fertility Centre. We were hoping you could come in to see Dr. Myers. We've had notice of an issue that needs clearing up. A…" Samantha's voice faltered. It was that hesitation, that squeezing of the throat, that sent a shiver of possibility through Tess. "A rather serious issue regarding your IVF procedure."

Despite the two years that had passed, a part of Tess itched to call

Hyeon-Jun. It was possible a mix-up could have involved him, if it happened with her second or third procedure. But to call now, before she knew anything, would look pathetic, desperate. Tess's hand gravitated toward her abdomen, as it so often did, making her even more conscious of the emptiness there.

She had laid her hand on her belly the same way when her sweet baby girl somersaulted. Kicked. Punched. Declared her life—her will to live. Each move, each jab, no matter how hard, had sent a thrill through Tess. Each flutter had signaled hope.

Then the moves stopped.

When Tess realized it, she wasn't sure how many hours had passed. Four? Five? Few enough that the reasonable part of her mind told her it was nothing but a long nap. She felt stupid, heading to Emergency, certain they'd tell her to go home, have some fruit juice, give the baby a little sugar high, shine a flashlight. But she'd already done all of that, and still nothing. So, as she placed her hand on her belly, she'd whispered to the child within it. *Please*...hoping that small life would hear her...*stay*. Then, sitting in those large comfy chairs at the IWK Health Centre, the cramping started. *No*, Tess had mouthed. But she knew—before the moan erupted from her throat, before the receptionist was at her side calling for help, before the blood pooled on the floor. Her baby. Her sweet baby, who'd swum and twisted and lived those past twenty-one weeks, was gone. Eight eggs. Four fertilized, and this, the one embryo who'd made it to day five—this had been her last chance.

There were doctors and nurses. A gurney, lights, and halls and blood. So much blood. Holding on to blind hope, Tess refused to push until her body forced her, until there was no more pushing. No more anything. When she woke, her baby was gone. So was her uterus.

Standing outside the wellness center, Tess tried not to hope, but hope grew in her the way her babies never had, full and ready, threatening to burst out.

5

KATHERINE

THE AIR IN THE CENTER FELT THICK, AS IF IT WERE PRESSING IN ON them, keeping them motionless. When the news segment ended, they all stood still until, as if someone had flipped a switch, voices filled the space. As phones were pulled out and screens lit up to no missed calls, relieved laughter joined the buzz.

Bile rose in Katherine's throat. Upon first hearing the voicemail, she had jumped to this conclusion: a switch. Something gone awry. The confirmation—after all the days and nights of pushing away the fear—that her daughter was not her daughter. Not in the way people thought mattered most.

Katherine backed away from the screen, the cluster of women spreading like ripples on water. The voices around her lifted, an unintelligible thrum, as Katherine bumped into one woman, then another, her movements heavy, like pushing through mud.

Thanks to the Facebook group, Katherine knew many were free of fear. They'd done IUI or taken drugs to regulate or prompt ovulation. The lucky ones had used Saadia's treatments and lifestyle changes only. But more than half of the "infertility mamas" in the room were VitaNova IVF patients.

Katherine listened, silent, as the thrum thinned out into individual voices.

"There were so few details," said one.

"Like, when did this switch, or switches, happen?"

"How many people were involved? Did anyone hear that? Did they say?"

"No, and they said, 'Will be contacted,' which means maybe they haven't even made the calls yet?"

"Has anyone received a call?"

Those in the clear put their hands on the shoulders of the ones who weren't, assuring them there was nothing to worry about, because surely the clinic would have called anyone before the news was released. Surely they wouldn't let anyone find out like this.

Yet no one had received a call, they said. Katherine hadn't received a call either, or so she said.

Still clutching Rose, Katherine waved her arm, as if brushing off the news.

"Don't worry." A face Katherine should have been able to name but couldn't smiled too sweetly. "Rose has so many of your features. Truly."

Katherine nodded, then turned away, forbidding her lip to tremble. If there was one person in the room who had the greatest reason to fear, Katherine was it, and every single person present knew it, had probably thought it even before today.

Katherine stared at Rose, who looked like Patrick. Only Patrick. Months ago, Katherine had brought it up casually at playgroup, saying it as a joke—"We know she's *his* child, but it's not often the mother has to wonder if the baby she birthed is *hers*"—the way Patrick so often had. The moms assured her it was one hundred percent normal. It's some biological safety net, Tiffany had said with a laugh. Babies looked like their fathers, at least for the first four months, so fathers know the child is theirs.

But those four months were long past, and not much had changed. Rose's eyes had shifted to a green with flecks of amber and gold. Striking, they changed with light and mood. Her skin had darkened. It was darker than Patrick's, but still no one would ever come close to calling it tan. Yet, so said everyone, she had Katherine's smile. Katherine's cheek structure.

Katherine didn't see it.

She had put it out of her mind, as much as she could. An only child with parents who worked too much, she was the girl who'd played for hours with her baby dolls, spent her afternoons in front of the TV watching siblings bicker and laugh, mothers who were home to guide and comfort, make after-school snacks and fully balanced meals. She'd seen the loyalty those televised brothers and sisters had for each other and wanted it, if not for herself, for her own children. She wanted a home full of laughter and energy, family dinners, family game nights, family vacations.

She became the woman who judged potential partners on the likelihood they'd be good fathers, who thought about her future children's names, *ooh*ed and *aah*ed over every baby she saw, eager for her turn. She wasn't about to risk it all by going back to the fertility clinic, asking if it was possible they'd made a mistake, because a child who looked like Rose coming out of a woman who looked like Katherine *was* possible. She'd seen it in families where the mother had given birth with no scientific intervention.

She told herself Rose was hers, her miracle child, that any fears to the contrary were ludicrous. She hoped their three remaining embryos would give her that full house she and Patrick dreamed of, but in case not, in case this was her one shot to get parenthood right and raise a happy child, she would never let herself slack on being the best mother she could be. She would never let herself give in to those fears for more than the briefest of moments.

And she wouldn't today. She stood, saying words of encouragement and dismissal, just as everyone else was, knowing she couldn't be the first to leave. She kept a mental tally as the IVF mothers departed, many within minutes of the segment ending. With each one who left, the tightness to the air dissipated, replaced with a subdued hysteria as a palpable throbbing of excitement filled the space.

Oh, to be so close to such a scandal, everyone seemed to be thinking. What if, moments before, they had been chatting with a mother whose child wasn't hers? What if their child had been playing with one who, for months or years, had been living with the wrong family?

Katherine filled a small plate, forcing each delectable bite of food down her throat. She chatted and joined in the speculation, eyes wide with incredulity while feigning confidence. She listened as women brought up stories they'd read, articles about court cases, families torn apart, devastation.

"Just months ago," said one mother, "a clinic somewhere in the U.S. put two babies from two different mothers into a third woman's womb. That's why I got mine tested." She shook her head as she rubbed her belly. "When this one comes out, she'll be tested too. After reading that, I couldn't sleep without knowing." A shudder. "To unknowingly raise another woman's child…"

At last, when Katherine couldn't hold her smile, when she'd stayed long enough that leaving wouldn't be an admission of fear, she collected her jacket, wished Saadia well, and fled as slowly and confidently as she could.

At home, with Rose napping down the hall, Katherine sat in her living room and pulled out her phone to listen to the voicemail. Three more were there—from various friends and relatives—and several Facebook messages, all asking if she'd heard the news, hoping Katherine was all right, hoping it had nothing to do with her and Rose. Katherine stared, anxiety pushing at her like water pressing to take down a dam. She typed hastily, *Yes, I heard. Oh my goodness! It's awful. Those poor families!* then copied and pasted it to everyone, deciding a text was sufficient for the voice messages too, and if any more messages came in, that's what she'd say.

Then, with trembling hands, she keyed in her voicemail code again, listened to the clinic's message. Samantha's shaking voice, her hesitation, sent a fault line of fear through Katherine: "A rather serious issue regarding your IVF procedure. Please call as soon as you can."

She closed her eyes and pulled the phone from her ear, telling herself she was being dramatic. VitaNova saw hundreds of women a year—maybe thousands—women from all over Atlantic Canada. Dozens could be sitting at home listening to this same message, torturing themselves for no reason, as Katherine was now. Katherine took a long breath. The phone vibrated. Tracey's photo lit the screen. Katherine dismissed the call, not sure if she could say another word without her voice cracking.

Another vibration. Her mother, who wanted a larger role in Katherine's life now that she'd retired and was no longer distracted. Katherine wanted it too, but it was hard fitting Elvira into a space that had been so empty for years. Then Patrick's face appeared. His third call since she'd arrived home. She stared at the screen, her finger hesitating above it. She set the device to silent and slid it away.

6

TESS

TESS LEFT THE PARKING LOT AND TURNED ONTO THE STREET, already heading in the direction of the clinic as she called, knowing before she did there would be no answer, their lines tied up with reporters. Adrenaline coursed through her, propelling her forward.

A rather serious issue. A switch. Which could mean…

Tess could barely formulate the thought. She approached the building that housed the fertility clinic, thinking again of Hyeon-Jun, wishing he were here beside her. Though it wasn't him, exactly, she wished for, but his position—husband, partner, friend. All the things he should have been. Seeing several members of the press already outside, she tried the clinic's line again. Busy. She hesitated before getting close enough that the media might notice her, suspect her destination. If she'd expected them to swarm this quickly, she may not have come. But here she was. Tess strode past them, her gaze on the security guard keeping them at bay.

"Hi." She smiled.

The guard's grim expression softened. "Hey there. An appointment?"

Tess nodded and walked past the reporters, who held out mics, questions flying as she raised a hand to cover her face. Inside the multipurpose building, she walked the halls to VitaNova, pushed through the glass doors, watched as Samantha stood from her spot at reception, knocking her empty thermos to the floor.

"Tess." Samantha walked around the desk, picking up the thermos as she came. "I thought you'd call."

Tess gestured to the ringing phone.

"Never mind. Come with me. Dr. Myers is with a patient, but well… come with me."

Tess walked through the waiting room, past the mothers and hopefuls, past the partners holding their hands. "If you could just tell me—"

"Follow me," said Samantha. "You need a swab."

"A swab?" So they needed her DNA. Tess's pulse quickened.

Samantha glanced back, not slowing her step. "There's a notary in one of the offices downstairs; we'll see if she can come up."

"Please tell me what's going on." Tess upped her pace as she trailed Samantha past rooms she'd spent so much time in, from the pretreatment tests to the daily ultrasounds before her rounds of retrievals, and then to the day she'd first seen Hanna, looking like a gummy bear, bouncing around in that dark world, no longer a distant dream. "The news said there was a switch," said Tess, her insides aching with the loss, "and then your call. My egg, was it transferred into another woman? Is that why?"

"I can't tell you anything." Samantha kept walking.

"Do I have a child out there? Or will I?"

Samantha stopped so abruptly, Tess almost bashed into her. She knocked on the frame of a half-open door.

The woman at the desk, hair disheveled, a phone tucked under her ear as she typed, looked up.

"Theresa Sokolowski is here."

The woman spoke into the phone. "I'll have to call you back… I must. One of the mothers is here… Yes… No… Do what you think is best." She rose from her chair and crossed the room, her smile clenched. "Mrs. Sokolowski." She grasped Tess's hand. "We're so sorry you have to be here, but so glad you've come. Samantha, go find Dr. Myers."

As Tess followed the woman along a corridor she had never ventured down before, Hyeon-Jun surfaced in her thoughts once more. He wouldn't have followed passively, letting them ignore her questions. He took what he wanted, demanded to be heard. She'd first seen him on the benches outside the engineering department at Dalhousie, where she ate her lunches. He assumed she was a student, and she hadn't bothered telling him she'd dropped out almost two years earlier, was only on campus for a short-term temp job, digitizing records. Three days after he'd introduced himself, he told her he was taking her to dinner. Rather than being turned off at the assumption, she said yes, excited at the prospect of a meal out.

A year after the recession, jobs were scarce. Cast out from her parents' protection, Tess struggled to pay her bills, despite downgrading to a North End apartment close to the harbor and known for its rat infestations. She'd thought her family was poor growing up, but it wasn't until she was on her own that she knew struggle.

Hyeon-Jun changed all that, her new, great struggle adjusting to his wealth, to living with a man who—if she was honest with herself—she'd never really loved. It was the not being alone that she'd loved: the protection, the security, the knowledge that bills would be paid and the heat would remain on and she didn't need to worry about any of it.

Instead, she worried about his disappointment after their first loss, and then the second. He told her to stop temping, that maybe it was too much stress, and they didn't need her money anyway. Her job, he said, was to give them the family she wanted just as much as he did. Which had brought them to VitaNova for round after round of fertility treatments.

When they arrived at a small office, the woman seated herself at a desk and gestured to another chair.

"You're testing my DNA?" asked Tess.

"Yes. We'll need your consent first." The woman started to hand Tess a form, then pulled it back. "Sorry, I…" She shook her head. "It's not filled out. Just a minute."

"You're testing my DNA," Tess repeated, trying to keep the wobble out of her voice. "To see if the switch happened with my eggs. And based on how freaked out you are, someone's eggs got switched, didn't they? And a baby was born? Is that—"

"We don't know what happened," said the woman. "That's why we're—"

"But there was a switch," Tess insisted, her voice cracking.

"Alleged," the woman asserted.

"But if there was, if there's a child out there, and that child is mine—"

"Then we need to find out." Tess turned her head at the sound of a new voice. Dr. Myers pulled up a chair beside Tess. "That's why you're here. To find out."

As they had her sign the forms and took the swab, Dr. Myers told Tess that a nurse, Irene, had confessed to switching the eggs of Tess and another woman.

"It was intentional?" Tess choked on the words.

"Doctor," said the office woman, her voice a fraction too high, "no details! Not yet."

"So, I'm one of only two women?" asked Tess.

The doctor's brow furrowed.

"Who is she?"

Dr. Myers shook her head, her gaze on the forms in front of her.

"Why did Irene—"

"I don't know," the doctor sputtered.

Tess leaned back, realizing she knew, or at least had an idea. Irene, her former university classmate, had been the sonographer at her final appointment before retrieval.

Hyeon-Jun had left less than a week before. Tess, full of all those drugs, ovaries swollen and tender, and emotions amplified, had watched as he stood before her in their minimalistic, professionally decorated living room, saying he was sorry, but not looking it. Saying he was tired of her stubborn refusal to accept she would never have a baby.

She'd stared at him, oscillating between the desire to scream and the urge to turn back time. Fix this. Fix all of it.

She had spoken slowly, placidly, surprising herself with her ability to appear calm. "I'm days away from the retrieval," she said. "My eggs are almost ready. I need you."

And that's when he'd said it, after a long sigh, as if she were the one being unreasonable, as if even her presence were a burden. He was already going to be a father. He'd met someone. Their baby was due in the spring.

Tess collapsed. She'd heard about that, people's legs giving way. She hadn't realized it was an actual thing.

The spring. So she, this other woman, was at least four months along. Further than Tess had ever been.

"It's already paid for." Hyeon-Jun shrugged. "Do the retrieval if you want, but I can't give you my sperm."

Tess screamed, then threw the ridiculously expensive glass-blown elephant the decorator had convinced him was classy. Hyeon-Jun dodged, and the figure smashed into the wall, glass shards and a distinctive chunk of trunk flying.

She'd told Irene all of this, lying in an exam room, gel on her belly.

Some of what had come before, too: why she felt her body was putting her through this. Tess cried in the stirrups, hiccuped, revealing how after six years of losses and fertility diets and yoga and acupuncture, Hyeon-Jun had impregnated this other woman, presumably by accident, then walked away from Tess and her swollen ovaries to start a new life, a new family.

Irene, eyes full of empathy, had removed the ultrasound wand from Tess's body and pulled the sheet down over Tess's legs. She put her hand on Tess's shoulder, rolled over a stool, sat. They'd been friends all those years ago. They'd had study dates, they'd eaten lunch at the same table, laughed over Professor Mulder's quirky ways.

Tess, at twenty-one, had been studying to be a nurse sonographer, while Irene wasn't sure where her degree would lead. If Tess hadn't left the Halloween party early that night, she might have been the one on the stool, comforting some other woman. She and Irene might have still been friends, colleagues, even. Without a doubt, Tess's entire life would have turned out differently.

"We all wondered why you dropped out." Irene's empathy-filled eyes glazed over, one tear, then two, falling. "You were doing so well. You blew my test scores out of the water."

Irene shook her head when Tess went into detail about the three miscarriages before they'd even tried IVF.

Now, guilt coiling around her, Tess stared at Dr. Myers's still-furrowed brow, resisting the urge to confess. Though Tess hadn't asked Irene to do anything. She'd only wished for a miracle.

Dr. Myers looked up from her papers and swallowed, looking like she was going to be sick. "Looks like we're just about done here." She nodded to a woman who'd entered with Samantha—the notary, apparently—and handed her a form.

When requested, Tess handed over her license, then stood, willing her legs not to shake.

"We'll get the results as soon as we can, two, maybe three days," said the doctor, "and hopefully this is all a big misunderstanding."

Tess hoped the opposite.

She'd told Irene, "I need this to work," her voice cracking, desperate, as she imagined a life of solitude—no parents, no husband, no children. She'd explained to Irene that this was her last chance. She would never be able to scrape together the money for another round of IVF on her own. "I have donor sperm." A laugh burst out of her, cold and sharp. "If only I could have a donor egg, too. Maybe that would do the trick."

A joke. Not a request. Tess never thought for one moment Irene would take her seriously.

KATHERINE

K ATHERINE?"

Katherine turned from the counter where she'd been standing, not prepping dinner like she'd intended.

"I've been calling. Did you see the news?" Patrick stopped, staring at her. "You've heard?"

She waved a hand; it shook.

"It's probably nothing. I mean…" He hesitated. "What are the odds?"

"I got a call."

"Oh." His shoulders sank. "And?"

"I'm not sure." Katherine stood straighter, one hand resting on the counter behind her. He must be afraid. Here he was, home from work two hours early. "I didn't call back. It was a voicemail, saying I needed to speak with Dr. Myers."

"You didn't call back?"

There it was: disappointment. She wasn't sure the first time she'd seen it in Patrick's eyes. Several years into the trying, for sure, when he realized she wasn't the perfect woman he'd imagined. And then when she'd become so obsessed with conceiving that it became her core focus—the dietary changes, the yoga, the supplements, the constant researching.

It crushed her, that look, almost as much as the failure to conceive had. She'd worked her whole life trying to please, to make sure people weren't disappointed in her.

"No, I...I thought it was nothing," said Katherine. "I figured I'd wait till you got home. In case they wanted to see you, too, so we could compare schedules." A lie. She hadn't thought of that, though it made some sense. "And it was before Saadia's party. I was already running late. Looking for the keys."

"Oh, sorry." A quick grin flashed. "I try to remember." Patrick's expression fell. "Well, are you going to?"

"Call, you mean?"

He nodded, the disappointment still there. Just as it had been when she'd had so much trouble breastfeeding but refused to use formula. When, in those first few months, he'd wanted to show off the baby—to his parents, his brothers and sister, his colleagues—and she struggled to find the time or energy to get dressed, or shower, or leave the house, but wouldn't let him take Rose without her. When she didn't have the energy to clean but refused to have anyone see the house in the state it was in—see how horribly she was failing.

"Sure. Absolutely," said Katherine, wanting to wipe that expression off his face. "I was thinking I'd make dinner first."

Patrick's voice rose. "What?"

"I said I'd—"

"No, I mean, shouldn't you be calling the clinic first? Besides, it's Chuck's birthday. We're going to Mom and Dad's for dinner tonight, instead of this month's lunch."

"We're—? Damn." Katherine put her hands on the counter. It was hard to handle Patrick's family at the best of times—with their awkward references to all things Black culture (a misguided effort to connect, she imagined), their inside jokes, their thinly veiled criticisms—but with the news of the switch looming in her mind, which they'd all want to talk about…?

"Tell them I'm sick. Or that I have a headache."

"They'd still want Rose and me to—"

"Tell them we've got food poisoning," Katherine snapped as her phone lit.

Patrick grabbed it. "It's the clinic." He swiped to answer. "Hello?"

"Give it to—"

"This is her husband." A pause. "Yes." Another. "She's right here. I'll put it on speakerphone."

"Katherine?" Dr. Myers's voice.

"I'm here." What would happen if she snatched the phone, hurled it against the wall, ran, and kept on running?

"This is Dr. Myers. I'm so sorry I couldn't get in touch with you sooner. We had no…" Dr. Myers stopped. Her voice, which was usually so friendly and positive, so inviting, sounded distant. "We didn't want people to learn about the incident like this. The media shouldn't have… Anyway, well, have you heard about the…uh…incident?"

"We have. Yes." Patrick speaking for Katherine, as if she couldn't speak for herself.

"Okay. Well, as you can imagine, this is all deeply disturbing. It's unprecedented, so we're not exactly sure the best way to handle everything. We have protocols, of course, but not for something like this."

"Okay," said Patrick, as Katherine mumbled, "Of course."

"I'll need you to come in for DNA testing as soon as you can, to the IWK Health Centre, actually, since we're just about to close."

"You think…" Katherine tried not to let her voice tremble.

"Come in for the testing, Mrs. Matheson. There's no need for worry or fear until we know if there is something to worry about."

"What about me?" Patrick leaned in, holding the phone aloft in his hand.

"No. Uh, that won't be necessary. The incident—if there was an incident, we don't know for sure—only involved the eggs."

"So Rose could be mine and not Katherine's." His voice sounded incredulous, yet this was what he'd joked about. What Patrick had found so funny as he sat there, positive Rose was his.

"Yes. And Rose, you'll need to bring her in, too."

"Wait." Patrick swallowed. "Does this mean some other woman could be raising Katherine's biological child, that—"

"Rose is my child," Katherine snapped. She backed away from the phone. The floor felt soft, the tile moving under her.

"Please," Dr. Myers pleaded. "Please, come in. We don't know anything yet. If there is anything to know." Dr. Myers cleared her throat, authoritative again, like someone who was going to take care of them, make all the bad things go away. "Those questions can be answered later, if necessary."

Silence, from all of them.

"When?" asked Katherine. "When do you want us to come?"

"Tonight." The doctor's voice rose an octave.

After setting up a time, Patrick disconnected the call. "So no birthday dinner." He grimaced. "Food poisoning, you said?"

Katherine's hands shook. Her voice quavered. "Yeah."

In the lobby of the IWK, Katherine, Patrick, and Rose approached Dr. Myers and the two women on either side of her: a lab tech and a notary. Only Rose seemed pleased about the gathering. "Hi. Hi," she squealed.

Dr. Myers's face twitched. Her eyes glazed over, like she was trying not to cry.

Katherine's lip quivered. Before visiting the fertility clinic, she'd overhauled her life trying to get pregnant, hoping each new trick or tactic or miracle method would be the answer, the fix, so she could stop feeling so hopeless, so broken. And then, eventually, she'd come to this woman, put her life and her future in her hands. This woman, who had let a mistake happen under her watch. Who couldn't even look Katherine in the eye.

Katherine turned from the doctor as the notary confirmed both her and Rose's identity, checking and rechecking Katherine's license and Rose's birth certificate. Katherine and Patrick signed, allowing consent for Rose's swab. The young tech swabbed their cheeks and tucked the samples away.

"We'll put a rush on it," said Dr. Myers. "You'll know in a day or two. Three at most." She brushed off Patrick's questions: How many mothers were being tested? How did the switch happen? How did they find out? And finally, were they sure he didn't need to be tested?

It was the only question the doctor acknowledged with more than "I can't say at this time," or "We'll discuss it later, if needed."

"Would it make you feel better," she asked, "if we test you, too?"

Patrick nodded.

"Not a problem," said the lab tech. "I always bring extra." She swabbed Patrick as the notary checked his license. Katherine couldn't speak.

The entire process took less than ten minutes. When it was over, Patrick rubbed a hand along his jaw. His shoulders slumped, as if a weight too heavy to carry had landed on them with a thud. "This could be bad, Kat. I think it's bad."

Katherine swallowed, the fear in his voice hitting her like a punch to the throat. "You said it probably wasn't a big deal. You said—"

"Where were the other women? Where were the piles of forms? The notary, did you see? Her folder was practically empty."

Katherine shook her head. "In her office...or someone's office. In—"

Now Patrick shook his head. "Dr. Myers looked like she was about to cry. You'd think if she'd done this dozens of times, she'd be a bit more... numb to it."

Katherine swallowed past the dryness. "Another doctor could have met people, or not a doctor at all. Maybe the other women were from PEI, New Brunswick, Newfoundland. Anywhere."

"Maybe." Patrick wrapped his arm around Katherine's shoulder, squeezed, then dropped his hand to push the stroller, his grip so tight his knuckles went white. Her theory didn't make sense. Not enough sense, anyway.

"Patrick?"

"Yes?"

"Dr. Myers. I mean..." Katherine hesitated. "She wouldn't answer anything you—"

"Legally, it's the smart thing to do," said Patrick. "Privacy. And not wanting to tell us anything we could use against her in court. She didn't even apologize. No admission of guilt." His voice was tight. It was the voice she'd heard him use on late-night work calls.

"Court?"

"There's no point in us worrying about it now. I'll start calling lawyers. I'm not even sure which—"

"Lawyers?" said Katherine. "What? To sue?"

Patrick stared at her. He sighed. "That too. Maybe." He lifted one hand from the stroller and entwined his fingers with Katherine's. "Most likely, none of this will matter. The test will come back showing what we've known all along. Rose is ours. Both of ours."

Katherine wanted to express her agreement, laugh away their fears, jump ahead to the day the test would confirm Rose was hers. Instead, she squeezed Patrick's hand.

After getting the call, she'd thought only of the possibility that Rose may not be hers, not the consequences. Not until Patrick hinted at it—Rose could be someone else's. Someone who would want her back.

8

TESS

TWO DAYS AFTER HER DNA TEST, TESS WAS BACK AT THE CLINIC, sitting in front of Dr. Myers, being told the results were in.

She had a daughter.

"But not with the sperm donor?" asked Tess.

"No." Dr. Myers cleared her throat. "Your egg, you see, it was switched, fertilized by another one of our patients."

"Who?" Tess leaned forward. "Who has my child?"

"Matheson. The father's name is Patrick Ma—"

"What!" Tess clutched the chair. Her breath came in short, quick bursts, like she was seven years old again, breathing into a paper bag, inhaling stale bread crumbs and trying not to choke.

Tess had a baby girl. With Patrick Matheson. Katherine's husband. Tess's arms shook. Her chest tightened through the effort to breathe. She'd been pregnant with Katherine Matheson's baby.

Tess spoke, not a question, but a statement of fact. "Rose. Rose is mine."

Dr. Myers's voice hitched as she spoke. "You know her? Them?"

Tess nodded, a smile finding its way to her face, pushing away the shock and disbelief. "I held her. Two days ago. Rose is mine?"

Dr. Myers coughed, then took a sip of water from the glass in front of her. She swallowed. "Biologically, yes, Rose is yours."

Tess leaned in, her hands still gripping the armrests, hardly able to believe it—after so many miscarriages, after the choice she feared had led to those losses, she finally had a child. "Which means I'll have rights, doesn't it?" she asked, her voice pulsing with hope. "Some kind of shared custody, or more, maybe?"

"Well, it's not that simple, but—"

"But I'll have rights. She's mine, too."

Dr. Myers stared. She nodded. "Yes, you'll have rights."

"Can I see her? Now, I mean? Or soon? Can you set up a meeting?"

Dr. Myers blanched. She opened her mouth, then closed it. "No. I can't set up a meeting."

"Then how?"

"Well, uh…if you know them, I suppose, well…well…maybe I shouldn't have revealed names." Dr. Myers blew out a stream of air. "There'll be proper channels. I'm not sure of those channels. You'll have to find that out yourself."

Despite Dr. Myers's lack of help, Tess walked out of the clinic as if the ground beneath her were shifting. She had a baby. A laughing, babbling, about-to-take-her-first-steps, and already-saying-her-first-words baby. She wasn't alone.

In the clinic, just days ago, when they refused to answer her questions, Tess had tried not to think about what else it would mean, that the baby she'd lost, the baby she'd delivered—only to hold so tiny, so fragile, yet lifeless in her arms—had not been her baby at all.

But now the thought came back to her: Hanna, her last egg, her last chance, hadn't been Tess's. She was Katherine's. And Rose was Tess's. She wanted to run to the Mathesons', proper channels be damned. She might have, if she knew where they lived. She could call her brother, see if Mikolai had the address. But what would she say? "Remember that nice family I introduced you to at that infertility picnic you came to, and it turned out you'd gone to high school with the husband, who then invited you to join his soccer team? Guess what? We have a kid! Their baby's my baby—and I want her back."

Tess hit the button to cross the street, waiting patiently while every fiber in her wanted to jump and scream. She didn't know how to handle this, but knew, based on the doctor's reaction, showing up at the Mathesons' door wasn't the way. There were proper channels. Channels Tess—and Dr. Myers—knew nothing about.

But Tess would figure them out.

A few blocks from the clinic, Tess sat on a nearby bench, head down to shade herself from the view of the people walking along Spring Garden Road, where on a typical day, it was rare not to see two or three people she knew, or at least knew of. She took out her phone, debating whether to contact Mikolai. Not to get the Mathesons' number, but to have someone to talk to, to tell this life-changing news. She'd barely spoken to him in the last year and a half, had only seen him a handful of times, always pretending she was doing better than she was.

He saw the Mathesons—or Patrick, at least—every week, so he wasn't the best choice. But she needed to talk to someone, a person who would listen as she worked through all the thoughts and feelings roiling around inside her.

She turned in the direction of the wellness center, not knowing where else to go. Thankfully, Saadia was at reception. "Tess"—Saadia glanced at her computer and clicked—"do you have an appointment?"

"No, uh…" It was embarrassing, Tess knew, showing up like this without an appointment, so desperate for someone to talk to that she'd come to her acupuncturist—a person she paid to pour her heart out to as she lay on a table, her body pierced with needles. "I…" Tess was worried that Saadia would think she was pathetic. Her insides swirled with fear, nervousness, excitement. "I need to talk."

"Ah."

"I could make an appointment."

Saadia looked at the clock, smiled. "You know what?" She walked to the coffee maker, filled two thermoses. "It's time I took my break—maybe a long one. Let me get Mandy to cover the desk, and we'll visit the Public Gardens."

Once within the gated walls, they walked to a shaded bench in a far corner of the garden. "My favorite spot," said Saadia. Large deciduous trees loomed above them, their fallen leaves dotting the path in rich yellows and oranges. Although the rush of cars sounded behind her, in front a hush seemed to settle. Tess exhaled, her diaphragm contracting fully as she lowered to the wooden slats.

"Tess?" Saadia shifted toward her. "What's going on?"

Tess bit her lip, then released the words. "Hanna wasn't mine." She swallowed. "Not really."

"Oh wow." Saadia sat, letting silence surround them, as she so often did—allowing herself to process or the other person time to expand on their words. When Tess didn't speak, Saadia nodded. "I wondered, after seeing the way you rushed out the other day, after the news segment. So the switch, it happened to you?"

Tess nodded. "I have a child." A smile danced its way across Tess's face, pushing out the mix of other emotions. "I'm a mother."

Saadia squeezed Tess's hand. "This is huge. It's unbelievable. And you're happy about it?"

Moisture sprung to Tess's eyes. "Thrilled."

Saadia's voice filled with awe as she met Tess's gaze. "This is incredible. What are you going to do?"

"I'm not sure." Tess half laughed, half sighed. "Of the steps to take, at least. The doctor didn't have any solid advice. She said there were proper channels if I wanted to see my daughter, have her in my life."

"Definitely," said Saadia. "Legal channels. You'll probably need a lawyer."

"You think?"

Saadia rubbed a hand along her chin. "I could ask my father if he knows someone."

"Your father?"

"He used to be a family practice lawyer."

"Right." Tess looked away, thinking of the cost. After Hyeon-Jun left, she'd sworn to herself she'd build her own life, rather than rely on a man. To get there, though, meant sacrifice. She rented a far cheaper apartment than she could afford, a closet of a spot, though not so cheap it came with rats. She wasn't dealing with that again. She cut coupons, living as frugally as she could, stayed in the apartment even when she secured a job at the lab. The pay wasn't much more than her fast-food gig, but the hours were consistent and the overtime meant she could pay her bills and save the rest, so one day she could get a degree or two, and never have to live that way again.

A lawyer, Tess knew, could make her months of savings disappear.

"Or there is legal aid," said Saadia, presumably sensing Tess's distress. "I remember my father not liking those cases because it slowed the process down, putting his clients on edge. Still, it may be an option."

"Uh-huh." Tess tried to qualify for legal aid during the divorce but wasn't approved. Hyeon-Jun's income—which he'd split between them on their taxes—made her ineligible. Not able to afford her own lawyer, she represented herself. They were in love once, she thought. They were both good people at their core, she thought. They could figure it out.

Figuring it out meant Tess got nothing and Hyeon-Jun got everything. She wished she'd realized, before making that decision, that what she felt for Hyeon-Jun had never been love—that what he felt for her likely wasn't, either. If she had, maybe she would have fought the way she should have. She'd come into the relationship with nothing, and at the time of the divorce—so entrenched in her grief over Hanna she couldn't think straight—she figured, why shouldn't she leave the same way?

But not this time. She had a chance at her child, a chance to live the life she'd always wanted. She'd fight tooth and nail. "I could hire a lawyer," said Tess, even if it meant depleting her savings. "If I had to."

"Explore legal aid first," said Saadia. "They're in the Halifax Shopping Centre, I believe, and they must have a website. Unless—" Saadia hesitated. "Do you think you could discuss it with the parents? Try to handle it among yourselves? Do you know who they are?"

"I don't think I should say."

"That seems wise." Saadia placed a hand on Tess's shoulder and squeezed. Tess looked at her. This was also why she'd gone to Saadia—her uncanny ability to listen, rather than push. Mikolai would have been on his feet by now, pulling Tess along, devising a plan. He would have insisted on knowing the names of the other parents.

When she'd called him up after the retrieval—the first time she'd heard his voice in almost eight years—she told him how Hyeon-Jun left, about their fertility struggles, and that she was going ahead on her own. He'd called every night after that to see how she and the embryos were doing, then went to the embryo transfer and held her hand.

Two weeks after the transfer, he'd joined her at the infertility picnic she was too nervous to attend on her own but felt she needed to be at—to meet other mothers, to learn how to cope. He attended her first and second ultrasound too, then insisted she move in with them after losing Hanna, to heal and rest and be taken care of. He was wonderful but overwhelming, as if he were trying to make up for all the lost years in one fell swoop.

After the two and a half months Mikolai and his wife had insisted she stay, Tess decided it was time to leave. She needed space, needed to limit contact and communication. Their bustling family and seemingly unending joy to be alive when she found it hard to even get out of bed was too difficult to bear.

If she'd told him what she was about to say now, he would have found a way to arrange a meeting with Irene, gotten Tess her answer. An answer she wasn't sure she wanted.

"I'm worried it's my fault," said Tess.

"Why?"

Tess looked at her hands, told Saadia what she'd told Irene—about Hyeon-Jun, his mistress, the donor sperm.

"That's a lot." Saadia exhaled. "A lot to have lived through, and I'm so sorry for you, but I'm not seeing how that makes this your fault."

Looking at Saadia, Tess shrugged. "As you know, I never had much trouble getting pregnant. Staying pregnant was the challenge."

Saadia merely nodded, knowing that part of Tess's history intimately.

"When I told Irene I wished I could use a donor egg, that must have given her the idea. Must mean I'm to blame," said Tess, "for this happening."

Saadia shook her head. "You're not responsible for Irene's choices, even if you'd specifically asked her, which you didn't."

Tess sighed, hope and uncertainty warring within her. If the Mathesons found out what she'd said, or a judge, if it came to that, would they agree?

9

KATHERINE

THE ROOM SEEMED TO SHRINK, THE WALLS OF DR. MYERS'S OFFICE closing in fast. Sweat trickled down the small of Katherine's back, beaded across the bridge of her nose. She tried to take a deep breath, right down to the floor of her belly, but the air got stuck…

"Mrs. Matheson? Katherine, are you all right?"

The doctor blurred in front of her.

"Katherine."

She was inhaling, or she felt she was inhaling, but nothing. She couldn't breathe. Why couldn't she…?

"Katherine!" Patrick's voice—commanding. Solid.

Everything snapped into focus. Katherine straightened. Her gaze zeroed in on Dr. Myers. "I don't understand… She did it on purpose? You're saying she intentionally switched my eggs with another woman's?"

Dr. Myers nodded. "That's what she said."

"But why?"

"She didn't say."

"Then why confess? It doesn't make sense!"

"None of this does, Mrs. Matheson. But the fact is—"

"This is ridiculous. You made a mistake once… What's to say—"

"But the switch wasn't a mistake." Dr. Myers swallowed, her face flushing. "Not according to Ms. Connor. And the test results, they're conclusive. I assure you there was no error."

Katherine saw herself standing, storming out, but in reality, she sat there, listening to the words. *Rose is not your child.*

"But *how* did this happen?" Patrick shouted. "Why was a nurse even near the eggs! Aren't the lab techs supposed to—"

"It's not something I can discuss," said Dr. Myers. "Legal reasons."

Katherine braced her hands on the arms of the chair, her breath still coming fast.

"Do you have a lawyer?" Dr. Myers asked.

"Do you?" Patrick shot back.

"Wait," said Katherine, "is there another baby? From the switch? Do I have—"

Dr. Myers shook her head, a wave of sadness seeming to displace her defensiveness. She spoke slowly. "There could have been, but no, there is only Rose."

Katherine leaned back. Only Rose. She closed her eyes, her head suddenly pounding. Most rounds of IVF didn't even result in a pregnancy, especially in women nearing thirty-five or older, even fewer in a live birth. So, there was only Rose. All she had to think of was Rose.

"Rose's mother…" Dr. Myers cleared her throat as Katherine's eyes snapped open, her face contorting. "Her *biological* mother is eager to meet Rose. She was quite excited to learn… She seemed to think… Well, I, we, the staff weren't quite sure what to say… We should have had lawyers in these meetings. We realize that now, but we didn't for hers and, well…" Dr. Myers pulled at her collar, folded her hands on her desk, then laid them flat. "She thought she could see Rose right away. We don't know the process, but she'll have rights. Some, at least, if not—" Dr. Myers stopped. Her face flushed, and rightly so by the babbling, absurd mess of words she was spewing. She took a breath, then spewed more. "She asked about her legal rights."

Katherine sat incredulous, furious at Dr. Myers for not thinking things through, for telling this woman about their daughter before telling her and Patrick, for being a flaming idiot who let all this happen under her watch.

Patrick bolted from his chair. "She's mine," he barked. "Right? What if I don't want her to meet Rose? What if I refuse? I'm Rose's father. What if I say no? Damn!" He pounded a fist against the wall. Dr. Myers flinched and Rose yelped in her sleep. "I shouldn't have let her be tested. I should have called a lawyer first. I should—" Patrick stopped, the vein in his temple pulsing, the tendons in his neck exposed. He returned to his chair, sank, and crossed one leg over the other, his foot bouncing.

Dr. Myers swallowed again, uncertainty and embarrassment rolling off her like fumes. Her eyes kept shifting to her computer, her desk, anywhere but Katherine and Patrick.

Katherine couldn't quite register what was said next, not exactly. She gazed at Rose, the sweet peacefulness of her expression. The perfect pout of her lips. Patrick was shouting. Dr. Myers was talking.

Something about the technicality of it all, what had happened, how, when. The nurse switched the dishes that held their meticulously labeled eggs—the other woman's and Katherine's, eight eggs each. This was the only reason the doctor had for why Katherine and why that woman. They were the only women to have the same number of eggs retrieved that day—it was the only way a switch could have happened during the few minutes the embryologists were out of the lab without them knowing there was a problem when they returned. The only way they could have unintentionally used Patrick's sperm to fertilize another woman's eggs, and a sperm donor's to fertilize Katherine's.

Rose squirmed and cried as Katherine lifted her into her arms, tried to settle her. Patrick stood again, still shouting, demanding something: the name of the woman who was trying to stake her claim on—

"Theresa," said Dr. Myers. "Tess. Sokolowski."

Patrick fell to his seat. Dumbstruck. Katherine gripped Rose closer as the room seemed to spin.

"I shouldn't be telling you that, but when she asked, I told her without thinking." Dr. Myers raised her hands in an expression of surrender. "So, I suppose it's only fair I tell you as well."

Tess, who had been pregnant…with Katherine's baby. The baby Katherine had mourned *for* Tess, sympathy flowing through her at the thought of Tess seeing that positive line, getting that call with a positive blood test, only to learn, days or weeks later, that her little baby wasn't going to be her baby after all. A geyser of emotion rose in Katherine as she imagined that baby, Tess's baby, hers, theirs…

Dr. Myers sighed. "We don't have a protocol. Not for this."

"Maybe you should have figured that out," snapped Katherine, the geyser pushing, throbbing to release at the thought of that small defenseless life, cut off too soon. *Katherine's* little ba—no! Not Katherine's baby. Rose was Katherine's baby. Only Rose. "Before contacting us at all."

"You're right," said Dr. Myers. "Please know we're putting protocols in place about more than that, about how the lab is run, the security around it, so nothing like this can ever happen again."

"Not that it will do us any good." Patrick put out a hand, as if warding the doctor off. He shook his head, his energy deflating like a limp balloon.

"Any further discussion with you will be through our legal representation," he said, his voice full of more acid than Katherine imagined possible. "Expect to be sued."

They left minutes later, with more awkward not-quite-apologies from Dr. Myers and subdued rage from Patrick, with Katherine just trying to put one foot in front of the other, to breathe.

Hours later, after Katherine put Rose to bed, cuddling her in her arms long after she'd fallen asleep, the words still seemed impossible: *Rose is not my child*. She tried them on in her mind. Played with them, using different intonations, different speeds, yet they never seemed possible, no matter how she said them. They didn't make sense. So she tried other words: *My child was lost*. But those didn't make sense, either. Because Rose *was* her child. She bent and picked up a gray plush elephant. Of course she was her child. If she wasn't, why would this elephant be in her hand? Why would this rattle be on the floor beside her feet?

But the doctor had said it. The test results proved it.

Katherine picked up the rattle, fluffed and ordered the couch cushions, went to the kitchen, and wiped down the counters, the breakfast table, the sink. She wouldn't think of that other child again. She opened the fridge and started hauling things out, scrubbing, scrubbing, though the shelves were already clean.

After she'd finished, she looked toward Patrick's office, where he'd been half the evening—making calls, trying to find the best lawyer, which was difficult, because how do you find the best lawyer for something that, as far as they knew, had never happened before? Not like this. The few times he emerged, he hadn't looked at Katherine. He looked above or below or to the side of her.

When Katherine should have been heading to bed, she headed to Rose's room instead, as she so often did since they'd stopped co-sleeping, each night away from her baby making the distance between them seem greater, each night plagued with the fear that if Rose were out of Katherine's sight for too long, something bad would happen, something that, if Rose were in arm's reach, Katherine would be able to prevent…yet she hadn't been able to prevent this.

Katherine stepped to the crib, stared at her girl, who wasn't quite her girl after all. She laid a hand on Rose's chest, caressed her cheek, and tip-toed out of the room silently. She returned to the kitchen, then set to work scouring the near-spotless oven so vigorously her hand cramped. She stopped, letting the sponge drop, resisting the urge to scream.

She wanted to talk to Tess, to tell her, *Rose is my baby, no matter what the tests say, so kindly walk away. Please.*

She wanted to erase Tess from the face of the earth.

She wanted to go back to the moment before that voicemail and stay there forever.

10

KATHERINE

O N THE SURFACE, THE DAY AFTER LEARNING HER DAUGHTER WAS not her daughter was like any other. Katherine cooked breakfast for herself and Rose. She made sure the house was spotless, and then— because children need proper stimulation no matter what their parents are going through—they went to the park. Katherine was avoiding the library, where they usually spent an hour playing before their Tuesday morning mom and tot group. She was putting it off—all the moms inevitably talking about the IVF scandal, wondering if anyone they knew had been affected, if Katherine had. She debated forgoing the playgroup altogether, to avoid having to pretend her life hadn't just imploded. But she'd have to face it at some point, and besides, all the books said children needed consistency in their lives to foster a sense of security and order, as well as socialization.

After leaving the playground, Katherine turned onto their tree-covered street, the leaves a splendor. She maneuvered the stroller up the driveway, unstrapped Rose, and lifted her out. Their gazes met and Katherine looked away, a shaft of pain slicing through her. She looked back into Rose's eyes, which she now saw were Tess's. Rose's expression turned serious, perplexed perhaps by the lack of a smile on Katherine's face.

Katherine swallowed past the thickness in her throat, then pasted on a smile, pushed out the words she'd usually say. "Okay, sweetie. Time to get in the car." She buckled Rose in and stared at her girl, this sudden stranger before her, with someone else's face and expressions.

Minutes later, settled in between Tracey and Tiffany, Katherine held Rose up for a boisterous rendition of "We're Going to the Moon." When the group leader announced free play, Katherine set Rose down, her arms shaking.

"How's it going?" asked Tracey, whose youngest scrambled after Rose. "You haven't returned my calls."

Katherine kept her gaze on the kids, discomfort and guilt rising at the concern in Tracey's voice. "Sorry, day by day, you know?" She glanced at her. "Life is busy."

"Day by glorious day." Tiffany laughed as she adjusted her daughter in her lap, lifted her shirt to nurse, then sent Katherine a wink.

Katherine smiled her acknowledgment, then looked back to Rose, who plopped to her bum, shaking a bumpy ball between her plump hands with a vengeance before popping a knob of it into her mouth. Katherine averted her gaze, pushing away the urge to dash across the room, pull the toy from Rose, and wipe it down before handing it back. But germs were good, the books said. Necessary to establish a robust immune system. She looked at Tracey. "How are you?"

"Pretty good." Tracey gestured toward Fletcher. "Teething, so…"

Katherine offered a sympathetic smile. "Hope he gets through it quickly." She hesitated. "How was the rest of Saadia's party? Did your father show up?"

"He did," said Tracey. "A bit awkward for me. I've only seen him a few times, and he still barely acknowledges me, which I get. The great embarrassment and all."

Tracey gave a laugh, clearly trying to hide the pain behind it. *Awkward* had to be an understatement. Tracey was in her late twenties when she met her father, a married man who'd impregnated Tracey's teenaged birth mother, then refused to have anything to do with either of them. "But he looked proud of Saadia," continued Tracey. "And humbled, maybe. He saw that what she's devoted her life to isn't just some quack's endeavor, that she has a community of people whose lives she's changed for the better."

Katherine nodded. "It's about time he saw that."

"Yeah." Tracey let out a little sigh. "But people are who they are and don't easily change."

"Your mom changed," said Katherine. "When you found her, she wanted you. She put the work in to build a relationship, even though she'd given you up all those years earlier."

Tracey nodded. She smiled. "True."

"And the news report?" said Katherine, not wanting to know, but also needing to. "How did that affect things? I know it took over for a while."

Tracey let out a half laugh, half sigh. "Well, there was no shortage of conversation, that's for sure."

"What I want to know"—Tiffany leaned past Katherine—"is if that hubby of yours has any inside knowledge into the scandal?"

Katherine's throat constricted. Her gaze darted to Rose, pulling herself up on a kitchen play set, banging pots on the toy stove—not at all looking like Katherine's daughter.

"Not really," said Tracey. "Adrian said the media doesn't know anything more than they've revealed in the latest reports. The nurse, Irene, she confessed—that's the only reason anyone knows—and she said it was just once."

Were Tracey and Tiffany thinking it right now? It would take more than two hands to count the number of times some curious stranger—seeing Katherine with Rose—had asked if Rose was hers, thinking that Katherine was merely a friend, an aunt, or the Black nanny. And now, biologically, Katherine had no connection to Rose. She was married to Rose's father, but that was a legality, not genetics. So what did that make Katherine? A stepmother? A surrogate? She almost wanted to blurt the truth, to ask if that's how Tracey and Tiffany would see it too.

"The clinic released a statement saying they've contacted the families concerned and the matter will be dealt with privately, which makes sense."

"So we won't know anything about it?" Tiffany sighed.

Tracey shrugged. "Things slip. Depending on the situation, Adrian said the family may want the media to know, but he's thinking they'll want all the privacy they can get. We would." She shook her head. "I can't imagine… After everything the women involved would have gone through with IVF, all the years of struggle, and then—" Her voice cut off, breaking.

Tiffany offered a small smile, her cheeks flushing. "Well, at least you know it wasn't either of you." She squeezed Katherine's knee. "That's a relief."

A relief. For every mother but her. And no one knew why. That's what Katherine wanted to know. Why?

"Oh." Tiffany kept her hand on Katherine's knee. "Did you hear Chrissy's kid has hand, foot, and mouth disease?"

"No, I—"

A boy yanked a pot from Rose's hand, throwing her off-balance. She stumbled backward, tripped, and banged her head into a table leg. A pause of silence, and then the scream. Katherine leapt from the floor and crossed the room. She scooped Rose into her arms as she hollered, held Rose against her chest, rocking her, murmuring assurances as she bounced her daughter in the way she'd seen mothers doing for years, which had come naturally to her, too.

She kissed Rose's forehead. The "why" mattered less than the fact that it happened, that Rose was here now, that Katherine would not give her up.

In her car after playgroup, Katherine sat, hands steady at the wheel, fingers gripping so hard it hurt. This accident, no, this *crime*, was a crime against her family. The family she'd suffered for, worked for as hard as she'd ever worked at anything. The part of her that was scrambling to understand what was happening, the part that felt like her feet had been swept from underneath her—she would send that part away.

Katherine navigated the late-morning traffic and turned up her street. In the driveway, she tapped the brake; Patrick's car sat in front of her. Her chest tightened, nerve endings firing. Patrick home in the middle of the day, after the week they'd had, was not likely to be good news.

Rose on her hip, Katherine walked through the door. She pulled off their jackets and boots, putting them in their proper place, then set Rose down in the playroom and latched the gate. She crossed the hall to the breakfast nook and stood, staring down at her husband.

"What is it?" she asked, hating the sight of his head leaning on his hand like that, his shoulders slumped, as if in defeat. She could do this on her own, but it'd be a hell of a lot easier if she didn't have to support him, too, if she had him by her side, fighting fiercely.

He sat straight, surprise crossing his features. "Sorry, I"—he gave his head a shake—"I didn't hear you. I was…thinking."

The chilled fingers of fear seemed to play across Katherine's skin. She'd seen this before, the way Patrick could sink into himself during times of emotional distress. He'd done it about three years into their attempts to conceive. But he'd bounced back. He'd been a rock, not holding her up, exactly—she'd held herself up most of the time—but standing beside her, offering support. That was the Patrick she needed.

"About what?"

"I talked to a lawyer this morning. Kerra. Her advice was to use her as little as possible. She suggested a mediator would be our best bet. Hope Tess isn't looking for sole custody, that she doesn't want to go to court. Whether or not we go to court, the most likely scenario, she thought, would be either shared custody, fifty-fifty or, fingers crossed, that all Tess wants is weekends, alternate holidays, a couple of weeks each summer."

"No."

"I know." Patrick shook his head again. "I don't want her in Rose's life." His eyes moistened. "In our life." Defeat dripped from him. "You're Rose's mom. I'm her dad. We're her family." His voice trembled. "If I had my way, we'd keep this a secret from Rose forever. We'd never let her know, the way we never would have known if that meddling nurse had kept her mouth shut."

Katherine backed away. "Do you think that's a possibility? Keeping it a secret?"

"No." Patrick stood, stepped toward her.

"But…" Katherine turned, thinking, then spun back. "What if we could? Handle it like a closed adoption. I can't imagine the powers that be would let us keep it secret forever, but maybe until she's eighteen, and then, if she wanted, Rose could contact Tess."

"Based on what Kerra was saying, I doubt it." Patrick let out a sigh. "The one good thing Kerra said was that because this happened at the egg stage, not embryo, because I'm the biological father, there's almost no chance Tess will get sole custody."

"Sole custody?" Katherine shook her head. "Ridiculous. We're her family. We're raising her. I gave birth to her."

"I know," said Patrick. "But there's no precedent, not that she could find on such short notice, at least. Nothing in the media in Canada, and if anything like this has happened privately, it's family court, so…well, she's looking into it. If anything crops up, that may help us know where we stand, but she said judges generally side with the biological mother in custody cases where that mother hasn't signed away her rights."

"She didn't even know she had rights to sign!"

"I know."

"And usually that biological mother was also the birth mother!"

"Exactly," said Patrick. "Kerra's hoping there'll be some precedent with a surrogate mother, though she doesn't think it's likely, because in Nova Scotia a surrogate needs to use another woman's eggs, either the intended mother's or someone else's altogether, to ensure there is no genetic connection to the surrogate and child."

Katherine rubbed her brow. "But a surrogate would have specified advance intent to give the baby away. My intent was to have and raise my child."

"I know." Patrick rocked on his heels, then looked at the floor before meeting Katherine's gaze. "There's something else."

"What?" Katherine stared at him. "What is it?"

He sat back down. "I told the lawyer… I mentioned…well…"

"What?" Katherine sank to the seat across from him.

"I told her you were Black. I wanted to know if—"

If that would make the difference. If all of Katherine's fears, from the first moment she looked at her child, would be realized because of this pivotal detail. Katherine waited, not urging him to speak.

"Anyway, she said it wasn't likely the case would hinge on that, but it certainly wouldn't help. It…well…she said it could be an issue of culture." He hesitated. "And if it were to get in the media, on social media, not that a judge would bend to that but…people would talk. People would have opinions. There could be pressure. It could become political. So Kerra advised doing all we can to not let this get out."

They stared at each other. Patrick reached for Katherine's hand. "We're going to find a solution." His face twitched, some emotion he was trying to push down making its way to the surface before he stuffed it away again. "I am so sorry this happened, but we are going to figure it out. No one is taking Rose away from you." He emphasized the name. "*Tess* is not going to take Rose away from you."

Katherine held Patrick's gaze, thankful to see him rising again—determined.

"She won't," he said again. "Look at us. Loving couple. Stable home. Security. Tess can't give Rose that."

"No. She can't give Rose that." A chill went through Katherine. Stability, a loving home: it wouldn't be enough. She'd read about the importance the courts put on family connection: how derelict fathers were still allowed a role in their children's lives; how mothers who had given their children up were able to get them back; how if there was a roof over a child's head, enough money for food in the fridge, a parent could have joint custody, and if they couldn't afford that, then visitation. Parents living in shelters had been granted visitation.

Katherine closed her eyes, searching for the strength she knew was inside. "What do we do? What's the first step? You've got the lawyer, now what?"

Patrick squeezed her hand. "We wait."

"Wait?"

Patrick let out something between a grunt and a sigh. "What we should have done initially. Not willingly given them our DNA, but waited for a court order."

"We could have refused?"

"It doesn't matter now. It wouldn't have changed anything. Just delayed it." Patrick crossed a leg over his opposite knee, his bottom foot bouncing. "We have Rose. We don't need to do anything. Tess will have to contact the courts, start an action. The lawyer said if Tess is smart, if she takes the advice given her, we'll be contacted for mediation. Until then, we do nothing."

"Nothing?" The word caught in Katherine's throat.

"Nothing."

11

TESS

TESS SIGNALED HER STOP, STEPPED OFF THE BUS, AND MADE HER way to the doors of the Supreme Court of Nova Scotia, Family Division—a mottled brown-brick building that looked more fit for a prison.

That morning she'd stood in front of the mirror, scissors in hand, trimming away the ragged ends of hair that hadn't seen a salon in…she didn't know how long, since before Hyeon-Jun had left, for sure. She'd almost laughed when Katherine had mentioned it at Saadia's party. It wasn't a new hairstyle; it was neglect.

"Tess, uh…Theresa Sokolowski." She leaned against the receptionist's desk. "I'm here to see Maeve."

Less than a week after learning about Rose, and here she was, taking action, seeing a lawyer—literally one step closer to holding her daughter in her arms. She'd looked the number up online and called the receptionist after leaving Saadia, worried she'd hear the same dismissals she'd heard the last time, but instead, the person on the phone had continued asking questions, told her where to find the forms and how to fill them out. Now Tess followed the receptionist's directions down the halls to Maeve's office. She smoothed her skirt, pulled at the sleeves of her blouse, put a hand to her freshly cut hair. Since Hyeon-Jun, the many men she'd encountered—in dimly lit rooms where music blared and drinks flowed, and whose beds she'd snuck out of before morning's first rays—didn't care how she looked, but a judge might. Not that Tess wanted to see a judge. From what she'd read, if all went well, she wouldn't have to.

"Theresa?"

"Tess." Tess smiled.

"Come in." Maeve waved her into the cramped office, which she apparently shared with two others whose desks were currently empty, save for the piles of paper and manila folders. "You're looking to start an action?"

Tess nodded.

"And you don't have a lawyer? Hoping to qualify for legal aid?"

Tess sat, confusion passing through her. "I am."

"Mm-hmm." Maeve rifled through some papers. "Looking at your financials, I don't think that should be a problem, but before we dig in, let's talk about your situation—work, home, family, friends. Make sure we understand what you have going for you, what you need to work on, and what going for custody will entail. Then hopefully we can get you that lawyer."

"Wait," said Tess, "aren't you a lawyer? I thought I was coming in today to—"

"I am," said Maeve, "but not your lawyer. My role is to assess your situation. See if you qualify. Then, if you do, I'll put forth your application for approval."

"Oh." Tess leaned back. "And how long will that take, getting a lawyer?"

"Weeks if you're lucky, months if you're not."

Tess's expression fell.

"The good news," said Maeve, "is I can start an action. Which means the other party will be contacted, mediation set up. If all goes well there, you may not even need a lawyer."

"Right." Tess's stomach twisted. "And the chance of that?"

Maeve smiled again. "If you're both reasonable, it's possible. But in case things don't work out that way, tell me all about you. Hold nothing back."

Tess laid it out as Maeve took notes—her job, what her apartment was like and where. She sucked in her breath as if slurping from a large straw, trying to push away the embarrassment. "I don't have many friends." *No friends* was the accurate answer. At work she kept to herself: labeled tubes, followed protocols, ate lunch at her desk. Outside of work… Well, she wasn't about to say anything about that.

"No one you see regularly?"

Tess shook her head.

"And your family?"

Tess shook her head again.

"You don't have any family?"

"Well, I…I don't see them. Not my parents, at least. Not for years."

"A falling out?"

"You could say that."

A disowning, really. Tess averted her gaze, stared at a gray-brick wall and one spindly tree outside. She rarely yearned for them anymore—the smell of her mother's kitchen, the sound of her father listening to classical music on the radio as he read in their cramped living room, or the even dearer sound, when he set his cello up beside the window and, head cocked to the side, created beauty so painful it made her shiver, the vibrations over her skin like a caress.

"So they don't know about this? Any of it?"

"I'm not sure they even know I was married. My husband, my

ex-husband, convinced me to send an invitation, but they didn't respond. So maybe they didn't get it."

"Do you have any siblings?"

"A brother." Mikolai hadn't come to the wedding, either. He'd wanted to, he wrote on the RSVP, but Karina's sister's wedding was the same day. In Poland. They'd already booked their flight. It wasn't until after Hyeon-Jun had left that she reached out again. "I contacted him during my divorce." She looked to Maeve. "He...was there for me. I pulled away after the stillbirth. But I could reach out again."

"That would be good." Maeve looked at her file. "If you could patch things up with your parents, that'd be better."

Tess bit her lip.

"Could you contact them? See if they want to meet their granddaughter?"

"Well..." Of course she could, in theory. She could say she was sorry for not being the daughter they raised her to be, for all of it. But it wouldn't surprise her if Jasia closed the door in her face. It was her mother who'd cut Tess off, her mother who'd reminded Tess of the "first commandment with a promise"—"Honor thy father and thy mother"—and then said, "If you don't go back to school, if you don't at least tell us why, you don't come back to this house."

It was her mother who'd stood, a hand on her hip, chastising Tess in Polish—as she always did when she disapproved—who'd called Tess a liar. Which was accurate. Tess had lied when she'd given her reason for leaving school. The truth wasn't something they could handle. It would hurt them worse than the lie.

"No." Tess returned her gaze to Maeve. "No, I don't think so."

"Well, think about it. It's not what the case would hinge on, but showing you have a loving family, showing family is important to you, it would be helpful."

"Mm-hmm."

Maeve rubbed her temple, as if the effort to be this genuine, this optimistic in the face of Tess's situation, was wearing on her.

"Regular contact with your brother. Reinitiate contact with your parents." Maeve looked at the forms in front of her. "And these work hours, you typically work up to sixty hours a week." Maeve looked at Tess over the top of her glasses. "You'll need to do something about that."

"I'm trying to save up. So I can go back to school full-time."

"That's great, Tess. Admirable. But it's not going to work with a child."

Maeve was right, but Tess had hounded her boss, Carl, for those guaranteed overtime evening and night shifts for months. He wasn't going to be happy if she wanted to drop them. "What if I worked nights?" said Tess. "Have Rose sleep at the Mathesons'? Then I take her in the morning and have her all day?" She paused. "Until I can arrange a new schedule."

Maeve laughed. "And watch that little girl on no sleep? Nope."

"Oh, yes." Tess bit her lip. "I hadn't…well—"

"Change your schedule. Pronto."

Tess nodded. "What about having Rose weekends? A few evenings a week. To start, I mean. Until I can figure things out."

Maeve sighed, placing her arms on the desk. "Stability is key. There are lots of single parents out there, but for a single mom with no strong support system…" She shook her head. "Having your life set up, ready to bring this child into, is key. No judge is going to hand over a child and say, "Okay, here you go, figure it out." They want to know you've already got it figured out. So make sure your living space is adequate. Get a job with solid hours. Doesn't have to be nine to five, but regular hours that won't leave you exhausted and will allow you, as much as possible, to maintain the waking and sleeping schedule your daughter already has."

A warmth flowed through Tess at the words: *your daughter*. She nodded vigorously. "But what if I don't have to see the judge? If I set up a plan, and the Mathesons—"

"That would be wonderful. Either way, your life needs to be ready for this child. And, Tess, if the girl were yours, I mean, if you'd had her all along, do you think you'd hand her over, especially knowing the situation she'd be going into?"

Tess bristled. Her situation wasn't *that* bad.

"You want to look as appealing as possible when you go to mediation," said Maeve. "And before your trial—if you go to trial—secure childcare. A reserved spot, something solid. Make sure your living space is child-friendly. Asking for weekends, a few evenings a week is great to start, to ease your daughter into it, but if you want more, you need to be ready for more."

Tess swallowed.

"This isn't going to be easy," said Maeve, "but people make it work. You can, too. If you want it enough."

Tess had given in, given up so many times. Her life defined by loss after loss after loss. She was not going to lose anymore. She met Maeve's gaze. "I want it."

12

KATHERINE

TWO WEEKS AFTER LEARNING ROSE WASN'T HERS, KATHERINE packed Rose's bag for her bimonthly day at Grandma and Grandpa's. Katherine had been evasive in response to her mother's messages, the same way she'd been in the years of trying, too devastated by her inability to bear a child to talk about it. So she delayed her replies two, sometimes three days, knowing Elvira would wait at least that long before sending a follow-up. To her mother's message the day of the news report, asking how Katherine was doing, Katherine had replied two days later: *Fine. Hope you're good too!* To the message about whether Katherine was busy planning for Rose's birthday party: *Of course. I'll get you the details when I have them. Life's just so hectic :)* It was the wrong thing to say; her mother knew her, knew by now Katherine should have had everything organized. And she would soon, but the idea of all those people—people who had likely wondered before if Rose was hers and would have even more reason now— made Katherine freeze every time she tried.

Not long after, the message Katherine had been waiting for came: a voicemail this time, not a text. "I know you joked about Rose. I just…

with the news. Call me. Okay? Let me know everything's okay." Which Katherine, of course, couldn't do. The shame she'd felt all those years about not being able to conceive flooded back whenever she thought of the switch. All those years of not just disappointing herself and disappointing Patrick, but disappointing their parents: hers, who were desperate for grandchildren; his, who seemed to take her lack of fertility as a personal affront. And then there were their friends, who kept asking when their little bundles of joy would get more playmates. To admit the truth of Rose's parentage to any of them, to say it aloud would be like admitting all over again that she was a broken woman. It was her fault they'd never conceived naturally, and giving birth to a baby that wasn't biologically hers felt like her fault, too.

Katherine had called back at a time her mother wouldn't be able to answer and apologized with breezy joviality for the brevity of her texts, saying life was so busy, but she was fine—they all were. And were her parents still good to watch Rose that Thursday? She hated the lie almost as much as she hated the truth, but the lie was easier to say.

"Are you sure you've been all right?" Elvira asked as Katherine dropped Rose off. "If there's any way I can help…with life being so busy, tell me, okay? I'm here."

Katherine smiled. "I'm fine. I'm managing." She hugged Rose, then hugged her mother, the lie more difficult to speak face-to-face. She made the exchange brief, hoping Elvira wouldn't ask about the switch specifically, but would continue with vague questions that allowed vague answers.

After returning to her SUV, Katherine jumped at the ding of her phone broadcasted through the car's speakers. She reached for the device, then clicked on the flashing tab, opening the group thread for her book club, remembering that this month's pick was hers, which meant she was the host.

She read through the nonspoiler comments on the book she was a good twenty chapters away from finishing, and the questions about book-themed appetizers and drinks. She couldn't join in, pretend her life wasn't in the process of imploding. With a heavy sigh, she typed, *Sorry ladies! Hate to do this to you, but someone else will have to take the lead. Rose caught hand, foot, and mouth disease, so no coming here and I better not venture out either, unlike that wretched Chrissy! ;)*

She set down her phone and pulled her SUV onto the street. Patrick had scheduled the first visit with the lawyer a half hour after Katherine dropped Rose off at her parents, and if she lingered any longer, she might be late.

Hand in hand, Katherine and Patrick stepped out of the elevator into the swanky, glass-walled lobby of Campbell and Sebold Family Law. After waiting in plush seats, green tea in Katherine's hand and a sparkling water in Patrick's, the stiletto-heeled assistant led them to Kerra Campbell's office.

Kerra, in a perfectly fitted, perfectly pressed dark-gray pantsuit, put out her hand, first to Patrick and then Katherine. She told them to sit.

"I'm not one for preamble." She crossed her legs, leaned back in her chair. "I called the assigned mediator after receiving notice of the action. Tess wants shared custody. She didn't say that specifically—rather that she wants a significant role in her daughter's life." Kerra raised her hand. "The word *role*, as opposed to *custody*, is strategic."

Katherine shifted in her seat. It was the words *her daughter's* that had made her flinch. If those were the mediator's, Katherine imagined they were strategic, too—as if Tess was the one cut open, the one to stay up all those nights holding a baby who refused to sleep if not in direct contact with Katherine's body, as if Tess's heart had been the one to break at the mere thought of anything bad happening to her baby girl.

"To start," continued Kerra, "I want you to consider the possibility that having Tess in Rose's life may not be such a bad thing. Maybe an extra person to love Rose could be wonderful."

Patrick leaned forward. "That's not—"

Kerra held up her hand again. "Readjusting expectations can do wonders in these cases. Save thousands."

"Money isn't our concern," said Patrick.

"I still—"

"Do you have children, Ms. Campbell?" Katherine smiled, staring Kerra down.

"A boy."

"And what if a woman showed up saying he was hers, saying you were no longer your son's real mother?"

"That's not exactly—"

"What if you had to share your son?" Katherine leaned forward now. "Miss birthdays or Christmases? What if another woman told your son to call her Mom?"

"People figure it out," said Kerra. "Divorce, remarriages, they do what's best for the child, what would be the least traumatic. That means putting what they think is best for themselves aside."

"This isn't a divorce." Katherine's hands, folded in her lap, clenched. "And what's least disruptive would be Rose not having to know about any of this."

"Listen," said Kerra, "I see this time and again. Children are adaptable. Children, if loved, gravitate toward happiness. So long as they aren't used as ploys between their warring parents, children, generally, are fine."

"*Generally.*" Katherine scoffed. "You want us to hang our daughter's happiness on a word like that?"

"I mean no offense." Kerra imitated Katherine, folding her hands on her desk. "I understand this is an impossible situation. It's my job to help you through it, but it's also my job to give you realistic expectations."

"It's your job," said Patrick, "to do your best for us, work for us and what we want."

Kerra's nostrils flared, her smile stunning. "It's good we get these tensions out here. They won't be helpful in mediation, and they won't be helpful in court. You're right, Patrick. It is my job to work for you, and I will. But with all due respect, it is also my job to ensure you have the full picture and are aware of all aspects of this situation." She pulled a folder from her desk and handed a paper to Katherine. "Here are the details for the mediation. It's time to discuss what you should and shouldn't say, the plan you're going in with, and what you should expect. And when you go, take something, a photo or a copy of Rose's baby album if you want to be generous."

"Why?"

"To show you're not hostile. That you accept Tess has a connection to Rose."

"What if we view it as a closed adoption?" said Katherine. "Reveal the switch to her when she's eighteen, let her know she's not biologically mine, and then if Rose wants to know about Tess, we tell her. If she wants to meet her, she can."

"Do you honestly think Ms. Sokolowski would go for that?" Kerra shook her head.

Katherine looked at Patrick, then returned her gaze to Kerra. "If the other option is losing to us in court, never seeing Rose again…maybe?"

The lawyer's voice was as soft as her smile, filled with a pity Katherine could see in her future—on the faces of friends, family, strangers—when the word got out. Because it would get out, eventually. "Whether you like it or not, Rose is Tess's biological daughter, and you're going to have to acknowledge that with more than an offer to see her in seventeen years."

13

TESS

TESS CHECKED THE LABEL ON A VIAL BEFORE CAREFULLY PLACING IT in its holder. She picked up another, measured out the sample, precise to the half milliliter, placed it, and picked up another, trying to keep her gaze away from the clock. She wanted Rose in her life, and as much as she dreaded the meeting she'd scheduled at the end of her shift, the best thing to do was to do it and have at least one task accomplished before the mediation. She'd already procrastinated long enough, fearing the no, fearing failure.

Drawing her attention back to her work, Tess sighed. This was not what her years of study had been for—doing scut work, work anyone with sufficient training and a mind for attention to detail could do. She had dreamed of more. The work was tedious, but not mindless. It required focus, and if she focused, she could push the bad thoughts away, ignore the fact that life never worked out the way she imagined. So that's what she did—she worked. And on the nights she wasn't working, she did other things to take her mind away. No time for thought. No time for pain.

Tess closed her eyes, thinking of Rose: her eyes, her smile, her solid existence. Hanna had felt ephemeral—barely there, barely real—which, Tess supposed, she had been. After Tess woke from surgery, the nurse, an older woman with dyed brownish-red hair, tiny teeth, and smooth hands had said Tess would be okay. A lie. She'd asked if there was anyone Tess could call. There wasn't. Mikolai's dogged optimism was not what Tess needed in that moment. Then she asked if Tess wanted to hold her daughter.

Tinier than any child Tess had ever seen, the bundle in her arms was more like a doll than a baby. She had a perfect nose and pouted lips. She was wrapped in a receiving blanket, only her face exposed. Tess stared at her, felt the scarce weight of her, then slowly, delicately, she unwrapped the blanket. She traced a line along each perfectly formed finger. She smoothed a palm over her baby's belly, distended, alien-like, but still perfect. She kissed each foot, then wiped off her tears.

"Would you like to name her?" the nurse had asked. Tess looked up, shocked. She'd never thought of it, naming her dead babies. She breathed. "Hanna."

The nurse smiled. "That's lovely." She paused. "We have a kit. You can take her weight. Measure her. Do footprints. We have clothes if you'd like to dress her. I can take pictures. We'll print them off before you go."

Tess started to shake, a tremble that reverberated through every inch of her and made her breath short. She felt cold, colder than she'd imagined a person could feel. The nurse grabbed a prewarmed blanket. With a smile on her face, she snuggled Tess and Hanna up, like a kindly grandmother, like this was some normal day, normal moment, three generations basking in the joy of new life.

"There's no rush." The nurse adjusted Tess's blanket, patted her shoulder. "We can do it when you're ready."

Tess didn't believe her: every minute that passed, she expected the nurse to return and tell Tess it was time. Every time someone approached her room, she knew that would be the moment. *Enough now*, someone would say. *Hand her over*. But no one did. During what must have been about the twelfth check-in, Tess spoke. "I'll take that kit now," she said. "And some clothes?"

The nurse stayed while Tess dressed Hanna. She cooed over the delicate footprint. She was patient as Tess posed with her baby, suggesting various positions. She didn't ask if Tess was done. She didn't tell her it was time to say goodbye. Tess knew, though. She kissed Hanna's forehead. She kissed her nose, her fingertips, her feet. She wrapped her in the blanket again and handed her over, as she handed over a part of herself she'd never get back.

Until Rose.

Tess wouldn't lose this second chance at motherhood, of having a family, of finding—for the first time in years—a reason to be happy. Starting now, she would do whatever it took to have Rose in her life. Better hours. Better accommodations. Family—not just Mikolai, but her parents, too, if that's what it took.

Another look at the clock. Ten more minutes. Tess directed her concentration on the vial she was placing. When the sample tray was full, she carried it over to the mass spectrometer. Sometimes she didn't even hear the shaking, the repetitive drone. Other days, it set her teeth on edge.

Shift complete, Tess set about tidying her station, the thought of her failures still pulsing in her mind. If only she'd fought harder for at least a small share in Hyeon-Jun's wealth, fought at all. If she had, she could have finished her degree by now, been working on a second one or in a solid job—rather than this entry-level monotony—transforming herself into a woman who could care for Rose even without her ex-husband's funds, instead of one who was about to grovel.

Tess stood outside her boss's office. Carl was an all-right guy, though he had a chip on his shoulder. Setting down the phone, he waved Tess in and pointed to one of the two chairs across from his desk. "What can I do for you?"

Tess sat, her hands under her thighs to quell the sudden urge to bite her nails, an old habit she'd picked up again in the past week. She swallowed, thinking of how she'd hounded him for consistent overtime hours, how he'd been resistant to it, afraid if she worked that much, the quality would suffer. But he'd eventually given in. "I need to cut back," said Tess. "No more overtime."

Carl leaned back in his chair and crossed his arms. The conversation went the way Tess imagined it would: him talking about how he'd already reworked the schedule once for her, her thanking him, him suggesting she could work only night shifts if she wanted fewer hours, her explaining how that wouldn't work. School, she'd decided, would be her reason. But that was a "her" problem, he said, one she'd need to figure out herself, because it was damn hard to find people who regularly wanted to fill the evening slots now that upper management expected them. "And besides," he said, "the new semester is months away, so what's the rush?"

Tess bit her lip, then released it. Carl sighed. "I'd love to help you out. You're a sweet kid. You keep your head down, get the job done, but I don't see how I can make only daytime hours work. Not now, anyway. Oh shit, don't cry; come on, this is a—"

"I'm not crying." She wasn't. Not yet. She could feel the moisture pooling, the hopelessness and frustration bubbling up and fighting for release at this, her first real challenge, her first clear, focused task, which she was already failing.

"It's not just school." Tess folded her hands in her lap. She twisted them, fighting back the tears. "You know the IVF scandal? The mix-up?"

She hesitated. "That was me. I mean my eggs, and it turns out I have a little girl." As she spilled it all out, her trepidation turned to strength, and resolve flowed through her; if Carl wasn't willing to help, she'd get another job.

"This is incredible." Carl leaned forward. "Crazy, hard to believe, but... how are you handling it?"

Tess let out a slight laugh. "It's a shock. But also incredible, as you say. I have a child. I'm a mom, at last."

"Right. Congratulations." He nodded, rubbed the back of his neck. "I have a little girl, or she was little once, so I get it." He smiled. "It won't be easy, but I'll figure it out... Do your best to find out exactly when this needs to happen, and if you need proof or something, when the time comes, if I haven't figured it out, I'll write to the judge, let him know the day you have that girl in your life, you'll have the hours to make it work, even if I have to take the overtime myself."

Tess swallowed, the moisture spilling from her eyes as relief washed in. "Thank you." She stood and turned from the desk, looked back, and smiled again, knowing she'd done this one thing right.

14

KATHERINE

THE MORNING OF THE MEDIATION, KATHERINE RUBBED HER EYES and took a sip of her tepid tea. The flavor, along with the soothing scent of chai and ginger, had long faded. She pushed the mug away in distaste, weariness cloaking her like a shroud. She stared at the computer screen, fighting the creeping paralysis of defeat. At Kerra's insistence, Katherine tried to imagine letting Tess be a part of Rose's life, but she couldn't. She couldn't see herself packing a bag and sending her daughter off with a hug and a wave.

And yet, if the articles Katherine spent hours reading last night and returned to again this morning were what a judge would base his or her decision on—stories of IVF mix-ups, of switches in hospitals, of adoption and surrogacy cases gone wrong—then Tess did have reason to stake her claim, to think of Rose as "her daughter." The precedent Katherine kept seeing affirmed biology wasn't everything, but it was a lot. Katherine had known that before she sat down, but she'd searched anyway, racking her brain for new ways to phrase her searches, hoping for a different outcome.

Katherine clicked on a saved tab, the one article about Irene that had popped up in her searches the night before. It revealed the nurse was facing the potential of a $250,000 fine and five years in prison, that it was an unprecedented case. But nothing in the article indicated why Irene had done it. Nor was there any speculation, thankfully, on the families involved. But this was new—Katherine leaned in closer—only two families, it said. The media had finally confirmed it: only one switch, one child.

Katherine swallowed and scrolled to the comments.

So horrible. That poor mother!

Which mother?

Could you even imagine? Obviously the biological mother should get her baby back. It's her baby.

So what about the one who carried the child, does that count for nothing?

That nurse should be in prison! Put her away.

Why would she do this? What's the story?

Katherine looked for someone suggesting a reason, an answer. But no one knew. No one could even speculate, apart from hypothesizing that the nurse had switched one of her own eggs, or the eggs of a family member or someone she knew, that the nurse and one of the mothers were conspiring.

Katherine sat back at that. Maybe it wasn't preposterous to think Tess had something to do with the switch. Katherine pulled up her search screen then typed in *Theresa Sokolowski + Irene Connor*. Her finger hovered, poised to hit Enter, when Patrick entered the room.

"Babe, what are you doing? You should be dressed."

Katherine pushed the computer screen closed. "Nothing, I—"

"We have to leave in thirty minutes."

Katherine sighed, feeling ridiculous. What was she thinking? That she'd type in the names and there it would be, evidence Tess was complicit?

In her room, Katherine stood in front of the closet. Thankfully, she'd done her hair before coming down for breakfast. She ran her hands over the row of seasonally categorized and color-coordinated clothes, but none of them seemed right. She'd carefully chosen everything in her closet: most of it could mix and match for whatever flawless look the day's events required, but what did you wear to sit in front of your daughter's mother and politely ask her to stay the fuck out of your lives?

Katherine had only used the babysitter twice. It was rare for her to go anywhere without Rose, and if she did, her parents or Patrick's were usually the ones they called. Them or Tracey. But they weren't able to choose the date or time for the mediation, and Katherine didn't want anyone asking questions about why they needed a sitter midday. It was easier not to say anything than feel the need to lie, yet again. Plus, as far as Tracey was concerned, Rose had hand, foot, and mouth disease. She'd even sent over a care package after Katherine's book-club message—a basket full of chocolates and cheese, a bottle of wine, and a handwritten note: *For a little treat during your isolation. Fingers crossed she doesn't spread it to you! xoxo.* Katherine's insides had twisted with guilt as she texted her thanks.

Katherine stood on the babysitter's porch, waving goodbye as Rose reached her arms out, tears flowing, her face a scream. Katherine turned to Patrick. "Should we bring her?"

He shook his head. Katherine stepped back, resistance at abandoning her girl flowing through her, especially now. Katherine kissed Rose again, squeezed her hand. In the car, she sat clenching and reclenching her jaw. She looked to Patrick as he turned the ignition. "We could skip it," she said. "Not have to see Tess. Handle it all in court. Let the lawyers do the talking."

Patrick rolled his eyes. "You have to get over this." His voice was tight, trying to hold back the derision she knew he felt. It was an age-old fight: Katherine trying to hold on, Patrick pushing her to let go. "Rose will be fine."

"She's not fine. She's crying. She's terrified."

His hands clenched, the same way they did when Katherine refused to sleep-train Rose, instead waking six to ten times a night to nurse and comfort her, and spending every nap with Rose sleeping on her chest, or when, in those newborn months, she insisted he pull the car over if Rose started crying. He couldn't understand the way Katherine's body ached when she was away from Rose for too long or if Rose was upset. Even when they were in the car, less than four feet apart, if Rose started crying, each yell cut into Katherine, causing physical pain, the firing of nerve responses making her writhe in her seat.

"She's all right." Patrick put his hand on Katherine's thigh, as he had so many times before. "She's fine." Physically, he meant. That's what Patrick didn't get. Rose was crying because she was frightened her parents were leaving her with a stranger. She wasn't about to die, as Patrick had said more than once, but that didn't mean she was fine. And if things didn't go well today, Katherine might be forced to hand her baby over to a stranger every few days, forever. She was not fine. None of them were.

Patrick put the car into drive and pulled onto the street. Katherine stared at him, wondering not for the first time in recent years what had drawn them to each other. They were so different. After all those years of struggle, why had they not drifted apart or imploded, as so many "infertility couples" did? It wasn't because of any great enduring passion. They weren't soulmates—though in the beginning, bleary-eyed with new love, she'd felt certain he was "the one." Now, sometimes, he didn't even seem like a person to her. He was a statement. A role: Husband. Provider. Partner. Sometimes he wasn't even that, seeming less significant than furniture. Had he felt that over the years? Recognized the moments when he meant so little to her, her all-consuming yearning for a child overpowering all else? Perhaps that was why they touched so infrequently. Why he rarely looked at her the way he used to.

But he was a good man. A kind man who maybe sometimes viewed her as a role, too, who maybe stayed because that was what good and kind people did. Katherine resisted a sigh, resisted the urge to pull his hands off the wheel, turn the car around, collect her daughter, and leave the city, the country, the continent, if that's what it took. Leave him, if he wasn't willing to come along, which she knew he wouldn't be.

Instead, she sat motionless, hoping for the sake of their marriage, their family, that he had no idea how she felt. She breathed deep as he pulled into the parking lot, opened the car door, and reached for her hand with a smile that looked frightened. They entered the building the way they'd started their marriage. Together. A team.

She hoped.

15

TESS

AS TESS STEPPED OFF THE BUS ON HER WAY TO THE MEDIATION, HER pocket vibrated. She pulled out her phone, swiped to the messages.

It was from Saadia. *The mediation's today, right? I believe in you. Here's to avoiding a trial. Stand strong. All will work out for the best!*

Tess let out a puff of air and shook her arms as she entered the building, Saadia's words bracing her for what lay ahead. In front of the mediation room door, she stood tall and pushed back her shoulders. She could do this.

Tess placed her hand on the doorknob, a surge of terror coursing through her at the prospect of facing the Mathesons. She pushed the fear aside, envisioning the last time she'd seen Katherine and how, out of all the women in the room, Katherine had been the one to seek Tess out, to say hello. How she had placed her daughter, their daughter, into Tess's arms with hardly a thought. Katherine was a good person, kind; she'd want to handle this in the best way possible.

Tess took one more breath, then opened the door, surprised to see she was the first one there. Large paintings, likely purchased from Winners or Walmart, hung on the walls—water lilies, a waterfall, a lake at sunrise. Tess glanced at the clock. Seven minutes to spare. She stared at the chairs. It shouldn't matter which one she took. That was the point of round tables. But position mattered. From two chairs, you couldn't see the door. From another, the sun glinted in and would half blind the occupant. From three, you couldn't see the clock. It wouldn't look good to pull out her phone if time seemed to stand still.

Tess chose one of two chairs that gave a clear view of the door and the clock. She sat, the *bang, bang, bang* of that most precious organ slamming against her chest. She closed her eyes, drawing in calm by visualizing the reason she was here.

Rose.

With her eyes closed, she could still feel that solid little body in her arms, marvel at the little grin that, now that Tess thought about it, was so much like the grin that stared out from the few baby pictures she'd seen of herself.

Tess wished she'd known at the party. Instead of letting her guilt over the past, the shame over her losses overwhelm her, she would have focused, made each second an impression that would last forever—her first time holding her daughter. Maybe Tess had known on some level. Maybe that's why, despite every reason she shouldn't have, she reached out, made the offer, held Rose close, why she could still recall the moment so clearly, smell the warm scent of honey and vanilla.

As the door handle clicked, Tess's gaze snapped to attention. A woman with shiny brown hair, cut chin length in a style that swished across her face like a fan, rushed into the room.

"So sorry." Her smile was radiant. She seemed young, younger than Tess.

Tess sat straighter. "No problem." She smiled. "You're not late." Tess liked her. That easy smile, the way she laughed at herself.

The woman stuck out her hand. "I'm Chelsea."

"I'm Tess."

The grip was firm, friendly. This was a woman who would be on her side. The door clicked again, and Tess turned her head, her hand still in Chelsea's.

Katherine stepped into the room, every curl in place, her outfit fitting as if it were made for her, the warmth of her smile easing some of Tess's worry. Patrick entered behind Katherine, shut the door. The introductions were made, the guidelines laid out. They were here to work together, to find the best outcome for an impossible situation, a situation no one should have to experience. But they were all reasonable adults. They could see outside of their own wants and needs, hear the other person, come to an understanding.

Chelsea spread her arms. "Who would like to go first?"

Katherine's delicate-looking hand raised ever so slightly. It lowered to the table gracefully, the nails shiny and shaped: no ragged cuticles, no bitten edges. Tess slid her hands from the table and hid them in her lap.

"Katherine, tell us, what is your best-case scenario?"

"Before I do"—Katherine reached into her purse and pulled out an envelope—"I just wanted to give Tess something we thought she should have."

A flicker of uncertainty lit in Tess's belly as she reached for the envelope and flipped it open. Her breath caught at the sight of Rose: her broad, toothless smile, the wisps of hair glistening in the light that shone on her.

"She's about five months old there," said Katherine.

Tess continued to stare, aching to have heard the laugh that must have gone with that smile, to have tickled that belly. She raised her gaze to Katherine, her eyes moist. "Thank you. So much. I...thank you."

"You're welcome." Katherine nodded and pressed her lips before letting out a sharp breath. "So, our best-case scenario. You see, Rose is a sensitive child. Just now, before coming, we had to leave her crying with the babysitter." She gave her head a slight shake. "It's heartbreaking. I almost couldn't leave her, but I knew to bring her here would be worse. So confusing."

Confusing? Tess straightened. Rose wasn't even one. She wouldn't know what was going on. She'd be sitting in a room with her parents. What was so confusing about that?

"That's our goal," said Katherine, "to have this whole situation be as nondisruptive for Rose as possible. We don't want to see her confused. We don't want to see her torn between love and loyalty to two different families. Tess." Katherine turned her gaze from the mediator directly to Tess's eyes. "I cannot even imagine how hard this is for you." She tilted her head. "When I think of the baby you lost, the child that, well—" She stopped, closed her eyes, inhaled. *Was this an act? It looked genuine, but...* "I know you must want the best for Rose, too. I know—"

"Katherine," interrupted Chelsea, "it's best not to tell people their feelings or thoughts. Speak for yourself; that'll help our progress."

"My apologies." Katherine smiled at Chelsea before returning her gaze to Tess. "Patrick and I have discussed it, and if we knew there would be no emotional or mental disruption, no damage, obviously we'd want to do everything we could to foster a relationship between you and Rose, to let Rose know her biological mother." Katherine's voice wavered at the word, as if it took effort to push it from her throat. "But we don't see how that's possible. To take Rose from the only home and family she's ever known, even for a time...could be traumatic. So we think"—she reached out, interlaced her fingers with Patrick's, who, for the first time, met Tess's gaze—"it's best if Rose knows nothing about you. Not until she's older."

Tess stared. She could sense the atoms in the room vibrating. Waves of sound from the clock, the radiator slammed into her.

"And until then, we can send pictures. Updates. Whatever you want. We know—" Katherine glanced at Chelsea. "Sorry, we *believe* you want to be a part of Rose's life, and we think this will be the best way. For everyone."

Tess closed her mouth, which she realized had been hanging agape. *Pictures? Updates?* "For a time." Tess's throat went dry. "How long a time? What do you mean? I want to see her. I want to see her now."

Chelsea put her hand out. "Tess, Katherine has expressed her best-case scenario. How about we hear yours?"

Tess set her feet flat on the floor and clenched her hands under the table, her jagged nails digging into her palms. She looked at Patrick, whose gaze was on the table, discomfort seeping from him like sweat. She looked at Chelsea, smiling warmly. She looked at Katherine, who stared directly at Tess. *She doesn't see me,* Tess thought. *She sees a woman trying to steal her child. What would she think if she knew my words had led to all of this?*

"I want to see my daughter," croaked Tess. "I want to know her." She licked her lips, trying to mask the broken, chapped skin. "I realize the transition could be awkward. Uncomfortable, at first. But it doesn't have to be. We could start with visits, with you there, Katherine, or both of you." She didn't bother looking at Patrick. He, clearly, was not the one in charge. "We could let Rose get to know me. Be comfortable with me. I could be Tess, at first, and then...I don't know, Other Mommy?" A strangled laugh erupted from her throat before she could stop it. "I read that somewhere. It's silly. But what does she call you? Mom? Mommy? I could be Ma or Mama or Mamusia—that's Polish."

Tess stopped. She needed to make Katherine see she wasn't the enemy. She was a woman who wanted to know her daughter, who loved her daughter, someone Katherine could have been if the situation were reversed. "Eventually, maybe within six months, a year, however long seems reasonable, I want to be a staple in Rose's life. I want to be what I am, one of her mothers." Tess swallowed past the dryness, her voice strengthening. "I won't try to take that role from you, Katherine. It's a role we can share." Tess looked at Chelsea, the smile still there, every feature on her face attentive. "Best-case scenario would be shared custody, fifty-fifty, and we can figure out how to make that work, with time, holidays, everything.

"And it wouldn't always have to be split," continued Tess. "We could all do Christmas morning together. I would be willing to do that for Rose. Happy to. Or firsts, you know, first dance class, first swimming lesson." Tess's voice wavered again, her confidence falling at the sight of Katherine's blank stare and placid smile. "We could make it work if we try. We can make this a…a…blessing." The word felt foreign in her mouth, a word her mother would use. "Two mothers. Two people to love her. Support her. There's no reason that can't be better than one."

The room went silent. Patrick raised his head, and with a look, she tried to make him remember the night they'd run into each other at the high school reunion gala after she'd lost Hanna, when she'd poured out her pain, her anger, her fear. How he listened, shared his pain with her. Two grieving parents. Two broken people. His stare dismissed all of it. "That isn't going to work, Tess. Rose is ours. Our child. You need to step away, accept she's never going to be yours."

Chelsea leaned forward. "Patrick—"

"Well, then." A battle drum, hard and strong, reverberated in Tess's chest. "I guess I'll see you in court."

16

KATHERINE

A S THEY DROVE TO KERRA'S OFFICE FOR A DEBRIEF, KATHERINE thought back to the moment she first stepped into the room, when Tess half stood, her body facing Chelsea, their hands grasped. Upon seeing Katherine, Tess looked like a deer in the headlights. She looked sweet. She looked like a woman who'd been through the wringer and come out standing. Katherine had placed a warm and compassionate smile on her face because she knew that's what should be there, that Tess shouldn't be her enemy. If the situation were reversed, Katherine would want the child Tess had carried. She'd feel that baby was hers. Tess wasn't asking for anything Katherine wouldn't have asked for. But by the end of the mediation, Tess's air of shocked innocence had shifted as she made it clear she, too, wasn't giving in without a fight.

Tess shouldn't be Katherine's enemy. But she was.

Kerra looked between them. "So, it didn't go great?"

"We couldn't have expected it to go much better." Katherine crossed her legs. "We knew she wanted Rose."

"She wants shared custody." Kerra spoke slowly, emphasizing her words in a way that made Katherine's fists want to clench. "That's what I told you. And she's willing to take it slow, ease Rose into it, have family events together."

Katherine took a sharp breath.

Kerra exhaled. "She's willing to be reasonable."

"It's not reasonable to think I'm going to let another woman raise my child."

"Except"—Kerra rubbed a hand on her neck—"Rose is also Tess's child." Kerra raised her hand as Katherine's mouth opened. "I know you don't see it that way. I know. I get it, but part of my job, my role, is to advise you in a way that gives you the best chance of keeping Rose in your life with the least amount of stress and pain. It's clear you want sole custody, but you have to realize that's highly unlikely. I've said it before, and I'll say it again: what's likely is you'll go to court, spend a lot of time and money, and end up no better off than if you agreed to Tess's offer in mediation. Potentially worse." Katherine opened her mouth again. "However," Kerra emphasized, "I will fight for what you want. I'll do my best, and I am one of the best. This isn't going to be easy. It's not going to be fun, but if you're determined, we'll give it our all."

"There's a chance, though, right?" said Patrick. "For sole custody."

Kerra nodded. "There's always a chance."

Katherine leaned forward. "What's our first step?"

"You need to show you're not merely the best choice for Rose, the best parents, but the only choice. You already have strong family support, friends in your lives. Foster that. Make it clear you have community. Show your involvement and enthusiasm for Rose and your family life.

"More importantly, we need to show that Tess isn't parenting material. That having her in Rose's life would be detrimental. You need to show she's an unfit mother. Without that, there is no chance you will get sole custody without visitation rights. Do you know anything compromising about—"

"Oh, come on." Patrick raked a hand through his hair. "Is this really…?" He sighed. "She's been through a lot, and—"

"She's been through a lot, and what? We should make it up to her?" Katherine glared at Patrick. "Let her raise our daughter?" She bit her lip and closed her eyes, disgusted at the tone coming out of her mouth. "Mikolai's never said anything?" Katherine placed a hand on Patrick's leg, her voice soft. "You mentioned once she was estranged from her family, right? Did Mikolai say why?"

Patrick looked away, shook his head.

"Please." She hated this, understood why Patrick did too, but she hated more the thought of Rose in Tess's arms, waking in Tess's house, sitting at Tess's table while Katherine and Patrick sat alone. "If you know anything—" Her voice cracked. "Anything that could help us keep Rose."

Patrick let out a huff of air. He thumped a foot on the floor repeatedly, the way he always did when in a situation he wanted out of. "She dropped out of school," he said at last. "Even though she was doing well. Top of her class. Things were said. As far as I know, she hasn't been a part of her parents' lives since. Hardly even sees Mikolai."

"Why'd she drop out?" asked Katherine.

"I don't know. I'm just saying what Mikolai said. I'm not going to go dredging up—"

"Well," said Kerra, "we're not asking you to. That's not your role."

"But that's good, right?" Katherine turned to Kerra. "She doesn't have family support."

"It's a start." Kerra tipped her chair back. "She's divorced, so she'd likely be a single mother to Rose, with no family support system. It's an advantage, but not enough to make a real difference as far as shared custody is concerned. We need to find out more. We need to know all we can: where she works, her job history and stability over the years, her home situation, her financial situation, how she spends her time, with whom she spends her time, and what they'd say about her." Kerra leaned forward. "We'll want to know why she's divorced, why she dropped out of school, why she's estranged from her family. We'll want to know anything unsavory, anything that could bring into question her ability to be a good mother." Kerra paused. "Scratch that. We want anything that could question her ability to be an *acceptable* mother at all."

"How are we supposed to find that out?" Patrick clenched his jaw, a vein over his temple pulsing. "Go digging around? Do a web search? I mean, come on."

"No." Kerra opened a folder on her desk and pulled out a piece of paper. She placed it in front of Katherine and Patrick. "There are people who can do that for you. With more access and avenues than you'd ever have."

"A private investigator?" Patrick picked up the paper.

Katherine eyed the page. A private investigator, to dredge up anything worth dredging. To hurt this woman who had already been so hurt.

"Do you have a suggestion?" Katherine took the paper out of Patrick's hand, scanning the list.

"Adeline Sanchez is particularly good," said Kerra. "But she's in high demand. Pricey."

"Price isn't an issue." Katherine scanned the list until she found Sanchez. She looked to Patrick.

"I don't know about a private investigator." Worry tightened his voice. "It seems…" He hesitated. "Excessive."

"It's fairly common," said Kerra. "There's a good chance Tess will hire one, too, to expose any of your dirty laundry. Which brings us to you two."

Kerra folded her hands on the desk. "If there's anything a PI could dig up, it's best I know now. To get ahead of it."

"We have nothing to hide." Katherine looked at the page again. "Sanchez is the best?"

"In my view."

Katherine placed the paper on the table. "Let's call her."

17

TESS

IF TESS HAD A CAR, SHE'D BE SITTING IN IT NOW, WINDOWS ROLLED up, hands gripping the wheel. She would scream, release then clench her hands, pummel the forgiving rubber. Or if it were later, she'd head to a bar, drink until this frustration numbed, find some man to take her away, help her forget the feeling of sitting there, having the Mathesons look at her like she was nothing. Instead, she had to rein it all in, walk down Spring Garden Road with her head held high, gait measured, looking perfectly normal as every cell within her felt as if it was exploding.

Chelsea had tried to smooth things over, make them see reason. She'd talked about the benefits of working something out, of being flexible. But Katherine and Patrick were steel rods, arrogant in their certainty, sitting there like the battle had already been won, like Tess didn't have a chance. Well, she did. She was Rose's mother.

As Tess passed a bar, again the urge for liquor and its calming caress swelled through her. She could slip inside, pace herself to make it to the night. But day drinking, hooking up with random men wasn't exactly stable behavior. Stability, Maeve had said, was Tess's best chance of securing the most time with Rose.

It had all been stolen from her: carrying Rose, birthing her, seeing her grow these past eleven months. Tess had let go of Hanna, she'd let go of the five babies before her, because she didn't have a choice. She would not let go again.

Her chest pounding, a tingle shooting up and down her arms, Tess switched directions, propelled herself past the bar and onward, block after block, until she hopped on a bus and let it transport her the rest of the way. She entered the building where Mikolai worked, walked down the corridor, and knocked on his door. She'd been putting off seeing him, afraid she wouldn't be able to conceal the news of the switch, because she wasn't ready for him to know, to try to take over the situation. She wasn't ready for him to see how weak and fragile she still was. The scars from Hanna, from Hyeon-Jun—maybe not so visible to others—would show on her face as fresh wounds to Mikolai.

"Hi!"

Her brother looked up, his smile broad. "Tess!" And that did it—fresh liquid rising to the corners of her eyes, on the verge of leaking out.

"Hey." Tess smiled back, drawing on all the resolution within her. She could do it, talk to him and establish connection, without revealing why. "Sorry to barge in like this. I was in the area and…it's been months and, well…" She stepped forward. "Have time for lunch?"

They sat across from each other in an upscale restaurant on the Bedford Highway, which, from the outside, looked more like a rec center than a restaurant—small and modern. Wine glasses, cutlery, and cloth napkins were set on the table. Thankfully, coming from the mediation, Tess was dressed for the occasion.

"You look nice." Mikolai leaned in, a twinkle to his eye. "Any particular reason? Last time we talked, you said you were interviewing for jobs—got a new one that requires new attire?"

Tess kept her smile firm, guilt jumping within her. She'd had the job at the lab for almost a year now. Had it been that long since they'd had a conversation? "I did get a new job," she said, even though it didn't answer why she was dressed up. She told Mikolai about it. As she saw his smile growing larger, pride flowing off him in waves, Tess caught a glimpse of their father, and occasionally their mother, too. She wondered which of those features she'd see in Rose as she grew, telling herself she'd be there to see them. If Rose had Jasia's characteristics, Tess hoped it would be her green thumb or her uncanny ability to throw random ingredients together and produce a delicious meal; those were the best memories she had of her mother. Even when Tess was a child, they hadn't been close. Jasia was so often chastising, expecting Tess to be a certain way—steadfast, focused, a devout child with her mind on the Lord, rather than on earthly things.

Tess always imagined a different story with her own children. That she'd be the type of mother who encouraged. Who took the time to listen and understand, even if the way her children saw the world was different from her own. She'd give hugs freely, daily, not just for special occasions, not as if they had to be earned. She'd be okay with a noisy house, laughter and running feet, even if those feet occasionally tracked in mud or knocked over lamps. She wanted love—both from her children and for them. She wanted to douse them in it.

"And what about you?" asked Tess, once Mikolai had asked all there was to ask about Enviro Lab. "How are you? And how are Karina and the kids?"

"Busy." Mikolai paused as the server set down their meals. "But so good. Tomas is very into soccer right now. Me joining that team sparked his interest. He'd kick the ball around night and day if we let him. Oh, and get this, he's all about Raheem Sterling! Which means he cheers for Manchester. I've tried to get him interested in Lewandowski or Szczesny, show some Polish pride, but nope!"

Tess laughed, imagining it—little Tomas, his face contorted with focus, practicing his drills, cheering for an opposing team. "And Jannie?"

"She's good," said Mikolai. "At last month's dinner, Mama taught her how to make chałka, and she's made it three times since then, wanting to perfect it for this month's dinner."

"Wow." Tess tried not to let the twinge show on her face. Her mother had rarely had the patience to bake with Tess, though Tess had asked dozens of times, wanting to be close to her, to have something that might make her mother look at her with pride.

"She's changed," said Mikolai, his head tilting. "Softened. Maybe you should reach out, see if—"

"Maybe," said Tess, too quickly. She took a bite of her flatbread pizza, focused on chewing so she wouldn't have to speak.

"They were angry," said Mikolai. "They didn't understand why you dropped out like that, especially when you were doing so well. I didn't understand."

Tess shrugged, trying to give off an air of dismissal as the pain reared up. Jasia hadn't dug or pushed to figure out what the reason was; she simply believed Tess was a flake, the disappointment she'd always expected her to be. "It wasn't for me."

"Tess."

"I thought we had an unspoken agreement we wouldn't talk about this." She forced a laugh to her voice, then looked at her plate, trying to push the feelings back down.

Mikolai nodded, sipped his soup. He swallowed, dipped his spoon once more, then set it in the bowl. "Maybe we should dissolve that agreement. I know it was awful, them cutting you out of their lives like that."

"They disowned me," Tess snapped, bringing her father into it for not standing up to her mother, for not pushing for the truth, either.

"I know." He paused. "But I don't think they thought it would turn out like this. They thought it'd be a method, a way to…I don't know, encourage you to go back to school."

"Pretty drastic method."

Mikolai sighed. "Try to think of it from their perspective. Poor immigrants who struggled to settle in a new country, who left their friends and family, went decades without traveling home so they could save the money to give their children a better life. You dropping out, to them, to Mama, it was like you spit in the face of that."

Tess looked away. She *would* contact them; Maeve had made the importance clear. But she had time to work up to it—she hadn't even been assigned a lawyer yet.

Tess looked back to Mikolai, whose gaze was still on her. "I'd love to see the kids, and Karina. Maybe I could come by for lunch."

Mikolai's smile held a hint of disappointment. *Don't press,* Tess asked him wordlessly with her eyes. *Just drop it.*

"Sure." He nodded. "That'd be great. They'd love to see you."

18

KATHERINE

ON THE DRIVE HOME FROM THE LAWYER'S OFFICE, KATHERINE twisted in her seat to look at the baby mirror. Her daughter slept, her nose upturned, her little lips a rosebud. Katherine turned to the sound of Patrick's sigh. "What?"

He squinted, his gaze on the road, his lips pursed, so like Rose.

"The PI?" asked Katherine. "It makes sense. We need to know if there's anything to give us an advantage."

"It's dirty."

"Dirty?" Katherine raised an eyebrow.

"Yeah. It's not who we are, digging into Tess's past. And I don't like the idea of Tess digging into ours, as if we were criminals. None of us did anything wrong."

Katherine looked at the road, a raw pull at the back of her throat. "It's not our fault, you're right. And it's not hers." She took a deep breath, the cool air making her nostrils flare. "But we can't think of it like that, not if we want a shot at keeping Rose. We have to think strategy. We have to think of our family." Katherine looked to Patrick. His jaw held firm, jutted slightly. "And if she's innocent, if she's perfectly lovely with no skeletons in her closet, we're just wasting our money. No harm done."

He gripped the wheel harder, glanced at her, then back at the road. "I still don't like it."

"This could mean the difference. This could be the reason a judge decides Rose should be ours."

"Rose is ours."

"Exactly." Katherine's shoulders tensed. "So we have to do whatever we can to keep it that way."

Patrick shook his head. "We can focus on showing we're the right family for her."

"We'll do that; we are that."

"Well, that's all we should do."

"What if it's not enough?"

He hesitated, his jaw twitching. "We shouldn't look for the worst. Go sneaking into someone's life, their past, the things they'd rather keep hidden. Things that are painful or embarrassing, things a lawyer could twist."

"And what if one of those things could affect Tess's ability to be a good caregiver, jeopardize our daughter's safety or well-being, and if we don't uncover it—and the judge sides with Tess—we hand our daughter over to…to…who knows what?"

"It's not like we put a PI on the babysitter." Patrick's Adam's apple, which Katherine rarely noticed, bobbed unattractively as his voice rose. "Is that who we are? Would that make"—Patrick glanced at the back seat—"her proud?"

Katherine closed her eyes. "We're people who want to keep our daughter as our daughter." She raised her chin. "Unless there's some specific reason to keep Tess out of Rose's life, Tess will be in Rose's life. Rose will know I'm not her mother. Not in—" Katherine's throat tightened, her eyes burned. "Not in the way people think matters most."

Patrick sighed, then reached across the gear shift and rested a hand on Katherine's thigh. He squeezed.

"People cheer when a biological mother and child are reunited," continued Katherine. "Think of every made-for-TV movie about adoption or switched babies at birth, think of the news articles you've read. Biology means something to people. It's blood. It's connection. It's understanding where you come from."

Silence filled the car. Katherine looked away. Everyone thought it. She would have thought it, before.

"Kat, I hear what you're saying, but our best bet is to focus on us, show we're the right choice." Patrick tapped the wheel. "But we can think on this more, talk about it later." A forced smile entered his voice. "Speaking of focusing on us, Mom messaged me yesterday asking for details on Rose's birthday party, saying she hadn't heard anything from you yet. That if we wanted to make sure people weren't previously engaged, we'd better lock down a date soon." He paused. "It made me realize we've barely even talked about the party since all this started."

Katherine looked at him, then turned away.

"You were all about it," said Patrick, "before."

Katherine gripped her wrist, imagining the smirk on Susie's face as she wrote that text, subtly pointing out that Katherine had dropped the ball on such an important event. She wouldn't be surprised if Susie had made a "colored-people time" joke to her husband. But she was right, Katherine couldn't put it off any longer.

"I'd still like to throw a party, obviously," said Patrick, "but do you think you're up for it?"

The world raced by. Their earlier conversation wasn't over, but he was right: for now, they could put it aside. "Absolutely. We should throw a big party." She kept her voice firm. "A celebration." And it'd be more than that. "Show we have a strong community, like you said. People who love and support us, who love Rose. Show that we're the best and only choice."

The next day, Katherine held up her remote as an on-air reporter told viewers to tune in for the latest news on the IVF scandal. She muted the screen just as Irene's face appeared, then stared at the guest list for Rose's party. Despite her fear that the more people, the more likely it would be that someone would figure out they were the "switch parents," as the media had been calling them, Katherine decided it wasn't worth the mental energy to toil over who was worthy and who wasn't, so she invited everyone she could think of. Step one to reinforcing their strong community. A community of 103 people. If everyone came, their house and property would burst at the seams, but it would burst with joy, love, hope. It would be a celebration. It would also be strategic: strengthening friendships, renewing connections they'd let slide, celebrating their girl.

Still, there was one name she'd crossed out, written again, erased. Hearing Patrick in the kitchen prepping his coffee for the morning ahead, Katherine called out to him.

"What do we do about Mikolai? I saw you added him to the list."

"Yeah." Patrick came in and sat in a chair across from Katherine. "I wasn't sure. But he's on the team. I'm inviting everyone on the team. Some of those guys are my closest friends from university days, a couple from high school, even. And I see them every week. To invite them but not him…"

Katherine nodded. "It would look weird."

"Like we were singling him out."

"What if you just invited the ones you knew from before the team?"

"I'd be inviting all but two guys. And technically, I knew Mikolai before, too."

Katherine stared at the empty line where Mikolai's name had been. "It won't be weird, having him here?"

Patrick offered a slight smile. "For us, maybe. But no one else. He doesn't even see Tess anymore, barely talks to her."

"But he is Rose's uncle. Biologically."

"And no one will know but us."

Katherine stared at the empty line in her notebook. "What if he knows?"

"Then I doubt he'd come." Patrick paused. "If you don't want to, we won't, but you said you didn't want to exclude anyone. Risk—"

"You're right." Katherine inhaled, deciding as she scrawled his name once more. "It'll be fine."

Patrick stood, leaned over, and kissed her forehead, shocking Katherine with the tenderness of the action. She met his gaze, smiled, grasped his hand. He squeezed hers, returning the smile, then stepped away. It wasn't much, but it was something, more intimacy than they'd shared in months.

Katherine stared at the page, telling herself everything would be fine, trying not to think about the other reason for this party: if custody turned out the way Kerra suggested it might, Katherine wouldn't be there for all the other firsts.

What might she miss? First steps? First time using the potty? The first day of school? But this, they had—Rose's first birthday.

Katherine looked at Rose, who sat studying an alphabet book as if it were a graduate studies text, her brow scrunched and her tongue stuck out at the side of her lip. Her daughter—Tess's daughter—still here, still hers, but not in the way she had been just days ago. Not in the way she ever could be again.

Katherine noticed the muted TV screen. Irene's image was gone, but it'd be back. So far, Irene hadn't talked, at least to the media, had given no reason for what she'd done. Katherine watched as VitaNova Fertility Centre's doors lit the screen, followed by the shot, again, of Irene being taken into the courthouse. She confessed, Dr. Myers had said, but why had she done it?

As Dr. Myers's face filled the screen, Katherine reached for the remote and pressed Volume. "We're appalled," the doctor said, voice contrite, expression somber. "We're a team here. A family. Our mission is to provide exceptional care. Part of that is attention to detail and stringent protocols to make sure no mistakes happen, ever. But this wasn't a mistake. It was a blatant switch by a team member we all loved and trusted. This is a tragedy for all involved. One we have already made sure, through the implementation of new protocols, can never happen again."

The screen cut back to the reporter, mic in hand, asking why the nurse had made the switch. Dr. Myers shook her head, told the reporter she wished she had that answer, but the important thing now was preventing anything like this in the future. As the image transitioned back to a reporter at her desk, Katherine clicked the remote and the screen went blank. Dr. Myers had assured them she wouldn't tell the media anything Katherine and Patrick didn't know, so anything more the reporters said would be speculation. Useless noise.

After giving the kitchen counters a wipe, washing and putting away the items that couldn't go in the dishwasher, then sweeping the floor, Katherine checked her watch; her appointment with Adeline Sanchez was in a half hour. Rather than feeling excited for taking the first positive step in this ridiculous nightmare, she felt chastened by Patrick and his disapproval in the car the other day, and by his withering stare at breakfast the following morning, when she told him she'd booked a meeting.

Katherine's stomach churned at the thought of the argument they'd been having, in various versions, for years: her trying to do what she thought was right, and Patrick making her feel like she was doing something wrong because of it.

But there was no time for that, not now.

Trying to push aside her preconceived notion that PIs were nefarious folk, working in dark alleys, using criminal methods to get their information, Katherine drove into Halifax's North End and pulled her SUV into a spot on Maitland Street. Adeline's office was beside a chiropractor Katherine had seen years earlier, a brick building squeezed between rows of gentrified town houses. Katherine flipped down the visor, adjusted her curls in the mirror, applied a touch of matte powder to her face, and exited her SUV. Noting the ramp leading to the door, she put the car seat in the stroller. If Rose got fussy, Katherine would be able to push her back and forth and avoid having to whip out her breast.

Inside, light flooded the lobby. Large art covered the walls: a lion with a man's face lurking behind it, wearing a baseball cap; a psychedelic owl smoking a pipe; a woman reminiscent of the Virgin Mary wearing glasses, her arms outstretched, whirls of smoke and color around her. And in the middle of it all, a man who seemed more suited to life in the woods, also wearing glasses, sat at the reception desk in front of a MacBook.

Katherine adjusted her purse on her shoulder. The design was…unexpected, but she'd reserve judgment. She stepped up to the man. "I'm here to see Adeline Sanchez."

"Greetings." He smiled, such a welcoming and unassuming smile. "I'll see if she's ready for you." He passed through an open doorway and reappeared moments later, arm outstretched. "Come on in."

"Thanks, Roland." Adeline nodded to the man as Katherine entered the room, and then turned to Katherine. "Call me Adee—only ever Adee."

Adee stood, all five-foot-nothing of her, looking even more minuscule after Katherine had seen Roland's girth and height—yet she took up the room. Only two words could describe her hair, which cascaded past her shoulders in waves, wild and voluptuous. Her skin was lighter than Katherine's, but with a definite tanned hue. Her lips were dark and her eyes darker. She wore laced burgundy leather boots over torn skinny jeans and a baggy T-shirt with a clownish skull on the front. She put out her hand and Katherine took it. "This your kid?" Adee stepped toward Rose and waved her fingers, a joyful smile igniting her face. "She's a beauty."

"Thank you." Katherine returned her grip to the stroller handle. She hadn't known what to expect, but Adee wasn't it. She wanted professionalism. She wanted ingenuity. She wanted calm ruthlessness.

Adee gestured toward two chairs under a window. "Take a seat."

"The website didn't say…" Katherine wheeled the stroller toward the chairs. "You've been doing this how long?"

"Ten years." Adee sat, crossing one booted foot over the opposite knee. "I started young, and I'm older than I look."

"Mm-hmm, and—" Katherine racked her brain for the questions she should ask, the lists she'd seen online. Not that she needed to rack her brain; she had them written in her notebook, a hand's reach away, but she didn't want to pull it out in front of this woman who seemed hardly more than a child but had a presence and easy confidence Katherine envied. "You have a receptionist, clearly, but beyond that, do you work alone?"

"I have a staff of three," said Adee, "and contract workers, occasionally. I'll be the primary investigator. It's me out in the field, doing the work. My crew exists for the tech: compiling my results, transcribing, administration. That sort of thing. They're there when I need them. They also help to keep costs down. For you, I mean."

"Right. And your methods...for surveillance?"

Adee tapped a hand on her knee. "I take it you're a lady who's done her homework, knows not all PIs are the same. I use a mix of high-end, top-of-the-line technology and old-school sleuthing, which means sometimes I work in the gray areas—never black—but those are strictly for reconnaissance. If I can't sit in court and tell a judge exactly how I got the information, I may still tell you, but it's not going in the report."

"I see." A quiver of relief shot through Katherine. Rose whimpered. "So you go to court, then?" Katherine pushed the stroller and pulled it back, rocking. "You're comfortable being called as a witness?"

"Absolutely. And I don't go like this. Blazer, dress pants; I clean up real nice."

"Right. Okay." Katherine sat straighter. She suppressed a grin.

"You said on the phone this is a custody case?"

"Yes."

"The standard things to look for, things that would influence a justice, are substance abuse—drugs, legal or otherwise, alcohol—and criminal activity of any kind. Outside of that, has your daughter been left with people you haven't approved or didn't expect? Left alone? Which, of course, would be a safety issue. Are there any other safety issues? Well-being issues? Abuse—verbal or physical? And before I go any further, I need to make this clear: my job is to investigate the other guardian, but if, in that process, I uncover anything shady about you, anything that could jeopardize this little sweetheart, I will make that information available to the courts, too."

"I'm not worried about that."

"Not even a flinch. Good. Okay. Those are the people I'd rather not work with." Adee leaned forward. "So, Mrs. Matheson, with all of that, are you ready to move forward?"

Katherine hesitated. Tess was meek at times, not exactly an achiever, but from all Katherine knew, she was none of the things Adee had mentioned, which meant this would likely be a waste of money. But the point was, Katherine didn't know. She nodded. "Yes."

"All right." Adee clapped her hands. "It's time to tell your story. Start wherever you like—with the love story, with the way your former partner's a bastard, issues of substance abuse, criminal activity, neglect, or—"

"There's no love story," said Katherine, her gaze still on Rose, "and it's not about my partner."

Katherine explained it all, about the IVF, Irene, the switch. Adee's mouth formed a little O when she got to that part, whispered a cuss. When Adee asked if Katherine had anything on Tess, any hint of drama or trauma or shady situations, Katherine pulled out her notebook, told Adee about the unexplained dropout. The estrangement with Tess's family. The divorce. The ex-husband, now with another woman. She laid out the question she'd decided not to google but leave to a professional—whether Irene and Tess knew each other, whether there was something, anything that could have made Tess complicit.

"That's all you have?" said Adee. "Beyond not wanting to give up your daughter, you have no legal reason Tess shouldn't have shared custody?"

Hope, Katherine wanted to say. That's all she had.

"That's it," said Katherine.

"It's okay," said Adee. "It's a start. We can proceed, so long as you understand my cost is the same, even if all I discover is that Tess is a stand-up woman with a beautiful life waiting for your daughter."

Hope was why she went through the fertility treatments and the IVF, despite her doctors saying there was almost no chance. Why she started treatment with Saadia, despite thinking it wouldn't make a difference. And why, when Adee stared at her like this was a long shot, more than a long shot, Katherine stared right back.

"I understand," said Katherine. "Proceed."

19

TESS

LESS THAN A WEEK AFTER HER LUNCH WITH MIKOLAI, TESS STEPPED off the bus and turned up the street, nerves and excitement all wrapped into one. Everything was falling into place. Carl had agreed to make her hours work. She'd booked apartment viewings for late next week. She had meetings set up with a day home and two day cares to talk about reserving a rotating spot for Rose, which would be tricky, she'd learned. Most places wanted full-time, or at least required you to pay for it.

But Tess would figure it out. She wasn't the only mom out there who had her child part-time. She'd have to lock down a schedule, find another family to split the childcare hours with. She'd sent a message to Saadia, letting her know of her progress, and received a GIF in return, the words *Breathe in, breathe out, you've got this!* flashing above a cartoon taking deep breaths. She'd laughed, warmth flowing through her at the hope that their relationship was transitioning from practitioner and client to friends.

Tess hadn't yet worked up the nerve to contact her parents, but she would soon. Maeve had laid out the steps she needed to strengthen her case, and one by one, she was checking them off her list.

Guilt still trickled over her because of the subterfuge with Mikolai, not telling him the real reason she'd reached out. Deep down, she'd wanted to reach out long before finding out about the switch, but her grief over Hanna was too raw to make that step. In the weeks she'd stayed with Mikolai and his family while recovering, each smile, each laugh highlighted what Tess would never have. Their effervescent joy made her pain all the worse.

The grief hadn't left, but the hope over Rose, the possibility that one day she'd have the joy of parenting her child, had given her strength. Today she would reconnect with Mikolai's whole family, establish connection with the cousins who would grasp Rose's hand once she started to walk, who would run around the yard, their squeals of laughter mixing with hers.

Tess placed a beaming smile on her face as she knocked on the door and waited for Mikolai's boisterous greeting. Never one to disappoint, he pulled open the door, his smile and body movements larger than life, the only person she knew who always seemed excited just to wake up in the morning and realize he was breathing.

He motioned for Tess to come in, wrapping her in a one-armed side hug as he carried Tom under his other, the laughing boy horizontal, with his legs kicking behind him and his arms straight in front.

As Mikolai's arm fell away from her shoulders, Tess bent down and kissed Tom's cheek. She cupped his face. "You flying?"

He nodded with a broad grin. Tess laughed and stood, then followed Mikolai and his soaring boy into the kitchen. Karina stood in front of the counter, her hair swept up in a messy bun, her lean tan arms kneading dough for pierogies. Karina's smile lit up at the sight of Tess. "Welcome," she said, waving Tess over and planting a kiss on her cheek. "It's so good to see you."

Tess smiled back as Karina elbowed her. "Get in on this."

Tess turned to the sink, washed her hands, and then stood beside

Karina. Sinking her fingers into the warm dough, Tess was reminded of the life she'd wished for, the life that now, one day, she might have. Jannie entered the room, all arms and legs, and slid onto a chair at the island across from Karina and Tess. "You've grown!" said Tess.

"My little beanpole." Mikolai laughed. "Like you were at that age."

Tess grinned, remembering the awkwardness of her body growing so fast she didn't know how to move or walk properly anymore, a stranger in her own skin. "You're beautiful," she whispered to Jannie, as the girl offered a shy smile.

"Mikolai told me about the new job," said Karina, her shoulder bumping Tess's. "That's great."

"It is. Thanks."

"And it's because of your studies?"

"Well…" Tess hesitated. "Yeah. I suppose so. Would have been better if I had the degree."

"But you got the job."

"I did." A surge of pride welled in Tess. She'd never looked at it that way—she'd gotten a job usually reserved for university grads. Yes, for them it was a stepping stone, which it wouldn't be for her unless she finished her degree, but still, she'd gotten it. "And I'm going back to school." The words tumbled out of Tess's mouth before she'd considered them—her desire to reveal something true and real amidst all this withholding making her speak.

"You are?" Mikolai's features transitioned from surprise to glee. "When?"

"Well…" Tess hesitated as she tried to think of a way to explain the delay without having his excitement wither. "I haven't figured that out yet, but it's my plan. I've been saving. I've saved quite a bit. Enough to cover my final semester and most living expenses, too, but I'd like to save more so I'll have no debt. I could start next fall. And then maybe go on to a master's, too."

"Oh, Tess." Mikolai plopped on the stool beside Jannie. "That's fabulous. But why wait? If you have the money now, start now. Or next semester, at least. It doesn't even have to be full-time. You could take one course, or two, while you're still working. You only have three credits left, right?"

"Well, yes, but—"

"So do it, Tess. Don't wait. Get the degree, and then you can get a better job or move up in your current one. Isn't that what you said? That with a degree, you could move up?"

"Yes, but—"

Karina swatted Mikolai with a dough-covered hand and rolled her eyes. "Leave the girl alone," she chastened. "Let her do things her way."

Tess smiled her thanks at Karina. Mikolai had a point—and in a way, it made sense—but Tess had been out of school for a decade. She didn't want to risk starting and then realize she was no longer cut out for it, no longer had the skills to take notes, study, ace her tests and lab assignments. And if she were tired, if she were juggling work and school, failure would be a stronger possibility.

"I don't understand why anyone would *choose* to go back to school," said Jannie, "if they didn't have to."

"So they can get a good job," said Karina, "have a better life." She turned her gaze to Tess. "Do you plan to continue with the same major?"

"Yes," said Tess. "It means I can get my degree a lot sooner, as long as all my credits are still valid. I'm guessing it's possible I may have to redo a few, although, thankfully, most of the specialization would have come later."

"A sonographer," said Mikolai. "Are you sure that's still a good idea? I mean, after all—"

"Mik!" Karina shook her head.

"Well…"

Tess swallowed. "Mik's right," she said. "It may be hard. But there are other avenues I could pursue, and sonographers do a lot more than look at babies. I could work in a cancer ward."

"Other avenues." Mikolai winked. "Dr. Sokolowski has a nice ring to it."

"Don't think so." Tess attempted a smile, then pressed her hands into the dough, kneading.

"Tata said you're smart!" said Tomas, bounding into the room.

"I sure did!" Mikolai grinned.

"But that you don't apply yourself."

"Tomas!" said Karina, as Mikolai pulled the boy to his side and cupped a hand over his mouth.

Tess shrugged. Their father had said a similar thing more than once, including the day she told them she'd dropped out. *Apply yourself,* mój kwiatuszek. *If you do, you can do anything.*

"Do you want to be a doctor?" asked Tomas.

Tess shook her head. Seeing her affinity toward science—all through junior and senior high, she was at the top of her class or close to it—her father had talked about her becoming a doctor. Either an MD or a professor, he thought, would be fine. Her mother, doubting Tess could handle it, thought a nurse would be better. A solid, respectable job for a woman that wouldn't allow her to feel too high and mighty.

In a bio class in high school, when a sonographer had come to her classroom and Tess had first seen an ultrasound, that little life swimming inside a dark and undefined world, she'd been entranced. She couldn't see herself standing in front of a classroom lecturing or tending to patients, as her father wanted, and she didn't want to be a nurse—touching all those strange people, ooze and sickness and ailment. Holding an ultrasound wand between her and her patients seemed the way to go, being there for the first glimpse of life, sharing in her patients' joy. At the time, she hadn't thought about being there for the hard times, the lives gone wrong too soon. She hadn't imagined being on the other side of that wand.

"I'll be proud of you no matter what," said Mikolai, "and Mama and Tata will be, too."

"Mik." Karina again.

"Changing the subject"—Mikolai straightened—"I've been meaning to ask, you going to the Mathesons' party for their little girl? I thought we could all arrive together."

Tess tensed. "I didn't know about it."

"Really?" Mikolai popped a carrot in his mouth. "I thought you and Katherine were friends. Anyway, it's the Sunday after next. Patrick was telling everyone at soccer. You should come."

Tess swallowed. If she was going to tell him, this should be the time. "I don't know if—"

"Oh, it's fine." Mikolai grabbed another piece of carrot. "They're inviting everyone. The more the merrier, Patrick said."

A chance to see Rose… Tess knew she should say no and give some excuse, or bare it all now and tell Mikolai what she should have told him already, be honest with the one person most likely to have her back. The words were in her mouth, fighting to roll off her tongue. "Sure," she said instead, "that sounds great."

20

KATHERINE

TWO WEEKS. TWO WEEKS AND NO WORD FROM KERRA. NO WORD from Adee. No word from Tess. Katherine shook her head at Patrick. "Tess said she wanted Rose."

"She did." Patrick picked up a pack of crayons, a mini book, and a gluten-free, sugar-free, peanut-free packet of vegan cookies and dumped them in a goodie bag, then shifted down the assembly line Katherine had organized.

Katherine looked back to her computer, where she was organizing the RSVPs. So far seventy percent of the guests had responded, several of them using the opportunity to ask if there'd be other IVF families there, if Katherine knew anything about the switch or who was involved, if the thought of what happened made her sick. *Your ploy makes me sick!* she wanted to say, but instead she kept to variations of her original copy-and-pasted reply. A lie, without technically lying.

Rose's birthday would be a bash, but the work to put it all together, organizing caterers and entertainment, goodie bags and layout, was a burden rather than a pleasant distraction. Normally Katherine loved this stuff, thrived on it, but not this time.

Katherine looked at Patrick again. "Well, what's going on?"

"These things take time."

"Time?" Katherine shook her head. "Kerra said Tess's next step was to apply to the courts for access. How long could that take?"

"Maybe she's preparing."

Katherine had an uncharacteristic urge to throw the mouse at Patrick for how calm he sounded, how calm he'd seemed for weeks. Not that it should surprise her. This was Patrick. The more on edge she was, the more relaxed he became. Katherine resisted a sigh. "Preparing for what?"

"I don't know. Her life. We were told to make sure our lives represented the best possible environment for Rose. Maybe she was, too. I don't think she got much in the divorce. Mikolai's not in contact with her much, but…I don't know. She's probably been going through hard times."

"So that's good, then, if she—"

"Katherine, geez." Patrick shook his head.

"I mean for us. For custody. Not that it's good she's going through tough times, but—"

"Okay. Okay." Patrick waved a hand, then let it fall. "Maybe she's just waiting on a lawyer. It's only been a couple of weeks. Things don't move quickly when you're not paying the big bucks. Tess probably has to wait on legal aid."

"Mm-hmm, and that is…" Katherine's stomach clenched, her breath catching with nervous hope. "I mean, her chances with…"

"Legal aid lawyers are good. They're passionate. Devoted. They have to be to take on the level of work they do."

Katherine exhaled, frustration spreading through her. She wanted news, an update. When Katherine texted Adee to check in a few days ago, she said she'd been busy with other cases and assured her she'd get her team on the preliminary work during any downtime. She'd feed Katherine relevant intel as it came, but she wasn't available to dig in yet. Custody cases take time, she'd said. Katherine was supposed to tell Adee when they received the date of their first hearing, and then she would shift Katherine's file to a higher priority.

No news was good news, or so they said, but no news was also torture.

Reading her expression, Patrick paused his packing. "Try not to stress, Kat. It's just been a couple of weeks. Put it out of your mind. Enjoy this time. Enjoy this party and all that comes with it. We'll stress and worry when we have to."

Katherine returned her gaze to the RSVPs. How many two-week waits had she had? Seven years' worth. And only the one that had given her her baby had ended well. This one was worse than them all, because now that she had her baby, she might lose her.

Katherine jumped as her phone buzzed on the table. She swiped the screen.

It was Adee. *Nothing big, but I've had a bit of time to get started, so thought I'd get in touch. Tess has a steady enough job. Been there almost a year now. Okay pay.*

"Who's that?" asked Patrick.

"Adee," Katherine answered as she typed. *So that's good?* She paused, then: *For Tess, I mean. That's all that matters? That she's employed? That she can provide?*

Adee responded: *She certainly won't be able to provide for Rose in the way you and Patrick do, but yeah, she'll be able to meet Rose's basic needs, which is all a judge cares about. She is living in a pretty rundown place, though. Wouldn't look good. So, there's that.*

Katherine sighed. *Okay. Thanks.*

"What is it? What did she say?"

Katherine slid over the phone.

"Wow." Patrick let out a laugh that made Katherine's teeth clench. "So that's what we're shelling out the big bucks for. Riveting stuff."

"She's just getting started."

Patrick held his finger up as his own ringtone sounded. He pulled it out of his pocket. "It's Kerra."

"Speaker." Katherine leaned forward.

He held the phone out, then pressed the Speaker button. "Patrick, hello. Kerra Campbell here."

"Yep. You've got Katherine on the line, too."

"Wonderful. How've you both been?"

"Oh, plodding on," said Patrick. "We're prepping for Rose's birthday party, though it's not for a week and a half."

Katherine resisted the urge to let his comment annoy her. "It'll be a good crowd," she said.

"That's wonderful," said Kerra, "foster that community. So…" Winding up the chitchat, she deepened her tone. "I need to keep this short. I've been in contact with a lawyer on the Irene Connor case, asking him to keep me in the loop and whatnot. I expected this, and these things move slowly, so it won't be for a while, but I wanted to let you know that both Katherine and Tess will be called as witnesses for her trial. Likely Patrick, too. Now, unlike your case, Irene's is going to be public and reported on heavily. The media is having a field day. This isn't the first time there's been an IVF mix-up in Canada, but it's the first time it's been in the news, and certainly the first time it wasn't a mistake." Kerra paused as her words sank in.

"The problem is," she continued, "it'd be best for everyone if your story is kept private. You don't want people delving into your business. You don't want anyone with an old grudge saying something unsavory or looking for their fifteen minutes of fame by giving an interview about you, how they know you, anything like that, whether it's good or bad. Not just for your case, but for Rose, in the future. This situation is not the world's business, and it's best to keep it that way."

Patrick's foot thumped. He let out a loud sigh. "Okay, but if Irene's case is going to be heavily reported on, is keeping it private even an option?"

"Well, in a situation like this, some people would want it to be the world's business, to make sure not just Irene but the fertility clinic is held to account, to warn other families, share their story so this never happens again. But I don't think that's the best route here."

Katherine spoke. "So are you saying I shouldn't testify?"

"No, no, not that. And I should say, if you wanted to share your story publicly, if you've weighed the pros and cons for Rose, that's fine, that's your prerogative, but not until after the trial. Your trial. So when you get the call to testify, my advice is to request a publication ban. One on behalf of both your names, and Rose's and Tess's as well, whether she requests it or not."

"That means our names can't be in the papers?" asked Katherine.

"Exactly. Not in any reported media. Your requesting Tess's name will be more tricky. Hopefully her lawyer advises her to request it herself, but if she doesn't, you can do it on behalf of Rose. You may not get it. It's supposed to be 'necessary for the proper administration of justice,' which will be hard to argue for Irene's case, but we'll try. And if not your names, we'll be able to keep Rose's out of the media mess as she's a minor, assert it would be detrimental to her and her mental health to be known as the child of this scandal. So the key is making sure none of you make her name public."

"Could we choose not to testify? If they don't grant the ban?" asked Katherine.

"That might be considered obstruction of justice. Victim testimonies could go a long way to conviction and full sentencing. A long way to scaring off copycats seeking some godlike power-tripping thrill, to making sure no one tries this again."

"Right," said Patrick, "and when we get the call, should we call you?"

"Sure. I'll put you in touch with someone better placed to guide you through the process."

"Okay," Patrick and Katherine said in unison.

"And in the meantime," said Kerra, "not a word of this to any press or anyone connected to the press. In fact, I'd tell as few people as possible. If your identities get leaked and it's traced back to you, it could mess things up."

"How, exactly?" Patrick looked at Katherine, his brow raised.

"Breaking the ban. Just don't talk about it. If you already have, let those people know this is a private family affair."

"So—"

"Listen, I have to go. Don't wait for the call. It could be weeks. Months. But when they call, you know what to do."

"Wait." Katherine leaned in farther. "Have you heard anything about a court date for the custody hearing?"

"No." Kerra let out a little laugh. "I don't even know if Tess has gotten a lawyer, but when I do, you'll be the first to know. Just remember, these things take time. Have a nice day."

"But—" The call ended. Katherine looked at Patrick, exasperated.

He smiled. "What did you say? Crayons are for two and up or three and up?"

Sometimes she wanted to smack that carefree smile off Patrick's face. He must be stressed, but it was just like before. He went through the days, the weeks, the months as if none of it was life-altering.

"Two."

Katherine's insides twisted. She stared at the man who had been her husband for over a decade, but who so often felt like a stranger, stuffing the goodie bags, throwing items in rather than placing them so the bag sat smoothly. She resisted the urge to stop him, explain, again, the way each item should be packed so there were no unsightly bulges, no items sticking out the top. Instead, she watched that Zen-like expression on his face.

Once, after yet another negative pregnancy test when she'd been late, when she'd dared to hold out hope, he'd said what he always said, with a smile, "We'll try again." Several hours later, she walked into the bathroom, saw him standing, hands gripping the sink, staring at his anguished face in the mirror. He'd caught sight of her reflection, stood straight, and smiled, any trace of sorrow gone. So he wasn't immune to the pain she felt, even when so often he seemed to let the trials of life roll off his shoulders. What she didn't know was whether his apparent ease was a coping mechanism or an act to settle her, assuage her turmoil. Either way, unlike her, he certainly didn't try to control every aspect of life to make up for the fact that life was anything but controllable. Instead, he pointed out the bright side.

It was why she loved him—his dogged optimism. He was good for her; he balanced out her nerves. But it was also why she had these moments, these flare-ups, of hate.

21

KATHERINE

SEVERAL DAYS HAD PASSED SINCE KERRA'S CALL ABOUT THE PUBLI-cation ban, and there was still no news of Tess, no indication the custody case was moving forward. The unknown pricked at Katherine, tainting every moment, erasing any opportunity to feel happy, relaxed, at ease. And now she had to have lunch with Patrick's family. Katherine hefted a massive salad bowl out of the car. "It's not too late to cancel. Say I'm not feeling well. Or Rose isn't."

Patrick made a sound between a laugh and a groan as he walked around the car and opened the door to retrieve Rose. "We're already here."

"I'm not sure I can handle it, pretending everything's normal. Pretending we're okay."

"You're going to have to handle the birthday party. Think of it as practice." Patrick gave Katherine's shoulder a squeeze. "Family, right? Kerra said that was important."

"Mm-hmm."

Katherine cast her gaze at the house where she'd had family dinners once a month for over a decade. She followed Patrick up the drive to his parents' front door. He pushed it open and called out his greeting as two dirty-blond flashes darted past them, Nerf guns in their arms.

When they were a few months into dating and he'd invited her to family dinner, Katherine had thought she'd like it. His three siblings were nearly always in attendance—and when occasion called, a host of aunts, uncles, cousins. But over a decade later, she still felt like a guest, like she was on the outside looking in, not unwanted, exactly, but close.

"Patrick!" Susie rushed to her son, wrapped her arms around him, and held on tight. "Katherine." Susie smiled, displaying alarmingly white teeth for a woman her age. "So lovely to see you." She hugged her lightly, giving an air-kiss to the side of Katherine's cheek. Letting go, she waved her fingers at Rose, then promptly turned to the kitchen. Katherine followed, salad bowl in hand.

"You shouldn't have!" Susie's smile was broad, her expression one of forced surprise and delight. "A regular one this time, or fancy-schmancy over-the-top?"

Katherine pressed a smile. "Just regular." She brought salad almost every month. In the early years, she'd mixed it up: kale and arugula with pine nuts and Parmesan, or a ginger-spiced cabbage and lentil. But after hearing Susie laugh to another daughter-in-law about Katherine's "creations," she stuck to romaine or iceberg lettuce with standard vegetables: tomatoes, carrots, cucumber. Still, every month, Susie questioned her. Katherine set the bowl on the island and unwrapped it, her gaze on Susie's back as the woman shuffled in front of the stove.

Katherine rubbed her arm, debating whether to offer to help, even though Susie always waved her off. She resisted a sigh, not wanting to be here, to play into the charade. Not when Irene's case was in the news and likely to come up around the table.

Patrick said he hadn't told them about the switch, but that they should still know enough not to mention it, knowing just the topic would make her uncomfortable. Not that that had ever stopped them before. In her seven years of infertility, the comments and jokes had felt ceaseless. Initially, it'd been the questions: "What are you waiting for?" and "Better get on it; Katherine's clock is ticking!" Once Katherine started treatment, and it became impossible to brush off the inquiries with throwaway replies, such as "When the time is right" or "One day," the jokes had shifted as they all watched the darling firstborn unable to continue their line, knowing he'd picked a wife who, in this most important of ways, was a failure.

Though they hadn't said it outright, Katherine knew that's how they saw it, as her failure. She could hardly blame them; it was how she saw it, too. When Patrick announced they were starting fertility treatment, first the drugs, then IUI, and eventually IVF, his mother offered pinched smiles, sent articles about stress reduction, dietary changes, and old wives' tales "that often worked!" Patrick's brothers joked about his lack of virility, knowing it was her, not him, who was the problem.

His sister didn't have much to say about any of it, so consumed by the five pregnancies she went through in the time it took Katherine to have one. While Heather complained about morning sickness, swollen ankles, and nighttime wakings, Katherine offered her sympathies, inwardly wishing she were so lucky, yearning for the discomfort.

Once, Susie had sent Katherine an article about cleaning supplies, how the wrong ones could affect fertility. *You keep such a nice house*, the note had said, *just want to make sure that's not the cause of your troubles. Look at these great alternatives!* As if Katherine hadn't thought of that. As if she hadn't thought of everything.

Rose crawled in behind Katherine, grabbed her leg, and pulled to standing. "Mama!"

"Hi, sweetie."

Susie turned, her smile broad, a cookie in her hand. Before Katherine could stop her, say to at least wait until after lunch, Susie passed it to Rose, whose face lit up. "Kee!" she squealed.

Katherine held her smile as Susie turned back to the counter. She'd given in on the sweets fight months ago, despite initially insisting Rose wouldn't taste sugar until she was two. Rose didn't have it at home or at Katherine's parents', but after too many tension-filled moments here, too many postlunch arguments with Patrick, who'd told her to let it go—at least with his family—Katherine had acquiesced.

Katherine stepped forward, wanting to show she wasn't simmering. "Can I—"

"No. No," Susie answered without turning. "Go sit, darling. But thank you."

Katherine smiled back, unexpected moisture building behind her eyes. Patrick had told her more than once that besides their differing opinions on issues such as sweets and junk food, the tension with his family was all in her head. In moments like this, she wondered if it were true.

Katherine entered the living room and sat as Patrick's youngest brother, Chuck, plopped on the couch, his feet on the coffee table. "How's it hanging?"

"It's uh…" Katherine hesitated. "All right."

"Cool." He grabbed one of his nephews running past and ruffled the boy's hair before releasing him. "We got the birthday invite."

"Yes." Katherine pushed out a smile, uncertain what else to say. Of course they got the invite, they'd RSVP'd. "Glad you're coming."

"Well." Chuck laughed. "We'll make an appearance, but five hours for a party? That's a bit long, don't you think?"

Katherine kept her smile firm. The words *Drop-in style!* were right at the top of the invite. "It's a drop-in," she said, "you're not meant to—"

"Food's ready!" Susie entered the living room, her smile bright.

Katherine stood along with Chuck as all ten adults, Rose, and her youngest cousin settled around the table. The older kids were in the kitchen. Katherine kept quiet, smiling when necessary as the roast beef, potatoes, and vegetables were passed around. "Did I hear you mention Rose's party?" asked Susie as she sat.

Katherine nodded.

"I was so glad to see you'd finally gotten organized. Left it a little late, I thought."

Katherine pressed a smile.

"Grilling up some burgers and dogs?" asked Patrick's brother Ronny. "I'd be happy to man it if you like. We all know my culinary skills far surpass yours."

"Actually," said Katherine, "we hired caterers so we won't have to worry about it."

"Caterers?" Chuck laughed. "For a one-year-old's party? What are you getting? Sushi and tapas?"

"Well, yes," said Katherine, her jaw tensing. "Along with some other foods more suited to children."

Patrick looked at her, shook his head. They'd argued about food for the party: Patrick wanting simple fare, as Ronny expected, and Katherine wanting not just caterers but serving staff, too, so there'd be one less thing they had to worry about. Katherine knew, deep down, Patrick would have been happy to have the staff. It was this he'd been concerned about—the ribbing from his brothers. They'd made comments in the past about Patrick and Katherine's spacious house, their two off-the-lot cars, the professional photos of Katherine while pregnant and again of Rose as a newborn. As if they should hide their wealth, as if success wasn't something to be proud of.

"Let me guess," said Chuck, "mini wieners baked in artisanal sour-dough bread."

"And aged Romano cheese on sprouted multigrain crackers," said Ronny.

"I'm surprised you know what those are," said Patrick under his breath as Susie flicked her hand at his brothers.

"To each their own," she said. "Even if their own is a little hoity-toity for my tastes!" She chuckled.

"Oh, this is something you may find interesting." Ronny glanced at Katherine, who wished, as she so often did, that these dinners were yearly instead of monthly. "I read an article the other day about babies conceived artificially, then grown in artificial wombs, for women who couldn't carry babies and for male partners who couldn't find a surrogate."

"What?" Patrick's father shook his head. "That type of thing should be outlawed, scientists taking life into their own hands like that. That's God's role." Jerry shook his head again. "An absolute abomination."

Katherine, heart racing, opened her mouth to speak. She moistened her lips, leaned forward, but before the words came out, Patrick's voice carried over the room. "Is Rose an abomination?" Everyone looked at him, eyes wide or mouth open. Jerry winced as his shoulders lifted. He started to speak but Patrick raised a hand. "Rose wouldn't exist without those scientists. She was conceived in a petri dish, just like those babies. We were lucky Katherine was able to carry her, but other women aren't so lucky. So what's the difference?" Patrick rested his arms on the table. "Is that what you think, Dad? Rose is an abomination?"

Jerry paled. He kept his gaze away from Katherine, from Rose. "No. Of course not." And he didn't think it, Katherine was sure of it. Jerry loved Rose. But in the way his voice wavered, the way he wouldn't look at her, wouldn't even look at Patrick, she knew what she'd suspected all along. He thought the method of Rose's conception disturbing, unnatural, perhaps even sinful. Now that she was here, he loved her, but he thought the science that created her shouldn't exist.

"It's different," said Susie, her voice high-pitched, desperately conciliatory. "Absolutely different. Rose may have started in a petri dish, but she grew inside of you." She turned to Katherine. "She shared your blood, she heard your heartbeat. It's comparing apples and oranges."

Except apples and oranges were both fruit.

"Yeah, but if you think about the fact that—ow!" Chuck reached a hand under the table and cut his eyes at his wife, then groaned. "Charley horse."

Katherine swallowed, her skin prickling, the conversation far too close to the switch, which they all must have heard about. She pictured a family conversation before she and Patrick had arrived—would they bring it up, or wouldn't they? Even if they weren't wondering if Katherine and Patrick were involved, they must be itching to talk about the fact that they could have been. It, most likely, was why Ronny had come across the article: researching about the switch, trying to glean information. In Rose's early months, Patrick had made his favorite little joke in front of them, too, and at least half the people in this room had commented on how Rose looked like Patrick.

"Oh, she's so fair!" Susie had proclaimed the first time she saw Rose. "Look at that creamy skin."

Katherine had stared—glared, more like. Susie had looked at her and at Patrick. "Not that it matters," she said, her grin still broad, looking back at the baby. "It'll just make her life easier. And that's a fact."

Now, in the silence that persisted far too long, Katherine looked around the table, desperate to know their thoughts. Desperate, also, to get out of that house and away from all those eyes staring at her or trying not to look.

"What I want to know," said Chuck, at last, "was who caught that Leafs and Bruins game last night? What a shit show."

Ronny laughed and Jerry pounded the table. Katherine picked up her fork, placed it in her mouth, and chewed.

Once they pulled onto the street after leaving his parents' house, Katherine turned to Patrick. "Do you think they know about the switch? And wonder if it was us? Could Ronny bringing up that article have been about trying to get answers?"

Patrick rubbed a hand through his hair, then looked away from her, a flush covering his face.

"What? What did they say?"

Patrick kept his focus on the road. "They've known, Kat, from the day of the DNA test. When I called to tell Mom we couldn't come to dinner. The moment she answered the phone, she asked if we'd heard about the switch. If we'd been contacted."

"And you told her?"

"Well, yeah. I didn't want to lie to her. And of course, she's been asking for updates since."

"So you lied to me." Katherine shook her head, feeling as if she'd been punched in the gut.

"I just didn't want you to stress." Patrick took a long breath. "I knew you'd be annoyed I told them, but they're my family, too."

"Which makes it okay to lie? Why are they always the priority? *This* family has to be the most important." Katherine put a hand to her chest, then gestured toward Patrick. "We're what matters right now. A united front. Partners. You don't lie to your partner."

Patrick glanced at her. "Well, it meant you didn't have to talk to them about it."

"Look how that turned out."

"Kat."

"They all sat there, knowing, while I was in the dark. Like a fool."

Patrick pulled to the side of the road and parked the car, his voice cajoling. "Them knowing is not a big deal."

"Not a big deal for you, maybe." Katherine's hands shook. "Rose is your daughter. You're her father. No one's trying to take that away."

He rubbed a hand along his temple. "I know. Please. I said I'm sorry."

"No." Katherine turned to him. "You didn't. You explained why you did it, but you didn't apologize. You justified yourself by defending your need to make them the priority. That's what you do. That's why I hate going there."

"You hate going there?"

"They're this insular little clique. Everyone who's not blood is on the outside."

Patrick shook his head. "You're blood, Katherine. You're my wife. You're Rose's mother."

Katherine's jaw clenched. Patrick put his hand to his forehead. Neither of them spoke the truth he'd let slip.

"Katherine."

"They're probably glad."

"What?"

Katherine spoke the words, knowing she shouldn't even as they spilled out. "Glad she's not mine. Glad their precious granddaughter isn't tainted."

Patrick's voice held a steel edge to it. "Not this again."

Katherine's thoughts returned to Susie's pleasure over Rose's pale skin. It wasn't an isolated opinion, either. Years earlier, at their rehearsal dinner, Katherine had heard Patrick's aunt Jenny whispering with another guest. "Think of the children," she'd said. "Not that there's anything wrong with Black people," the aunt emphasized.

"Oh, no, of course not," said the other woman.

"But it'll be so difficult." Aunt Jenny's voice dripped with jubilant concern. "His children's lives, I mean."

"Katherine's beautiful," the other woman said, "and so well-spoken."

"Many of them are these days," said Aunt Jenny.

"Maybe the children will pass," said the lady. "Isn't Katherine a mulatto?"

"Yes." The aunt sighed. "She is. So, hopefully."

Aunt Jenny had gotten her wish. Susie, too, apparently. Rose passed. Because she wasn't Katherine's. Because she was created in a way that some—like Patrick's father—thought should never exist. Just as so many, too many, thought Katherine shouldn't exist, thought her existence was in some way obscene or, at the least, an inappropriate mixing. Katherine still remembered the first time she'd been called mulatto—not as an insult, but as a neutral descriptor—remembered looking the term up and discovering the connotation that she was a mix between two discrete species and, as a result, constituted a third, separate species of her own.

Not for the first time, Katherine feared that one day Rose would resent her parents' choice to put her life into the hands of scientists. That this, the scandal, the mix-up, would be a taint that followed her always, akin to the perceived taint of Black blood in so many who "passed."

"Katherine." By the sound of his voice, Katherine could tell Patrick was speaking through clenched teeth. "My family loves you. They don't care that you're Black. They don't have any issue with Black people, as I've told you time and again. They just…" He paused. "They think Black people are different culturally, and it's confusing for them that you're not different in any definable way, so they say stupid things sometimes. But it's nothing more than that. And"—he shook his head—"I can't. I can't keep defending them. This is on you now."

"I—" Katherine gripped the door handle, anger and frustration and terror mixing inside her. "I'm scared. Scared that people *will* care, that no one will be able to see Rose as mine because—"

Patrick reached for her hand, grasped it. "Put that thought away, okay? No one questioned before—"

"They did."

"They didn't, Katherine. They wondered, the way we did. But outside of that, I promise you, it won't matter. You're Rose's mother, you birthed her, and race has nothing to do with it. It won't have anything to do with it."

Katherine looked at their hands, their fingers entwined. She wanted to believe him.

"And I'm sorry. About lying. You're right. I shouldn't have lied to you. I do put my family above our family sometimes. I don't mean to." Katherine met his gaze and he grinned—that half smile that had made her fall in love with him. "A lifelong habit is hard to break." He squeezed her hand. "I'll do better."

Katherine's lip trembled. "You did good tonight. Standing up for Rose to your father. For us."

Patrick leaned back. "That was awful. Speaking without thinking, I promise you."

"I know."

Patrick tilted his head. "Have you told your folks yet? About the switch?"

"No."

Patrick's lips shifted to the side. He stared, as if he pitied her. "They'd want to know."

Katherine drew her hand away, not wanting to reveal the deeper reason she hadn't told her parents.

"I'll tell them when I'm ready."

"Okay, I just think—" Patrick's phone on the dash lit up. "Kerra again. Should I?"

Katherine sighed. "Yes."

He grabbed the phone and swiped, rather than activating the car's speaker. He nodded into the device. Nodded again. *Why, oh why, did he nod into the phone?* "Yes…well…I understand. We expected that…of course… and so now?" More nodding. "Okay…yes, I'll tell her… Thanks, you too." He put the phone back on the dash's holder and turned to Katherine. "It's begun."

"Tess applied for access?" He nodded. "And?"

"The judge is ordering court-appointed mediation."

"But we already—"

"She wants us to try again."

22

TESS

Tess sat on the curb outside her apartment waiting for Mikolai, who was already a few minutes late. She hadn't needed him to come, but when she mentioned she was looking for a new apartment, he'd jumped at the opportunity, insisting a second set of eyes was pivotal when making such an important decision.

She placed her hands on the hot concrete and leaned back, the wait giving her time to go over the meeting she'd finally had with her court-appointed lawyer. After perusing the reports from Maeve, John Messineo had been pleased to learn that Tess had reestablished contact with her brother, had confirmed better work hours, and would be looking at apartments. Pleased, too, to know she was going for shared custody. "You'd have to prove you were the better parent if you went for full," he'd said, rifling through her files. "Which may be impossible."

Tess had tried to maintain her smile, though she imagined it looked more like a grimace.

"Contact with your parents?" he'd asked, his clean-shaven, round, and rosy cheeks lifted in a hopeful smile. She'd had to shake her head, tell him not yet, but she would.

She'd just figure everything else out first.

Tess looked up the street again, the tightness in her throat making her anxious for Mikolai's arrival. "How much time do I have?" she'd asked Messineo, hoping that having her own lawyer would now get her a solid answer. But the answer was the same. "These things move slowly. Line everything up now, as soon as you can, because when they stop moving slowly, they sometimes move incredibly fast."

He'd wanted to know, too, if Tess knew anything about the Mathesons that could work in her favor. Something she'd overheard in the fertility group with Katherine or that her brother had picked up from Patrick at soccer. Anything unsavory. Gossip, even, that could lead to something solid. Tess looked away as Messineo sighed. "Would visitation be an option?" he'd wanted to know. "To start, at least? Regular visitation, rather than going for shared custody right away?"

Tess shook her head. She'd already offered to start with visitation, and the Mathesons had spat in her face. If the judge decided on visitation to ease Rose into it, Tess would be fine with that. Support it, even. But as far as her legal expectations now, she wanted it clear her intention was shared custody. An even, fifty-fifty split. It was her right.

Seeing Mikolai's car turn up the street, Tess popped up. He pulled up beside her, then jumped out, racing around to give her a hug. "Sorry, sorry." He laughed.

Seeing the kids in the back seat, Tess leaned over to wave.

"Tom's soccer coach had one of those boot casts on, and Tom insisted on helping him pack everything up before we left."

Tess smiled, shaking her head. "Like father, like son."

Mikolai paused, grinning. "I guess so."

An hour later, Tess, Mikolai, and the kids followed the property manager through an apartment. The fourth apartment. Technically, they were all fine. But one was too dark, one too small, one too full of cats—even if she scrubbed the floors and walls, the smell might never leave, Mikolai pointed out. None felt right. Tess needed it to feel right. She needed to walk inside and picture Rose running down the halls, sitting in a patch of sun on the floor, playing with her dolls or blocks or whatever she played with. She needed to breathe the air and think, *Rose could be happy here.*

By the way Tomas was looking around, nose scrunched up, mouth twisted, this wasn't the one, either. "Do you have anything with a yard?" Tess turned to the property manager. "And not so many steep steps?"

Veronica, whose hair was in a high ponytail, curls bouncing on her shoulders like a high school cheerleader's, stared at her phone, her voice flat. "If you didn't like these, you won't like them."

Tess usually cowered at the first hint of confrontation or displeasure, but not this time, especially with Mikolai here, ready to take the lead if Tess wavered. She stood taller. "Do you think another management company would have more access? You are the first I've tried." She turned, walked to a window, and looked out. Jannie and Tom followed and leaned against her, one on each side. Tess placed her hands on their shoulders. "We need a yard," she said, her gaze on the view below: a street, thick municipal bushes, a fence, and then train tracks. "It doesn't have to be big, but enough room for a child to run around, lay out beach towels on a sunny day." Tess could see it so clearly, her and Rose. Tess rubbing sunscreen on those firm little arms and legs, making sure Rose's hat was on tight. She'd buy a plastic kiddie pool. In the backyard on a hot day, a kiddie pool would be perfect.

Veronica sighed loudly. "There is one." Veronica sounded bored, annoyed, even. "It has everything you said you're looking for: two bedrooms, laundry facilities, off-street parking, near a park, downtown, yard access, and no steep stairs."

"And don't forget large windows," said Mikolai, "for all that studying you'll be doing." When Mikolai had brought that up two apartments ago, Tess nodded, agreed with Mikolai, though inwardly she'd been thinking more about Rose than textbooks. Light to study Rose—each amazing aspect of her.

"It has good light," said Veronica, "which you didn't add until after I set up these viewings."

"Perfect." Tess fought to keep her smile firm despite Veronica's obvious lack of enthusiasm. "Can we go see it?"

"It's not in your price range."

"Oh?"

"And smaller than the places you've seen…though the design is better. More open concept." She paused. "It's in the South End, which jacks up the price."

"How much out of my range?" asked Tess.

"Two-fifty."

"I could—" Tess held up a hand and shook her head to silence Mikolai.

"Or you could keep looking," he said, "book again for next week, see if anything else opens up."

"I can handle it." It was a lot, but not astronomical, and Tess needed to secure a place soon; all the ones she'd seen wouldn't even be available for two to three months. Plus, being in the South End, she wouldn't need a car. Not that she couldn't bring Rose across the city in a bus or taxi, but it'd be easier not to. She pictured the apartment, a few blocks from the Mathesons—a quaint little place, with sun and a yard and a future. Tess's smile turned from forced to genuine as she shifted her gaze to Veronica's bored face. "Let's see it."

After leaving the fifth apartment, the one she had decided on, Tess sat with Mikolai on the lawn of the Commons, watching Jannie and Tom kick a soccer ball with a few kids Tom had roped in. Mikolai draped an arm over Tess's shoulder, squeezed her to him. "I'm proud of you, kiddo."

Tess flushed, awkwardness and warmth creeping over her. "Thanks."

"No, really." Mikolai dropped his arm and leaned back. "New job. Going back to school. This stellar apartment."

"I'd hardly call it stellar." Tess laughed.

"It's good, though, Tess. It's great. It's progress." He smiled again, gazing at the kids. Tess smiled, too. The apartment wasn't perfect, but perfect could come later. It was bright and airy. The yard had a sandbox, a climbable tree, and was big enough for a small swing set and a little garden where they could grow flowers or veggies. They'd laugh as dirt fell through their fingers, as Tess showed Rose how to place each seed and pat the earth over it, the way her mother had shown her. *Yes.* Tess smiled. It was the type of space that said, *I have my life together.*

Tess leaned back. She shifted her gaze to watch Mikolai as he watched the kids. She wanted to tell him he had a niece out there. Tell him that, as broken as she still felt, she finally saw a light at the end of so much darkness. She wondered what he'd say about the conversation with Irene. Whether he'd encourage Tess to contact her, find out—once and for all—if that was the reason Irene had done it, if Tess was the one to blame. If she was, would the law hold her responsible? More than once, she'd considered reaching out to Irene, but she didn't want to risk it affecting her chances of getting Rose.

Every time she opened her mouth to tell Mikolai, fear reached up and wrapped around her—fear that she wouldn't make it work, that when she sat before a judge, she'd be found wanting, and all that pride she'd seen in his eyes today, all that hope he had for her, after so many years of letting him down, would disappear. So she would wait as long as she could to tell him, until she knew she had shared custody, if she could hold out that long. She'd wait, too, to find out whether she was the one to blame, if Irene had done this unthinkable thing because of her. She would do all she could to not let him, or herself, down again.

"That's my boy!" Mikolai cheered and clapped. He turned to Tess. "Did you see that?"

"No, uh…what?"

"That juggle!"

"Oh! Missed it." Tess offered a shrug as Mikolai stared at her.

"You okay?"

"Uh-huh."

Mikolai turned his face back to the children. "I've been meaning to say, Karina, she, uh…thought maybe I shouldn't have told you to come to that party. Thought it may be hard for you, being around all the babies likely to be there."

A shiver ran through Tess. "Oh?" She bit her lip, shifted her gaze to the kids as she sensed Mikolai turning his to her.

"You're still welcome to come with us, obviously, but no pressure. I don't want you to feel uncomfortable."

Tess nodded. "There are babies everywhere, though, right?"

And in less than a week, despite the Mathesons acting as if she had no claim, Tess would see hers, hold her. Best of all, with all those people there, Katherine and Patrick wouldn't be able to do a thing about it.

23

KATHERINE

THE DAY OF ROSE'S PARTY, KATHERINE STOOD ON THE BACK PATIO, her mother beside her.

"She's having a ball!" Elvira chuckled as Rose sat in the grass, clapping as her cousins and several other kids ran around her, bubble wands waving amidst peals of laughter.

"The bubbles are a hit." Katherine smiled as she surveyed the yard. About half the guests had arrived, and thanks to her setting up and decorating until two in the morning, everything was perfect.

Patrick had been making the rounds while Katherine greeted guests and double-checked the food. Now he stood laughing with a friend he hadn't seen in years, his hand clamped on the man's shoulder, looking relaxed. Katherine turned at the sound of her name to see Tracey and her boys approaching.

"Hello! Welcome!" Katherine embraced Tracey, a waft of coconut and sandalwood enveloping her. "I don't believe you've met my mother. Elvira Reddick."

Introductions made and hands shaken, Elvira excused herself. "You two catch up." She grinned. "There are a few people I should say hi to."

"This is fabulous." Tracey adjusted a barely awake Fletcher in her arms after saying goodbye to Katherine's mother. "I tried those date and goat cheese hors d'oeuvres on the way in. Heavenly."

"They're good, aren't they?" Katherine beamed. They may be going to court, but look at this gathering. Look at this community of support.

"A bouncy castle, too." Tracey laughed as her older son dashed across the yard. "I don't think I'll be able to pull Jackson away from it." She gave Fletcher a jostle to rouse him, then set him down. "Look, sweetie. Bubbles." The boy, a few months older than Rose, rubbed his eyes, then dropped his arms at the sight of the bubbles. His face lit up with joy as he did that distinctive wide-legged toddler run Katherine was dying to see from Rose, prayed she wouldn't miss.

"You all right?" Tracey rested her hand on Katherine's arm.

"I'm great!" Katherine grinned. "Wonderful. A little sentimental." She looked at Rose, perfect in the green grass, her gaze following the bubbles.

"I know." Tracey gave Katherine a side hug. "It's a cliché, but they grow up so fast."

"It's true." A surge of emotion welled up, tears threatening to follow. "Adrian couldn't come?" Katherine asked, now eager to redirect the conversation.

Tracey shook her head. "Big story. He wanted to…said to wish Rose a happy birthday."

"Katherine."

Smile faltering, Katherine turned at the sound of her mother-in-law. Then, catching herself, she brought her smile back wider than ever.

"The sushi in the living room is out." Susie clasped her hands in front of her. "It's so early. I hope you have extra."

"Yes, Susie. Thank you."

"I didn't think you'd want me checking the fridge to replenish. But it's been so long since the plate's been sitting there with not a scrap of fish on it."

Katherine held her smile. "No need. I'll take care of it." She turned to Tracey. "Enjoy, okay? We'll catch up later."

Katherine made her way to the kitchen, teeth clenched. The trays wouldn't be empty if they'd hired servers. Just one or two—someone to see to replenishing, someone to take the occasional tray around to the guests—and then Susie, less than an hour into the party, wouldn't have been able to bring up the lack of food: one more way in which Katherine had failed.

"I'm happy to help." Katherine jumped at the eager voice by her shoulder. She opened the fridge and pulled out the top tray of sushi. "It's no problem," continued Susie, who never would have let a tray go empty. "I know you have so much on your plate."

Katherine smiled, trying not to vilify her mother-in-law, to read into her voice, her smile, the words she could almost hear—*I know you're not your daughter's mother. I know, because you couldn't get pregnant, my son may have to share his child.* "Thank you." Katherine's voice came out as friendly and at ease as she intended. "I've got it. You go enjoy yourself."

Relief washed over Katherine as Susie left the kitchen. She transferred the rolls, creating a concentric design that soothed her. As she lifted the tray, Tiffany's voice caught her attention. Katherine paused to listen. Tiffany was talking to one of the Tuesday moms from their library tot group. Katherine could almost place the voice, the musical lilt indicating she was from the South Shore, but a few of the Tuesday moms had that lilt. Katherine listened a moment more, trying to match the voice to a face, and then she tensed.

"It's just so bizarre. Taking your eggs out of you, swirling them around with jerked-off jizz. I would never do it. I couldn't. And then putting it back into you." The woman laughed and gave a shiver. Katherine stood frozen. She knew the voice, but only registered the words. "And now this. What a scandal! I wonder who the other woman is. To think, she's trying to keep her!"

A wave of heat flooded Katherine. Her throat went dry.

"Well, she's her mother," said Tiffany. "She went through—"

"Not really," said the other woman. Chrissy, of course it was Chrissy. "Apparently, nine times out of ten, the courts favor the biological parent."

Katherine turned. She had to walk by them to get to the living room, but she wouldn't say a word. Except she was—the words coming out of her mouth, her voice low yet shrill. "How dare you?" Shock covered their faces, their eyes widening. "Why did you even come?"

"Katherine?" Realization seemed to cross Tiffany's features.

Katherine was sweating. Not a glistening glow. Sweating. Droplets slid down her back, gathered under her bra. "Wait, what were you talking about?"

"Just about this girl who works for my brother-in-law, Carl," said Chrissy, "how she's the biological mother of the kid in the IVF scandal. How—" Chrissy raised her hand and pointed toward the door. "Her. That's her. Oh my gosh, that's her!"

24

TESS

AS MIKOLAI PUSHED OPEN THE DOOR TO THE MATHESONS', TESS stepped through to see Katherine turning, visibly flustered. The tray in her hand shook so much she almost dropped it.

Outside the Mathesons' house, which was even bigger than Tess had imagined, cars lined the street, at least two dozen of them. With balloons on the lawn and streamers on the front porch, it wasn't simply a party, it was an event. So maybe, Tess had thought, it wouldn't be such a big deal that she was here. Maybe Patrick and Katherine wouldn't even notice or would be too busy to care. Clearly, she'd been wrong.

Katherine stared at them, as if unable to move. Then, like the flip of a switch, a smile spread across her face. She thrust the tray into the arms of a woman standing near her, then strode toward them.

"Katherine!" Mikolai exclaimed, walking to meet her, arms outspread.

"Mikolai!"

As Katherine walked into his embrace, gave Karina a brief hug and air-kiss, and then beamed at the children, Tess kept her gaze on two women who watched the interchange. They leaned forward, as if absorbed in a riveting play. What were they looking at? Could they know? The switch was still in the news. Tess had scrolled through several articles that morning, read the comments below each one. Everyone wanted to know who the mothers were. She'd even heard coworkers talking about it in the lunchroom, discussing the ethics of in vitro fertilization, whose child the baby really was.

But according to the articles, nobody knew their identities. And how could they? Irene wasn't talking. Tess wasn't talking. Katherine and Patrick wouldn't be talking.

"I hope you don't mind." Mikolai's arm fell across Tess's shoulder. "I brought my sister. I'm sure you remember her."

"Yes. Of course." Katherine's voice was several octaves higher than normal. A frenzied, manic look to her eye. "Tess." She leaned forward, giving Tess the lightest embrace. "Welcome!" Her voice was too loud, practically effervescent. "Come in, please." She swept her hand toward the living room. "The party's through here. We have food and bubbles. A bouncy castle." Again, she beamed at the children.

"A bouncy castle?" said Tom.

"Yes! Go ahead," said Katherine, her voice still elevated. "Find Patrick. Say hello!"

As Tess passed Katherine, she glanced up, saw the terror in Katherine's eyes. Tess looked away, feeling it, too. Before coming, she had stood in front of the mirror, smoothing her hand over her dress. She'd changed her outfit four times. Ridiculous, she knew. Rose wouldn't care, Rose wouldn't even know who she was. But as this would be the first time she was meeting her daughter as her mother, she wanted to look her best, to be the perfect picture of the perfect mother.

She'd contemplated calling Messineo, asking if it was a bad idea, if this would come up in the court-appointed mediation as a mark against her, but he was the one who had told her to show she had family ties. What was more familial than going to a birthday party with her brother, her nieces and nephews, and her daughter?

So here she was, being swept into the house in the wake formed by Mikolai's family. As Tess slowed, taking in the space, Jannie ran back and grabbed her hand, tugging her forward. Tom, not wanting to be left out, grabbed Tess's other one. Warmth flushed through Tess.

Despite her fear, her hesitancy, these children were on her side. Bolstered by their affection, Tess stood taller as she surveyed the living room. It was perfect, like walking into a design room at Ikea: it had flow, a presence of calm, beauty, wealth.

Black-and-white photos of Rose hung on the walls, but there were no toys, no smudges, no crumbs. Tess was eager to find her, but not just her, signs of her: her room, toys left in the middle of the floor when a book grabbed her attention, her towel strewn across the tub, still scented with soap and warm skin, her handprints, sticky smudges on the kitchen counter. She wanted to crawl into her crib, wrap her arms around Rose's favorite stuffed animal, and breathe in her smell for all the nights she couldn't, all the days and hours, the year she had missed.

Mikolai and his family passed by tables laden with food. They stepped through patio doors and onto the spacious back porch, fronting a large corner lawn still richly green. Tess looked back to the house, yearning for that glimpse of Rose's life, yet she stayed near Mikolai. His presence would prevent a scene. She couldn't be grabbed or told to leave with him by her side.

Patrick stood not far from them, talking to guests. His laugh was loud and relaxed. And there in front of him, legs in the grass, dressed in a pale-pink onesie, matching headband, tights, and tutu skirt, was Rose. Tess caught her breath. Rose, aptly named, with her sweet rosebud lips and, Tess now saw, green eyes. She hadn't noticed it before, but it was unmistakable, the sunlight emphasizing notes of amber and gold. Rose had her eyes. Tess's body tingled. Moisture threatened to blur her vision.

She walked forward.

Mikolai's hand landed on Patrick's shoulder, and he turned, smiled brightly as Mikolai wrapped his arms around him. Patrick's gaze fell on Tess, his smile vanishing, the blood draining from his face. He recovered quickly, kissing Karina's cheek, ruffling his hand on Tomas's head, and chucking Jannie under the chin.

"And you remember Tess?" Mikolai put his arm around her shoulder, hauled her in close.

"I do. Of course!" Patrick hesitated, then put out his hand, cordial. "So good to see you again. Glad you could make it." He dropped her hand before she had a chance to grasp his.

Mikolai, too forward, too friendly, as if he still lived in their tiny village in Poland where people raised each other's children, bent and picked up Rose. "Look how she's grown!" He bounced her in his arms as she stared, wide-eyed and frightened, and then, captivated by this grinning, love-filled man, smiled back. "She's a beauty."

"She is." Patrick looked from Mikolai to Tess. From Tess to Mikolai. Was he thinking what Tess was thinking—how much Rose looked like her, how quickly she took to her uncle? Or was he debating a way to get Tess out of here with the least disruption to his guests and reputation?

"She couldn't have been more than a couple of months old last time I held her." Mikolai shifted Rose to his hip. "After our big win last season."

"Dad!" Jannie pulled on Mikolai's shirt. "The bouncy castle. Please. Now."

Mikolai laughed. "Anyone want the birthday girl?"

Tess stepped closer, too afraid to speak.

"Me!" Karina held out her arms.

Tess glanced from Rose to Patrick. "I brought her a present. It's just small."

"Presents are in the living room." His voice held a firm edge. "There's a table."

Tess pulled the small bag out of her tote, not looking to Patrick for approval. "I'd like to give it to her now, if you don't mind." She stepped toward Karina, her body trembling. She was inches from Rose. "Here, sweetie." Rose looked at the bag, sparkly tissue paper poking from the top. She grabbed the paper. Squealed. Scrunched it between her fingers. Tess's heart skipped a beat.

"You better take that paper away from her." Karina laughed. "Show her the gift inside."

Tess hesitated, not wanting to pull the paper from Rose's hands. Karina did it for her. So the child's frown didn't turn to something worse, Tess angled the bag toward Rose. Rose's smile bloomed as she reached in and pulled out the crocheted fox Tess had paid forty dollars for. It was handmade. One of a kind. Rose bounced it in her arms, then squeezed tight. Warmth flooded Tess. It was worth every penny.

"Looks like she's a fan," said Karina.

"Yes." Patrick's voice, tight and clipped. "Thank you." He reached for Rose, smiled at Karina. "I'm sure you want to see your kids in that castle." He set their daughter in the grass.

Karina's voice held an odd uncertainty to it. "Okay. Well, sure."

Patrick stepped to Tess. "We need to talk." Tess nodded without looking at him. She couldn't take her eyes off Rose. Those pink cheeks, that laugh. A tiny furrow between her brows. "Privately." Her eyes. Her chubby legs. The way she stood—wobbly. Rose's leg lifted, one step, two, three.

"She's walking!" an older woman exclaimed, her voice a squeal. "Patrick. She's—"

Patrick spun and crouched down, gasping.

"Katherine," said the woman. "Where's Katherine?"

Tess froze. Rose's first steps. And Tess was here. She was seeing it.

Patrick stood up. He looked from Tess to Rose, Rose to Tess. He shook his head and crouched back down, his smile wide as Rose approached. It was six steps now. Seven. She collapsed just short of him. He clapped and cheered, lifted her up, swung her in the air. Everyone who had seen it joined in. There were hoots, choruses of "Well done" and "The birthday girl!" Tess stood silent, her lip trembling, her cheeks tight with the grin she couldn't wipe from her face if she tried.

25

KATHERINE

KATHERINE HAD RESISTED THE URGE TO LOOK BACK TO TIFFANY AND Chrissy, to see if they were still standing there while she spoke to the Sokolowskis. They knew Tess was one of the women involved in the IVF scandal, and Chrissy, by the way her face lit up when Tess walked through the door, was anxious for a look at her, titillated by the gossip. And Tiffany's expression… Had they thought Katherine's outburst was nothing more than righteous anger for a fellow IVF mom, or did they suspect it was her? Were they sitting there now, reveling in the turmoil unfolding before them? Katherine pictured the news spreading through the party like wildfire. She had to douse it. Immediately.

As the Sokolowskis headed toward the living room, Katherine glanced at Tess, that frail, fragile slip of a girl. Only she didn't look so frail anymore, and she didn't look like a girl.

Once the Sokolowskis were past, Katherine looked back and saw Tiffany's and Chrissy's heads snap toward each other. *Too late, ladies*, she wanted to say, *I caught you gawping*. Instead, she smiled and walked back to them. "So sorry about that."

Tiffany pulled on her shirtsleeves, her gaze not meeting Katherine's. Chrissy's eyes were wide and focused.

"And for that outburst earlier." Katherine let out a short laugh. "The stress of party planning." She waved an arm. "You know us IVF moms, we stick together. I…with all Tess has gone through, I don't like the thought of her being talked about like that."

"We didn't mean to offend." Tiffany passed the sushi tray back to Katherine.

"Did you know when you invited her?" Chrissy now. Her voice low, thank goodness.

"I…"

"Carl, my brother-in-law, said she was having a custody battle with the other mother. Did they find a solution?"

Breathe, Katherine. *Think*. Her energy deflated, her resolve to lie, to cover up, threatening to fade away. But despite Tiffany's narrowed gaze, Katherine wasn't caught. Not yet. "I don't think it's figured out yet." She took a breath, deciding how much to reveal. Part of her wanted to tell someone, anyone, to not have to hold it all in. The other part wanted no one to know, ever. It didn't make sense, but she was ashamed, embarrassed, as if giving birth to someone else's child—and not knowing it—was her own personal failure, an indication that she wasn't the mother she should be, that maybe she didn't deserve to be one at all.

And there was more to it than that; there was everything Kerra had warned them about if the news got out. "It's not something I'm comfortable talking about." Katherine glanced at the empty hall. "I'm shocked Tess came." She leaned in toward the women. "I didn't invite her. I thought she'd want to keep a low profile, that a party right now, with so many moms and babies, would be too much for her. Patrick and Mikolai, her brother, are on the same soccer team, and we invited the whole team. Mikolai invited

Tess, I guess." Katherine stopped, checked again to see if anyone else was in earshot, lowered her voice. "Still, it would mean so much if you kept this to yourselves. These issues, they're meant to remain private."

Tiffany nodded.

Chrissy wore a smile that looked like it was meant to express sympathy. "Do you know the other mother?"

"No." Katherine shook her head. Her hands clenched the tray. "Tess told me there'll be a trial. With the nurse. Tess and the other parents will be called as witnesses. They're requesting a publication ban, but if it looks like Tess was talking about it, not keeping it to herself, then it'll get in the news. That could be disastrous." Katherine hesitated, resisted the urge to wipe her brow. "For the child, especially. Imagine if it got out. If, when she gets to school, everyone knows her as that IVF baby who got switched."

"So it's a girl," said Chrissy.

"We won't say a word," said Tiffany.

"Actually, I've already told several people." Chrissy shrugged. "I didn't know it was such a secret."

Katherine's heart raced and her throat went dry. They'd be unlikely to get a publication ban if the word was out before they applied, which would mean not only these guests but the whole world would know the truth, have a chance to voice their opinion. The story would be plastered across headlines and social media, vans and reporters parked outside their house. Everyone knowing, everyone talking, forever.

Katherine inhaled, the air passing through her windpipe like sandpaper. Her vision blurred.

"Katherine?"

She needed to breathe but the air scratched and burned.

"Katherine!"

Someone grabbed her arm. Her body shuddered as the room, the sounds, the scent of barbecued chicken, curry, fresh fruit, and grilled fish came into focus.

"Katherine, she's walking." Katherine's mother gripped her arm, tugging her toward the living room. "You're missing it."

Rose! Katherine dashed past her mother in time to see Patrick spinning Rose in the air. A crowd of people looked on, beaming. Patrick caught sight of Katherine. He stopped, settling Rose on his hip, his face aglow. "Katherine. She walked. She took her first steps." He smiled. Katherine smiled. Tess, standing less than four feet from him, smiled.

A mallet seemed to pound on Katherine's chest. Tess had seen Rose's first steps. Not Katherine. Tess. Because Katherine had been inside, paralyzed.

And here she was again, frozen. She wanted to scream at Tess, tell her to get off her property, stay away from her daughter. But everyone was here, everyone was looking. She wanted to run to Rose, take her in her arms, set her down, encourage her to try again. She wanted to turn back the clock.

"Katherine." Had Patrick even seen Tess standing there? "Come over. Let's see if she'll do it again."

Katherine, regaining her limbs, moved forward. She crossed the space between them. "Mama." Rose waved her arms. "Mama."

Patrick set Rose down when Katherine was still at least six feet away. Katherine stopped, crouched, put out her arms, and Rose, finally not afraid, was ready to do what Katherine had known she had it in her to do for weeks now. With a wobble that made Katherine's heart burst with pride, Rose walked toward her and into her arms.

26

TESS

THERE WAS ANOTHER ROUND OF APPLAUSE AT ROSE'S SECOND first steps. A crowd had gathered, but here was Tess, only watching. This should be her moment. Rose should have gone from her father's arms into Tess's. Tess was her mother, and she deserved to be here, be a part of the moments yet to come. She stepped forward.

Rose still in her arms, Katherine shifted her gaze to Tess, her face transitioning from joyful wonder to something else entirely.

Tess jolted out of the trance that had propelled her forward. The crowd surrounded them, staring, smiling. Then, as word must have traveled from ear to ear, some of those smiles turned to confusion, shock, an almost macabre interest in the scene unfolding, in Tess walking toward Rose.

"Katherine!" Patrick gestured toward Tess. "Look who showed up. It's your friend, Tess!"

Katherine held Rose tightly as she stood and scanned the guests. Tess scanned, too. Some still focused their eyes on them. Others were chatting among themselves, turned away to tend to their own children or get more food. The few who remained looked interested, likely with goodwill. Likely, the looks she thought she'd seen were all in her head.

"I'm so glad." Katherine spoke more quietly than Patrick. Tess understood. There was no need to shout; the people in earshot could hear either way. "You disappeared online. I didn't know how to get ahold of you." Katherine smiled. She said what she would have said if the switch had never happened, if her failure to invite Tess had been as simple as that.

The three of them stood close. Patrick dropped his arm. Tess reached out hers. "Can I hold her? The birthday girl."

Katherine clutched Rose to her, then relented. She wouldn't make a scene, though Tess could see setting Rose in Tess's outstretched arms took all of Katherine's willpower. The look on her face was as if Katherine were tearing her heart out and placing it in the grasp of her greatest enemy.

Tracey glided toward them. "Tess, so nice to see you again."

"Yes," Tess answered without looking at Tracey, her gaze on Rose.

"You must be so proud." Something seemed odd about Tracey's voice. "First steps."

"Yes." All three of them—Tess, Katherine, and Patrick—answered. Tess lifted her gaze at the silence that followed, then drew her attention back to let Rose grasp her finger. To tickle her chin.

Tracey's hand settled on Tess's back, drawing her focus away again. "I hate to do this to you. I can see you're enjoying this little sweetheart, but Katherine's father was asking about Rose. His knee is bothering him and he'd rather not come outside, but he wants to see this girl on the move."

Tess held Rose closer as Katherine reached out. Tracey intercepted. "Stay." Her voice was warm, calm, directed at Katherine. "I'm sure you've been run off your feet today. I've got her."

No! Tess wanted to scream as Tracey pried Rose from her arms. *No, I just got her. No, please.* But she said nothing, her lips pressed tight. This wasn't the way to go about it. She knew that. She, too, wouldn't make a scene. Instead, she watched, wordless, as Tracey carried her daughter away.

Patrick gripped Tess's shoulder, the pressure a fraction away from pain. Without a word, he led her to a shaded part of the yard.

27

KATHERINE

KATHERINE LOOKED AT TRACEY CARRYING ROSE AWAY BEFORE turning to follow Patrick and Tess to a shaded part of the lawn, far enough away from the party to be free of prying ears, near enough to not seem odd. They could be stepping out of the sun or showing Tess the burning bush they were both so proud of.

"What are you doing here?" Patrick fumed.

Tess's vividly green eyes, which Katherine stared at every day in her little girl, were wide. "Mikolai invited me. He said you wouldn't mind."

She must be stupid.

"And does Mikolai know that you're taking us to court? Trying to take our daughter?"

"Trying to take my daughter!" Tess leaned in, looking larger, stronger than Katherine had ever seen her, as if she were the reasonable one and Patrick and Katherine were acting inappropriately. "I don't want to go to court. You've left me no choice." Desperation on her face, she stretched out her arms, as if in supplication. "She's my child, too."

"You don't even know her." Katherine's voice rose, but she reined it in. "You didn't feel her kick in your belly, didn't wake through the night to nurse her again and again, hold her for hours pacing the floor, or let her sleep on your chest. You didn't teach her how to hold a spoon or practically put out your back going up and down the hall holding her hands so she could learn to walk." Her blood pounded as she felt it all again: the love, the frustration, the exhaustion so deep at times she thought she may die. "You want a baby, I get it. But not Rose."

"I don't just want a baby"—Tess stepped toward her, her hands still outstretched, palms up—"I want *my* baby."

Fear enveloped Katherine. Her hands shook as rivulets of sweat trickled down her spine. "You're not a part of her life."

"But I should be. I'm going to be. She's mine."

Katherine backed away, the words hitting like a slap. "She's not." Tess had already taken so much, and yet she had the nerve to come here, to hold Katherine's daughter, to witness her first steps. A vein in Katherine's forehead pulsed. She felt like she could strangle Tess, like she could kill. "You have to leave. Now."

"What if it were you?" Tess's voice was so confident, so soft yet full of authority, as if she were negotiating a hostage release or trying to talk Katherine down from a ledge. "What if the situation were reversed? If Rose had died and Hanna had lived." A pause. "Would you be content to get letters and pictures? Would you sit back and let me raise her all on my own?"

"Hanna?" Katherine's rage fizzled.

"My baby." An expression of love covered Tess's face. "Your baby, the one I lost."

Katherine stepped back. After that first day, she had barely thought of that baby. Her other baby—the one Tess had carried. She hadn't allowed herself.

Tess had named her. Hanna.

A strange sensation came over Katherine. What if it *were* reversed? If Hanna had lived and Rose had died?

Katherine closed her eyes and shook her head. She wouldn't think of it. That wasn't what had happened. "It's not me," said Katherine, hating the petulant sound of her voice. "You lost your baby. I—"

"Okay." Patrick raised his arms. "This is what's going to happen." His voice started with a slight tremor, then solidified. He looked between the two women. "Tess, you're going to go inside, have a bit of food, chat with some people." He didn't wait for a response. "And after twenty or thirty minutes, you're going to find Mikolai, tell him you have to leave. You're sick. You forgot about some work thing. Then you'll leave. Quietly, as if none of this has happened. As if everything is fine."

Tess looked from Katherine to Patrick, silent for one breath, two. Katherine imagined the cogs turning as Tess debated her next step. "Okay." Her chin lifted. "But I'm not backing down."

As Tess walked away, Katherine slumped with exhaustion. She rubbed a hand across her temple.

"It'll be okay," Patrick murmured in her ear, the tremor resurfacing.

Katherine nodded as they walked toward the party, then split ways—he toward some friends on the lawn, her toward the house, her limbs trembling, her heart still beating fast. A buzzer vibrated on Katherine's wrist. Cake! It was time for cake. She passed through the living room, a broad smile pasted on her face as she acknowledged one guest and then another. She stopped before the fridge, realizing she had to focus, do this right. She couldn't just haul the cake out. She needed to get Patrick, have him tell people to gather. She wouldn't let frustration and overwhelm from Tess's presence ruin this perfect party.

Katherine made her way back through the living room, taking in the clusters of people laughing and talking. The buzz sounded again on Katherine's wrist as Patrick sidled up beside her.

"It's going to be okay." He gave her a squeeze. "We'll get through this. Let's do our best to have fun—or at least look like it."

"You'll gather everyone to sing?" asked Katherine.

"And you'll come in, candle lit."

Back in the kitchen, Katherine opened the fridge. She paused, staring blindly at the contents, weariness pulling down on her. She set Rose's smash cake on the counter, lit a candle. She had to snap herself out of this; she had to enjoy it, as much as she could, and not let Tess steal that, too. With a deep breath, Katherine lifted the cake and turned as she started the chorus of "Happy Birthday," delighted in Rose's clapping glee, and told herself it was going to be okay.

28

TESS

HOME FROM THE PARTY, TESS STEPPED INTO HER APARTMENT, PAST the muffled sounds of her downstairs neighbors fighting, and into her bare-walled room. She peeled off the dress she'd taken such time deciding on.

When Patrick told her to leave, talking to her as if he held all the authority, as if she were some child, she'd wanted to fight back, yell, scream. But that wasn't the way; it would hurt her case, not help it. Standing in the Mathesons' yard, she'd thought back to Dr. Myers's advice about following the proper channels, to Maeve's and Messineo's guidance on how to get her life together, to show herself as stable, responsible. Crashing her daughter's birthday party probably didn't show that, and making a scene definitely wouldn't. So she'd agreed; she'd done as he asked. But still she fumed that Katherine had said those things, dismissed Hanna. Katherine was wrong to have looked at Tess like that, but Tess was wrong, too. She saw that now. She shouldn't have gone. Yet—she smiled, remembering—she couldn't regret it. She'd seen Rose. Her first steps, her smile. She'd heard her laugh, held her, breathed in the sweet scent of her baby girl, who was barely a baby anymore.

Tess sat on the edge of her bed now, phone in hand, staring at a photo she'd taken of Rose. She swiped, zoomed in on the next. Rose laughing. Swipe. Rose sitting in the grass, eyes wide as she watched bubbles. Swipe. Rose with her cake—fingers, mouth, cheeks, and nose covered in icing. That was all Tess had risked. Four photos.

The icing was made with sweet potato. Tess had overheard Patrick's mother telling someone that Katherine had made it herself. By the sound of her voice, his mother seemed to think it was funny, unnecessary. Over the top.

Tess understood, though. Katherine wanted the best for Rose. Tess wanted the best, too. She could make icing out of sweet potatoes. She'd slip vegetables into smoothies and sauces. She'd do whatever it took. Tess wiped her fingers across her cheek, smoothing away the tears. Tess's life had fallen apart in pursuit of this child. She'd lost Hyeon-Jun, she'd lost her home, and following the grief after Hanna, she'd lost touch again with Mikolai, Karina, her niece and nephew. Whatever else she lost, it'd be worth it to have Rose beside her.

She'd worried, as she walked up to the Mathesons' door, that she'd not see Rose as hers. That the child she'd decided to fight for would seem a stranger. While Tess may not have felt Rose's kicks in her belly, the magical undulating motion of her flipping within her, and everything else Katherine had referenced, she was still Rose's mother. She felt it the moment she saw her, that undeniable yearning, that exquisite joy.

Tess navigated her phone to the tab with the latest articles on Irene. She scrolled to the comments; she'd read them that morning but wanted to see the words again. The support. The assurance she wasn't insane in thinking she had a shot. There were people out there who saw things the way she did, who believed she deserved her daughter.

So horrible. That poor mother!

Tess smiled.

Could you even imagine? Obviously, the biological mother should get her baby back. It's her baby.

Tess read on, each comment in her favor—and most were—bolstering her confidence, her outrage. Biology mattered, the overall opinion shouted. Tess's child had been stolen. Tess and her baby were the victims.

Tess set her phone down, decision made. She had tried to be reasonable, but if the Mathesons refused to cooperate, she wouldn't, either. She was Rose's mother, and didn't mothers always win?

She reached for her phone again and scrolled through her recent calls until she found Messineo. She'd tell him about today, and that she was changing her plan of attack. She would go for sole custody, let the Mathesons have regular visitation—she wasn't cruel—but nothing more. Rose was hers.

29

KATHERINE

AS AFTERNOON'S LIGHT SHIFTED TO THE DIM BEFORE DUSK, Katherine realized Tess was gone. Though exhaustion pushed down, making her limbs heavy, her breath shallow, Katherine breathed easier, as slowly—in groups of two and five and seven—people walked through the door and the party grew quieter.

Katherine checked the food table once more, then headed to the kitchen to refresh the trays for the couple dozen stragglers still out on the lawn or spotted throughout the main floor. A hand fell on her arm.

"Katherine." Tiffany's eyes were wide. "It's you, isn't it? You're the other mother in the IVF scandal." Tiffany shook her head, her cheeks flushing. "There I was, running off my mouth, first at the library group, and then today."

An explosion of cold burst at Katherine's center and spread. "I don't—"

"It must be horrible. It must be—"

"Who told you?"

Tiffany rubbed Katherine's arm, that look of pity Katherine feared upon her face. "No one had to tell me," she said gently. "I saw her holding Rose, and with how you reacted earlier, it…well…it was obvious."

Katherine's pulse raced. She gulped for air, tried not to think of the publication ban being denied—if the word got out—and their names plastered across the internet, a search away, forever. Tried not to wonder who in this room had been wide-eyed and satisfied to know that they'd been right all along, that Rose—green-eyed, fair-skinned Rose—had never been Katherine's.

"Does anyone else know?" asked Katherine, her hands gripping Tiffany's arms.

"No, I…I don't know; I mean, maybe people suspected? I heard several people talking about the fact that Tess was one of the mothers, and… maybe they're wondering?"

"Well, don't tell anyone. Don't confirm it." Chrissy's smile flashed in Katherine's mind, her shrug as she admitted she'd already told several people about Tess, the thrill of gossip lighting up her features. "And tell Chrissy to keep her mouth shut."

"Okay. Yeah, well, she suspects, too. Is talking like it's fact. But I will."

Katherine crossed into the kitchen, the cold that had pulsed through her body transitioning to heat, her face on fire. She braced her hands on the counter, the gentle thrum of conversation from other rooms wafting to her ears. Katherine opened the freezer and let the icy air blast.

"Katherine."

Katherine spun at the sound of her mother's voice, saw the shock and pain on Elvira's face, and her father behind Elvira, Rose asleep in his arms.

"Is it true, what that woman just said…the IVF scandal?"

Katherine swallowed and opened her mouth, but didn't know how to speak. She nodded, a tear sliding down her cheek.

Elvira pulled Katherine to her, then pushed her away, hands on either shoulder. "This means…" Elvira stepped back. "Rose isn't yours? Not really?"

"Of course she is," said Katherine's father. "Elvira, I don't think we need to discuss this right now."

"Then when?" said Elvira.

"The bouncy castle people are packing up," said Patrick, entering the kitchen. "I was wondering about a tip for—" Patrick stopped. "What's going on?"

"They know." Katherine's pulse raced and her head throbbed. She rubbed her fingers under one eye and then the other. "About the switch."

"That's goo—"

"I didn't tell them," she snapped. "Not really. People are figuring it out."

"Ahh…" Patrick's face fell. "I heard people talking about Tess. Apparently, Chrissy is the sister-in-law of Tess's boss."

Tracey and Susie entered, platters in their arms. Susie looked around the room, from Katherine and her parents to Patrick. "So it's out," said Susie, setting down her tray. "About time Russell and Elvira knew." She put her hands up. "I didn't say a word, even when I heard people talking. I just walked away."

Katherine's jaw trembled, her limbs tensing. She looked at Tracey, who looked both uncomfortable and concerned. "Did you know, too, or did Susie just confirm it?"

"No, I…well…I heard as we were walking in just now. And people are talking. Or are wondering, at least, but I don't think anyone knows for sure. They figure if it was you, you wouldn't have invited her."

"Why *did* you invite her?" asked Susie.

"We didn't invite her." Patrick sighed. "She showed up."

Russell rubbed Rose's back as she shifted. "I wish you'd known that you could have told us. Even if there's nothing we could have done to help.

You don't need to protect us." His voice shook. "We're supposed to be the ones…"

"Now that we do know," said Elvira, "please tell us what's going on. Have you gotten a lawyer?"

Patrick nodded. "Yes." He stepped farther into the room. "Right away. We're doing what we can. We'll do all that we can."

"I still don't understand," said Susie. "When she showed up, why didn't you tell her to leave, especially when you're taking her to court?"

"Court?" said Elvira. "Is that a good idea? Could you lose Rose altogether?"

"We're not taking her," said Patrick. "She's taking us. And as to losing Rose, we're told it's unlikely."

Katherine put a hand to her head, the words, the questions, swirling around her. "So not everyone knows? They only suspect it's us, but everyone knows about Tess?"

"No, I don't think so." Tracey stepped closer. "Even the news about Tess didn't start to spread until the last hour or so, after a lot of people had left."

"Well, Tess, is it?" Susie hesitated. "I knew it was her the moment I saw her. Rose is the spitting image."

Silence fell.

"Well, those eyes, and her coloring," said Susie, backtracking. "Based on that, no one would have thought Rose was Katherine's."

"And no one would have thought Katherine was mine?" Elvira's voice was sharp, her shoulders held back.

"I'm just saying, it's obvious that—"

"Mom!"

"Anyway," said Susie, "the point is, it's so evident Tess is Rose's mo—biological mother. And I read an article about the number of colored…" She glanced at Russell. "Or…I mean, Black children who need to be fostered or adopted, and how it's so hard to find Black families to put them with, but how important that is…so you'd think it'd work the other way, too. You'd think the judge would want—"

"He might," said Patrick. "But our lawyer doesn't seem to think it'll be a determining factor."

More silence.

Tracey spoke now, her voice soft but commanding. "Maybe it would be a good idea if we stopped all this before someone else walks in. We can round up the final guests—there's less than a dozen out in the yard. We'll tell them the birthday girl's fallen asleep, the party's over, then leave ourselves. Katherine, Patrick, this was wonderful, and I'm sure you're both exhausted, too. I'm sure you could use some rest."

Katherine looked at Tracey, thankful she said the words Katherine couldn't speak.

"She's right," said Russell. "We should all get going. Anything you need, kids. Anything at all, okay? You know where to find us. Even if it's just to talk, have a sounding board. We all love this girl. And we all love you."

Hot tears pooled behind Katherine's eyes as she stood there, needing to escape. "Thank you for coming." She scanned the room. "Thank you for your concern." She scooped Rose out of her father's arms. Her girl curled into her chest, resettling, fitting perfectly. "I'm going to take her on up. Have a good night."

Settled in one of their two handmade Adirondack chairs in the backyard, Katherine stared at the lawn covered in shadow as the last rays of sun slipped below the horizon. The house was empty by the time she came down from putting Rose to bed, the furniture back where it should be, the dishwasher running and another pile stacked neatly by the sink.

Needing solitude, Katherine had slipped through to the backyard without talking to Patrick. The news hadn't spread as widely as she feared, but still, Katherine wondered how quickly speculation would turn to rumors, and who—of all the people who knew for sure—might confirm rumor was fact. Chrissy, Katherine imagined, or one of Patrick's brothers, speaking without thinking as they so often did.

Katherine's phone buzzed. It was Adee. *This just in, I'm sure not what you want to hear, but Tess recently put down a security deposit and signed a year lease for a much nicer apartment. Two bedrooms, good neighborhood. A couple of blocks from you.*

Katherine tasted something metallic in the back of her throat. First she came to her house, and now Tess was infiltrating her neighborhood. *A couple of blocks from us?* she texted back.

Yeah. Smart move. Not only the better place, but that she could say she's looking toward the future. It will make pickups and drop-offs that much easier and, when the time comes, smooth the decision of where Rose goes to school.

Katherine sighed. *If she gets shared custody.*

Yes, exactly.

You haven't found anything else? Katherine asked. *Something that would work in our favor?*

Three dots, blinking, blinking, blinking. *Nothing definite yet. At least, nothing I'm comfortable sharing over text. I'll set up a meeting once the information I do have is more solidified, once it forms a narrative you could present in court, and I have the proof to back most of it up.*

Katherine let that sink in. *So there's hope?*

I'm finding info that could help your case. Sit tight.

Katherine slid the phone back into her pocket and leaned against the chair. She tensed at the sound of footsteps behind her, not wanting to talk to Patrick, risk saying something she'd regret about his mother's views on "colored" people and how it was "so obvious" Rose couldn't be Katherine's. She shifted in surprise at the sight of her mother.

"I thought you'd left."

"I did. Then I came back." Elvira sank to the chair beside Katherine. "You threw a wonderful party."

Katherine let out a laugh.

"The guests had a good time," said Elvira.

Katherine shook her head. "Who wouldn't, right? Free food, games, a bouncy castle, and to put the icing on the cake—thrilling gossip."

"Pun intended?" Elvira smiled.

"Uh-huh."

"And don't forget"—Elvira put her hand on Katherine's arm—"the birthday girl walking for the first time, for all to see."

"For Tess to see," said Katherine, her gaze on the deep indigo of the night sky, "before me."

The rustling of the leaves and distant traffic softened the silence between them. Elvira sighed. "I'm sorry for pouncing on you like that earlier, when I learned…but I was shocked. Overwhelmed." She turned to Katherine. "What I should have asked is, how are you doing?"

Katherine let out another laugh, one that sounded more like a cry.

"I know, awful." Elvira gave Katherine's arm a squeeze. "But dig in… tell me."

Katherine looked into the settling darkness, not knowing what to say. All those years trying for a child had broken her. On the surface, she'd kept up with the charade. She built her business. She kept fit, kept house, playing the role of perfect daughter, perfect daughter-in-law, and, as best as she could, perfect wife. Not letting anyone, even her mother, know her pain. Katherine shook her head, wanting to speak, but afraid of letting herself be that vulnerable, of looking weak.

Elvira took her daughter's hand. "Katherine, you can tell me. It's okay to talk about it, whatever you're feeling, whatever you've felt."

The corners of Katherine's lips twisted as resistance flared within her. She looked at Elvira, then exhaled, letting the words tumble forth with the released breath. "I was embarrassed." She waited for Elvira to nod before continuing. "By how much it crushed me, not being able to conceive, to fulfill the most simple, elemental role of a woman. And that embarrassed me, too. The embarrassment embarrassed me." Katherine shook her head, sighed. "That's why I didn't tell you about it until we started the fertility treatments. Why I didn't tell anyone."

"Because if you were independent and strong, you should be happy whether you were a mother or not," said Elvira. "You should find your fulfillment elsewhere."

"Exactly," said Katherine, surprised at how perfectly her mother had described it.

"It's a struggle women have been facing for years," said Elvira. "Not whether they could, always, but whether they wanted to have a child, or whether they wanted to have more. And if they did, what that might mean for who they were outside of being a mother."

Katherine nodded. "Even after Rose, so often, I've felt like I was failing. I'm not the mother I thought I would be."

"None of us are."

A light breeze made its way over the yard, creeping along Katherine's shoulders, making her shudder. She stared at the spot where Rose had first walked and felt her joy split with frustration, fear, anger—because of Tess.

"When I finally saw those two lines on the pregnancy test, despite the fear, despite the uncertainty, I felt I could be happy at last, legitimately happy, you know? Fulfilled. And I have been, in many ways. I had done it—with the help of science, of course—but still, I had done it. Fulfilled my dream, what I felt born to do. I was carrying my child." Katherine took a long breath. "Except I wasn't. I didn't."

"Oh, Kitty Kat."

Katherine closed her eyes, saw Tess with Rose. "Their eyes, Mom. Their smiles."

"I know, baby."

"She's not mine." Katherine's voice quavered. "She never was."

"She is. No matter what happens. She's yours."

Katherine opened her eyes and stared into the darkness. "What if we don't win?"

She turned to her mother, whose lips were pinched. "You'll still have her," said Elvira. "With Patrick the biological father, you couldn't possibly lose custody entirely, could you?"

"What if Susie was right, that in the judge's eyes, it would come down to culture, or what that would really mean, that I am Black and Rose is not."

"Then we'll show them us."

Katherine let her head fall into her hands.

"I wondered, you know," said Elvira, "when I heard about the switch. I thought it brought up those fears you had when Rose was a newborn, and that's why you didn't want to talk about it, not that you were the mother and Rose was the child. But you'll figure it out, my love. Like you always do. It won't be what you expected, but you'll make it work."

"I'm sorry I didn't tell you. That I—"

Elvira raised her hand, shook her head. "It was your news to tell. In your own time. You've always been a private person."

Katherine's lip trembled. "We planned on doing another transfer shortly after Rose turned one, but now, with this—" The thought slammed into Katherine like a violent wave, almost knocking the wind out of her. "Our embryos," said Katherine. "They're not mine."

How could she not have thought about it before? How could Dr. Myers have said nothing? The switch happened with the eggs before fertilization. Eight healthy-looking eggs, five properly fertilized, four surviving to day-five freezing.

"Oh." Elvira shook her head. "But what about Tess's? Did she…? I mean you…well—are there any left?"

"I don't know. But they'd be mine and some sperm donor's. Not Patrick's." Katherine shook her head, fear rising in her throat. "I can't do it again, the whole IVF cycle from the start." Katherine had grown so many follicles that the doctors hadn't even given her the option of a fresh cycle, the risk of ovarian hyperstimulation syndrome too high. When, from all those follicles, they'd only retrieved eight healthy-looking eggs, it'd been a shock. She was a "poor responder," they said, the other eggs not developing properly, which was probably why she'd never conceived. "It was awful."

"I know, sweetie."

The way her ovaries had ached, swelling to twenty times their normal size, and then after, when the ovarian hyperstimulation syndrome hit, the leaking fluid had caused her abdomen to expand larger than it had been at seven months pregnant. "But if we ever want another child…"

"Don't think about that now," said Elvira.

A sob worked its way up Katherine's throat. She choked it down. "The injections, the drugs, the hot flashes…" And then there were the symptoms she hadn't wanted to talk about, the debilitating waves of medically induced sadness that lasted for days.

"Don't think of it."

Katherine pulled her legs up to her chest, hugging her knees.

"You two coming in?" Patrick's voice drifted across the yard.

"In a minute." Katherine shivered and rubbed her hands on her arms, a reflex that did no good. She looked at her mother. "He wanted a big family."

"He wanted you."

Katherine twisted in her chair to see Patrick's silhouette through the patio doors. She pressed her lips together, pulled them in, noticing the soft wetness. It'd been so long since she'd felt anything like that, felt more than the quick, dry kisses she and Patrick exchanged when he left for work in the morning—out of habit, not love. She stood as the silhouette lifted a hand and waved.

"I hope so."

30

TESS

AFTER STROLLING THROUGH THE PUBLIC GARDENS, HOPING THE views of nature would put her tensions at ease and instead having everything wrong with her life suddenly amplified, Tess stood at her kitchen counter, a bottle of Soplica—her favorite vodka—in hand. She took a swig, wanting to forget her meeting with Messineo: his tone, his condescension, the way his anger and frustration had burst out as he looked at her like a piece of shit stuck to his shoe.

When, full of resolve and gusto, she'd called him and told him she'd gone to the party, that she had a new plan, he insisted they meet in person, despite it being the weekend. She'd paced between the trees of Victoria Park, waiting, hoping he'd be on her side.

His voice started out calm and mellifluous, like liquid metal. He emphasized that she needed to be the reasonable one, that that's what she would have going for her at the court-appointed mediation. But as their conversation continued, as he chastised her for going to the party, for thinking that she had a chance at sole custody, that voice shifted. He talked down to her, asking whether she really wanted sole custody, telling her a child was a big responsibility, and expensive—as if she didn't know, as if she hadn't spent five years of her life fighting to get pregnant!

If she'd had her baby, live and kicking in her arms, no one would have asked if she'd thought this through, if she was good enough, well-off enough, stable enough. The baby would have been hers, no questions asked. Yet because of a mix-up, because her body didn't work the way other women's did, she needed to prove she was worthy. Needed to compete.

His face had twisted into a grimace as she restated her resolve, insisted she wouldn't budge, told him he worked for her, and if she wanted to go for sole, that's what he had to tell the courts. He'd practically shouted at her as she stood there, her limbs rigid and trembling. A rush of adrenaline coursed through her system as she fought not to shout back at this man who was her best shot, but who told her, with disdain dripping from his voice, that she hardly had a shot at all. "Don't ever do something as stupid as that again. Crashing their party!" He shook his head, raising his arms in exasperation. "They'll wonder what else you'll do, if you're a flight risk. You've got next to no chance of sole custody. If you even want shared, stick to the plan." He raised a finger to emphasize each point. "Life in order, strong connections, and for God's sake, contact your parents already."

She was planning to, despite her frustration, despite wanting to chase after Messineo when he left, tell him he had no idea what she was going through. No idea what it was like to miss so much of her child's life. To hold her in her arms, only for a moment, then be cast out. Instead, she'd decided to head to the Public Gardens, calm her nerves before making the trek to her parents' house.

And then, only minutes after stepping onto the trails, she'd seen it. More than anything Messineo had said, more than the shame of being told to leave Rose's party, what made her reach for the drink was a bright-eyed toddler turning onto the path ahead, and a few paces behind him, a man who had to be Hyeon-Jun—the same haircut, trimmed to perfection every two months, the distinctive gait, arm in arm with the mistress, who was now the wife, her hand on an unmistakable baby bump.

Tess had darted to a side trail, her pulse racing, uncertain whether they'd seen her, afraid but also desperate to find out—was it him? Living the life Tess had always wanted? Her chest constricted. Her body tingled and crawled. It didn't make sense why some people got it all, and others…

She cut to another path, her pace as fast as she could make it without running, turned so she could glance back, see the face that wasn't Hyeon-Jun's.

She'd fallen against a tree in relief. Yet her husband…ex-husband…was out there somewhere, with a baby and a wife, and possibly another child on the way. And she was alone.

Back home, Tess's face contorted in pain at the memory. She took another swig of Soplica, knowing the drink alone wouldn't be enough to make her forget. She walked to her room, placed the bottle on her bureau, then let her clothes fall to the floor before sliding a skintight dress over her slim frame. She smoothed lipstick over her mouth, ran a lengthening mascara over her lashes, stared at her reflection. She'd never been a natural beauty, but sometimes, though she couldn't seem to manufacture the moments, she was striking. Tonight, she couldn't see it.

Tess took a final swig of Soplica. Most men, she figured, didn't need those rare moments of fleeting beauty to be interested. She had a vagina and was willing. So any time she wanted a night of distraction, she got it. No need to worry about that.

Tonight she wanted distraction.

She shook her head and grabbed the Soplica again, desperate to shake the memories of the past few hours. Of that beautiful little boy, the could-be mistress, the huge satisfied smile on the face of a man who could have been her husband. Who was someone's husband, giving his wife a look Tess had stopped seeing years before Hyeon-Jun left, if she'd ever seen it all.

Tess guzzled the drink until she had to stop to breathe.

Hyeon-Jun had always wanted to be a father—felt obligated, even. It was the way he was raised: family above individual happiness, family above all. You procreated, continued the genetic line. It was the point of life. A point Tess had failed at again and again. That Hyeon-Jun, after learning her secret, had seen as her failing.

She'd never quite understood why Hyeon-Jun had chosen her—he was so rich and successful; she was barely making ends meet. It didn't make sense. Not at first, anyway. As time went on, and she had the opportunity to think, analyze, propose a testable hypothesis, and tear apart the facets of their relationship piece by piece, it made more sense. She was weak. Easy to control and easier to mold. She made him feel powerful, a knight in shining armor.

During those weeks and months of dissecting their relationship, Tess always came back to that moment when she'd told Hyeon-Jun the truth about her past. She wasn't sure what aspect bothered him most. Perhaps it was what she'd always feared herself—that because of the choice she'd made, all their babies had died.

Despite knowing it wasn't a great idea, that she'd have to be stronger when she had Rose, find a different way to push away the pain, Tess took a final sip—the desire to numb this ache stronger than anything else—and stepped into the night. She'd forget, then sleep, then find new strength in the morning, keep fighting for her daughter, even if it meant doing the thing she feared most.

The wind whipped Tess's hair across her face, the cool sea-kissed air making her shiver, but she walked on until she reached the Hideaway: one of a handful of places she frequented on the nights she used sex as a means to forget, to let go, if only for a moment, of the pain and emptiness Hanna's absence had left. The first time she'd done it, the sex hadn't been planned. The first time, silence had surrounded them, making every touch, every sound they'd produced more potent. Tonight, though, strong bass notes vibrated through her, keeping time to a hip-grinding beat. The air, hot and oddly balmy, held a thickness to it. Unlike the lounge two floors below, whose clientele was mostly university students, here the crowd was older, more professional, but just as desperate. Here, Tess could find anonymity.

Two laughing women in stilettos and dresses even slinkier than Tess's bumped into her as they walked by, no apology, as if she were invisible, an atom floating through air. Tess slid onto a stool and caught the bartender's eye. "A vodka and tonic, please."

He nodded. "It's been a minute. You hitting other joints?"

"Something like that," she shouted above the din before averting her gaze.

When the drink was in front of her, Tess guzzled it back in one go, then placed it on the bar, refusing to catch the bartender's eye.

"Ready for another?"

Tess pivoted. She glanced at the speaker's left hand. Bare. She draped her arm over the back of his chair, smiling in the way men enjoyed. "Sure."

The man offering a drink was probably ten years her senior, but he'd do. They'd chat. Maybe dance. They'd leave. And for a few blessed minutes, maybe even hours, she'd forget.

31

TESS

TESS STOOD IN FRONT OF THE HOUSE, STILL NURSING A SLIGHT hangover from the night before. Nursing, too, her disappointment in herself. She closed her eyes, tried to swallow away the bitter taste in the back of her throat. She'd told herself those outings would stop—for Rose. That she'd focus on stability. But after all that had happened the day before, the dismissal at the party, Messineo's censure, and then thinking she'd seen Hyeon-Jun's beautiful growing family—realizing the actual family was out there somewhere—she felt so low she couldn't resist the urge for one last night of forgetting.

It would be the last, though. That wasn't who she wanted to be. Should she tell someone of this lapse? Mikolai, maybe. He'd jump in for sure—probably have her signed up for some program before she even had a chance to explain she didn't need that. And she didn't. She could go weeks without drinking, months probably, if she really wanted to. She shook her head. She'd stop on her own. Last night was the last night.

Tess opened her eyes and gazed at the house. It was as flat and squished as she remembered, sharing walls with the houses beside it. The siding needed refreshing, but the lawn was meticulous, the small patch of yard full of bushes and carefully cultivated rows of greenery with pops of color from the strategically placed fall blooms. The window boxes, though not as boisterous as they would have been a month ago, still held patches of bright orange and yellow and red. It amazed her, her mother's knowledge and passion for making things grow in the best way possible, for the best visual effect. It was art. In another life, Jasia could have been a landscaper, a botanist, a florist. In this one, she had worked in the laundry at a downtown hotel.

She didn't want to walk up those steps, but Messineo's words rang in her ears. Last night certainly wasn't a sign of a life in order, but this would be. She hoped. Tess should have called, but she couldn't risk it, the possibility that they'd hang up the phone, tell her not to come, say, yet again, they no longer had a daughter.

She got it. She did. Mikolai hadn't needed to remind her at their lunch. Their parents had slaved in this country, neither of them living up to their potential, all so that their children could thrive. And to them, Tess had thrown it all away—as far as they knew—for nothing. Because she didn't "feel" like going to school anymore. Because she wasn't sure what she wanted to do with her life. "Just finish," her father had pleaded. "Three credits, *mój kwiatuszek*, only three credits. You can do it, and then you'll have a degree. Then you'll have a good life."

But she couldn't, and she couldn't tell them why. It would break her mother's heart. Tess couldn't even imagine how many rosaries Jasia would feel the need to say for her sinful daughter. She'd probably find it easier to disown her forever, resign Tess's wayward soul to hell.

A heaviness poured over her, making her limbs inert. Today, she'd have to give them a "why," not for the past, but for being here now. Unlike with

Mikolai, who was eager to have her back in his life, no questions asked, her parents, Jasia in particular, would require a compelling reason for why she'd shown up at their door.

Tess kept her gaze on the same lace curtains that had hung since the day they moved in, hiding her parents from the world while letting them look out unseen. They could be staring at her now, arguing about whether they'd let her in or close the door in her face. Perhaps they wouldn't even open it.

She moved toward the steps, her legs like clay, wanting to turn back but hearing Messineo's words in her head, that if she wanted even a chance of sole custody, family support was the missing piece of the puzzle. On the porch, Tess swallowed, hesitated, lifted her fist to knock as the door swung open. There her father stood—the crinkles around his eyes deeper than she remembered, his shoulders stooped. He must have been standing at the window, watching her decide, waiting.

"Cześć, Tata."

"Theresa." He opened the door wide, his smile wider, his eyes bright. "Mój kwiatuszek, come in."

Tess took the few steps toward the kitchen, the smell of spices heavy in the air. The house had been dated when they'd bought it, the previous owners having done their last remodel in the early seventies. And still, nothing had changed. The same wallpaper with the large orange and brown flowers. The same linoleum, scrubbed so many times you could hardly see the pattern. The same still and silent halls of her childhood.

Tess had asked her mother once, embarrassed to have her few friends see the museum that was their home, "Why don't you redecorate?" Tess offered to help, said she'd tear down the wallpaper, repaint. Her mother had scoffed, embarrassed that she'd raised such a foolish girl who would ask such a foolish question. "It's good," her mother tutted. "Why pay money to fix something that does not need fixing?"

Tess drew her gaze from the green cupboards, yellow counter, and paneled walls and looked at her father. He was shorter than she remembered, but still he towered over her. His hair was grayer. His eyes just as kind. "I wanted to come," he said, his voice a whisper, his accent as thick as it had always been, "to your wedding. I wanted to come, but—" He didn't say more. He didn't have to. "Any grandbabies?" His smile was mischievous, expectant. Tess looked at the puke-green flooring to avoid his gaze. So Mikolai had told him nothing? She exhaled then raised her head.

"Is Mama home?"

"No." He looked at the clock, as if frightened. "She is at the church. A funeral."

Tess nodded. She walked past him, into the living room. It, too, hadn't changed. Except… She turned to her father. "Where's your cello?"

He raised his right hand in a fist, extending the fingers slowly and then bringing them back in, the knuckles swollen and twisted. "I can no longer play." His face constricted in pain. "Not for a long time now."

Tess's heart clenched. Playing was Aleksy's life, his greatest source of joy after a long day of work, after a disappointment, a death. This was worse than all of it: the years of separation, the fact that her parents hadn't come to her wedding… This, her father without his music, made her forgive.

The urge to say she was sorry ran through her, but even though Jasia wasn't there, Tess could hear her mother's response, the derision in her voice. *Sorry for what? You think you gave him the arthritis? You think you took his music away?*

The inaccuracies of language. She could try expressing her regret in Polish, but she hadn't spoken the words in over a decade. She opened her mouth and froze, afraid to let those sounds pour over her tongue, afraid she wouldn't remember, and what a betrayal that would be. She let out a word that would never feel foreign.

"Tata." Tess stepped forward as his arms spread. She still fit, her head against his chest, his arms wrapped tight. He kissed her hair, smoothed it with his gnarled hand.

He released her and motioned to the couch. "Sit. Tell me your life." He strode to his corner chair, still seeming such a strong man. Yet, to see his hands.

Tess sat. "Hyeon-Jun and I…" She hesitated. "It didn't work out."

Her father's eager face fell. "But why? You talk. You work it out. That's what you do."

Tess sat, her ankles and knees together, her hands in her lap. "It couldn't be worked out."

"But, mój kwiatuszek—"

"He got another woman pregnant." The words fell out. *Irreconcilable differences* was what she'd meant to say, as if she were a politician and that was the party line.

Her father sighed. "Sometimes, some men…"

"He loved her, Tata, not me. They're married now. He wanted a child."

Aleksy kneaded his hands. "And you didn't? Is that—"

Tess shook her head and stared at the carpet this time.

"Theresa, what is it?"

She swallowed.

"Mój kwiatuszek, tell me."

Tess took a deep breath, raised her gaze, took in her father's kind eyes, his patience as he waited. "I couldn't." She bit her lip. "We tried. We went to doctors. We…lost babies. I couldn't…"

"…hold them in," Aleksy finished. "My sister. She was like that. Five little babies all slid out. Your shape is so much like hers. I wondered. I prayed."

"What?" Tess stammered. "The…the doctors, they didn't have an explanation. Everything looked fine."

184

"And my aunt, too," said Aleksy. "I don't know how many, but there were losses, and no children."

Tess felt a break in her chest, something hard and painful splitting. Those women wouldn't have done anything to start the losses. Not likely, anyway. They wouldn't have been the ones to blame. "I didn't know."

Her father made a small sound. "Sometimes knowing, it doesn't help. It makes worry. Makes life harder."

Tess wanted to reach out, lay her small hand in his large one. She hadn't planned on telling him this much, not without her mother present. But maybe it was better. Maybe her mother wouldn't have even sat long enough to listen. Tess leaned forward. "I wish I'd known."

Her father nodded. "I hoped you wouldn't have to."

She stared at the floor, not knowing what should come next. "That's why I'm here. We did IVF. In vitro ferti—" Her father nodded. "You know what it is?"

"IVF. Yes. A couple at the church did it. And it's been in the news."

"Yes." Tess took a breath. "The last time I did the procedure was without Hyeon-Jun. I used a donor." Tess looked at her hands. "I lost the baby. Again. But it wasn't mine, not biologically. My baby—" She was doing this all wrong, but how did you do it right? She raised her gaze. "My egg went to another woman." Her father leaned back, realization settling in. "And this woman had a girl. Rose. She just turned one. She's perfect."

"Oh, Theresa." His voice came out raspy, as if he were holding back tears. "What does this mean?"

"They want to keep her, obviously, and I want her, too. I tried to go for shared custody. I thought that'd be fair, easiest on Rose, but…" She paused. "They wouldn't agree. They offered me photos, yearly updates."

He tutted.

"So I'm taking them to court. I'm fighting for her."

Her father sat straighter. "On your own?"

"Well." Tess bit her lip. "That's why I'm here. I'm not asking for anything. Not financially. Nothing like that. But I want to know if you, you and Mama, if you want to know her, meet her, be in our lives." She stopped. This sounded bad. It sounded manipulative. All these years, and now, when she needed something, she was back.

But she hadn't decided to leave; she'd disappointed them, that was all. She would have come back any time they'd asked… "It would look good, better, if I had family around. If…"

"I understand." He leaned forward, rested his hand on hers. "I see. Me, you know it's… You know I…" He squeezed her hand. "But your mother. I will speak with your mother."

"I'm going back to school," said Tess, desperate to convince him, give him the means to convince Jasia. "I've been saving money. I'm going to finish my bachelor's. I'm working in a lab right now. It's a good job. I'll get a degree that will let me move higher up. After that, maybe even a master's."

The corners of his eyes crinkled in an expression that made her want to weep. "That's good, mój kwiatuszek. That's wonderful. I'll talk with your mother. Maybe you can come for dinner. You and Mikolai and the children."

As he stood, Tess realized that would mean she needed to tell Mikolai— before the dinner—see his disappointment that she'd hidden the truth, risk more disappointment if she wasn't deemed good enough to raise her daughter.

"Now you get up. Now you go," said Aleksy. "But I'll speak to her." He ushered her to the door, hugged her again, holding longer than he needed to. "Call Sunday after next, in the evening. Your mother is always in a good mood after seeing the grandchildren, and that will give her some time to adjust to the idea, set something up for the week after, perhaps. Yes, call then, and we'll see."

32

KATHERINE

KATHERINE STARED AT THE PHONE: TRACEY'S FACE WITH A PULSING light around it. Katherine had been ignoring calls and text messages since the party two weeks ago. She'd talked to her mother a few times, but no friends. She'd sunk into herself, drained by the party, the whispers, the fact that every morning she awoke terrified of seeing their faces plastered across the screen—her fear, her lack on display for all to see. Every morning she was reminded of how weak she'd felt in those years of trying, how alone and broken, how she worried losing Rose would send her to an even darker place than before. But enough was enough. She swiped beneath Tracey's image. "Hello."

"Katherine. Hi! I'm so glad! I didn't think, I mean… I'm happy you picked up."

Katherine let out a slight laugh.

"I've been worried." Tracey's tone quieted. "How are you?"

"I've been better." Katherine sighed.

"I can imagine. How are things, uh…going?"

Katherine hesitated, letting the silence sit between them, deciding whether she was ready to talk. "We have another mediation tomorrow."

"I see…" More silence on the line, then, "How are you feeling about it? The mediation."

"Oh." Katherine shook her head, stared where light hit the veins in the spotless marble of her countertop, making it glisten. "Thrilled. I'll have to listen, again, to someone try to persuade me to be reasonable, to hand my daughter over." Katherine waited for Tracey's response, for some form of chastisement for her bitter tone. But none came, only a soft noise of acknowledgment to indicate Tracey was there, listening. Katherine looked at the ceiling, her eyes moist, so tired of holding it all in. "I feel at a loss, Trace. It all feels so out of control. I'm doing all I can, all I can think of, but ultimately…"

"Ultimately, life, all the time, no matter how we try to deceive ourselves, is out of our control."

"I know." Of course she knew. They both did.

"But you like feeling like you're doing something about it, and you should—try, I mean—while knowing, accepting, that ultimately the outcome is out of your hands." Another pause. "It must be unbearable."

"It is."

Tracey's voice trailed across the space between them, wistful. "I've been thinking about you, this horrible situation, and well…there's so much I could say, but I'll just say this, and I know it's not the same situation, it's not at all, but when I went looking for my birth mother, I was afraid to tell my mom, afraid of what it would even mean—finding this other woman, maybe loving her, and if I did, whether the love I had for my adoptive mother would change. Lessen. I think my adoptive mom was afraid of that, too. But something I learned, that we both learned, is love doesn't split when you share it. It grows."

Katherine breathed, wanting to tell Tracey that it wasn't the same, not at all, but she knew Tracey was just trying to help…and that was nice, to have this friend who cared.

Tracey sighed. "Maybe I shouldn't have mentioned my own experience. It's just, if things don't work out the way you want, remember that. Having to share Rose, it doesn't mean you'll lose her love." She paused. "More than anything, Kat, I'm sorry you're going through this. All of it. It's awful. It's all our greatest fears. I know those words mean nothing. It doesn't help, and there's probably nothing I can do to make things easier, but if there is, even if it seems silly, like bringing over a meal so you don't have to cook, tell me."

"No." Katherine leaned against the counter. "It's fine, thank... Actually"—she straightened—"could you watch Rose during the mediation? I'm sure she would rather stay with you than the babysitter."

"Yes," said Tracey. "Absolutely. Any time."

Katherine smiled at Tracey's eagerness, relief flowing through her that this one thing would be a little easier. "Thank you."

"Of course." Tracey hesitated. "How's Patrick? How's he handling it?"

Katherine stared at the counter again, a sigh escaping. "I don't know."

"Uh-huh."

Katherine could almost see Tracey's nod. She was the only person who knew about the problems in Katherine's marriage. The lack of communication. The lack of sex. Throughout the whole nine-plus months of pregnancy, they hadn't been intimate once. Katherine was worn out from the long months of fertility treatment. She feared what sex could do to the baby, though their doctors assured her it was fine. And though Katherine knew they should, they hadn't had a proper conversation about it once.

"So, things still aren't going that well?" asked Tracey. "Have you guys been, uh, intimate yet?"

Katherine turned from the counter. "We've tried, but...no. Not since before Rose."

"Katherine, you've got to. You've got to talk to him, too, but sometimes,

I don't know…" She let out a short laugh. "Sex can break the ice. Create that intimacy to open up to each other. You need each other if you're going to get through this."

Katherine swallowed, knowing Tracey was right, but afraid it wouldn't make a difference.

"Listen, how about I take Rose tonight? You guys can order dinner, get some wine."

Katherine tensed. "No. Rose has never done an overnight before, not even with her grandparents."

"Okay, then after she's in bed. Even if you're tired, just…this isn't good, Kat. I know it probably feels like everything else is more important. But this is important, too. And I'm sure you could use the stress release!"

Katherine laughed, then sighed. "Look, Trace, I've got to go. But I'll think about it. Thanks. Is two good? To drop Rose off?"

"Yeah, sure. And good luck, okay? With all of it."

Later that evening, Tracey's final words in her mind, Katherine stepped into her bedroom. The sun's last rays filtered through the sheer curtains, casting speckled light on the floor. Rose was asleep. Patrick was at work. Katherine pulled a box from the closet that she hadn't opened in at least five years.

All month, her body had felt wound up, her nerve endings on high alert with the stress of the switch, the mediation and impending trial, the near radio silence from Adee, the fear life as she knew it would never be the same. She needed release, as Tracey indicated, a chance to step outside of her raving, consumptive thoughts. But more than that, she and Patrick needed to find a way back to each other. Katherine rifled through the flimsy items, her hand lingering over the delicate fabric. She needed to know that with all they had been through, all they were going through now, they were still them, still lovers, still wanted and needed each other. And after, maybe, they would be able to talk in a way they hadn't since long before all of this began. Maybe she wouldn't feel so alone.

By eight o'clock Katherine had her hair styled, her makeup on, her body squeezed into the most forgiving pieces of lingerie she owned. At the sound of Patrick's car in the driveway, she turned off the TV, positioned herself on the couch, her body displayed to best advantage, and placed a seductive smile on her face.

She listened as he tossed the keys on the bench by the door—not in the bowl, by the sound of the dull thunk rather than clink—kicked off his shoes, and pulled wide the fridge door. The ting of a beer can opening sounded through the quiet house. Silence, as he must have been swallowing, then footsteps.

"Oh!" Patrick stopped short as he stepped into the living room.

"Hi." Katherine kept her voice low.

"You look…I mean… Wow."

"Come on over."

Patrick stood, unmoving. "I've had a hell of a day."

"Let me make that better."

Patrick's shoulders slumped. He came to the couch. Katherine shifted, then once he'd sat, she climbed on his lap, straddling him.

"I'm so tired," he whispered.

"Me too." She kissed him. "We need this."

"I—"

She kissed him again, his closed mouth slowly opening, his tongue exploring, his hands gripping her bottom, bringing her closer. Katherine's heart raced. She was so wet, so ready, but it'd been forever since they'd drawn out foreplay—years. Tonight, she wanted to enjoy the yearning, wait till she was desperate. She pulled back, then started working her mouth along his neck, the tip of his earlobe. He groaned.

After the mandated six weeks following Rose's birth, they'd tried, at Katherine's insistence, to finally have sex. But it hurt too much. And she was tired. She'd been touched all day and through most of the night, attending to Rose's needs. She'd initiated, for Patrick's sake, yet he'd seemed to understand intuitively that the last thing she wanted was to be touched more.

But she wanted it now. She moved back to his mouth, their tongues locking, her hands in his hair. She moaned as he gripped her thighs, ached for his fingers to reach her clitoris.

It hadn't been like this in years. The conception efforts were rote, lacking intimacy. Lacking fun. An obligation. By the end of those first five years of trying and into the next four—after the doctors declared her infertile—sometimes they didn't even kiss. Sex became a job, the rhythm consistent, each of their roles known.

Tonight, though, he slipped his fingers into her as Katherine gasped with a surge of pleasure. Not able to wait anymore, she reached between his legs as his body stiffened. She sat back, her hand releasing the flaccid penis she'd gripped. "Patrick?"

He grabbed her waist, lifted her off him, and shifted away. "I told you I was tired."

"But—"

"I was trying for you, okay? I never said I wanted it."

Katherine pulled her knees up, covering her body, which suddenly felt exposed. Patrick started to stand, and she reached her hand out, grabbed his wrist. "Wait. It's okay. Don't leave." Except it wasn't okay. "We can take it slow."

He sighed, leaned his head against the couch, hands at either side of his head. "Another night."

Katherine sucked her lip, then whispered, physical frustration pounding through her, "How many times have you said that before?"

He looked at her sideways, then averted his gaze, his expression pained. They lived as roommates, not lovers, an odd tension filling the air where passion used to sizzle.

"I thought we—"

"This is a weird time, Katherine. That's all. Even weirder now. I'm sorry, okay? I just—"

"You don't have to apologize." Except it felt like he should. "We'll get back to"—she hesitated, wishing she had a blanket, a sweater, something to wrap herself in—"us. Won't we?"

"Of course." Patrick leaned over, kissed the top of her head, the way a father or brother or uncle would.

"Maybe you could just sit? And we could talk. We don't really do that anymore."

Patrick's distress twisted his features. He opened his mouth, closed it, shook his head. "It's been a long day. A long week. We'll pick this up again soon, okay?"

"Okay." Katherine nodded as Patrick rose.

"I just need to do a few things in my office, then how about we watch a movie? Your pick." He reached for his beer.

"Sure."

He walked toward the hall, not looking back, as Katherine stepped from the couch, opened the ottoman, and grabbed a throw to wrap around her.

She was sure he loved her. But was love enough?

For months now, almost every interchange between them had been about Rose. If they lost her, even partially, the glue that seemed to be keeping them together, would they last? And if they didn't, would Katherine have any real claim on Rose? Without Rose, without Patrick, who would Katherine even be?

Katherine stood to return to her room, get dressed. She trailed her hand along the oak stair rail she'd chosen specially, then stepped into their bedroom and approached her closet yet again, feeling more alone than ever. Feeling as if her marriage was on the verge of collapse.

33

TESS

WHEN THE MEDIATION WAS OVER, TESS STOOD AND WATCHED as the Mathesons left the room, Patrick's arm over Katherine's shoulder, Katherine shrugging it off. Tess stayed behind, not wanting to walk the halls with them. As expected, the whole affair had been a massive waste of time, except for one thing—the record. It had been hard, keeping her cool when there was so much to say, when so much of her wanted to be combative. But she'd done it, with her reasonable suggestions for the way Rose should be eased into a relationship through visitation, then to extend those visits. Suggestions that—apart from wanting sole custody rather than fifty-fifty—lined up with the recommendations from Robert, their new mediator.

Katherine, on the other hand, with her tone, her stubborn resistance to compromise, her words, which more than once referred to this situation as a fight, had made herself appear just short of hysterical. It was a side of Katherine that Tess wouldn't have imagined existed just months ago, but just months ago, the life Katherine envisioned for herself wasn't in jeopardy.

The meeting fell apart, just as the first had. Robert reminded the Mathesons of the exorbitant cost of a trial, the unlikelihood they'd ever get sole custody—appealing to Patrick, keeping his gaze away from Katherine. He went over the basics of what would happen next: a hearing with the judge, likely court-mandated visitation so Tess could establish a bond with Rose, so the supervised access workers could observe their connection. Then they were done.

As the door closed behind the Mathesons, Tess turned to Robert, keeping her voice light as he shuffled his papers into a briefcase. "Mediations go down like this a lot?"

"Not often. Occasionally, when one of the parents, usually the mother, feels she's been betrayed by her former partner, she wants her children to have nothing to do with him. More vengeance than anything else." He finished shuffling papers into his briefcase, then looked at Tess. "If there's a legitimate reason to not have shared custody—abuse, neglect, criminal activity—the cases don't come to me."

Tess nodded.

"I've never had a case like this one." Robert smiled, then the corners of his lips fell.

Tess smiled back, sensing his embarrassment. "Who has, right?"

He nodded.

"So it's up to the judge."

He picked up his briefcase. "Good luck, Ms. Sokolowski. I'm sorry I wasn't more help. I have to say, though, the Mathesons' notion that they could keep Rose from you, at this point, is ludicrous. I read your intake files and the updates, how you've made such efforts to ready your life. You'll get her, at least part-time." He put a hand on her shoulder, warm and heavy, like a father's. "It's just going to take longer and cost more."

Tess nodded as Robert left the room. Relief, expectation, and more than a bit of pride thrummed through her. She had readied her life. Patching things up with her mother was the final piece of the puzzle, but she'd do that soon…or at least try. If Robert was right, she'd get interim visitation rights before long. Supervised, but that was fine. It was great. She smiled, lost in thoughts of Rose. They'd meet in a provincial building, most likely. There'd be toys and games, but Tess would buy some, too, just in case. She'd have to figure out what a one-year-old played with. Dolls? Stuffed animals? Those colored stacking rings? Tess exited the building, walked down the length of it, and stopped.

"Rethink it?" Katherine's voice, louder than Tess had imagined she'd speak in public. But Katherine hadn't acted the way Tess imagined she would through any of this.

"Yes. Maybe we should rethink it." Patrick, so quiet Tess could hardly hear. She should turn around, walk in the other direction. She eased toward the edge of the building. "Maybe we need to give in a little—like an eighty-twenty split? So we look reasonable. So we don't end up with fifty-fifty or less."

"That's what you want? To have alternate holidays, birthdays, to see your daughter every other weekend?"

"No." A groan. "But it looks like we'll have to split time no matter what—that a judge will order supervised access."

"Which we can fight."

"I don't think we can. Look, maybe us initiating visitation, us being the ones to decide the terms would be better. Based on what the mediator said, it seems typically—"

"It seems like you're giving up before we've even started." A strangled, frustrated sound burst from Katherine. "And all this 'typically' nonsense. He was talking like there were only two parents. Like this was a 'typical' situation. But it's not. This isn't an estranged mother battling for custody.

I am Rose's mother. I grew her. I birthed her. She's still nursing. She is my child. Tess is no more than an egg donor. She's not Rose's mother. Not in the ways that matter."

"I know."

"If my baby had lived," cried Katherine, "would the sperm donor have been sitting around that table? No!"

Which would make you no more than an egg donor for Hanna, Tess wanted to yell, *and yet you said, "My baby."*

Patrick again. "Just calm down, okay? And lower your voice."

"Calm down?" Katherine's voice rose as she backed away from Patrick. Tess could see her now, the back of her curls bouncing as she spoke. Tess pressed against the wall. "I don't want my daughter having some broken life," choked Katherine, her voice shaking worse than it had in the mediation room. Tess imagined the tears that had fought to break out just minutes before now flowing down Katherine's face. "I don't want visitation. I want my daughter one hundred percent of the time, like any mother would. I'm sorry for Tess, I am. But not sorry enough to hand over my child. Not sorry enough to tear this family in two."

"I know, Kat. I know. But we may not have a choice."

"May. May," said Katherine. "That's the operative word. So maybe not." A pause. "Have you imagined it? As Rose grows, how would it work? Whose word would be law? She could undermine us, Patrick. We say no and Rose says, 'Well, Tess says I can do that, and she's my real mother.'"

"She's not. Rose wouldn't."

"You have no idea what Rose would do if her life's upturned. And Tess has no boundaries!" Tess pressed flatter against the wall. "Coming to our house like that. Taking Rose, holding her without—"

"Mikolai invited her."

"She could have said no. She's taking us to court and—" Katherine stopped. "Children need boundaries. She'll probably give her too much candy."

"Katherine." Patrick, a chuckle to his voice.

"And what if she's the favorite?" Katherine was definitely crying now. Her voice wobbled. She gasped for air. "What if Rose loves her more? She probably would. The fun mom. The mom who lets her skip school to go to the zoo and eat junk food all day."

"Katherine." Consoling now. Cajoling, almost. "That's not going to happen. Rose loves you. She's always going to love you, and Tess won't be some—"

"Stop it." A sharpness entered Katherine's voice. "You won't have competition. You're her dad. Her *one* dad."

"Well, who knows, with all of this publicity, that sperm donor could come out of the woodwork."

"Are you making jokes? Seriously? That's what you're doing? We may lose our daughter, and you're making jokes."

"No, I don't know. I just, I'm trying to make you smile."

A long sigh from Katherine. "I'm seeing the PI soon. I think she may have found something on Tess. Maybe we'll have a chance after all."

"Maybe." Patrick's hand landed on Katherine's shoulder, guiding her out of sight as their voices became muffled.

Tess stayed against the wall long enough for them to get in their car and leave the lot. She took a long and shaky breath. The PI? She looked to the sky. The scents, the sounds, the intoxicating and mind-numbing heat of her last night out floated to her consciousness. She couldn't remember the man's name, wasn't sure she'd asked it, she'd been that drunk. She'd left with him, walked the four blocks to a hotel. He'd given her what she'd needed, a moment of forgetting.

If the Mathesons used it in court, would it turn into a night she'd never forget?

But what would it even show—that Tess was unfit, that her drinking, going off with a stranger were a danger not only to herself, but to Rose? It wasn't. She wouldn't have done it if she'd had Rose with her. Yet it wasn't just that night, but so many others. Would that indicate a pattern? Would a lawyer be able to claim self-destructive behavior, an addiction that would no doubt continue? It wouldn't continue, but how could she prove that, and how far could a PI go back to glean information? Months? Years? Likely, she'd be able to determine that Tess and Irene had been classmates, friends. Would she accept that it was a coincidence or dig deeper?

Tess put a hand to her forehead and closed her eyes. A sickening chill spread through her. What other shames from her past would be called against her?

34

KATHERINE

KATHERINE PULLED OPEN THE DOOR TO ADEE'S BUILDING AND maneuvered Rose's stroller inside. The same bearded hippie man sat at the desk. The same light shone through the large floor-to-ceiling windows, illuminating those striking paintings. Only Katherine seemed different. She'd been nervous last time; this time, she felt sick. Sick about what she was about to learn, about what she might do with it.

"Katherine, hello!" Adee strode into the room in a checked miniskirt, bright-red leather tank top, and cutoff denim jacket, her hair under a chic cloche hat.

"Hello."

On the phone, Adee said she'd found skeletons. Not ones that would put the trial unequivocally in Patrick and Katherine's favor, but ones that could nudge it in that direction. Which was good; of course it was. Katherine wanted Tess to be unworthy of Rose. But she also didn't want Rose's mother, her biological mother, to be a train wreck.

"Hi, sweetie." Adee bent to Rose and wiggled her fingers. She waved Katherine into her office, then motioned to the chairs by the window.

"Up, Mama. Up."

Katherine unbuckled Rose from the stroller, balanced her across her knee as she dumped the toys she'd brought out of her bag, then set Rose on the floor beside her. Child-friendly voices singing about being nice, not just once or twice, filled the room. Katherine bent down and adjusted the volume on the bright-yellow bus.

"So." Adee laid out some papers and glossy photos on the table. "We've got drinking, promiscuity, out all hours."

Katherine leaned forward, took in the sight of Tess in a slinky dress, her lids droopy, her arm draped over the chair of a man who gazed at her like she was a juicy red steak.

"Could it be her boyfriend?"

"It's not."

Adee slid the pages over, showed her grainier images that appeared blown up, seemingly from the background of other shots.

Katherine's skin itched as if she were wearing a scratchy wool sweater. "How long ago was this?"

"The most recent was about two weeks ago. Others go back almost a year and a half."

"How did you—?"

"Facial recognition software that scans people's photos on social media, blogs, and various other media postings. And some clubs keep security camera backups for years."

"Wow." Katherine hesitated, her throat dry. "Almost a year and a half. So, not too long after the miscarriage."

"Mis—? Oh," said Adee, "you mean the one with your egg? That was early labor, not a miscarriage. Tess lost her uterus and the baby. It was a stillbirth."

Katherine froze and a tremor surged through her. A stillbirth? And Tess had lost her uterus.

"Twenty-one weeks along. Tess had a chance to hold her, take pic—"

"Stop." Katherine's voice erupted, high and thin. She braced herself on the chair, light-headed. Hanna had been big enough to hold. A miscarriage was horrible, but a stillbirth, a baby who, if given a few more weeks, may have made it in the outside world...

Since Tess had spoken Hanna's name, Katherine had been trying to push it away, push it down, pretend she'd never heard it. And now to know her baby had been big enough to hold, may have survived. Katherine closed her eyes, her jaw quivering.

"Katherine." Adee's voice was low. "I didn't think... I... Are you all right?"

"Yes." Katherine waved a hand, not looking at Adee, trying to calm her quaking. She thought back to the way she'd been in the mediation yesterday, the tone of her voice, her stubborn refusal to bend, and now this, digging into Tess's past, when Tess had lost so much... But it was exactly how Katherine should be, wasn't it? Regardless of anything else that had happened. Stalwart. Fighting for her child. Katherine swallowed, sat straighter. "I'll be fine, I—" She gave her head a little shake, raised her gaze, and then pointed to the photos. "These are all different men?"

Adee leaned back, her expression hesitant. "Seems she has three or four places in the city she frequents. 'Trolling,' said one of the bar staff. She's a woman who comes in for a reason. Sometimes she dances first, but even that seems part of the hunt. She catches the eye of some man, lets him get her good and drunk, then leaves on his arm."

The twist in Katherine's gut intensified as she battled to focus on Adee's words, leave all the rest behind. "Is there any proof she—"

"Proof enough," said Adee. "Hotel concierges who've recognized her, regulars who've seen her getting into cars."

Katherine let out a short burst of air. "And people just tell you this?"

"People like to be rats," said Adee, "especially when they think it's for a worthy cause." She shrugged. "And when they get their fingers greased."

"Mm-hmm." The sick feeling intensified. "Would a judge care? It's not as if she's doing this with a child at home. It's not as if it's a crime to enjoy sex."

"No," said Adee, "and to be honest, I don't like it, smearing a woman for her sexual choices."

Katherine winced. She pushed the photos away from her.

"But at the same time," said Adee, "it could be argued that this behavior, the frequency of it, presents a pattern, maybe even an addiction. Sometimes weeks, even months, would go by, according to the people I've talked to, but other times it'd be several weekends in a row, sometimes several nights in a row. Friday, Saturday, Sunday. With different men."

Katherine placed a hand on her abdomen. "I see."

"One bartender said it was sad, Tess seemed a sad woman, using the bottle and a man for escape. Clearly, it never worked for long."

Katherine inhaled. How could Tess not be sad? So many losses, a husband who left, and then to finally have a child, feel her grow in her womb—only to lose her. It was Katherine's biggest fear all through her pregnancy, a loss she doubted she'd recover from if it had happened. Katherine looked at Rose, her miracle child, her greatest source of joy. She swallowed, turned her gaze to Adee. "What else?"

Adee pulled back the photos and laid out new ones. "She's estranged from her family, like you said. They were poor Polish immigrants but have established themselves. They have an active church community, see their other child and grandchildren once or twice a month. Private people, secluded, but no real skeletons in their closets. Tess has reconnected with her brother, as you know. And she recently made at least one visit to her parents' place."

Katherine nodded.

"The estrangement happened after Tess withdrew from university. She was a top student, shy, said former classmates and professors, but studious. It shocked people, her dropping out. The last time most of them remembered seeing her was at a Halloween party"—Adee paused—"where she left with a fellow student."

"Okay." Beginning to regain her composure, Katherine picked up a photo: Tess, a young Tess, smiling, not looking confident in her own skin, but happy. Happier than Katherine had ever seen her, her arms draped over the shoulders of two women.

"This is interesting." Adee pointed to the woman to the left of Tess. "Do you recognize her?"

Katherine looked closer. She shot her gaze up.

"Yep." Adee grinned, her brown eyes sparkling. "Irene Connor. The nurse."

Katherine focused on the photo, her heart racing. "They knew each other?"

"According to another classmate, Irene was Tess's closest friend in the class, took her under her wing, helped to bring her out of her shell."

"But what does it mean?" Katherine's voice rose. "Why didn't she say anything? Do you think—"

"It's hard to know what to think," said Adee. "It could imply some kind of collusion. But there are still so many questions. Why would she want to switch her own eggs? What benefit would that give her? And if she were to make that switch, just to put it frankly, why the eggs of a Black woman?"

Katherine had wondered that, too, when she'd learned the switch was intentional. Eight eggs, Dr. Myers had said. Random chance. The only way a switch could be made without someone catching it. Katherine, frustrated she wouldn't get any more explanation than that, had brushed it off as a power trip by Irene, a bizarre urge, the type of thing you contemplated dozens of times, knowing it was insanity, something you'd never do, like stepping off the curb in front of oncoming traffic just to know what would happen. Except Irene had done it, taken the leap.

But now it didn't seem possible the switch was a coincidence, random chance, as Myers implied. Katherine rubbed her arm, incredulous. "It was Tess for a reason."

"It's certainly a possibility," said Adee. "It would be something for your lawyer to dig at, whether Tess was in on it, and why. Family court cases don't work quite like that but"—Adee tilted her head back and forth—"this knowledge, it couldn't hurt. Tess may say something incriminating. Something that might make her look less the victim, imply she knew she was getting someone else's egg, but now, since it didn't work out, she wants her biological child back."

Katherine's thoughts flipped, spun. What reason could Tess have for wanting another woman's egg? And why not get a donor egg; she'd already gotten donor sperm. Katherine looked again to Rose, her hands on a ring tower, trying to squeeze the smallest ring on first, biting her lip just the way Tess had when they'd bumped into each other the day of the retrieval, when she'd looked so alone and frightened.

But Tess knew Irene. Tess and Irene had been friends. It couldn't be mere coincidence…though the number of eggs had to be, which meant Tess couldn't have planned it ahead of time. "It doesn't make sense," said Katherine. "Why would Tess do it? As you said, what benefit could there be?"

"Well, that's the big question, isn't it? Even for why the nurse did it."

"Yes," said Katherine, "and I still can't fathom it, but if Tess had masterminded the switch, if she even knew about it, why wouldn't she have found some way to leak it as soon as she lost her baby, before Rose was even born?"

"Fear of repercussion?"

Katherine shook her head. "It doesn't make sense, Tess having any-thing to do with this. It just doesn't line up."

Katherine stopped and stared at the table, not understanding it, imag-ining she never would. "I could ask her, but…" She let out a strained laugh. "What would she say?" She shook her head again. "I'll think on it, and maybe Kerra will want to question her, but if there's nothing there, that leaves the one-night stands as our strongest"—Katherine hesitated—"intel?"

"So far."

Katherine suppressed a grimace. Tess was an adult, a consenting adult. Patrick certainly hadn't been Katherine's first. He hadn't been her second, either. She'd had one-night stands. Not many, but she'd had them. And she knew the pain of yearning for a child, the heartbreak when that child never came. Tess's pain could only have been worse. If she needed an escape, the distraction of a physical encounter, should Katherine be the one to judge?

Yet what if Tess's indiscretions weren't merely an escape, but a habit? An addiction? Katherine tried to be the perfect mother, to keep Rose safe, happy, and healthy, making sure she ate the right food, had the correct level of physical and sensory exposure as well as socialization. She kept a spot-less house because children needed order to thrive, and because she was terrified of some rogue virus or bacteria infecting Rose. Disciplining was a mystery, everything she read seeming to contradict itself. But she tried.

Would Tess? Katherine couldn't imagine Tess going so far as to leave Rose home alone to get drunk. She couldn't imagine she'd bring strange men into the house. But she didn't know. Which was why she was here, why she should pass all this information into the hands of the judge, let her decide.

"Katherine?" Adee's voice was soft. Softer than Katherine had ever heard it. She looked up, met Adee's gaze. Here she was, paying good money, a lot of money to expose another woman. Not just another woman, a woman who, one day, if things didn't go the way Katherine planned, Rose might love. "There's something else." Adee tapped her fingers on the table. "I don't know how useful it would be. It would depend on the judge." Her voice was different than before, the expression on her face as if she were tasting something rancid, as if she didn't want to speak the words she was about to.

"Tell me."

Adee sighed. "Around the time Tess withdrew from school, a few weeks after, actually, she had an abortion."

Katherine inhaled.

"And while I can't give you or the courts the documentation to prove the actual abortion, I know it happened. It's something your lawyer could dig into, question Tess about dropping out of school, mention the party, and if Tess told the truth, maybe use it to, well, argue that…"

"What," said Katherine, her skin heating up, her head starting to throb, "that because Tess ended the life of her first baby, she doesn't deserve this one?"

Adee pressed her lips together. "I don't think that. But this is the job, to give you the information. And where applicable, to help show you how to use it. I've seen people use this type of information before, in different circumstances, of course, when the father fighting for a child was actually fighting against the mother.

"In Tess's situation, well…" Adee rubbed a hand along her neck. "There was speculation about something happening the night of the Halloween party. The guy Tess left with was a bit of a player, and Tess, according to one of her friends, was very inexperienced. Since then, the guy has had two charges of date rape against him. No convictions."

Katherine closed her eyes. A thrumming filled her head.

"Put two and two together, and—"

"Yeah," said Katherine, her voice clipped, "I get it." She let out a shuddery breath, pressed her hand on the table. "No."

Adee sat silent. "No, what?"

Katherine looked at Rose, her throat clenching. "No, I don't want to use it."

"Which part of—"

"Any of it."

Adee hesitated. "There's one more thing."

"No!" Katherine shot from her seat, waving her hands in front of her. "I don't need this. Any of it. It was a mistake."

"Are you su—"

"Don't worry." Katherine bent to pick up Rose's toys, stuffing them into her bag. "You'll get your money. And thank you." She paused to look at Adee. "You've done an excellent job. If the court finds any of this out, fine. If they don't, fine. It's not coming from me."

Adee stood. "Mrs. Matheson…"

Katherine scooped Rose into her arms, settled her in the stroller, slipped the straps over her shoulders. It would be fine. Katherine and Patrick were the solid, stable parents. They had family, friends, a college fund established and growing daily. They were the right choice. Her hands shook as she tried to clasp the stroller's buckle. They'd focus on showing how worthy they were. It would have to be enough.

The photo of Tess in her early twenties flashed in Katherine's mind: so young, so inexperienced, leaving a party with a man she thought she could trust. Then walking into a clinic. Would her mother have been there, pushing her through the doors? They were Catholic. A vise seemed to clench Katherine's heart. Had that been the reason for the estrangement? Had Tess lost her innocence, her child, and her family, all from that one night?

Rose securely fastened, Katherine stood to her full height. Adee, who was collecting papers from the table, looked up. "You sure you don't want this? Any of it?"

Katherine shook her head and raised her palm.

Adee stared at Katherine, as if she was making a decision. She extended her hand. "Okay, well, I'll keep it in case you change your mind." A soft smile tweaked the corner of her lips. "It's been a pleasure, Mrs. Matheson, and I wish you the best."

Katherine nodded, fear and uncertainty rising in her throat. She dropped her hand, backed away, gripped the stroller. "Don't."

"Hmm?" Adee's eyebrow raised.

"Don't keep it. This is just between me and you. Burn it. Shred it. Whatever you do, just get rid of it. Please."

Adee shifted back, arms crossed. She was debating again, Katherine could tell, whether to say something to dissuade her.

"None of this is Tess's fault." Katherine's shoulders rose and fell, her throat so tight it was hard to speak, hard to breathe. "I don't believe she was in on it." Rose babbled, playing with consonants. *Ma-ma-ma, da-da-da.* "And I want my daughter. I don't want to share her, but…" She shook her head, still gripping the stroller. "Not like this. I won't do it like this."

35

TESS

TESS WOKE THE MORNING AFTER THE MEDIATION AND CHECKED her phone. When she got out of the shower, she checked her phone. At every work break she checked her phone, waiting for the call from Messineo that hadn't come. When her phone vibrated, she jumped, hoping it'd be the call, but it was Saadia, asking how the second mediation had gone.

Not too great, Tess replied, *though at least I kept my cool.* She debated telling Saadia about the PI, but she hadn't even told her Katherine and Patrick were the parents yet.

She slid her phone back into her lab coat, stood at her workstation, protocol beside her, drawing up samples of lake and pond water. As always, the work was exacting and important but repetitive. Measure, mix, spin, submit, wash, rinse. Measure, mix, spin, submit, wash, rinse.

Still, she needed to focus. Retrieving these samples sometimes meant sending helicopters to obscure and hard-to-reach locations in eastern Canada. One sample could cost thousands of dollars. Tens of thousands.

So, though Tess didn't even need the protocol anymore, there it sat, a constant reference as she checked each step before moving on to the next, unwilling to let her thoughts distract her, to make a mistake. She needed this job if she wanted a chance at sole custody—solid job, solid family connections, solid life.

Her feet aching, her skin slick with sweat, Tess measured out yet another sample. She set her 1-milliliter auto-pipette down and picked up a 50-microliter one. She spiked the sample. And on and on and on. She sighed.

At her first legal aid meeting with Maeve, Tess had been told these things take time. The system was overworked, and she should trust she'd be told whatever she needed to be told when she needed to be told it, that calling, pestering wouldn't help matters and could hurt.

She'd listened, waiting for Messineo's calls, stockpiling her questions for whenever they had a scheduled appointment. But one wasn't scheduled for over a week, and Tess needed to know.

The moment the clock struck the hour, signifying the start of her break, Tess set her instruments down and rushed outside to make her call.

"Don't worry," said Messineo. But Tess was worried; she was terrified. She heard the shuffling of papers, the slam of a door, murmured voices. "It's not uncommon."

"To hire a private investigator?" Tess leaned against Enviro Lab's brick wall, shielding herself from the onslaught of frigid wind whipping around the corner. "For a custody case?"

"Mm-hmm."

"But why would they—"

"To see if there's anything they can use in court. Usually it's for situations of abuse, child neglect, substance abuse, things that would endanger the child."

"Uh-huh." A heavy weight settled in Tess's stomach.

"You don't even have access to the child," continued Messineo, "so nothing to worry about there, and as to the other stuff, we've already talked about this. Model citizen. Living the life you'd live if the child were with you."

Rose, Tess wanted to say, *not "the child."*

"But what else?" she asked. "Things from my past? Choices I made or…indiscretions?"

"The past is the past," said Messineo. "Unless it reinforces present behavior, it's irrelevant or at least not very relevant. Just because you may not have been a suitable mother ten years ago doesn't mean you wouldn't make a wonderful one today."

But what about a year and a half ago? thought Tess. *What about two weeks?*

"Listen, Ms. Sokolowski, Tess, I'm sorry, but I'm on my way to court. I'll call you when I have news of the conference."

"Should I hire one?" Tess angled even more toward the wall, away from the prying ears of her coworkers. They'd started looking at her differently the past weeks, whispering. "Even the playing field?"

"You could." Messineo's voice was different now, farther away. He must have put her on speakerphone. A rumble of tires on pavement sounded in the background. "But it's not cheap. There's no legal aid for that, and you may not learn a thing." He paused. "Focus on you. Stable environment. Strong support system."

"But—"

"We'll speak soon, Ms. Sokolowski. Have a good day." The call ended.

Tess stared at her phone. "Damn." She slammed her hand against the brick wall, leaned her head into it. If the Mathesons were going to fight dirty, so should she—if she could afford it. She'd only qualified for legal aid based on her past year's income, because for most of that year, she'd still

213

been working at Wendy's. If the trial went on too long, they may reassess her, make her pay full legal fees, rather than the subsidized ones she'd lucked into.

Tess turned from the wall toward the building's entrance. Two of her coworkers, smoking on a nearby bench, whipped their heads away. "What?" She shocked herself with the deepness of her voice, the accusation in it. "You have something to say? Something to ask?"

Tim, who'd stopped mocking her and hadn't asked her out to dinner once since word (or at least suspicion) of the switch had clearly gotten around the office, shook his head. "Nope."

Tess walked past them, her fists clenched to hide the shaking.

Two days later, Tess sat on the edge of her bed, phone in hand, a strange vibration coursing through her limbs, reverberating in her chest, closing her throat. After work the other day, she'd spent two hours researching at the North Memorial Library, made ten calls, and found not one PI she could justify paying, not if she wanted to go back to school anytime soon. Which meant the Mathesons may learn the dirt on her, bring it up in court, and what would she have against them? She stared at her phone, thought of her father, the spicy-sweet scent of him, the way he held her in his arms. Would he ever hold her again, after learning who she was, what she'd done? There was a time she went to him with her problems, big and small, though back then, every problem had been small, comparatively. Still, he always treated her with kindness. It wasn't him who had created the decade of silence between them.

Tess bit a nail as she took in the sight of her apartment, looking even more pathetic than usual, everything she owned stuffed in boxes. As her father instructed, Tess had waited a couple weeks, plenty of time for her mother to process a visit after all these years. But would dinner be over yet? If tradition were kept alive, they would have been at the table by two, so now, at five, would her mother be sufficiently softened? Perhaps calling at six would be better. Or seven. She'd wait till—Tess jumped at the movement in her hand. She looked at the screen and swiped.

"Hi."

"Tess, oh, Tess."

Tess sighed as an invisible lump developed in her throat. "You talked to Mama and Tata. Guess dinner's over, then?"

"You could have told me. Why didn't you tell me?" Mikolai let out a soft moan. "And the party. That's what all the whispering was about. All the…awkwardness."

"Mm-hmm." Silence on the line. Tess sighed. "I was going to tell you before dinner next week, if they let me come." She hesitated. "How's Mama taking it? What did she say?"

Tess could almost hear Mikolai struggling to find the right words, wondered if he was angry or hurt by her withholding the truth. "She's willing to see you. To hear you tell your story." Another pause. "Tess, why do you try to do things all by yourself? Why can't you let us in?"

"You mean like when I went to Mama and Tata after dropping out of school and they disowned me?"

More silence, then a loud huff. "They didn't understand, Tess. All along you had these dreams, goals. You were smart. You were crushing all your courses and suddenly, 'Oh, I no longer feel like studying.' It was ridiculous. It was like spitting in their face, in the face of all their sacrifices."

"You sound like Mama."

"Well, Mama had a point."

More silence. This time from Tess. "What was I supposed to tell them?"

"The truth."

"And if the truth was worse?"

"Worse than throwing your future away?"

Tess turned to the bare wall. She wished she could blame the bareness on prepping for the move next week, that she'd taken down all her artwork and family photos and packed them carefully away. But the walls had always been empty. "Yeah. Worse than that."

"Tess, what's worse than throwing away your future? Worse than lying to the people who gave up everything for you? Who love—"

"Being raped." Tess stopped, shocked she'd spoken those words. Yet if the PI unearthed it, better Mikolai hear the full story from Tess than whatever fragments were revealed in court. She continued, slowly. "Having to see his face in class every day as if nothing had happened, as if I had asked for it. Feeling so powerless that—" The words caught in her throat, but she pressed on. "Night after night"—her eyes burned and her lips trembled—"I thought it'd be better to die."

"What's your apartment number?"

"Huh?"

"Your apartment number," said Mikolai. "Are you at home? Where are you? I'm coming."

"Yes, but Mikolai, no. It's fine. I'm fine."

"Theresa Sokolowski, give me your unit number right now."

36

TESS

TESS HELD OPEN THE DOOR AS HER BROTHER MARCHED THROUGH it, the first time she'd let him enter her apartment, previously insisting she meet him outside. He broke his stride, taking in the small space, the boxes, the old and peeling paint, and, she imagined, the slight moldy smell that, no matter how much she cleaned, never went away. He pulled her to him as she closed her eyes, her body stiff. Then, as he continued to enfold her, her limbs softened, relaxing against him.

She was flooded by memories of her childhood. He hadn't been a perfect big brother, but he'd been kind. He'd made her laugh, rarely excluded her, stood up for her. Why had she doubted he'd stand up for her after the rape? How different would her life have been if, all those years ago, she'd spoken the words she spoke tonight?

Mikolai let go, pulled back, his hands on her shoulders, and directed her to her raggedy couch, the only other seating option a single chair at a small foldable card table.

"Tess." His eyes were so focused, his voice soft. "Tell me."

At the Halloween party, they'd all been laughing, drinking, dancing. "It was a new world," said Tess. "I'd been to high school dances, but no house parties unless parents were present. No clubs. Never in a place where the drinks flowed." At twenty-one, she'd never even tried alcohol. *Drink up,* Irene had laughed as she pushed the cold frothing glass into Tess's hand. Tess had. She didn't know how many.

"I had four, five drinks, maybe," Tess told Mikolai. "Enough that I didn't have my wits about me, didn't question the safety of heading back to the apartment of a boy I barely knew." All she'd been thinking was how good she felt, how his hand caressing the back of her neck, his lips on hers were a wonder she'd only dreamed of.

Tess hung her head, avoiding Mikolai's eyes and the pity or anger or disgust she feared rested there. "Mama and Tata warned me of men, of what they wanted. But my friends insisted they were wrong. Insisted the choice was up to me."

We're not animals, Julie had said. *Just 'cause we start, doesn't mean it's impossible to stop.*

I stop all the time. Irene had laughed. *Whether they want to or not. It's me who decides.* Her hair had been long then, flowing. She was soaking up all that life offered her, enjoying each moment the way Tess never had. *If I want to kiss,* she continued, *we kiss. If I want more, we do more. If I want to stay the night and cuddle, that's what we do. None of that means he's getting in. No means no.*

Precisely, confirmed Julie.

But aren't there certain expectations if you... Tess persisted.

No.

But what if... She hesitated. *What if you say no and he says yes?*

You say no again, and then you leave.

"And so I thought," said Tess, "what do Mama and Tata know? They practically had an arranged marriage." They were next-door neighbors in

Ciechanów, playmates before her mother could even speak, married at nineteen and twenty-one. "These women—my friends—they were living it."

Irene had put her hand on Tess's knee. *Choose the right guy, that's all. A nice one. You'll be fine. You'll be more than fine.* She laughed. *You deserve some fun.*

"It was fun," said Tess. "Until it wasn't."

He'd seemed nice. Friendly. He was good-looking, too, in a way no other boy who had showed interest in Tess had been. It wasn't the first time a boy's hand had rested on the small of her back, but it was the first time she was in a boy's house—a man's house—with no one else around. He'd smoothed his fingers over her arm, and she shivered with the pleasure of it.

"I thought we'd kiss," she told Mikolai, "maybe a little more. Then I'd leave."

Mikolai shook his head, his face scrunched into an expression of concern. Tess looked away.

She had expected to enter a living room, but he opened the door into a room with a bed, a couch against one wall, and a TV in the corner.

"He led me to the bed," said Tess. He sat her on the edge of it, brought his hand to her face, drawing her in, touching his lips to hers. She let him, though more rigidly than before. "He pushed me down." Her skin crawled with the memory. "I said no." He'd silenced her with more kisses, pinned her arms down with his own. "I tried to get up." She pushed. She tried to kick. He held her down as she writhed. "He laughed, Mikolai"—her voice cracked, but she bit her lip and pressed on—"when I said no."

"Tess. Oh, Tess."

Tess looked up. "I should have screamed." She should have bit his lip, his tongue, before it had gotten so far.

"No. It's not your fault."

She should have kneed him in the groin. She tried. She was sure she'd tried. "I should have fought harder."

When he was done, he pulled his pants up, cinched his belt. *Want anything to drink?* he asked. She'd been frozen. So shocked she couldn't move, couldn't speak. He'd looked at her again, like she was deaf, dumb. *I said, "Are you thirsty?"* Her body sprang into motion. She grabbed her underwear, scrunched in a ball at the foot of his bed. She stuffed it in her purse and pulled her dress down over her hips.

Where you rushing off to? He seemed perplexed at her fumbling, at what must have been the look on her face. *I thought we were having a good time.* She must have stared at him, just for a moment, as he registered her shock. *Well, you came here.* He shrugged. *What did you think was going to happen?*

She still had one shoe on. She yanked on the other and lunged toward the door, undid the bolt, stumbled into the hall.

Mikolai shifted toward her, placed a hand on her shoulder tentatively, as if he were afraid to touch her. Her shoulders slumped as she met his gaze.

"Did you report him?"

Tess looked at her hands, the nails bit to the quick. "People would say my dress was too short. I went to his apartment. People would say I asked for it."

"If you said no, you didn't ask for it."

Tess let out a sharp laugh. "He said, she said." She sighed. "Besides, it would have meant living it all over again." Though she had anyway. She still woke from time to time, struggling and slick with sweat. "It would have meant Mama and Tata knowing."

Tess turned her gaze away from him. "You know how they would have reacted. How Tata would have looked—the disappointment, his daughter ruined. What Mama would have said. 'We didn't raise you like that. Nice girls don't go to those kinds of parties. Nice girls don't get drunk and go to men's houses. Who are you? Our daughter wouldn't do this.'"

She raised her gaze to Mikolai's, saw the confirmation on his face, heard it in his lack of contradiction. He leaned forward. "You should have told me. I would have helped you. We would have figured something out."

"Like what? What would we have figured out? I'd still have to go to class, see him every day. I'd still—"

"You could have deferred, picked up again the next semester. We could have told Mama and Tata you were sick. Overwhelmed. We—"

"Mikolai."

"Even now. We can report him. Maybe he's done this to others, maybe—"

"I don't even know his last name. I heard he moved after graduation anyway. He wasn't from here."

"Still. There'd be records. You could—"

Tess placed a hand on Mikolai's arm. "It's too late. It's over."

Mikolai stared, his eyes locked on hers, his expression strained. "I'm sorry." He took her hand. "I should have known. Should have pressed. You wouldn't have dropped out of school for no reason. That wasn't you. I should have—"

"It's okay." Tess cut him off. "It wasn't your responsibility."

"I was so busy, just out of grad school, starting at the firm, trying to make a name for myself, engaged to Karina." He paused, his teeth clenched, his jaw tense. "I told myself you weren't a child anymore; you could handle your own life."

"That's true. I wasn't. I could."

"No." Mikolai shook his head. "I failed you."

Tess looked away again, now holding Mikolai's guilt alongside her own.

She wouldn't tell him any more, not about the abortion, not unless she had to. If the Mathesons submitted that information to the courts—or anything else they learned—she wouldn't have a choice, but the thought of telling made her want to coil into herself: how all those years ago, when she saw two lines on the pregnancy test, all she wanted was *him* out of her—not so much the baby, but *him*. Him with his cocky grin, pretending he'd done nothing wrong. How if she had to, if she were back in that situation, she'd do it again…but still, it tore her to shreds.

Tess straightened. "What happened, happened. But that's not what matters now."

Mikolai looked away. He rubbed a hand over his face. "You're right." He turned back to her. "Rose is yours?"

Tess, at last, smiled. She nodded.

"Take me through it. All of it."

She told him about the switch, everything that had happened since the clinic's call, except for the fact that it was likely Irene had switched the eggs because of what Tess said. "I'm sorry I didn't tell you earlier, but I need your support," she said, "now more than ever."

"That's why you stopped by for lunch?" His smile was slight, unreadable. "Why you wanted to reconnect with us all?"

Tess nodded. He nodded back, his jaw twitching.

"If I have your support, Mama and Tata's, too, I'll have a shot. Maybe not sole custody, which is what I want, but a shot—Rose in my life."

He took her hand, held it in both of his. "You have it. I'm here, no matter what."

When Mikolai left, Tess secured the bolt and leaned against the closed door. He hadn't scoffed or turned away. He was by her side. She hadn't expected complete dismissal, but she had expected judgment, disappointment, a face that betrayed distaste.

There'd been none of it.

Mikolai, who was raised by the same parents, the same mother.

Tess closed her eyes and took a deep, cleansing breath. For the first time in a long time, she didn't feel quite so alone. She lifted her phone and dialed. If Mikolai could stand in support, then maybe, just maybe, the mother who raised them, who should have loved her no matter what but hadn't, could too.

37

KATHERINE

AFTER PUTTING ROSE DOWN FOR A NAP, KATHERINE SAT AT THE breakfast nook, her elbows on the table, her head in her hands, waiting for Patrick, who was about to return from a work weekend away. Her mind replayed the meeting with Adee, her own parting words. *Burn it? Shred it?* Katherine should pick up the phone, tell Adee she'd had a momentary case of madness. Tess was out getting drunk, going home with strange men, and rather than tell the judge, Katherine was—what? Respecting the woman's privacy?

But it wasn't about Tess. It was about Rose. And as much as Katherine wanted to, she didn't believe Tess would do anything to cause Rose harm. She saw now what Patrick meant, how one day Rose might resent the fact that Katherine hadn't just fought for her, but against Tess.

They'd have to do this his way. She'd have to tell him that after spending thousands of dollars gleaning this information, she wasn't going to use it. Instead, she was going to focus on doing what he'd said all along—showing they were the best choice for Rose.

Upon hearing Patrick's keys in the door, Katherine closed her eyes, readying herself, wondering if she should have told him over the phone with miles between them. If he ranted and raved, he'd be justified.

His footsteps stopped. "Katherine?"

"Mm-hmm?"

"Are you okay?"

She sat up, ready for the *I told you so* and the *What were you thinking?*

"I had my meeting with Adee today," she said.

"Uh-huh… Not good news?"

"Not good at all. I understand now why you didn't want me digging." Katherine made eye contact with Patrick. "We need to talk."

"Oh God." He collapsed in the seat across from her, his head falling, his hands rising to meet it. "I'm sorry. I messed up. And if it messes things up for us, for Rose…" Patrick inhaled, as if he were trying to gather up all the air in the room. "I'm sorry. It was a mistake. It wasn't planned and it didn't mean anything. I swear. It just happened. Once."

A mistake. Katherine's throat went dry as she processed his words. *Once.* She opened her mouth, closed it, opened it again—like a fish caught on the shore.

Patrick straightened. "I…wait. What were you going to say?"

"That I decided not to use anything Adee found," she spat. "That you were right, and we shouldn't be those people." She stood up and backed away as he stood too. Not once during all those months of celibacy had she thought her husband was a cheater. Her blood raced, her heart pounded. She registered, for the first time, the other words he'd said. Rose…if this messed things up for Rose, the trial. She wanted to scream. She threw her arms in the air, letting them land on her head. "Are you still seeing this person?"

Patrick held his hands out in front of him, wiping the space between them. "No. I swear. It was ages ago. A one-time horrible mistake."

Katherine pressed against the wall as Patrick stepped closer, not able to bear the thought of him touching her. Her skin felt tight; her jaw, she realized, was clenched. She released it, rolled her shoulders back, but still her voice trembled. "When? When did it happen?"

"A long time ago."

"When?" she snapped.

Patrick hesitated. "When you were pregnant. Seven months along." He rubbed a hand through his hair. "It wasn't planned, truly. It wasn't...any kind of...anything. It'd just been so long since we...and even then, with us, it'd become so robotic, so mandatory. And she was there, and I was there and...it meant nothing." He took another step forward as Katherine pressed into the wall, hearing the words but trying to block them out. Not wanting to hear any more, who or why or where or any of it. Not wanting it to be real.

"I hated myself afterward," said Patrick. "I wouldn't let myself touch you, even when you wanted, when I wanted... I got tested. Still, I felt so..." He stopped. "Unworthy."

Katherine kept her gaze averted, not wanting to look at him, this man who was supposed to be her partner, her lover, who'd taken vows then tossed them aside. She focused, instead, on three framed photos of Rose: wrinkly and perfect, curled up on a throw; her hand in Patrick's hand, the contrast striking; her feet cupped in Katherine's palms, the rest of her an aesthetically pleasing blur.

"I know you've been concerned, but that's what it's been about, Katherine, our lack of intimacy, my inability to...you know. I just felt so guilty."

She took in those perfect baby toes. Already they'd grown so much larger than they had been. Unrecognizable.

Patrick's voice quavered. "I want us to be a family, Katherine. We are. This doesn't change that, not for me."

She stared at him.

"I'm sorry, Katherine. Truly. We can do counseling. We can—"

Katherine stepped from the wall and turned away from him. "All I asked was when." Again, her gaze fell on those three photos. What mattered was Rose. Not Katherine's happiness. Not his. She turned back, her voice cold, her limbs rigid. "It's over?"

He nodded.

"Okay, then." She stood, her head tall, her shoulders back. "Go wake Rose, please. Take her to the park, or your parents. Wherever. Just leave."

"What?" Patrick stepped toward her, a vacant, wide-eyed look on his face. Why had she never noticed this, how stupid he could look at times?

"I want to be alone. Have her home for dinner."

"Oh, uh…okay. Yes. Sure." He stood, staring—vacant, wide-eyed, *stupid*.

"Now, please."

Once they'd left, Katherine flipped on the bathroom fan, then adjusted the showerhead to the strongest, loudest setting. She stepped in, let the scalding water pound her back. She slammed the side of her fists against the tiled wall, a deep, guttural noise bursting from her throat, rage pulsing through her veins. She slammed again and again as a scream burst out of her.

The life she'd planned, worked for, wanted more than she'd ever wanted anything was a lie—every aspect of it. She thought she hadn't known Patrick—she let out a caustic laugh, moaned, hit the wall once more. How right she was.

Destroyed. Her trust in Patrick. Her illusion that her daughter was her own, that their lives were or could ever be perfect. After a final slam, Katherine took a deep, slow breath. She exhaled, tried to force her pulse to settle, her breathing to ease, her mind to accept that, compared to the prospect of losing Rose, a one-night fling was insignificant. She adjusted the showerhead until a gentle flow poured over her. She washed her face, smoothed the soap over her arms and torso, finger-combed her hair, and then twisted it for easy manageability.

That night she made dinner, then put Rose to bed, Patrick by her side as normal. The next morning she undid the twists, applied fresh spritzes of moisture to release the coils. She took time with it, as she always did, making sure each curl coiled perfectly. She put on clothes that flattered, washed the dishes, vacuumed the floor, fed Rose. She smiled at Patrick, offered her cheek for a kiss as he left for work, as he hesitated, his face full of questions.

Her smile stayed firm. She would forgive. She would live as if she'd forgotten. The alternative was to walk away, sever the most important thing they had going for them—stability, a mother and father united in love, the only home Rose had ever known, a home that included her bio-logical father.

She dropped Rose off at her parents, was as truthful as she could handle as Elvira cupped Katherine's cheeks in her hand, told her she was worried, asked how she was coping with it all. Katherine's voice shook and her eyes watered as she admitted life was rough lately, harder than she'd thought it could be, but she was coping. She allowed herself to hold on to her mother longer than normal as they hugged, letting her lip quiver against Elvira's shoulder.

She drove to meet Patrick, to walk into the conference proceedings side by side, sit as the judge sat before them, talking about how this was unprecedented, expressing her sympathy for both parties, but that despite being victims of something unthinkable, they did not matter. The only person the judge cared about was Rose, what was best for her.

She spoke of the connection Rose already had with her parents, but how, at this young age, she could come to develop an equally strong one with Tess. As such, she was ordering regular visitation over the next few months, two, and then three times a week, first for an hour and a half, and then three hours at a time. At first, it would be in the court-appointed visitation center with trained professionals. Then Tess, Patrick, and Katherine would need to agree on someone to supervise.

Katherine sat, dying inside, feeling as if life couldn't get worse. First the affair, then news of the visitation—not just a possibility, but an actual fact, with a date and location cast upon them. Then, in approximately four months, a custody trial, where a new judge would ask questions of Katherine and Patrick, of Tess, of their friends, families, possibly even coworkers.

After the proceedings, they met with Kerra, who gave them the details about the first visitation, which would be in two weeks, and prepped them for what the trial would be like, how ugly it could get. She told them to finalize a witness list—people who could testify to their character, their exceptional parenting, their strength as a family. She asked if they had any questions.

"What if we don't agree on someone to supervise the visitation?" asked Katherine.

"It'll look bad." Kerra's voice was drawn. "You need to show you're willing to compromise, to consider the possibility that having Tess in Rose's life may be a good thing."

"If I were willing to entertain that possibility, we would have agreed at mediation."

A beat of silence. A repressed sigh. "This, obviously, is a—"

"Unique situation. Yes, I know." *Could Kerra have been the woman, with her full lips, her contoured legs? No, Patrick had said it happened too long ago for that. Then who?* Katherine pushed the question away. A name would only make it worse. If she didn't know, it could stay some abstract thing in the past—over, done with. She could tell herself it didn't matter.

"If visitation goes well, if Tess shows herself as competent and loving, you'll need to have faith the system works. It'll be best for Rose, too—provided the court decides to grant shared custody or even regular unsupervised visitation—if she's had this time to get to know Tess." Kerra paused. "Any other questions?"

Katherine shook her head, a sickening tension pulsing through her.

"Good. There's another reason I called you here today. The case against the nurse is underway. Both Katherine and Ms. Sokolowski, as expected, were called to testify. I know it's not your focus, but it would be prudent to decide soon whether you and Ms. Sokolowski want to launch a lawsuit against the clinic. Have you two discussed it?"

Patrick shook his head. "Barely."

Katherine avoided looking at him, hating the way his shoulders had slumped all through the day's proceedings, how he'd seemed so hesitant, so uncertain, looking at her one minute as if she were a bomb that might explode, the next like a dog with its tail between its legs.

"You could get millions," said Kerra. "It's not about that, I know, but the case, the inevitable coverage if you filed a lawsuit, would set a precedent. This, all of it, it's not only about you or Tess, about the nurse or the clinic. Proper systems weren't in place, and if they weren't in place here, they're sure to not be in place elsewhere."

"But I thought we didn't want our story out there," said Katherine. "Isn't that the reason for the publication ban?"

"Yes." Kerra paused. "Which is why you need to think about whether you want to settle privately or go to trial."

"But if we settle, doesn't that negate all you said about setting a precedent?"

"Yes and no. You could make it part of your agreement for the clinic to issue a press release or statement, letting the public or their governing body know the results. No names needed. And I know this is expensive. I'm expensive. Adee was expensive. Recouping those costs is what you're due. It's what Ms. Sokolowski is due." Kerra leaned forward. "As awkward as all of this is, if you were to file together, you'd have a much stronger case."

Katherine let out a short breathy laugh.

"I know, I know, it seems weird, but it's how these things work. Also, you'll have more leverage if you file a suit beforehand, when it's uncertain whether you'll lose Rose entirely or have to share her."

Katherine's head throbbed. "You think we should have two cases going at once. A custody battle and a potential multimillion-dollar lawsuit. One where we're fighting against Tess, and one where we're fighting with her."

"I'm letting you know your options."

Katherine rubbed her temple. "Do we have to decide right now?"

"No, of course not. You just need to think about it. These few months before the custody trial will pass quicker than you think, so stay the course." Kerra tapped her fist in her palm. "Patrick's solid job. Katherine at home with Rose, a constant connection, the ever-loving mother. Your extended families a regular presence. This is what you have going for you."

Katherine sensed Patrick shifting. "What if something were to come up," he asked, "at the trial, just say? An indiscretion. Would that, uh, harm our chances?"

Shut up! Katherine wanted to shout.

Kerra's gaze narrowed. "What kind of indiscretion?"

A sound of uncertainty reverberated from the back of Patrick's throat. Katherine resisted the urge to grip the seat of her chair. She hadn't resolved to put aside her pride, her shame, her anger, and that tickling urge for vengeance so he could reveal their fractured lives.

"Does it have anything to do with your ability to be a good father?" asked Kerra. "Anything…criminal?"

"No." Patrick's voice was tight. "No. Nothing like that."

"Then it should be fine. It would be better, though"—Kerra looked first at Patrick and then Katherine—"if I knew what this indiscretion was, if I could help you reframe it."

Katherine smiled, an acrid taste at the back of her throat. "It was nothing." She waved her free hand, willing herself to believe it. "We're fine."

Later that night, Katherine accepted Patrick's offer to bathe Rose before bed—the least he could do—and sat in front of her computer. Like a track stuck on repeat, her mind returned to the indiscretion, not only because of what it meant for her marriage, but for what it might mean for Rose. She didn't want Kerra to know, even if it meant helping them reframe it. She didn't want anyone to know, ever. But what if someone did? What if Tess hired a PI who revealed this dirty secret on the stand?

She'd been resisting, but now Katherine opened a new tab on her browser. Apart from that one night when she'd given in, months ago, every time she saw a headline related to the switch, she scrolled past it. When she heard even a reference on TV, she turned the channel.

Tonight, she wanted to know whatever she could, if only for something else to think about. Katherine typed *Irene Connor IVF* into the search engine. She leaned back, overwhelmed at the number of hits. Yet, surely one would give a reason why…

A medical professional went on and on about breach of trust, professional misconduct, the stain on the medical community. Other experts talked about the emotional and psychological damage the nurse's actions caused, hoping counselors would be available for all those touched by this atrocity.

Katherine's eyes scanned article after article, but still no one had any idea why. Most didn't even speculate, saying Connor was unavailable for comment. The public did, though. Comment after comment. Hate-filled. Compassionate. Every emotion in between. The news crossing the continent, crossing the world. Everyone talking. Everyone wondering. And Katherine, where it mattered, as clueless as them all.

Katherine read on, seeing, amid the demands for an answer to why Irene had done it, support for Tess—the bio-mom—who everyone thought should have, if not sole custody of her child, an equal role. The comments stressed the importance of biology. But what they were forgetting was that Katherine *had* a biological connection. Rose wasn't grown in some artificial womb; Katherine had grown her for over nine months, had nourished Rose with her own body since then. Rose's DNA lived within Katherine. She'd read that somewhere, *Scientific American* or *Psychology Today*, how DNA passed through the placenta into the mother's blood. How decades later, that same DNA was still in the mother's brain. Rose was a part of Katherine. Literally. Genetically. No matter what anyone said. Not that motherhood was about biology, anyway. It was about love, and Tess, as much as she wanted Rose, didn't love her. She couldn't… She didn't even know her! Katherine wasn't a stepmother, as she'd worried before. Whether or not she stayed married to Patrick, she *was* Rose's mother.

Katherine looked toward Rose's room, her chest so tight it ached. She wanted to call Kerra, tell her the visitation was pointless, she'd never hand over her daughter. She wanted to kick Patrick out of the house for what he'd done, for what his selfish, adulterous actions may do to all of them. She wanted to run down the hall, pick up her baby, and hold her close, never let her go. She wanted to scream.

38

TESS

TESS ARRIVED EXACTLY ON TIME FOR HER FIRST FAMILY DINNER IN a decade. She accepted her father's embrace, anxious for the moment when she'd tell him—and her mother—that in just over a week, she'd see Rose, spend uninterrupted time with her. That, eventually, they could meet her, too. For now, she kept that news to herself; other words needed to come first. She followed her father to the kitchen.

"Theresa is here," Aleksy said, his voice louder than usual, his arm spread, as if announcing a visiting dignitary rather than their own child.

"I am aware," said Jasia.

Tess stepped forward, her gaze on Jasia's back, watching the rhythmic motion of her mother kneading dough. Her throat tightened, a knot building in the center of her stomach. But she was here, she'd made that step, she wouldn't back down now. "Cześć, Mama."

"Theresa." Jasia turned, dusting her floured hands on her apron. "You are very skinny."

"Yes, Mama." Tess gestured to the pile of braided dough on the counter—one of her childhood favorites. "Chałka?"

"It is for tomorrow's prayer group."

"Ah, I see." Her voice sounded with disappointment, though she tried to mask it. "It's good to see you, Mama."

"The circumstances are not so good, though, are they?"

Tess looked at her father, who gestured to the table. "All is done, is it not, mój najdroższy? Should we sit for dinner?"

Tess glanced between her parents. "What about Mikolai and the kids?"

"They will not come."

"Did something—"

"I thought it best"—Jasia walked to the table, taking the seat she'd taken Tess's entire life—"we were alone."

Thought it was best for Tess not to have backup, more likely, not have Mikolai's humor and the children's boisterousness to ease the tension. "Of course." Tess sat, willing her jaw not to tremble. They ate dinner with hardly a word, only requests to pass a dish and the sound of cutlery breaking the silence. It wasn't until the tea was on the table—not in the living room as normal—that her mother spoke directly to Tess.

"You have a child."

Tess sat tall. "I do."

"And so you need us to make it seem like you have a family."

Tess swallowed. "I do have a family. You are my family."

"Hmm."

Tess looked to her father.

"I told your mother what happened. About the IVF, the mix-up. How you are trying to get your daughter. How family support is important."

"Not just for the trial." Tess leaned forward, her arms on the table. "I want her to know you. Both of you." She looked to Jasia. "She's so beautiful, Mama. She has my eyes. And her smile…" Tess's rigidness softened, warmth flowing through her at the thought of Rose. "She's perfect."

"Why, though, Theresa? Why would you do this? Without a husband. Without support."

Tess shrugged. "I wanted a baby. To be a mother."

"But, Theresa—"

"It's done now." Aleksy rested a hand on his wife's arm. "We have another granddaughter."

Jasia shook her head, her face set in the grimace she always wore when chastising Tess in Polish. She spoke of Tess's rashness, her lack of planning, not thinking through the consequences of her choices. Tess's head ached with the effort of comprehending words and phrases she hadn't heard in a decade, of not letting herself be transported to the night she'd sat in the same spot she was sitting now, when her mother had told her if she wasn't going to return to school, she shouldn't return to this house, either.

"I can do this," Tess said once her mother's lecturing stopped. Jasia folded her hands across her chest, her gaze still as stone. "I may not have a husband—"

"'What therefore God hath joined together, let not man put asunder,'" said Jasia.

Tess hesitated, then continued. "And I may not have a degree, but I have a good job and soon a nice apartment. I have enough money to finish my degree. I messed up, but I'm doing better. I'm doing great. You should be proud."

"Proud?" asked Jasia. "What is there to be proud of? You are doing the things you are supposed to do."

Tess, again, looked from her mother to her father—love shone in his eyes—then back to her mother. "Are you saying you don't want me in your lives? You don't want us?"

Jasia tutted. She looked away, her arms still folded, her chin raised. "Come back in two weeks. Every two weeks. And when you can, you bring that girl."

Tess grinned, relief flowing through her. It wasn't much, but for now, it'd have to be enough.

39

KATHERINE

THE DAY OF THE FIRST VISITATION, KATHERINE STARED AT ROSE. SHE stared at the clothes she'd laid out in front of her, a tremor reverberating through her core. Rose needed to look tended to, but not too cute. An outfit that said, *Here is a well-taken-care-of, well-loved daughter.* Not, *Here is your daughter. Scoop her up.*

What combination could say one without saying the other?

"You're too adorable!" Katherine kept her voice light as that tremor turned to a burst of pain so intense she wanted to cry out. She scooped Rose into her arms, cuddled her close, willed herself not to let all that was bottled within pour down her cheeks. "Too precious." Katherine grabbed the checked top and pulled it over Rose's head, amazed at how much Rose was helping now, how she pushed her arms through the sleeves, tugged on her shirt to pull it over her belly. In these few short months, she'd changed so much. Katherine pulled Rose to her again. Despite her ache that this day had finally come, she grinned at the sound of Rose's laughter.

Going along with the judge's directives changed nothing long term.

She pulled socks over Rose's perfect toes. It was necessary to show herself as reasonable and cooperative before the impending trial. She smoothed Rose's hair back with a brush and secured it with a sparkly hair tie. It didn't mean she was losing her child. She twisted Rose around, hugged her once more, then stood. She could do this. She had no choice.

Rose snug to her hip, Katherine shook hands with the supervised access worker. She looked at Rose. "It's like going to a babysitter, except even more fun," she said. "There'll be a big room with lots of toys and maybe other kids, too. You'll meet a new friend, Tess, who is very nice. Tess gave you Fox." Katherine held up a photo of Tess, which the Supervised Access Centre had provided, and placed the toy in Rose's hand. Katherine had been tempted to throw it out, but Patrick shook his head. She'd acquiesced, and the animal had become one of Rose's favorites.

"You'll hold this nice woman's hand, who will take you to Tess, and this nice woman will stay there, too. You'll all have fun. Mommy will wait right outside, and soon we'll be together again."

Katherine had gone through this last night. She'd gone through it this morning. She'd gone through it minutes ago, before exiting the SUV. But Rose was one. What she actually understood, Katherine couldn't know.

Katherine stood in front of Luela, the access worker, and tapped her toe. Arms trembling, she talked about the weather, the price of cauliflower, desperate to delay the inevitable with forced chat.

"It's time," Luela said. She put a hand on Katherine's shoulder. "I know this is hard."

Katherine wanted to scream. She smiled.

"Rose?" Luela leaned toward Rose, her hand held out. Rose leaned into Katherine, and the desire to hold Rose tighter, to turn and flee, deepened.

But instead Katherine squatted, set Rose on her feet, gave her one more squeeze, and then, pasting the most convincing smile on her face she could muster, nudged Rose forward. "Go on, sweetie. You'll be fine. You'll have so much fun."

She handed over Rose's diaper bag and watched as Rose went, hand in hand with Luela. Rose looked back, nervousness clouding her features, the fox squeezed tight to her chest, but she went. She didn't cry, and something within Katherine that'd been holding on by a thread snapped and shattered.

40

TESS

THE MORNING OF THE VISITATION, TESS SAT BESIDE SAADIA ON THE bench in the small patch of lawn outside the Natural Ways Wellness Centre, their boots in the snow, their gloved hands gripping thermoses.

"Don't be nervous," Saadia said, her hand tapping Tess's knee. "You'll do fine. Your daughter will love you."

Tess smiled back, her lip quivering. "But what if she doesn't?"

Saadia squeezed. "She will."

Tess sighed, glad Saadia had texted to check in, as she had at least once every couple of weeks since this had all started. When Tess told her a few days ago about the upcoming visitation, how anxious she was, how she didn't know what she'd do with herself between the moment she woke and the moment she'd see her daughter, Saadia had told her to come by first, have a cup of tea to calm her nerves. But Tess's nerves were anything but calm. "So much is riding on this," she said. "The access worker will write up reports after every visit. The judge will use them to help determine custody."

"Don't think about any of that," said Saadia. "Think about your daughter, spending time with your daughter."

Tess looked at the covered thermos in her hand. She still hadn't told Saadia the whole story, weighing the fact that the fewer who knew, the better, and the fear that if she told her, Saadia's support would waver. She didn't think Katherine and Saadia were friends, exactly, but they knew each other, were friendly.

"I haven't spent much time around young children."

"Neither have most new mothers, until they have to." Saadia tilted her head back, the bright winter sun washing over her face. "You're doing everything you can. You reconnected with your family."

Tess nodded.

"You found a new apartment, hours that work, childcare. You're doing all you should be." Saadia sipped her tea. "Any more news about testifying? For Irene's case?"

Tess shook her head.

"Will you?"

"Yeah, I guess so." Now Tess took a sip, the smooth hot liquid warming her from within. "I mean, how could I not, right? Yet at the same time…" Her voice trailed off.

"You're thankful your child exists."

Tess shook her head, taking her turn to lift her face to the sun. "More than thankful. She made me a mom. It was wrong. It never should have happened, and I know Irene should face the consequences, but I'm not angry. I don't want to help punish her."

"It's complicated."

"It is."

Saadia looked at Tess, her head angled to one side. "Have you ever thought about reaching out to her? Asking why she did it?"

Tess bit her lip. "I have." She'd thought long and hard, wanting to know and not know, fearful of confirming the switch had happened because of her, afraid of how that could affect the custody case. "I'm not sure it would help," continued Tess. "What benefit would it have, and maybe, I don't know, could it make things worse?"

Saadia nodded. "That makes sense." She stretched out her arm and pulled up her jacket sleeve to check her watch. "I'm sorry to cut this short, but my next appointment will be here soon." She stood.

"Wait." Tess gripped Saadia's arm. "There's something else. Something I want to tell you." She swallowed. She wanted Saadia to know. Wanted to know whether Saadia's friendship would continue or fade away. More importantly, she wanted Saadia to be a character witness for her in court, which meant she had to tell her soon. The truth first, and then later, if Saadia didn't reject her, she'd ask for her testimony.

"All right." Saadia sat.

"The other family, the parents, are Katherine and Patrick Matheson. Their daughter is my daughter. Rose."

Saadia's eyes crinkled as she smiled. She squeezed Tess's knee again. "I know."

"What?"

"Word got around at Rose's birthday party that it was you. People suspected Katherine. I was invited but couldn't make it, and well, as you know, people talk when on my table."

"You've known," said Tess, "all this time? Why didn't you say something?"

"It wasn't my business to know, and it was yours to tell." Another smile. "But I'm glad you've told me."

"How do you feel about it?" Tess hesitated. "You know Katherine, right?"

"I do. And she's lovely. But she didn't reach out to me. You did."

Tess shook her head. "How did people at the party know? Did Katherine tell them?"

"From your boss, I believe."

"My boss?"

"Apparently his sister-in-law was there and told people about you. I don't know after that. Maybe people put two and two together. I'm surprised I hadn't figured it out earlier. I knew you shared a retrieval date, and Rose is a miniature you."

Tess let out a laugh, blown away. "She is."

"I do have to leave now." Saadia stood. "Go be with Rose. Hold her, play with her, make her laugh."

"I will." Tess grinned, imagining it, then stood as Saadia put out her arms for an embrace.

Saadia pulled away and winked. "And send me a note to let me know how it goes."

Tess stood in the entry to the visitation area. Then she sat. Then she stood. She'd changed her outfit three times. She'd worn her hair up, then down, then up again. She'd filed her nails and buffed them to a natural, healthy-looking shine—as if Rose would care about any of that. But she'd had to do something to fill the time her visit with Saadia hadn't. Tess looked at her watch. She stood again, paced, fear that something had gone wrong racing through her: that Katherine hadn't brought Rose, denying the court directives; that she'd planned to, but had been in an accident on the way; that the door would open and Rose would turn away from Tess, scream, cry. She wouldn't be able to handle the heartbreak.

A squeak of the door and Tess stood, brimming with elation at the sight of Rose in a checked sweater with navy-blue tights that hugged her delightfully chubby thighs. Rose stepped into the room, her hand in Luela's, the supervised access worker assigned to their case. Rose scanned the room, and then those eyes saw Tess. Rose's face lit up with recognition as she dropped Luela's hand and toddled over. "Fos!" Rose raised the animal in the air and smiled. Trying not to tremble, fighting the moisture behind her eyes that burned and threatened, Tess put out her hand. Rose looked at Luela, then back at Tess. She plopped her perfect tiny hand in Tess's, sending a burst of love through her.

Luela stepped beside them, a smile on her face, gesturing to the visitation area. "Should we head on in?"

Tess nodded, nerves tingling. The room was much as she imagined, like a day care classroom on one end and a lounge area on the other, with couches, armchairs, a large TV screen with various gaming consoles set up in front of it. A man and a teenaged boy sat, thumbs vigorously flicking controllers. Tess gestured to the side of the room that held blocks, an easel, and rows of shelved bins filled with toys and craft supplies. "What would you like to do, Rose? Do you like blocks?"

"Bocks!" Rose chimed, dropping Tess's hand and toddling over—so steady now, so self-assured, unlike the unbalanced teeter at her birthday party. Tess sank to the floor cross-legged beside Rose, who had pulled a bin of large foam blocks beside her and was stacking them into a haphazard tower. They fell, and rather than wince or cry as Tess feared, Rose clapped, stood, shouted, "'Gain!" and squatted to start the process over.

Tess watched, uncertain whether to join in or just observe, while pride, thankfulness, and amazement coursed through her. She glanced at Luela, who sat at a small table a few feet away. Luela nodded, making a gesture Tess took to mean, *Go on, go ahead, get in there.*

Done with tower building, Rose lined the blocks in a row. "What a lovely line!" said Tess, surprised to hear the high singsong tone she'd observed in other mothers emerging from her throat. Rose nodded, focused on her task. As the blocks came near to running out, Tess thought back to the developmental milestones she'd researched, wanting to make sure she didn't have unrealistic expectations or attempt play so simple Rose would be bored. "Rose," she said, "can you find a red block?" Rose looked at her, brow furrowed. Tess glanced at Luela, who nodded, still smiling. "Here it is!" Tess picked up the block. "Hmm." She set it down again. "How about the blue?"

Rose plopped her hand on a blue block and grinned.

"Good job!" Tess clapped.

Rose stood, walked to the easel. "Paint? Do you want to paint?" asked Tess. Rose looked at her, an expression on her face that seemed to say, *You tell me.* Again, Tess looked to Luela.

"We have smocks that should fit her, and here are the paints. At this age, I'd say just let her go at it with her fingers."

"It won't be too"—Tess hesitated, thinking of Katherine's impeccably clean house—"messy?"

"I have cloths for you to clean her up. It's up to you."

"Well…" Tess looked at Rose, looked at the paints, reminded herself she was Rose's mother, too, and if…*when* she had custody, she'd have to make much bigger decisions than this. "Let's do it."

A few minutes later and Rose was squealing as she dipped her hands in the paint, smeared her fingers onto the easel, dipped again. She covered three sheets before pulling at her smock and stepping away. Tess washed Rose's hands, then rubbed a cloth gently where the paint had landed on her cheek, her ear, her wrist. She paused in her work, taking a moment to savor the sweet scent of Rose, the fact that she was here, it was real. Again, Tess fought the moisture building behind her eyes, not wanting to startle Rose and not wanting to cry in front of Luela. "There," she said, as she removed the smock, folded it up. "What next?"

They played with cars, with animal figurines, and then Rose toddled to the books, grabbed one, brought it back to Tess, and climbed in her lap. Rose settled in as Tess read, her child in her arms, and her heart filled with a love so intense, so right, it was as if every emotion she'd had before this one paled in comparison.

When Luela came over and told her their time was up, Tess reflexively pulled Rose tighter. "Don't worry," said Luela, "you'll see her again soon. Just a few days."

Tess lifted Rose off her, smiled as she held her hand out once more. There'd be no months of waiting this time; she'd see her daughter in just a few days.

41

KATHERINE

WHEN THERE WERE TEN MINUTES LEFT TO THE VISITATION, Katherine exited her vehicle, where she had sat for the last hour and twenty minutes, staring blankly. Everything was moving so fast, and she couldn't do anything to stop it. Already, Kerra had mentioned the off-site visitation, which wouldn't be for at least a month. Tess had put in a request for the intermediary to be her brother. "You said you know him, he's a friend?" posed Kerra. Katherine and Patrick had nodded. Mikolai made sense. He was a good guy, a wonderful father, yet Katherine wasn't happy about it, wanted to refuse. But really, she couldn't refuse any of this.

She sat in the waiting room, her knees pressed together. She wanted Rose to be fine, but also wanted her to be distraught, wanted to hear Rose's cries sounding down the hall as she wailed for Katherine, only Katherine. When the door finally opened, Rose toddled through it, a broad grin on her face, still holding Fox. "Mama!" she proclaimed, happy to see Katherine, but not desperate, not as if she'd spent the last hour and a half in misery.

Katherine hugged her girl hard. "How'd it go?" she asked, trying to keep the squeak out of her voice.

"Good." Luela handed over Rose's bag. "I do reports once a week, so you can pick up this week's report at the start of next." She smiled, as if what had just transpired was nothing, as if it happened every day, which, Katherine supposed, for Luela, it did.

In the car she tried to ask questions, gauge how the time had really gone. All she got, of course, were one-word answers.

"What did you do?"

"Bocks!"

"Anything else?"

"Bocks!"

"Did you have fun?" Silence. "Was Tess nice?"

"Ess!"

"Did you like Tess?"

"Ess!"

Katherine stopped asking questions and focused on the road ahead, her mouth dry, her heart wrenched. A few more months, then they'd attend the custody trial, and, she had to believe, a judge would put an end to this madness, decide it was best for Rose, best for them all, if her girl's life weren't fractured in two.

Eyes burning, Katherine pulled into the driveway, put her keys in the bowl by the door, picked up Patrick's from the bench, and plopped them in, too, then lined up all their shoes in the rack.

She walked through to the kitchen, noting the crumb-filled plate on the counter, the peanut butter on Patrick's knife oozing onto the marble, the dishes she'd left unwashed, the way she'd failed to leave her house perfect as usual. She stepped to the sink, then stopped, made her way to the breakfast nook instead. She sank to the seat, leaving the mess for later, as she heard Rose squeal, "Dada!" from the living room, the sounds of her straining to clamber up beside him, and him shushing her.

Katherine pressed the space between her eyes. Did he not even remember where they'd been, even care? Was his world not falling apart at the thought of Rose in Tess's presence? Tess's arms? Katherine strode into the living room, stopped as he raised a hand in the air and pointed to the screen.

CRIMINAL TRIAL DROPPED, the news ticker read. NURSE IN IVF SCANDAL GETS OFF WITH SLAP ON THE WRIST.

Katherine inhaled, but the air seemed stifled. A chill ran over her as she lowered to the seat beside Patrick. "Has Kerra—"

"I tried calling. Shh…"

A law professor from Dalhousie University was being interviewed. "With no precedent for a criminal conviction, it shouldn't come as a surprise. These types of actions, they aren't deemed applicable to a criminal case. The nurse's actions don't fit the definition of any offenses within the Criminal Code. Even the Quebec fertility doctor who inseminated over a dozen patients with his own sperm faced no criminal conviction."

"But what about justice?" the reporter asked.

"Ms. Connor has had her license revoked," said the professor, "and the provincial medical board fined her fifteen thousand dollars."

"Fifteen thousand!" Katherine exclaimed. "That's less than our legal fees!"

"Shh!"

"And no jail time?" Katherine pushed into the couch, her throat closing, her eyes burning—that this woman, this woman who'd taken their lives in her hands…

Rose crawled over Patrick to Katherine. "Mama." Katherine pulled Rose into her lap, her gaze on the screen.

"Will that money go to the families?" asked the reporter.

The professor shook his head, looking regretful. "That's not how these things work."

Patrick's phone vibrated on the coffee table. "It's Kerra."

"Put it on speaker."

"Hell—"

"What about our testimony?" Katherine leaned forward as Rose squirmed. Katherine yanked off her bracelet and handed it to Rose, something to keep her occupied. "I thought we were supposed to—"

"I know." Kerra's voice came out tense. "A bunch of cowardly bureaucrats. I feared this would happen." She sighed. "I get the 'no precedent' thing, but precedent has to be made sometime, and with this case, the blatant intent—Connor admitted to switching the eggs—the testimony of all of you." Kerra paused. "It's just…the system's behind. When the laws were scripted, these types of actions weren't possible, so they're not technically crimes. Parliament needs to legislate new crimes, because the courts can't."

"But it is a crime!" said Katherine.

"Morally, but that's not enough."

"Is there anything we can do?" asked Patrick. "Appeal?"

"No, it's not—" Kerra let out a grunt of frustration. "It's not like that. You can sue. That's your option now."

"But that can't get her jail time," said Katherine, "or the quarter-of-a-million-dollar fine."

"You can get more money than that if you go for the clinic—especially if you focus on them, not Irene. Leaving her out of it, placing the blame on the clinic, you could get millions."

"But Irene walks," said Patrick.

Another sigh from Kerra. "Irene walks."

Katherine fought the urge to pull at her hair, punch the table. "This is ludicrous. Irene gets off as if she did nothing. You don't even want us to sue her?"

"Not nothing," said Kerra. "She'll have to start over: new job, new life. The fine."

"A pittance." Katherine slumped. She smoothed a hand over Rose's hair, knowing she couldn't let herself cry.

"This is just—" Patrick shook his head, his lip curling. "This is unacceptable. We have the wrong child! That woman needs to pay."

Katherine turned on Patrick. "The wrong—" She placed her hands on Rose's ears, her chest tightening. "We have *our* child."

"Look, you two have a lot to digest, I'm sure, things to discuss. I've said it before, and I'll say it again, if you want the most money with the least time and effort, you should file a suit before the custody trial."

"You're right." Katherine lifted Rose. "We have a lot to discuss."

"I can get you the names of excellent civil litigators; just let me know when—"

"Will do. Thank you, Kerra." Katherine reached to end the call. She carried Rose to the playroom, Patrick at her heels. She closed the door behind her and faced Patrick in the hall. "Don't you ever say that in front of her again," she said in a harsh whisper.

Patrick raised his arms. "Say what?"

"'The wrong—'"

"She is, though, Katherine. She is the wrong child. Because of Irene. Our baby—yours and mine—never even existed." Patrick's eyes watered. "Never even had a chance."

"What are you saying?" Katherine pushed his chest. "She's ours. Rose is ours!"

"I know." Patrick gripped her shoulders. "But—"

"It's not even Irene you blame, is it?" Katherine stepped out of his grasp. "It's me. Me, for pushing you into this."

"No."

"You never wanted to do IVF. You said we should stop trying so hard, adopt if need be."

"Kat."

"An adopted child wouldn't have been ours, either. Not in the way you think matters."

"Kat!" He grabbed her arms as Katherine struggled, pummeling his chest as she tried to push away.

"You wish none of this had happened," she cried. "Wish we'd never had Rose—"

"No, that's not—"

"Probably wish you didn't have me, either, that you'd chosen some other woman who'd given you a house full of children. That's probably why you—"

"No!" Patrick shook Katherine, then pulled her into an embrace. "I love Rose. I want Rose. I love you. Only you."

"If I'd been a different woman, popped out babies like—"

"No."

But it was her fault. She had the broken body. They were going through this nightmare, about to lose their child, which should have never been theirs, because of her.

"We don't have to sue," said Patrick. "We don't have to do anything you don't want to do."

But they would. They couldn't not. And she, whether she liked it or not, would have to accept it.

42

TESS

TESS WIPED AN ARM ACROSS HER FOREHEAD, SMEARING SWEAT AND probably some dirt, too. The air was thick with the promise of spring's first blooms, and though it was barely warm enough for shorts and a T-shirt, she'd worked up a sweat. A sweat that made her feel as if all the toxins of her past life were spilling out of her, making room for something new, something solid and lasting and good.

She leaned back to rest on her heels and surveyed her work. In the two and a half months since she'd moved into her new apartment, since she'd had that first visitation with Rose, she'd cleared moss and grass and rocks, and now, what had been a plain yard with one tree in the corner was shaping up to be a veritable garden.

Along the back fence, Tess had prepped the ground to plant peas and beans, tomatoes and cucumbers. She was practically dizzy with excitement at the thought of Rose running over—she could run now—picking those peas and beans and popping them in her mouth. Tess could almost hear the laughter as she crunched down. In the corner would sit a large strawberry patch with blueberry bushes on either end. And on the far side, a flower garden, built just the way her mother would have, with thought for the heights of the various flowers and bushes and the time of year they'd bloom, so bursts of color would always draw the eye.

Tess had asked her mother to come see, inviting her parents for lunch. Jasia declined, but there was still time. The trial was just around the corner, and things would be better, Tess had to believe, before her parents would sit on the stand and testify.

Every two weeks, Tess had gone to family dinner, and the judgment, the hard eyes, the offhand comments lessened with each visit. Mikolai, Karina, and the kids there to smooth the tension, Tess had seen her mother's face light up in laughter. Just a few weeks ago, as Tess was folding cabbage rolls, her mother walked past, patted Tess's shoulder, winked, and said, "You still have the touch."

Tess returned to the dirt, tilling the soil to mix in the amendments she'd specifically chosen for each new bed. After one dinner, she'd showed her parents photos on her phone from the supervised visits with Rose. They marveled at how much she looked like Tess as a girl, delighted at Rose having those same piercing eyes. Her mother tilted her head to the family photo wall, and two weeks later, Tess returned with a framed photo of Rose. Two weeks after that, when she'd walked by the wall, the photo hung right beside the most recent shots of Jannie and Tom.

"Tess!" Mikolai's voice, full of energy, burst through her thoughts.

"Hi!" Tess stood and wiped her dirt-smudged hands on her shorts. "What time is it?"

"Don't worry. I'm early. Thought I'd look at that shelving system before we go, just in case I need any tools I don't have." He held up the toolbox in his left hand. "We could pick them up on the way back."

Tess nodded. She reached for her phone and tapped it. Her alarm was set to go off in ten minutes. "I'll show you where it is, then head to the shower."

"Sounds good."

Tess led Mikolai inside, then retreated to the bathroom. She stood under the cool stream of water and closed her eyes. In a little over an hour, Rose would be here exploring the halls, seeing framed photos of herself, her cousins, and her grandparents on the walls; squealing with delight while Tess presented each new toy she had found at various secondhand stores; seeing her room, with a crib and mattress protector and Paw Patrol sheets, the paintings she'd done at that first visitation framed and hanging proudly.

It had taken longer than Tess had hoped to secure off-site visitation, but at least it was happening. For this first visit, Tess had considered taking Rose to a park or the waterfront—they had three hours instead of an hour and a half—but she decided on home. It felt right to bring Rose home.

43

KATHERINE

ALL THIS TIME WAITING, AND NOW KATHERINE FOUND IT HARD TO believe the trial was in less than a week, that for the past few months, she'd been dropping her girl off, letting her go with this other woman, each time as difficult as the time before. Even harder to believe that despite that, Katherine was on her way to meet Tess, speak with her, no mediators, lawyers, or judge present.

Katherine waved goodbye to Rose, mouthed a thank-you to Tracey, settled behind the wheel of her SUV, then checked her hair and makeup once more. After navigating through the midday traffic, she pulled up to her favorite café, Juniper's Java, fifteen minutes early. She'd chosen the spot so it'd be familiar territory, so she'd have the upper hand. She'd arrived early for the same reason, but there was Tess, seated by the window, sipping from a mug, a scone in front of her on the low table. She didn't look nervous. She looked contented, lost in thought, like a woman who was happy—or happy enough—a woman who had her life together.

Katherine exited her car and stood by the door, watching. Tess no longer looked like a woman needing saving, but Katherine sure felt like one. She inhaled, letting her shoulders rise and fall, then thrust them back, walking toward the café with long strides.

She hadn't seen Tess in months, since the conference proceedings, Katherine realized, as Rose, at each visitation exchange, was passed through the hands of first Luela and now Mikolai. It wouldn't last like this forever, Kerra had warned. Hoping for sole custody was one thing, hoping for sole custody without visitation, unless Tess showed herself to be grossly unfit, was little more than a pipe dream. After the judge's decision, visitation or custody switch-offs would be between the two families. No intermediary.

After listening to Tess's voicemail, asking if they could meet up, saying she had something she wanted to talk about, just the two of them, Katherine had texted back, asking what it was about. But Tess wouldn't answer, saying she'd rather talk in person, that it was important, and could Katherine please come?

Katherine had called Kerra. "What am I supposed to do?" she'd asked, exasperation flowing through her, nervous about why Tess would want to see her alone, what she would want.

"See her," Kerra had said, calm as could be. "What's the harm?"

"Won't it seem odd if the judge finds out?" Katherine had asked, but Kerra assured her no.

"It would seem like you were trying to work it out but couldn't," she said. "Open the lines of communication. You don't have to be her friend, but show yourself to be reasonable."

Katherine had wanted to yell every time Kerra used that word. Nothing about any of this was reasonable.

"At the least," Kerra continued, "you could discuss your thoughts about suing the clinic."

"Isn't it too late for all that?" Katherine asked. "To worry about it now, days before the trial?"

"Not at all," Kerra countered. "We could write up a quick proposal to the clinic, get the ball rolling, which would have its benefits."

And so Katherine was here, despite how much it irked her. She didn't want to launch a lawsuit yet, though she knew they would eventually. She didn't even want to think about it. The custody case first. That's all she wanted to focus on, but it was impossible. Irene's charges being dropped had been plastered across the news and blew up social media. All this time later, it was still a hot topic, the public as outraged as Katherine was. There'd been another switch recently (an unintentional one), somewhere in the U.S., that had renewed the fervor. With each day that passed, each expert weighing in, each additional comment or call for reassessment of the medical board's decision, the justice system's, Katherine's fear that someone would leak their identities increased. The only positive of it all was that, since Irene's case hadn't gone to trial, Katherine and Patrick hadn't had to see Tess, work out the details of a publication ban, decide, with a timeline looming, if they'd sue Irene as well as the clinic, and when.

They hadn't needed to be cordial. But now, with Tess instigating today's meeting, getting here first, and by all accounts, getting her life together rather than letting it fall apart, cordiality was a necessity.

"Good afternoon!" Katherine's voice came out light and bright, just as she intended. Tess raised her head, her brows furrowed, creating one delicate line in the space between them—the same line that formed on Rose's face when she looked at Katherine quizzically.

"Afternoon."

A sharp twang reverberated through Katherine's chest. "So." She sat across from Tess, crossed her legs, and leaned back. "What's this about?"

Tess tilted her head toward the counter. "Don't you want tea? Or coffee?"

"Not particularly." She did. A latte would be perfect.

"Water, at least." Tess stood and crossed the room to the self-serve water station. She came back with a glass for each of them and set them on the table, smiling.

Tess lowered her gaze, so childlike, uncertain. "There's a lot we should probably talk about." She raised her eyes, the smile more hesitant this time. "But the real reason, the biggest reason." The smile grew. "That photo of Rose as a baby, it meant so much to me. I look at it every day. I enlarged and framed a copy."

Katherine waited. Tess must want more photos. Katherine didn't want to share them, the moments with Rose that had been hers alone, but it was a request she could fulfill. It was being reasonable.

"And so"—Tess leaned down, pulled a folder from her bag—"I thought maybe you'd like the same."

Katherine's throat tightened. Her chest stilled. She saw the name on the folder...no, not folder, *album*. Tess held the book out, one hand on each side. "If you don't want it, that's fine, or if you want to look at it later, I understand. I just...this is a copy. You can have it. If you want."

Katherine nodded. As the album touched her hand, the breath she'd been holding escaped in a whoosh. Tingles ran through her body. She'd tried not to think about the baby. She'd told herself Hanna wasn't hers, because if she was, what did that say about Rose? But as she ran her fingers over the stenciled name, flipped the cover, and took in the first page, first picture, her heart wrenched. Hanna was hers. She was hers just as much as Rose was hers. "My God."

"She's tiny. I know. A little odd-looking. It's because—"

Katherine shook her head, her eyes filling with moisture. "She's perfect." She trailed her fingers over Hanna's face, her arms, wishing she could see her eyes, feel the rise and fall of her chest. Things not even Tess had felt.

She looked at Tess, their eyes locking.

44

TESS

TESS HAD AGONIZED FOR DAYS ABOUT WHETHER TO CALL. AND she'd debated: Did she offer the album over the phone? Send it with Rose after the next visitation? Or sit face to face, mother to mother? Someone, at last, with whom she could share her grief.

She'd hoped the album would be an olive branch. Tess's request for sole custody had included regularly scheduled visits with no intermediary, which meant that if she won, she'd see Katherine on a regular basis. A gesture could ease the hostility, show that despite the tensions between them, Tess was willing to be friendly, considerate.

The Mathesons hadn't included visitation in their request for custody. So if they won, Tess wanted the album to remind Katherine that they shared the loss of Hanna. Soften her, so she'd reconsider allowing access. She'd thought about preparing it weeks ago, but she procrastinated out of fear and anger. Then she realized if she didn't do it soon, Katherine might not agree to meet her after the trial.

Perhaps equally important, Tess realized, it was a way to speak face to face, find out what Katherine and her PI knew and what she would use in court.

"She's perfect." Katherine looked up from the album, their eyes locking.

Tess shifted her chair toward Katherine. "She was so light, barely a pound. She didn't feel real. Yet everything was there. Every finger. Every toe and toenail."

Katherine turned the page. "This was her handprint? And these her feet?"

"Mm-hmm." Tess had sobbed as she copied the pages. Part of her told her to give Katherine the originals. Hanna was Katherine's flesh and blood, but Tess wasn't a saint. That ink had touched Hanna's skin. She couldn't part with the tiny lock of jet-black hair she'd snipped—not even a lock, a few fine strands—but she'd taped a pocket that held one of the two booties Hanna had worn into Katherine's book.

Katherine pulled it out. She looked to Tess. "This was hers? She wore this?"

Tess nodded. "I kept the other one."

"Of course." Katherine stared at the bootie. She brought it to her nose, inhaled. "Oh my goodness. You must think I'm crazy."

"No." Tess shook her head. "No, not at all."

"I didn't know they did this." Katherine had her gaze back on the book; she turned the page. The last. Four pages to document an entire life. Only the last page showed Tess's face. In profile, she gazed at her baby, wondering how just hours before Hanna could have been alive and kicking, yet now lay in her arms motionless.

Katherine stared at that page the longest—at Hanna in Tess's arms. Katherine brought her hand to her cheek, wiping under first one eye and then the other. She reached forward, leaving her seat, and wrapped her arms around Tess. Tess stiffened, but Katherine held on. Slowly, Tess moved her arms around Katherine, felt the pressure as they sat, as their bodies pressed against one another in grief.

The air around them seemed to chill as Katherine pulled away. "Thank you so much for this keepsake, Tess. It was incredibly kind of you. So generous. I'll cherish it."

"You're welcome." Tess bit her lip. She shifted her chair back to its spot. "I hoped you'd appreciate it."

"I do!" Katherine closed the book and laid her hand on the cover before tucking it in her bag. "If you'd like more photos of Rose, I'd be happy to prepare an album for you. I should have thought of it before."

"That'd be…nice." Tess's smile wavered, the confidence she'd been cultivating wavering with it. It was time for the real reason she'd suggested they meet. Her mouth suddenly dry, Tess took a sip of water. "This isn't the only reason I wanted to talk."

Tess knew it was risky to bring it up, but she needed to know if Katherine knew and whether she'd talk, before Tess went into that courtroom, before she sat on a stand, so she could prepare for the fallout, if necessary, get Messineo to help her frame a narrative around it, tell her family…though how she'd do that, she didn't know. Still, better they hear it from her.

Katherine leaned back, her smile firm.

"My lawyer, he said, uh, well—"

"The lawsuit?" Katherine sighed. "I'll do whatever you want. I'd rather wait for the custody case to finish. I'd rather settle…but I believe, for this at least, it'll be best if we have a united front."

"Oh, yes, well." Tess glanced away, flustered. Of course that's why Katherine thought they were meeting. They needed to talk about it. But Tess, too, thought it should wait. She bit her lip. It'd be an easy out from the thing she'd come to ask, but if she took it, she'd never work up the nerve again. "I agree. But, uh, no, that's not it. He said you hadn't submitted any evidence. Any incriminating evidence. Against me."

Katherine tilted her head, her expression neutral.

"I know you still have a day or two, but, uh, I was just wondering about that."

"Were we supposed to?"

"Well, no, uh…it's just…" Tess looked at her hands, the nails rough and ragged once again. She swallowed, using all her effort to keep her voice steady. "I just wanted to know if you were planning to. I heard…I mean, I know you had a PI on me."

"Ah." Katherine gave a slight nod. Was that a twitch in her jaw? "Yes. Well."

A sheen of sweat broke out along Tess's forehead.

Katherine sighed, the veneer of cold control seeming to slip. "We all have things in our past," she said, "things we'd rather forget. Or things we regret. Ugly things." Katherine looked away. "I'm not perfect. Patrick's certainly not perfect." Her voice caught. "You're not perfect. We all have dirty laundry, but it doesn't mean we're not fit to be parents. The judge can decide. It's not good for any of us to be dragging each other's names through the dirt."

Tess leaned forward. "I wouldn't have dragged Patrick's name through the dirt." She almost laughed, relief making her giddy. Katherine already knew! She knew and wasn't planning to use it. "Obviously, I'd look bad, too, but he'd look worse, which isn't fair, but true. He's the one who's married. And my lawyer said—"

"What are you talking about?" Katherine straightened.

"The affair," said Tess. "Not that you could even call it an affair. It was just one night—"

Katherine pushed her chair back, toppling a neighboring one. She gripped the table, emphasizing each word. "How do you know about Patrick's affair?"

Tess's pulse raced as realization coursed through her.

Katherine stood. "No." She held an arm out. "No."

Tess stood. The blood drained from her face. "You said...I thought—"

Katherine backed away, her arm still out, as if warding Tess away, as if Tess were attacking her. Katherine grabbed her bag, stumbled over the fallen chair. Tess stepped forward. "I'm sorry. I..." Katherine had to have known. What else could she have been talking about? *Ugly things. Dirty laundry.* And then it hit Tess: the drunken hookups, the abortion, her friendship with Irene, which could have led to all of this, the rape, even? Tess had worried about these things, too, stressed over them, but they had been overpowered by this one fear the moment Messineo had explained to her how the evidence worked: if the Mathesons were submitting any evidence from the PI, it would have been courteous to submit it already. But if it were information either Katherine or Patrick knew firsthand, they didn't *have* to submit it at all. They could simply bring it up during testimony.

Her night with Patrick was the only thing they could have known firsthand.

Shame flooded Tess that she could have been so stupid. So careless. Again. "I..." What should she say? What could she? "I thought you knew."

Katherine yelled, her voice guttural as she turned for the exit. "No!"

45

KATHERINE

KATHERINE'S VISION BLURRED. THE ROOM SPUN, ROCKED, AND waved as she held her hand out, backed away from Tess, turned, and fled. At her car she struggled with the lock, dropped the keys, swore, then picked them up and tried again. Behind the wheel she paused, breathed in, out, in, then turned the ignition. She slammed the steering wheel, gripped it as she merged into traffic. All this time. All this time of telling herself she was okay with Patrick's "indiscretion," telling herself she held blame, too, that all couples had bumps.

They hadn't been intimate, but just last week, he'd rolled over in bed, and whereas usually she would have shifted away, she'd grasped his hand, guided it over her, and snuggled against him. It hadn't gone further, but she'd been pleased to feel the reaction it incited, hard against her bottom.

A few days before that, when they were watching a movie, he'd held out his hand and she'd taken it, leaned into him, thinking maybe they could make it work. That they were worth making it work.

The bastard. The lying, cheating bastard. She slammed the steering wheel again. Opening her eyes to the world in front of her, she realized she was en route to his office and changed course. There was still Rose. Still the trial.

"Hey, Google," she spoke into the car, "send text message to Patrick Matheson."

She listened to Google's response, then delivered her message. "Come home now. Emergency."

Katherine sat in the living room armchair for five minutes, ten, fifteen. She sipped her tea. By the time she'd arrived home, her eyes were dry. She'd stood at the bathroom mirror, adjusting her curls, wiping the salt lines from her face. Her phone had lit three times.

The faint sound of the car pulling into the driveway filtered through the house. The door opened. Patrick's footsteps, shoes still on, slapped against the floor. "Rose. Where's Rose? Is she okay? Are you okay?" He looked frenzied, his hair fluffier than usual, pit stains darkening his sky-blue dress shirt.

"What's going on?"

Katherine took another sip of tea, her gaze steady on him, then spoke. "It was Tess. You slept with Tess."

"Shit." He crossed the room and sat. "She told you?"

"That's your response?" Katherine laughed. "*She told you?*"

"That's not my response. I'm sorry. I'm so sorry."

"But not sorry enough." Heat built behind Katherine's eyes; the threat of a quiver pulled at her lips. She pushed it away. "Not sorry enough to tell me yourself. Not sorry enough to save me the embarrassment of sitting across from her all those times, looking the fool. Of hearing her speak the words you should have spoken."

"I tried."

Another laugh.

"I did. The day I told you…you didn't want to talk about it. You walked away. You never brought it up again."

"But you could have." Katherine closed her eyes. She wouldn't let him see her cry. She wouldn't let him hear her yell. "You could have told me. Anytime."

"I didn't see the point." He rubbed a hand against the side of his face. "To make it worse for you, so any time you saw her… If things don't go the way we plan, you'll see her a lot. At birthdays and graduation and Christmas. I thought it would hurt you more."

Katherine shook her head. "Well, you're right about that." Oh God. The thought hit her like a slap. "That's why you didn't want the PI. Why you didn't want us digging into Tess's past. In case it dug into yours, too." That's why he thought she knew.

Patrick ran his hands through his hair, looking sheepish, looking like the dog he was. "Maybe that was part of it." He paused. "I didn't want to hurt you. But I also didn't see the point."

"Ha!"

"Listen, I'm not perfect, okay? There's no manual for this."

"Don't fuck your daughter's other mother. Seems pretty simple."

"I didn't know."

"Oh, right. Yes, of course. How silly of me. If you'd known she was Rose's mother, you would have chosen someone else." Katherine sipped her tea again. Her arms tensed. "Well, how about only fuck your wife? Would make a short rule book, don't you think? Save any of these tricky complications popping up."

"Stop it."

"So now you're telling me how to respond? How I'm allowed to process this?"

"No."

She was being a bitch. She knew she was being a bitch. But she had the right, damn it.

"I'll say it again. I'm not perfect." Patrick leaned forward. "I can't be perfect. No one can live up to your standards."

Katherine opened her mouth to speak.

"I'm not blaming you. I'm not. Don't think that. It's just, all of it, it was hard. Incredibly. It'd been over eight months. I'm only human. And even before, all those years when sex…well, it was like I was a tool for you, like all you cared about was my sperm and getting it in at the right time." He paused. "It's just—"

Guilt pulled at Katherine. A tool. She'd made him feel like a piece of equipment. A sperm donor. It's how she'd thought of him, too—so many times.

"All you cared about was a baby. Then the IVF worked, you were pregnant, and I thought, okay, she's pregnant. It happened. We can go back to the way we were. We can have some fun."

She'd thought that, too. She'd read for some women, sex could be better when pregnant, orgasms stronger. She'd looked forward to it, thinking that with the first positive blood test, she'd be able to relax. Yet fear had crept in, festered.

"But you didn't want me to touch you, feared it would hurt the baby even though the doctor said it wouldn't. So…it felt like it was me you didn't want."

Katherine inhaled, then blew the air out in a cool stream. "You should have told me."

"Told you what?"

"That you felt that way."

Patrick's shoulders slumped. "Would it have changed things? You'd have given in, gritted your teeth, and bore it, like you had so many times before, but it still would have been obligatory, just in another way. I didn't want that."

"So you went to Tess."

"I didn't go to her!" Exasperation poured from him. "It wasn't like that."

Katherine locked her gaze with his. "What was it like?"

Patrick described the encounter with little detail. Katherine did not press. She wanted to, because her mind filled in the horrible blanks as he told her about the chance meeting at the high school reunion gala, when Mikolai pulled Tess over, then left in a hurry. How they were stuck standing there and, with nothing else to say, reminisced about high school days. Although Patrick had graduated two years before Tess's first year, they compared notes on the best and worst teachers, the principal with his shock of ear hair, what existence was like when they were teenagers and life was a vast ocean of possibility, when they thought the world would be kind.

Katherine focused on her breath as he spoke, those blanks sprawling across her vision. She remembered the night. Patrick in his deep-navy-blue suit, his silver tie and silver cuff links. She'd clipped his shirtsleeves as she apologized for not coming. She was tired. Her back hurt. She wouldn't know anyone, anyway; he'd have more fun without her.

He had.

"It was innocent," said Patrick. They kept talking as the drinks kept flowing, servers offering new glasses whenever theirs ran dry—as if that were an excuse. Sharing recent hurts, recent pain. It wasn't often he spoke about their fertility struggles, but with Tess, it'd been easy. Katherine's skin tightened as she imagined the intimacies of their life he may have told her, of their marriage.

They talked so long they were the last guests left, the catering staff clearing dishes and tables away. They were about to leave, went to retrieve their coats, but then—

Katherine cut him off, yelling, "Why didn't you tell me it was Tess?"

"You walked away!" Patrick flung his hands in front of him. "You didn't want to talk about it."

"I didn't think it was someone I knew!" She had wondered, but it was a thought she pushed away, didn't want to consider. But Tess? That had never occurred to her. "You could have told me. You—"

"I know." Patrick stopped, his head lowered, his voice shaking. "It's been torturing me. I didn't know what to do. Tell you? Complicate this already ridiculously complicated mess? Make it hurt even more every time you have to see her, speak to her?" He stopped. "If I could turn back time…"

But he couldn't. None of them could. Katherine stood, turned from him, seeing it all: the way she and Patrick had been in those first years, pulling at each other's clothes, making their way to the bed or couch in a tangled mess. How, slowly, it had changed.

Katherine squeezed her eyes shut, wanting to squeeze out the images—Patrick lifting Tess, holding her small body in his arms. Tess, arching her back against the wall as he thrust into her, again and again and again. Patrick calling Tess's name. It'd been years since he'd called Katherine's.

Katherine resisted the urge to put her hands to her ears, block out the sounds she could almost hear, the panting, the groans of delight. When it was some nameless woman—shapeless, formless—Katherine thought she could handle it. But now that it was Tess, with her perky breasts, her come-rescue-me eyes and mouth, Tess, who was her daughter's biological mother, bile burned in her throat.

A hand landed on her shoulder.

"No." Her voice was too loud. "No." She spun, faced him. "Don't touch me."

Tears streamed down Patrick's face. "I'd take it back if I could. It was nothing, Kat. It meant nothing."

Katherine's heart raced. *Nothing?*

"I love you."

Love? Day after day he'd looked at her, smiled at her, kissed her, this lie between them. And she hadn't seen it. Not when he mentioned he ran into Tess at the gala. Not all the times after.

Kat backed away from Patrick's pleading eyes, her entire life thrown into question. She'd believed in Patrick. Believed, above all else, he was faithful. Believed even if they fell out of love, he'd never lie. But he had, constantly. And now this, to say it meant nothing.

"No." Katherine shook her head, calm covering her like a blanket, clarity settling her racing pulse. She walked to the foyer, picked the car keys up from the bowl by the front door, her fist clenching, the metal digging into her flesh. "It meant everything."

46

TESS

AFTER KATHERINE LEFT JUNIPER'S JAVA, TESS STOOD IN PLACE, HER feet stuck to the floor as if she'd jumped in wet cement. She sensed stares boring into her back, her side, her face. The chatter in the small café ceased, then slowly picked up again. She took their dishes to the front of the café, certain that the other patrons' eyes were following her, trying to pretend they weren't.

Now, as she walked home, taking the time to think, she replayed the scene. How could she have blurted it out like that? Why hadn't she waited until Katherine had clarified what she was talking about instead of assuming she knew?

Because the unknown had plagued her. Because for almost two years now, every time she thought of that night, and every time she'd seen Katherine, the guilt sat there, sometimes barely acknowledged, below the surface of all their other tensions, but there, always, with the sinking fear of the moment her sins would be revealed—and the rising fear that the moment would come on the stand, on the most important day of Tess's life.

And what could Tess say? She was in the wrong. It didn't matter that

Patrick was, too; Tess had known he was married, to Katherine, who back then had never been anything but kind. That's why, with every late-night encounter since, Tess had checked for a ring. She refused to knowingly do again what she'd done to Katherine, what had been done to her.

Tess turned in the opposite direction from home, walked the streets until she climbed the hill to the Citadel, overlooking the city. She took the steps down the other side, and then the roads, down, down to the harbor, where she found a bench, stared at the inky-black depths.

Tess had relived the night over and over: when she'd seen Katherine at Saadia's party, before their mediation meetings, before coming to the café today, and so many times in between. She'd feared what it would be like to sit in the courtroom and hear one of her greatest shames revealed. But she feared almost as much the potential years of waiting for it to come out, the nervousness she'd feel before each interaction with Katherine, stretching on and on, until one day she was confronted. Deep down, had she wanted Katherine to know? So she could stop wondering, stop agonizing over the day when Katherine would look at Tess, justified hatred in her eyes?

Sitting there at the waterfront, Tess wanted to rise, find a pub or dingy bar, erase the past few hours, the look in Katherine's eyes, the feeling of guilt and dread that flowed like waves against the shore. She hadn't planned it with Patrick. Neither of them had. She'd gone to the gala with Mikolai, whom she'd barely seen since she recovered from surgery. After losing Hanna, she had hardly seen anyone, talked to anyone. Yet when Mikolai brought up the reunion, something sparked in Tess—the possibility of going back to a time before, to people who'd known her when her life still had potential. It could be healing, maybe, remind her of who she once was, back when she believed in herself, believed she would do good things with her life, be happy.

Or it'd be a distraction, at least, and get Mikolai off her back. He had been trying to get her to go out somewhere, anywhere, with him for months. So, only a little begrudgingly, she went.

Mikolai dragged her over to Patrick, reminding her he was her friend Katherine's husband. Not that she needed the reminder—she'd seen Patrick and Katherine around town and at various fertility events at least half a dozen times.

Minutes later, Mikolai's phone buzzed, his face paled. Tomas had a dangerously high fever. Karina was taking him to the hospital. Mikolai had to go.

They were left standing alone. Patrick told Tess that Katherine was at home, seven months pregnant and in no mood to go out, no mood to do anything except clean and read all the baby books she could get her hands on. He'd chuckled, but the sound lacked joy.

As they chatted, the liquor she was sipping coursed through her veins, the first she'd had in years. Tess grinned, licked her lips as he smiled at her, there in a dark-blue suit, his eyes electric, his shoulders broad. Before that night, she'd never noticed his dimpled cheeks or the clear blue of his eyes. Before that night, she'd forgotten what it felt like to have a man looking at her the way he was—not like she was a shadow of a person who could walk by unnoticed, but like a woman. An attractive woman.

And then, the alcohol probably making him more loose-lipped than he'd be otherwise, he asked if the transfer had worked, if she had a baby at home waiting. Her story, of course, was worse than his, but he went on to share the years of pain and frustration, the way he felt he hardly knew Katherine sometimes, hardly mattered to her beyond her mission to get pregnant. How the vibrant, loving woman he thought he'd married had seemed to fade away. In the unmanned coatroom, Tess tilted her chin, her eyes locking with his.

Before Patrick, she'd only been with two men. And one of them had raped her.

That night, standing in an empty coat check, she was in charge—master of her body, her choices, herself. She'd been the one to lean in, start the kiss she refused to stop. In that frenzied, panting, sweating moment, she didn't care that what they were doing was wrong, that Patrick was a married man with a baby on the way. She wanted what she wanted. And it was ecstasy. Oblivion.

She'd never come so hard.

When it ended, both of them sweaty and breathless, his pants around his ankles, her dress scrunched around her waist, he looked devastated, saying it was a mistake, saying he was sorry, saying he hadn't meant to. Yet she hadn't felt regret.

When she'd woken the next morning, however, the smell of sex lingering on her body, the regret had come and never left; he was a married man. Today, *regret* wasn't a strong enough word.

Now, ignoring her hunger, her thirst—most of all her thirst—Tess sat, staring into the harbor, wondering when alcohol had become this for her—her first thought when life felt too hard, the pain too deep. But she wouldn't give in. At last, when late afternoon's light shifted to evening's dim and she began to shiver, she stood, proud of herself for resisting the drink, and began the long walk home. As usual, Tess took a route that added an extra seven to ten minutes, to avoid walking down Patrick and Katherine's street. Even though she couldn't see their house as she passed, she looked in that direction, wondering if Rose's family, as she knew it, was tearing apart.

Tess climbed the steps to her unit. Inside, she gripped the sink's cool steel, held a glass under the tap, and downed three-quarters of it in one go, wishing it were another liquid, one to dim her senses, numb these throbbing, wretched thoughts. The night with Patrick came back to her. The ecstasy of it. She'd been chasing that feeling, that sweet oblivion, with each late-night encounter since, each falling short. A foul taste rose in her mouth, thinking of all the others—sweating, pawing, desperate men—thinking of who she'd become.

She wondered again if she should tell someone how much she ached for a drink, a man, the chance to forget. She wondered if she needed help. But she was controlling it. She was here, at home, surviving through the pain while clinging to this thought: that as bad as revealing the infidelity was, for Tess, it could be good. With the trial in less than a week, if Patrick and Katherine no longer presented a united front—Katherine moving out or forcing Patrick to—and if the judge saw their disdain for each other, he might give Rose to Tess. That was all the motivation she needed to stay sober, and if that were the outcome, she couldn't help but wonder, would she still feel regret?

47

KATHERINE

KATHERINE BREATHED IN, OUT, IN, TAKING DEEP BREATHS UNTIL SHE felt calm enough to drive, until her hands stopped shaking. She pulled out of the driveway, on her way to pick up Rose. Katherine closed her eyes, then sprung them open, reminding herself to focus. Putting aside how devastating it would be for Rose, dying in a car accident would make everything too easy—for Tess and for Patrick. There'd be no need for a custody case. The lovers could have passionate sex any time they wanted.

Katherine could almost see it, Tess walking into Katherine's life the way she'd walked into her house the day of Rose's party. Cooking in her kitchen, sleeping in her bed. Rose, living a life with her true parents, Katherine nothing more than a distant memory. Eventually, less than that.

Katherine pulled into a gas station and slid into a parking spot, wanting to erase Tess from their lives. She reached for her phone, scrolled through her texts, found the name she was searching for. Adee. *I want it back*, she typed. *All the dirt you had on Tess, and any more you can get.* She hesitated, her finger hovering over the send button. She screamed, banged a fist against the wheel—her jaw clenched and quivering, her eyes wet. She couldn't do it. Tess was still Rose's biological mother. She highlighted the text she'd written, her finger hovering, then deleted it as a sickening thought came over her.

Did you know? she typed. *That "one more thing" that you didn't tell me. Was it about Tess and Patrick? Did you know?*

She waited, watched the ellipses blink. Stop. Blink again.

I did.

Katherine's stomach clenched. She closed her eyes, forced breath into her lungs. *Why didn't you tell me?*

More dots, which came and went, came and went. *You told me not to. I do what a client asks. That's the job.*

Katherine let her breath out slowly. She put her phone away, then pulled onto the Armdale Rotary, focusing as she navigated the lanes of whirling traffic.

She clenched the wheel and hit the brake too hard at a red light, her body lurching forward. It wasn't her fault, the affair, but Katherine could see how it happened, why it happened, how a warm body listening, wanting, would be so appealing when all Patrick was getting from her was distance. She eased up on the gas, her calf muscles so tight her leg convulsed. She could see, too, why he hadn't told her, with all that had happened since that illicit night.

If she'd opened up, helped Patrick understand why it was so hard to let him touch her sexually during the pregnancy, how conscious she was of every movement made by their unborn child, told him of the terror that gripped when the life inside her lay still too long, maybe he wouldn't have looked for solace elsewhere. But he had.

Katherine pulled into Tracey's driveway, her eyes dry, her heart rate even, and her marriage—at least the way she'd always envisioned it—over.

Several hours later, Katherine stood at the sliding doors to the porch of her aunt's summer house. Rich hues of cerulean, magenta, tangerine, and crimson filled the night sky. Rose slept down the hall, lulled, Katherine hoped, by the beating surf. When Katherine called her mother, asking for the keys, the questions had come rapid-fire. Why now, with the trial so close? Why not wait until summer, until Russell and Elvira could join them? Why at all?

"I need a break," Katherine had told her. "Some time away."

"Then let me take Rose," Elvira pressed. "A romantic getaway for you and Patrick. Why not?"

"Time away with my girl," Katherine insisted. "Just me and my girl." Which raised another host of concerns.

"This won't be the end," her mother assured her. "Even if you don't get sole custody, you'll have lots of time with Rose. You'll be her mother, always." Then Elvira had asked, worry tightening her voice: "How long?"

Katherine couldn't answer. She simply knew she needed to go.

An amazing calm settled over her. She wasn't happy. Not even close. Sadness seemed a pool she treaded ceaselessly. But she also wasn't defeated.

Katherine walked to her handbag, the album untouched since she'd slipped it in at the café. She pulled it out now, flipped to the last page, Hanna in Tess's arms. Tess gazing at her child with such love, such pain. Katherine had realized, of course, what Tess had lost. But she hadn't *really* considered it. She hadn't sat and imagined what it would have been like for Tess to hold an unbreathing child in her arms, caress her face, know she'd never walk, talk, smile. Never progress past that one moment.

Any time her mind had started to go there, Katherine cut it off; she'd entertained that scenario enough times with Rose. Even in those early weeks of life, after she had Rose safe in her arms, she would check her chest, her cheek, hold a hand over her baby's face to make sure she was breathing.

Katherine swiped her fingers across her face. In the café, as she'd gazed at Hanna, Katherine had wanted to say she couldn't imagine the pain, and how thankful she was Tess had shared this small piece of her daughter. Their daughter. How sorry she was Tess had lived through this loss. How sorry she was for the pain she'd caused Tess, was still causing her. The trial. The by-the-book visitation. The refusal to accept that Tess had a right to be a part of Rose's life the same way that, if Hanna had lived, Katherine would have had a right, would have fought for it.

But she couldn't bring herself to say any of it, and now she probably never would.

Katherine lifted her gaze to the scene before her, the colors in the sky shifting and melding, sapphire with hints of salmon, rich shades of pumpkin, with amber and gold kissing the horizon, reflecting in the glistening obsidian sea.

As the kettle whistled on the stove, Katherine turned from the shifting hues. She poured the boiling liquid into a prepared mug and took it back to the porch, slid open the door, and curled up in the blanket she'd left on the armchair.

The chill salt air, mixed with the scent of cinnamon and ginger rising from her tea, soothed her. In all those years of trying to conceive, when Katherine realized they'd never have that house full of kids they wanted, when each grandchild that entered the Matheson clan emphasized Katherine's lack, she'd forgotten who she was. She'd turned into someone new. She couldn't remember what it was to not feel the pain of being a broken woman, to not have the desire to please and do everything she could to make up for her failures.

When the most important aspect of what she wanted from life was out of her control, she had controlled what she could, thinking her value came in how happy she could make people, Patrick in particular. When her dream had come true, she'd shifted that energy to being a perfect mother, resolved she wouldn't be like Patrick's sister, like his brothers' wives, like so many mothers she knew who walked around in sweatpants, braless, with their unwashed hair in a messy bun. Who let the housework pile up around them, as if you couldn't be a good mother without letting your house and yourself fall to ruin.

Even so, sometimes she'd envied those women—not just the babies on their hips, but the way they allowed themselves not to care. They'd joke about their apathy, post on Facebook about their seeming inability to fold and put away a load of laundry in less than three weeks, as if this were a problem they couldn't solve. It was not difficult. You just did it, and then it was done. You cultivated the life you wanted, and part of that cultivation— for Katherine—meant she didn't live with perpetual crumbs on her feet.

But her life, which she'd cultivated so carefully, worked so hard for, was a lie. And it hadn't made her as happy as she expected. Every thought, every action weighted by the constant awareness of how Patrick, his family, everyone around her would perceive it. Always the questions: Was she a good enough daughter, mother, wife, friend? Was she enough?

And she'd kept up the facade, lying these past months to everyone she knew about her and Patrick, about how they were getting each other through.

It was exhausting.

"Don't leave," Patrick had pleaded after she'd returned with Rose, only to pack their bags and then load them into the back of the SUV. He'd stepped toward Katherine, gestured to their daughter in the car seat. "Do what's best for Rose."

Katherine had closed the trunk, shrugged her shoulders. "It's best for me," she replied. "This isn't for Rose. It's for me."

For the first time in a long time, it was a choice that felt right.

48

TESS

TESS STEPPED AWAY FROM HER WORKSTATION, CARTED A TRAY TO the mass spectrometer, then returned to measure out the acetonitrile for the first sample of the next batch.

With the trial days away, Tess couldn't get her mind off whether Katherine knowing about the affair with Patrick would make her situation better or worse. If it destroyed the strongest thing Katherine and Patrick had going for them—a stable home, the mother and father Rose had always known living together in harmony—that would certainly help. But now wasn't the time to think of it.

Tess turned her attention to her work. She introduced five milliliters of acetonitrile into each tube. Her sample tray finished, she carried it to the centrifuge and set the timer. She signed out more samples, returned to her workstation, and started again. Even before learning of the affair, Katherine had wanted Tess wiped out of Rose's life, wanted her to be nothing more than a curiosity Rose could explore when she turned eighteen.

Tess measured out another sample, spiked it. Anger oozed through her, her limbs tensing at the idea that Katherine could think any sane judge would keep a child from a mother who loved her, who, through no fault of her own, had already missed out on so much.

Tess exhaled, focused on the task at hand, then switched to thinking of Katherine's rage, how she must have taken that out on Patrick when she returned home. Tess had gotten a cab and driven by their house three times in the past few days, walked by twice at night, a hoodie shading her face. Not once had she seen Katherine's SUV. It might not mean anything, but it might mean Patrick and Katherine had split, and if they had, Tess had a real shot.

As Tess was finishing her lunch, her phone buzzed. She pulled it out and tensed upon seeing the text from Carl: *Come straight to my office. Do NOT go to your workstation!* Tess read the message once, twice, three more times, a sick feeling rising while she packed up her lunch. As she headed toward her section of the building and stepped into the elevator with two coworkers who offered grim smiles, the feeling intensified. Could they have received the same message? But no, they stepped out of the elevator toward the lab, as Tess turned the other way.

Tess tried to tell herself it was nothing: notice of a new shipment of samples, or even a transfer. Tess had mentioned at her performance review that she wouldn't mind a new challenge. But then why the ominous text message? Why would he forbid her from going to her workstation? She traveled down the hall slowly, then stood at the open door.

"Tess. Come in." Carl waved Tess into the small space. Tess glanced at the woman standing in a dress suit and heels. Marilyn? Margaret? She was management. Higher up than Carl.

"Sit. Please." Margaret. It was definitely Margaret directing Tess toward one of two empty chairs in front of Carl's desk. Rather than sit in the other, the woman perched on the edge of the desk, looking down at Tess and making Carl fume, Tess imagined, as she asserted her dominance. "Do you have any idea why you're here today?"

Tess shook her head.

"Friday's batch." Carl's voice sounded heavy. "The last batch."

Tess stared. What about the last batch? She'd gone through all the steps perfectly, as always. Hadn't she?

"It's ruined."

A shivery tingle shot through Tess.

"You used the wrong amount of acetonitrile." Carl pushed the open binder on his desk toward her, pointed.

"No. There's no way." It was the protocol she'd been following for months. Following perfectly for months. "Five mils of—"

"That batch had a new ratio, Tess. Three mils of acetonitrile, using a five mil auto-pipette."

Tess slumped in her chair. Her arms seemed weighted down, her head too heavy to hold. She managed to nod. "I don't understand how—"

"Neither do we." Margaret leaned in. "What I hope you do understand is how serious this is."

"Yes, of course." Tess stared at the pages, her temples pounding. She looked at Carl. "Life's been so overwhelming. The custody case. You know." *Of course you know*, Tess wanted to add. *You clearly told people in the office, your sister-in-law, too.*

Carl rubbed a hand over his thinning hair. "Yes, and you haven't been focused lately. Your numbers are down." He sighed, glanced at Margaret. "I should have intervened earlier… I shouldn't have been letting you work all those overtime hours, but—"

"My numbers have been down?" asked Tess. "Are you sure? By how much?"

"Not much," said Carl, "but it's noticeable."

"I'm sorry." Tess's throat threatened to close. The trial, days away, loomed in her mind. *Are you employed, Ms. Sokolowski?* she imagined the judge asking. *How do you expect to provide for Rose, Ms. Sokolowski?*

"I'll pay for the samples." Tess leaned forward, an invisible weight against her chest. "Deduct them from my pay. I'll be more focused. I promise. Check and double-check and triple."

Margaret picked up the records charts, held them out to Tess, using a pen as a pointer. "This one sample, Ms. Sokolowski"—she tapped the sheet—"cost seven thousand dollars. This one." *Tap.* "Five thousand. This"—Margaret picked up a vial from the desk behind her—"retrieving this sample cost eleven thousand dollars. Can you do that math, Ms. Sokolowski?"

"Yes. I mean no. I mean—"

Margaret shook her head. "Offering to pay, to have your salary deducted, is not a solution. Not if you want a living wage. It would take years to recoup our loss."

Tess nodded. She clasped her hands in her lap.

"Mistakes happen, Ms. Sokolowski. But not here. We can't afford them. There's no room for being stressed or unfocused. You've got to leave all that at the door. Once, maybe. One vial. Two, and then you catch the mistake. You inform someone, and hopefully the entire sample hasn't been ruined. But you did not catch your mistake." She tapped her pen again. "You're lucky Carl did. The next batch of samples on your tray, they cost thirty thousand dollars to retrieve."

Tess swallowed, her heart racing. *I'm sorry*, she wanted to say, again and again and again. But *sorry* wouldn't fix this. Her mind turned to Rose. Rose's smile. Rose's laugh. "I'm so sorry." Stable, Messineo had told her. Squeaky-clean living. Solid employment. And here she was, an adulteress, a promiscuous, drunken club-hopper, likely unemployed.

"It's not just the money," said Margaret. "Some of those samples, with the timing, the season, the relation to previous retrievals, it's not like we can just send a copter back out, start over." Margaret turned to Carl. "I don't know what I'm going to tell Stan. This could be all our heads." She turned to Tess. "It's definitely going to be yours."

Tess left Carl's office and made her way back to her workstation. She stood in the place she had stood hour after hour, day after day, dreaming of the moment she would never have to stand here again. She'd never once dreamt she'd leave like this. Tess leaned on the table, her head down, her shoulders in a frozen heave. She'd worked so hard to make her life ready for Rose.

Realizing her motionless, dumbfounded stare might draw prying eyes, Tess snapped herself out of her stupor. She packed up the few personal items from her workstation in a crumpled grocery bag she found in her backpack and kept her head down as she left the floor. Her stomach twisted. She choked down the urge to vomit. She didn't need more rumors, people thinking she was hungover, sacked for drinking on the job, though the way word traveled, they probably knew the true reason anyway. A mess-up like this? It would spread like a virus.

Tess forced down a rising sob. Realized she *was* lucky. Not fired, but a two-week suspension without pay, during which time they'd figure out her continued punishment. Demoted to nothing but labeling and washing, most likely. It could be months before she was back to having her own workstation, if she ever got here again. Because of a mistake so stupid, so careless, she could hardly believe she'd made it. Suspended. From the best thing she had going for her, as far as the judge would be concerned. The trial was in three days, and Tess, for the time being, was jobless—she let out a caustic laugh as she exited the building. Was there nothing she couldn't mess up? Her best hope now was that Katherine would be such a wreck, so hateful and bitter and destructive toward Patrick on the stand, it would make Tess look great in comparison…so long as Katherine didn't turn that rage on Tess, decide to tell the judge those "ugly things" after all.

Tess stopped. She thought again of that empty driveway, Rose's family possibly destroyed, of how, in more ways than one, Tess was responsible. A sickening wave of guilt crashed over her. Here she was, thinking that if the night with Patrick helped get her Rose, she wouldn't regret it. But she hadn't considered the damage to her daughter if the parents who would always be in her life in some capacity hated each other.

Tess saw again the outrage in Katherine's eyes, the hurt, as she fled the café; saw that empty driveway. She imagined Rose, confused or frightened at the fight that must have occurred, at the ones sure to come, because of Tess. So much anguish, the upending of so many lives, because of Tess.

And it wasn't just the night with Patrick. Without Katherine's egg, would Tess's embryo have even made it to twenty-one weeks? Would Tess have gone to that gala, been so open about her grief, if she'd lost the baby halfway through the first trimester, as she had with all the others? If she hadn't lost her uterus along with the baby, would their whole lives have turned out differently?

She needed to know, once and for all, whether she was responsible for the switch—responsible for all that had happened because of it—and if not, why Irene had done it. Why she'd confessed, putting into motion all the events of the last eight months. It still might be bad for the trial if Tess had to confess she'd put the idea in Irene's mind. But if questioned, she would have to admit that it was a possibility anyway, that she'd said what she said. Knowing for certain whether Irene had made the switch to help Tess wouldn't harm Tess's chances any more than they already had been, would it? Certainly less than losing her job would harm them.

But how to find her? Tess couldn't imagine the clinic or any of their old classmates offering up Irene's contact info. The internet wouldn't be any help; Irene had shut down her social media accounts months ago. Tess turned, deciding to try the least likely option, or the most. She took a deep breath, switched directions, strode down one block, two, until her steps slowed.

The house looked much as Tess remembered, though the lawn and garden were horribly unkempt. Tess walked up the empty driveway, noting the closed blinds on such a bright and sunny day. Her shoulders sank, but she knocked anyway, despite how unlikely it was that the family would be here after a decade, let alone Irene.

"No press!" a ragged voice shouted from within.

Tess stepped back, her heart slamming against her chest. "No, it's… I'm not…" She swallowed, raised her voice. "It's Tess."

Silence, as Tess's heart continued to slam. Then the sound of the lock, the pull of the door. Irene staring, her eyebrows two fuzzy caterpillars scrunching on her forehead in place of the thin sculpted lines Tess remembered.

Irene stepped backward, head down, and waved for Tess to follow her inside. "I wondered if you'd come."

The house was less cluttered than Tess remembered, more modern, though she'd only been there once. "It's different," she said, not knowing what else to say.

Irene walked through to the kitchen, where empty takeout and frozen dinner containers littered the counter. She turned to Tess, her expression haunted, her voice devoid of inflection. "My mom died a while back. My dad moved to the valley to be nearer to his family. It's mine now."

"I'm sorry," said Tess. "About your mom."

Irene nodded.

"I like what you've done with the place."

Irene let out a sharp laugh. She turned toward a breakfast nook and slid onto one of the seats, motioning for Tess to sit across from her.

Tess sat. Irene stared. A cat slinked into the room, jumped on Irene's lap, and purred as it rubbed against her.

"I—" Tess's throat caught.

"It's not your fault," said Irene. "You didn't do anything wrong, just in case you wondered. This is on me."

"But—"

Tears glistened in Irene's eyes; she blinked them back. "I shouldn't say more than that. I just—the lawyers, and well, I guess I got off easy...but they still said don't talk. Never talk. No public explanations." Irene sighed. "It's all too complicated. They didn't think it would help."

"I'm not exactly public," said Tess.

"You could be." Irene turned her gaze to the wall. "I'm sorry, too. For your loss. The baby. I—" Irene's voice cracked. "I never wanted it to turn out like this."

Tess leaned forward. "I won't tell anyone. Not a soul. Just please tell me why you did it. It's been haunting me. Was it because of what I said?"

Irene closed her eyes, her head bobbing back and forth. "Mostly."

Tess's chest tightened. "Mostly?"

Irene inhaled, the tears leaking from her closed lids. "It almost happened to me, a few months after the Halloween party. That guy. Our classmate. I pushed him off. Ran. Then, at the clinic, when you told me about your abortion, about all that came after, I connected the dots to that night, to your dropping out of school out of nowhere." She looked at Tess, her face scrunching as if in pain. "I'm the one who urged you to go with him, after I got you drunk…knowing you weren't used to alcohol, to men. I'm the one who told you there was nothing to worry about. I didn't report him when he…with me… But someone did the next year, and then others came forward. He wasn't convicted, but still."

Irene rubbed her chest, a wavering smile on her face. "I should have connected the dots sooner," she continued, "you dropping out like that, when you were smarter than all of us. Maybe I did suspect when he tried with me…knowing you'd left with him that night. But I pushed it out of my mind. I didn't want to go there. I didn't want to think it had happened to you, and that it was my…that I could have—" Irene averted her gaze, shook her head.

Tess swallowed, her heart pounding harder. "Could have what? What he did, it wasn't your fault."

"I played a part."

"No."

"It wouldn't have happened if I hadn't pushed you. And then I went on with my life. Not checking up on you. Not trying to figure out why you dropped out, even after…" Irene raised her gaze to Tess's. "I should have been a better friend. I should have known you wouldn't have quit the way you did without a good reason." She hesitated. "When I switched the eggs, knowing it was your last chance, I was trying to, I don't know, make up for it, I guess. For the child you… That you had to go through that. I knew I could never make up for the rest."

Tess leaned back, her heart and mind racing. She had the answer. It wasn't random. The switch, everything that had come after it, all that still would, all the confusion and heartache for Rose, for Katherine, for Patrick, even, was because of Tess. Because she'd been a stupid girl all those years ago. Tess flinched, hearing her mother's voice in her head. How many times growing up had Jasia called Tess that? A stupid girl, silly, foolish. And that's what she was. Stupid. Naive and weak. Afraid to stand up for herself. Years later, still messing things up, blind to the damage her words, her actions could cause. It was a joke, not a request, but she'd been the one to ask for that egg in the ultrasound room. She was the reason Irene thought she needed to atone for an event that was never her fault—ruining the woman's life in the process…which was what Tess still didn't understand. "Why did you confess?" She shifted forward. "Knowing you could lose everything?"

Irene tilted her head, not looking at Tess, but just past her. She let out a long sigh. "I couldn't sleep." She lowered her gaze. "It started after my mom died. We were close. She was my…everything. And I just kept thinking of you—the child you lost, the utter agony in your eyes as you came in for your follow-up—no baby, no womb. I'd lie in bed at night, racked with guilt, thinking about the fact that you had a child out there and didn't know it. Then I saw Katherine Matheson walking through the park with *your* little girl. And I thought of her, of what I'd done to her. How, because of me, she would never know her real mother. If someone had done that to me…if I'd missed out on knowing my mom, I just—" Irene swallowed. "I couldn't live with it anymore. I'd played God, and as a result, your child was being raised by someone else. Mrs. Matheson's child had died." Irene paused. "My mom always told me to do the right thing. And I hadn't, and I knew I could never change that. But I could confess, accept whatever consequences were coming to me."

Tess stared, uncertain what to say.

"I'm so sorry," said Irene, taking Tess's hand. "I know it won't change anything, and I don't expect you to forgive me, but since you're here, for what it's worth, I'm sorry."

Tess looked at their hands. "I do…forgive you, I mean. I'm glad, now, at least, that it happened."

Irene leaned forward. "That your child, your biological child…" Irene's voice trailed off. The caterpillars scrunched again.

"I'm happy my daughter exists."

Irene nodded. "I hope you get her. I hope the custody case works out in your favor. I wish—" She stopped again. "Wishes don't matter at this point, I guess." She stood, looking as if she were about to be sick. "You should go."

Tess walked toward the entry, wanting to say more. Irene held the door open and Tess stepped out before turning back. "I think your mom would be proud."

Irene offered a weak smile, her eyes glistening. "I know it was insane. I know I shouldn't have done it. I just…I was only trying to help."

Tess opened her mouth, so many words hovering unspoken. It was insane, what Irene had done. It was unconscionable. But for Tess, it was the best thing that had ever happened. It had given her a reason to live.

49

KATHERINE

KATHERINE LIVED IN A STATE OF LIMBO. WHEN SHE WAS HUNGRY, she ate. When she was tired, she slept. When Rose needed something, Katherine provided it. Otherwise, she let Rose do what she wanted. They walked the beach, collected rocks and shells, buried each other's feet, built castles and motorways.

All this time, she'd tried to be the perfect mother, perfect wife, and what had it gotten her? A husband it hurt to look at, a daughter who wasn't even hers, another who was already lost.

She decided to stop striving. The laundry piled up. Dishes sat stacked in the sink from three, four, sometimes five meals past. She cleaned whatever dish or utensil she needed, leaving the rest.

She wore sweatpants, large, billowy shirts, and dresses her aunt had in the closet. She hadn't washed her hair since they'd been there; the curls tightening up and puffing out. She pressed her hand to the mass and smiled.

Katherine sat, her hands and feet in the sand, staring at the ocean, at Rose, who ran to the edge of the encroaching waves, then back again, squealing with delight.

These few days had changed something, shown her she could exist even when those she most loved thought she was making the wrong choice.

Rose stopped midrun, her face freezing and exploding into an even bigger smile than the one she'd worn before. Katherine turned in the direction of Rose's gaze the moment she squealed, "Dada!"

"Rose!" Patrick ran across the beach, arms wide.

Katherine tensed, her fingers digging into the sand. She stayed seated as Rose ran past, leaping into her father's arms.

As the two approached, Katherine looked up, shading her eyes from the sun. "I said I needed time."

"Three days is time."

Katherine dusted the sand off her hands, then stood. "Not much."

"I missed my girl."

Rose squirmed in his arms, and he set her down. She ran to the shore. "Dada. Watz!"

"I'm watching, sweetie."

Katherine stared at Patrick as Patrick gazed at Rose, smiled, clapped. She sighed. Rage took too much energy; the desire to claw his eyes out, throw sand in his face, yell, curse, scream, too exhausting.

He turned to her, his head tilted. "I like your hair like that."

She felt no anger, felt nothing for this person she'd shared the last decade with.

"Come home?"

Katherine shook her head.

"I noticed dinner's not started," he said. Katherine narrowed her gaze. "I brought Thai. If you're hungry. If not, that's fine."

"I could eat."

After dinner, Katherine sat across from Patrick, a pinot noir he'd found in her aunt's pantry on the table between them.

"We'll replace it." He pulled the cork. "A night like tonight needs a drink." He set a glass in front of her, poured. "How long is this going to go on?"

Katherine shrugged. "I don't exactly have a plan."

Patrick half smiled. "You without a plan. Huh."

Katherine's lips creeped up. "Crazy. Isn't it?"

They sipped.

"I told you how sorry I was, right? If I could go back in time, do everything differently, I would."

"Mm-hmm."

"But I can't."

Katherine shook her head. "You can't."

"Katherine, please." Patrick leaned forward, palms on the table. "Give me something. Yell. Just not this." He held his arm out toward her. "I don't know what to do with this."

Katherine arched an eyebrow. "With what?" She saw his exasperation, knew how he must perceive her. Cold. Unfeeling. But she wasn't. Unfeeling, maybe, but not cruel. She simply didn't know what she was going to do, and she was fine with that.

"I know you said you need time. And I respect that."

"Yet here you are."

"To see Rose."

"Fair enough." Katherine held the wine to her lips once more. "Rose is asleep, and still, here you are."

"Will you at least come home for the trial?"

Katherine scrunched her nose, as if smelling something foul. "I'm not sure."

"Do you still love me?"

Katherine paused. She set her glass on the table, looked toward the porch windows, the sun just starting its descent over the water. "I'm not sure."

Katherine turned her gaze back. Patrick's eyes were locked on her, the hurt, the desperation in them something she'd never seen. But there was something familiar, too. Love. Patrick, without a doubt, still loved her. She saw it now; she just wasn't sure she wanted it.

Katherine reached her hand across the table and Patrick grasped it—the touch as familiar as the sound of his sigh, as foreign as a stranger's grasp. "I need time. After that, I don't know." She looked at their intertwined fingers. "Until then, you can see Rose any time you like. But once she's asleep, I'd like you to leave."

Katherine stood. She walked toward the door, opened it, waited. After he left, she flipped the lock and returned to her drink. It was earthy and sweet, with just the faintest hint of spice. She angled her chair toward the setting sun and sipped.

50

TESS

TWO DAYS BEFORE THE TRIAL, TESS STARED AT HER PHONE'S SCREEN. A new article this time, prompted by a prosecutor's petition for the criminal law to be updated, full of more speculation on Irene's lack of criminal conviction and what, so said several journalists and dozens of commenters, was merely a slap on the wrist. *What about the families?* the commenters asked.

Some people mentioned the birth mother who'd lost her child, whose baby might still have been alive if it had been transferred to her own womb. No one mentioned the father, that the child in question *was* living with her biological dad.

Most comments centered on the "bio-mom," as they were calling her, the poor bio-mom, whose child was being raised by another woman, who deserved to hold her baby in her arms. Tess clicked back and chose another article, scrolled to the comments. She read, then navigated to Twitter. Reading comments had become a compulsion since she decided to go for sole custody—she needed validation she wasn't crazy, conviction that she was doing the right thing by wrenching her daughter from the only parents she'd ever known.

Barely a week went by when she hadn't searched for fresh opinions on this situation almost no one knew the details of, yet everyone thought they were an authority on. The overarching opinion never changed. Bio-mom was the biggest victim. Bio-mom deserved to have her baby back. Bio-mom, in the eyes of the internet, was a wronged saint.

But Tess wasn't.

She was a screw-up. A failure not even a husband or mother could love. She'd come online searching for the same confirmation she always did, that she deserved Rose, even with this suspension from her job, even as a homewrecker, even though all this had happened because she—not being serious, not expecting Irene to arrange it, not even knowing she could—had asked for an egg.

If the commenters knew who she really was, all she'd done, would they say the child should stay put? Tess closed her eyes, her lips trembling. Two days until the trial. She pressed the Call button on her phone. Two days to prove she was worthy.

Messineo's voice, thick and weary, sounded through the phone. "Tess. Hi."

"Hi."

A pause. "What can I do for you?" Music in the background. Brahms. Cello Sonata No. 1. Tess's heart clenched. It was one of her father's favorites. He'd play it on his quietest days as Tess would sit, the music reverberating through her, telling her all the secrets of his soul he couldn't bring himself to speak.

"Tess?"

The night she'd first heard him perform it, up on stage, while she sat in the dark amidst a sea of faces, she'd never felt so proud. And sitting there, she'd wanted to make him proud, too.

Regret shot through Tess at who she'd become, a woman who, following her urges toward a moment of forgetting, may have torn lives apart. Who, after trying so hard to fix her own life, had lost the most stable thing she had going for her.

"Tess?"

"Sorry. I was just listening."

"Excuse me?"

Tess spewed the words, the tightness in her chest rolling upward. "Can I come in?"

"The trial's in two days," said Messineo. "You're ready. We've been over—"

"No. I think we need to, uh, rethink."

"Tess."

"I've been suspended from my job. And I don't think, I don't know… Will this ruin things?"

A long sigh sounded through the line. "I'll try to fit you in over lunch. Come to the courthouse, Family Division, at twelve fifteen. Wait in the foyer. If I'm late, I'm late. But I'll be there."

"Okay. Great. Thank you. Thank you so much."

Over the sweet yet haunting sound of Brahms, Messineo sighed. "I'll see you at lunch."

After her meeting with Messineo, Tess stood outside her parents' house. She'd rehearsed what to say, taking Messineo's words and making them her own. She'd messed up, but it was a mistake anyone could have made. Another tray, another batch of samples, and it may have been several hundred dollars lost, not thousands.

Bad luck, she'd say. They hadn't wanted to suspend her—Carl's eyes said as much as he relayed the news—but the blame had to fall on someone.

Tess walked to the front door, knocked, was directed to sit. Her father in his armchair, her mother on a chair brought from the dining room table rather than on the couch beside Tess. Jasia's mouth formed a grim line, her arms crossed.

"I just need someone to back me," said Tess, borrowing Messineo's words. "So the judge will know if they don't bring me back, it'll be okay, the lights will stay on and there'll be food in the fridge." She looked between her parents. "They'll bring me back, though, I'm sure of it, and even if they don't, I have savings—"

"Savings meant for school," said Jasia.

"Yes, but if they did let me go, I'd find another job." Tess spoke with false confidence, pep to her voice. "And I'm applying to return to school. My lawyer told me where I could rent a laptop so I can get everything in order, write and send the application. I'm going to get it done right away, before the trial even, so I can tell the judge I've applied. My supervisor will give me a glowing reference, I'm sure. He's always been pleased with my work."

"Until now."

"Until now, but it was one mistake." Tess's trachea seemed to contract, letting in no more air than a straw. She'd never spoken to Carl about a reference. But he would, sure he would. He would have…

"It's just so the judge knows you're willing to back me financially." Tess tried to sound casual, though contrite might work better. "Not just emotionally."

"But you are not asking us to back you financially," said Jasia, "simply to say we will, even if we will not."

Her father looked between them.

"Well…" Tess hesitated. *Lying lips are an abomination to the Lord.* How many times had Tess heard that in her childhood, even when she'd been telling the truth? "You won't need to. I'm sure you won't. They're not firing me. And if they were, I bet I could go back to Wendy's until I found something better. But if I couldn't, if the savings ran out…" Tess swallowed. She looked at her father, then back to her mother. "Would you?"

"No." Her mother stood. "No, we would not. You are no longer a child. You need to make your own way in the world, as we did."

"Jasia." Her father.

"We will not tell this judge we would. Lying lips, Theresa, are an abomina—"

"Thought I'd ask." Tess stood. Her legs shook. She looked between them again. *I would*, her father's face seemed to say, *I will*. But he wouldn't if her mother didn't agree. Tess pulled at her shirt. It felt tight. Why did it feel so tight?

She'd asked Messineo if she should change her request to shared custody. *You should have kept it that way*, he'd said, *but now it would seem flaky. Or worse, that you're not as interested in Rose as you were before, that this time spent with her has opened your eyes to the reality of parenthood, a reality you may not want.*

Sweat slid down Tess's belly, pooled under her arms. Messineo had sighed, pity in his eyes. *There's next to no chance of sole custody*, he said. *There never was, but shared custody was what you originally wanted, and so long as everything else in your life looks good, you have a fair chance of that.* Tess's heart thumped heavily, all the things Katherine may know, may use twirling through her mind. She turned to her father. His hand was under her elbow, the other supporting her back. "Tata?"

"Mój kwiatuszek, come, sit." He held a tissue to her eyes, dabbing away tears. "You're having an episode," he crooned. "You are all right. You will be all right."

"An episode?" Her mother huffed. "That is what you call it?"

She struggled to breathe, each breath more restricted.

"My sister got them, too," said Aleksy, pushing Tess down as her heart continued to thump. How had she gotten to his armchair? Hadn't she been sitting on the couch? "The one with the problems."

"The one who frittered away her life," said Jasia, "disappointed her family."

An adulterer, a dropout, on suspension—likely with a cut in pay on the way, if she got to keep her job at all—no family support, and prone to drink to excess. The judge would laugh in her face.

"Breathe, mój kwiatuszek, breathe."

Tess looked at Aleksy, tried to mimic his ins and outs as he breathed, to focus on the wave of his hand as he brought it toward him and away, toward him and away. But her airway was so tight. She grabbed at her throat, pulling.

She was standing again, being led toward the door, down the steps. "I am driving her home." Her father's voice as Jasia stood on the porch, arms still crossed.

Aleksy opened the car door, buckled Tess into her seat, whispered soothing words in their mother tongue, reminding her to breathe. "This happened before," he said, first in Polish, then English. She turned to him, her hand on her chest, thinking, *This is it, I'm going to die,* on repeat. "When you were just a girl. Twelve, maybe." He looked at her, his hands firmly on the wheel. "You were okay then. You will be okay now."

Tess's heart thumped, her breath came in short, terrifying rasps, but she remembered breathing in a paper bag, the scent of stale bread, that it had ended, and she was still here.

In her apartment, Aleksy sat across from Tess, her head propped on a pillow, her feet in his lap, like they used to be. An hour passed of Aleksy coaching her, calming her, getting her to focus on her senses, the sounds and sights around her, rather than her fears, and, at last, Tess was breathing easy.

"How did you know?" Tess asked, every ounce of energy sucked out of her. "To do that?"

"My sister."

Aleksy motioned to the room. "This is a lovely place you have here." He patted Tess's feet. "I'm proud of you."

Tess shifted her gaze. "You are?"

"Of course, mój kwiatuszek. You've been through a lot, and you are still standing."

Tess let out a shallow laugh. "Barely."

"No." He squeezed her leg. "You are. You are doing well."

Tess looked away, to the picture of Rose smiling. "Mama doesn't think so."

Aleksy followed her gaze, a soft smile lighting his face as he looked at his granddaughter.

"Why does she hate me?"

"Hate you?" Aleksy turned to her. "No. That's not what you think?"

"What would you call it?"

"Love, mój kwiatuszek. She loves you."

"She doesn't." The way her mother looked at her, spoke to her… Tess could never imagine looking at Rose that way, no matter what her daughter did to disappoint her.

"It is love. It's—" Her father paused. "Regret. She feels she failed you. She wanted better for you. A good life. A happy life."

Tess shook her head.

"And she's angry with herself. Seeing you, it brings out that anger. Brings out the guilt."

"My life isn't her fault."

"I know. I tell her. Shame…it is a powerful thing." Her father paused, a silence she recognized as he looked for English words, the correct way to express thoughts he'd only had in Polish. "An ugly thing. It twists what should be beautiful." He leaned forward, rubbed her hand. "You, my dear, this life you're making for yourself, it is beautiful."

Tess wanted to believe him. Believe all of it.

"I should have told you that more." Aleksy stared at the wall. "I should have stood up to your mother. I know that. It's… She… There is much about her life—our lives—you do not know." He looked at her. "I am not a strong man, and your mother, well, she is strong, but I promise you this: we will not be out of each other's lives again. If your mother refuses, then I will come here." Aleksy raised his chin. "To your home. She will not stop me."

Aleksy looked at his hands. "I should warn you, though, or ask you… Is there any way for your mother not to testify?"

Tess pushed herself to a sitting position. "What?"

"She is angry, Theresa, about the way everything has happened. She thinks differently about the world, people, you…and she thinks she will be doing right, but I fear she will do wrong. I fear she will say things to make it more difficult for you, for getting your daughter. Can you make it so that she will not be called to speak?"

A chill slithered through Tess. "I don't think so. My lawyer stressed how important it was to hear from you—both of you."

Her father nodded. "I will try to speak to her. I will do my best to make it better." He stood, kissed Tess on the forehead, rubbed a hand along her temple. "You are okay, mój kwiatuszek, you are, and you will be. Go to bed now, śpij dobrze."

Tess stood, her legs still shaky, and walked him to the door. She returned to the couch and stared at the wall once more. Despite the photos, the paintings, the appearance of happiness, she saw an emptiness, vast and overwhelming, where her hope that life could be better, could be good at all, should be. The only bright spot was Rose. Rose, whose love, whose presence, would make Jasia's disdain insignificant.

Aleksy's love was precious. Tess knew that; she was thankful for it. But her mother's love—if it was love—crushed her. In her mother's eyes, her failures loomed. And, if her father was right, Jasia was going to lay it all out on the stand.

51

KATHERINE

T HE MORNING BEFORE THE TRIAL, KATHERINE WOKE AFTER A REST-
less sleep, a nagging feeling pulsing through her that enough was
enough. The advice she'd read was conflicting. Put your child's happiness
first, above all else. Or put yourself and your happiness first, because wit-
nessing it, basking in it, will be the catalyst your child needs to ensure her
own joy. It seemed impossible to do both.

Katherine closed her eyes and rolled onto her side, despite the awkwardness of having so much of the bed in front of her.

She'd experienced a sense of calm these past days. But it was time to
return home, for the time being, at least. She needed to make certain that,
with everything she'd lost, she wasn't about to lose Rose, too.

Intentionally, Katherine arrived while Patrick was still at work. She
walked into the house already tense, expecting dirty dishes piled in the
sink and on tables and counters, too. She expected suit jackets tossed on
couches and chairs, crumpled. She expected more reason to be angry.

But the house was clean. Not as spotless as she would have had it, but close, even though she hadn't told him she was coming, wanting the time and space to see if it still felt like home.

Rose squealed and clapped, running from room to room. In her play-room she seemed frantic, dashing to this toy then that. Picking one up, hugging it, dropping the item only to pick up another. Five days. They'd been gone five days. What if, after all this was over, Rose was gone a week, two, more?

Katherine walked the halls behind Rose, followed as she clambered up the stairs. She trailed her hand along the oak railing. It was home, as much as ever.

She spent the afternoon as if she'd never left, yet when Patrick's foot-steps sounded in the hall, she stiffened, resisting the urge to flee.

"Katherine?"

"Dada!" Rose ran to him, squeezing tight once he'd lifted her into his arms.

Patrick stared at Katherine as he kissed Rose's head, held her against his side. "Are you...? Is this?"

Katherine's chest clenched. She shook her head. "You were right. It makes sense, throughout the trial at least, for us to be here." Patrick frowned. "We won't have to lie about it, us living together." Katherine sighed. "We'll figure custody out, then we'll figure this out." She gestured between them.

"I was thinking couples counseling, that—"

"Maybe." Katherine hesitated. "But the trial first."

Patrick nodded, set Rose down. "I hadn't planned much for dinner, but there's most of a rotisserie chicken in the fridge. I could make sandwiches and a salad?"

"Sure." Katherine gestured to the space around them. "You hire a cleaner?"

"No." Patrick turned to the fridge, hauling chicken and cheese and mayonnaise out, then plopping them on the counter. "I can clean. Not to your standards, but I'm not a slob."

"No." Shame crept upon Katherine. "You're not."

That night, Patrick and Katherine went through the bedtime routine together, giving Rose her bath, reading her story. Patrick left, as always, when Katherine and Rose settled in to nurse. As he pulled the door closed, the room seemed to open up.

Katherine stayed longer than usual, and with each additional minute on the clock, the air thickened, a weight upon her shoulders. She couldn't pretend everything was fine, not like before. So when she placed her sleeping girl in the crib and stepped out the door, Katherine didn't know what should come next.

She walked down the stairs and toward the living room, feeling like a guest in her own home, out of place and uncertain. She'd considered going straight to her room, their room, which didn't seem like theirs anymore.

Patrick stood in the hall. "I wasn't sure what you'd want. You can relax in the living room if you'd like." He gestured, as if reminding her where it was. "I can go to my office or the rec room."

"I'm pretty tired." Katherine cleared her throat. "I wasn't sure…"

"I just put fresh sheets on our bed. You can stay where you like, in our room or the guest room. Whatever you want."

"Oh." Katherine considered. She was the one who'd left, but he, more obviously, was the reason for the leaving. She didn't want to set a precedent, make it seem like this was his house and she was the guest. She also didn't want to lie in the bed they'd shared, wondering if they ever would again. "I'll take the guest room." She forced a smile. "Thanks."

"No problem." He opened his mouth, poised for words he didn't say. He nodded, sat back on the couch. "Have a good sleep." He paused. "I love you."

Katherine turned from him, now the one to open her mouth then close it, refusing to speak the words she'd spoken thousands of times, which she was no longer sure were true.

52

KATHERINE

KATHERINE TURNED OFF HER ALARM. SHE HADN'T NEEDED IT. IF she'd slept, it was for scant and fitful periods. Today was the day she'd been both dreading and yearning for for months, though it wouldn't be a one-day affair, the billable hours piling up.

The psychological assessments had finished weeks ago. The visits with the social worker, too. As far as she knew, the interviews of their friends and family would be heard for the first time in court. But how long could they take?

She pushed herself out of bed, almost viciously pulled up the sheets, tucked them tight, then arranged the comforter and throw pillows on the bed.

She wanted a verdict.

When she'd truly believed their home was the superior one, the life they could give Rose the best one, she'd been frightened. Now, the feeling went beyond fear. She didn't know what was best: for Rose to grow up in a home with parents together only for her benefit, tiptoeing around each other; to have parents living separately because of their broken vows; to live with Tess, whom Rose had grown to love; or something else, traveling between all three of them. No outcome felt right. No scenario the best choice. But Rose being with her had to be what was best.

Katherine bent to smooth her hand over the comforter, then stopped, letting the wrinkles sit there. She turned toward the bathroom. She'd shower, dress, head downstairs. It was how she'd get through this. One step, and then the next, and the next, keeping from her mind that possible final step, the one she feared would break her.

Just as Katherine finished styling her hair, a loud yell sounded down the hall. "Mama!"

After lifting Rose from her crib, giving a quick kiss and cuddle, Katherine set her down. Rose ran toward the stairs, her ponytail bopping.

"Wait, sweetie." Katherine dashed after her and grasped Rose's hand just before she reached the top of the stairs.

Rose pulled away. "Sowf!"

"Hmm?"

"Do id sowf!"

Katherine stepped back. Rose was close to being able to do the stairs on her own. She had the mechanics, had finally grown tall enough that her knees were higher than each step, a necessary component for success. But she was far from able to reach the railing. Katherine went down the first few steps backward, watching Rose, there to catch her if she stumbled. "Okay. Do it yourself."

Rose took the first step, teetered a bit, then regained her balance. She went slower on the next one, pressing her hand against the wall to steady herself. She continued, step by step by step, with each one her confidence growing, her pride radiating.

"Good job!" Katherine clapped. "Way to go!" She lifted Rose, swung her in the air, then drew her in. These were the moments. Rose laughed, squirmed out of Katherine's arms, and ran to the kitchen.

They ate breakfast as a family, dropped Rose off at Tracey's as a family, and then drove to the courthouse, the family of two they'd been all the years before Rose entered their lives. They stepped onto the path to the courthouse door and Katherine put out her hand. Patrick looked at it, his eyes narrowing in confusion. "A united front," Katherine whispered. "We'll figure out the rest later."

His sweaty palm met hers.

53

TESS

KATHERINE AND PATRICK WALKED TO THE COURTHOUSE DOORS hand in hand, looking like the perfect couple they weren't. Tess waited until they'd entered the building before approaching. It could be a show, the hand-holding. If it was, Tess wouldn't be the one to lift the curtain. She wanted Rose, in whatever way she could have her, but not at whatever cost. If Patrick and Katherine were determined to make it work, move past this, Tess wouldn't be the one to announce to the world they were living a lie. She hoped Katherine would feel the same.

Dizzy with fear and uncertainty, Tess focused on her breath. She commanded her legs to move through the hall and into the courtroom, noting the faces of her supporters in the crowd: Mikolai, Karina, her parents—or her father, at least—Carl.

Tess looked again. Carl? She'd given him as a work reference, not character. The psychologist could have suggested he come, called him to testify, or the Mathesons' lawyer. Why else would he be here? How would he even have known?

As his head turned toward her, Tess whipped her face forward and walked past a sea of people, mostly faces she vaguely recalled from Rose's party. She'd hoped Saadia would be there—to show she had at least one friend—but she had to fly out of the country to be with her ailing grandmother, so she'd written a sealed letter before she left, to pass on to the judge. Saadia warned Tess she'd mentioned Katherine as well, felt she had to, seeing she knew her character, too, treated her, too, had been in business with her off and on for a decade. Tess only hoped that despite this and despite the job loss, with all the progress she'd made these past months, Saadia's praise of her would be enough.

Judge Cormier began his speech, emphasizing the difficulty of the case, the uniqueness, his disappointment they couldn't figure things out on their own. However, he continued, he understood. He passed his gaze from Tess to Patrick to Katherine. "None of you set out to be part-time parents. The psychological evaluations, though raising some issues, presented nothing that should unequivocally determine custody. No matter the home," the judge declared, "I'm confident Rose will be cared for with love.

"The timing"—a hitch sounded in his voice—"makes the case all the more difficult. Had the switch been discovered in utero or shortly after birth, which has so often been the case with lab mix-ups in other countries, the decision may have been easier. But Rose having lived almost a year before the truth came to light, eight months having passed since then..."

Cormier turned to the Mathesons. "In Rose's mind, you, without a doubt, are her parents. Yet she is young enough that if sole custody were granted to Ms. Sokolowski, the psychological damage would likely be minimal. I cannot deny the importance of biological connection, and the reports reveal"—Judge Cormier smiled at Tess—"Rose and Ms. Sokolowski are developing a strong and important relationship."

Tess kept her gaze on the man as he spoke. She wanted to hate him and all his posturing, but it didn't seem like posturing. It seemed like confusion, uncertainty, a desire to make the right choice when it seemed there was no right choice to make, which meant she had a chance.

"I have to admit," he continued, "giving sole custody to either party is distressing. As emphasized in the appearances, we'd hoped you could work this out, determine a way to turn this horrid situation into a positive. To put your own wants and needs aside and agree on what's best for the child. But that responsibility has fallen to my hands." He paused.

"I don't want to separate this child from any of you. In the words of a social worker I greatly respect, when you pull a child from their family, they will rebel because they won't know who they are, where they're from, what their roots are," he continued. "No matter the outcome, I hope to give Rose a connection to her roots. All of them. Be it through shared custody, mandated visitation, or a more flexible solution. Unfortunately, that isn't what any of you want."

Tess looked at Katherine. She sat, hands in her lap, back straight, eyes pointed forward—a placid, unreadable expression on her face. Patrick seemed less confident. His foot tapped under the table. Every few minutes, he rubbed at his face or pulled at his neck.

The judge let out a short sigh. "These proceedings, and time, will tell. So let us begin."

54

KATHERINE

KATHERINE SAT, FOCUSED ON PROJECTING AN AIR OF POISE AS FIRST her parents and then Patrick's took the stand, were examined and cross-examined. Their words were kind, encouraging, painting a picture of a loving couple, adored by everyone they met. A couple who had tried for years to start a family, and now that they had one, wanted to live in as much peace as they could, with as little disruption to their and their daughter's lives as possible.

Her parents had not a negative word to say, no matter the question, and beamed with pride for Katherine, the husband she chose, and the child they birthed.

When it came to Patrick's parents, particularly Susie, Katherine's chest welled with confusion and shame. Either Katherine had misjudged the woman, or she was a more skilled liar than Katherine imagined. From the words she said, Patrick couldn't have chosen a better partner and Rose couldn't have a better woman to raise her.

When asked questions designed to bring aspects of Patrick or Katherine's personalities, parenting, or relationships into question, each parent spoke honestly, but always in a way that made any perceived faults nothing more than the unimportant foibles or challenges that plagued everyone.

Katherine fought tears, almost wishing they knew the lie, so she could drop the subterfuge, talk to someone, anyone, about the fact that her life was falling apart.

Tess's father, as quiet and restrained as Katherine's, seemed just as proud of his daughter. Just as loving. But when Mrs. Sokolowski took the stand, a chill ran down Katherine's spine. The woman seemed in every way the opposite of Tess. Broad and sturdy where Tess was fragile and lithe; hard and unemotional where Tess was soft, her fears and hopes and pain flitting across her face like a veil in the breeze.

Katherine held her breath as Kerra approached the woman. "My focus today," said Kerra, "is to determine whether Tess will be a suitable mother to this child. I'd like to know more about the estrangement." Kerra turned from Mrs. Sokolowski, addressing the court before turning back. "We know the core reason was her dropping out of school. That shows a lack of commitment. Are you certain Tess wouldn't show that same lack of commitment to Rose?"

Mrs. Sokolowski leaned forward. "I am not." The words hit like a slap. Katherine resisted the urge to look at Tess, see if she'd been struck. "My daughter makes poor choices. Rash choices. She is unfocused. She has the ability to focus, but…" Mrs. Sokolowski shook her head. "Other things get in the way."

Kerra stepped closer. "What things, specifically?"

Mrs. Sokolowski sighed, tutted. "I wish I knew. She is secretive. Does not open up." She crossed her arms in front of her. "Most secrets, if you ask me, are dirty. If they were not, why would they be secrets at all?"

Katherine stole that glance, the motherly part of her wanting to reach out, take Tess's hand, squeeze it. She drew her gaze back to the front of the courtroom.

"She dropped out of school, as you said," continued Mrs. Sokolowski, "dishonoring her father and me, and this girl, my own child, would not tell us why. After we paid all that money. For people like us, it is not cheap. But we worked. We sacrificed for years, for both of our children. We did not want them to start life indebted. Then she comes to us, no explanation, and tells us she is 'not feeling it.' Those are the words she used, if you can believe it." Mrs. Sokolowski changed her tone, lightening it as if imitating a Valley girl from an eighties teen movie. "'I'm just not feeling it.'" She shook her head, leaned forward again, her hands on the railing in front of her. "It frightens me. What if, after a few years, she is not feeling being a mom? What if she decides she is tired of Rose, too?"

A pin could have dropped in the courtroom, startled every ear. Kerra paused, one second, two, three. "Does that concern you, Mrs. Sokolowski? That your daughter wouldn't be a reliable parent for Rose?"

"Yes, it concerns me." Mrs. Sokolowski looked toward the judge, her eyes moist. "That is what I am saying. And it shames me. I have racked my brain, trying to figure out what I did, where I went wrong. But her brother is wonderful. The perfect child. So I do not know." She stopped, looked at Tess, then back at Kerra. "Maybe it was not me at all. Maybe it is just her." The hard, almost vindictive tone she'd started with left her voice, defeat taking its place. "Her husband left her. Yes, they had struggled. Yes, she could not have a baby. But…" She paused. "It does not seem a reason to leave if she was a person worth staying married to. If you are satisfied with your wife in other ways, if you think she will be a good mother, why not adopt?"

Katherine's stomach twisted. An unnerving sensation rose within her, tingling up and down her arms. Though this testimony could help her case,

319

she fought the urge to walk up to the stand and yank the woman down. Shame her for talking about her daughter that way.

"Do not get me wrong," said Mrs. Sokolowski. "I love my daughter. All mothers do." Another shake of her head, her lips pressed tight. "She was suspended from her job last week. That has not yet come up." Mrs. Sokolowski raised her gaze to the ceiling. "She was unfocused, again. Made a large mistake. And then she came to us, asking us to come here"—she turned to the judge—"and tell you we would support her financially, in case they decided not to take her back. She assured us she would find a job, she would not need our support, she has savings." She placed her hand on the railing in front of her. "So why would we say it? Why would she ask? Because it looks good?" She raised her brows and her voice, the bright overhead lights making the moisture in her eyes glisten. "It looks good to lie?"

Kerra started to speak, but the woman interrupted her. "There is one more thing. The, uh"—Mrs. Sokolowski blushed—"egg that resulted in Rose. The treatment. This happened after her husband left her. She got a donor for the…male's part. I assume you know that?" The woman looked to the judge again. He nodded, his expression grim. "She was a single mother. No father for her child, no benefits, working at fast food, no support system in place. Living, I am told, in a hovel of an apartment." Mrs. Sokolowski paused. "What if the child had lived? What life would that have been? For her, for the baby. She did not think it through. She does not think things through. She lets her emotions control her actions. The intention to bring a baby into that situation, it…and it pains me to say this, to speak this way of my own child." She closed her eyes. "It was despicable."

Katherine looked at Tess, her head held high, her gaze straight ahead, her clenched jaw quivering.

55

TESS

Tess sat, her ragged fingernails digging into her palms as the judge left the courtroom and people stood, murmuring while they made their way out.

"Tess?" Messineo, already standing, leaned toward her. "It's just one day. Just—" He sighed. "Let's go get something to eat. We can regroup. Discuss."

Tess raised her gaze. "I'm not on the stand next time?"

He shook his head.

"Then there's nothing to discuss. You go. I need a minute."

He clamped a hand on her shoulder, gave it a gentle squeeze. "Don't worry, okay? This isn't over. One testimony isn't going to make or break a case."

But if that testimony was from the person who raised her? The person who should have been her prime example of what a mother should be?

Tess sat as the room emptied out, her body feeling as if it were about to crumple in on itself, her blood coursing through her, fast and strong and frantic. A whimper traveled up her throat, but she held it back, stood, made her way out of the empty courtroom.

She scanned the hall, the foyer, the parking lot. Across the lot, her parents were getting into their car, her father opening her mother's door, as he always did. She ran across the asphalt, shoes slapping loudly, grabbed her mother's shoulder, and spun her.

"Why?"

Time stilled as her mother stared back, shock and then resignation crossing her features. "Why did I tell the truth? I hoped by now you would understand."

"Don't you want Rose in your life? If you don't care about me, don't you care about her? Your granddaughter?"

"I do care." Jasia held her purse tight against her chest, as if Tess were a thief, apt to snatch it. "That is why I said what I said. Do not think I took pleasure in it."

"Then why?"

Aleksy put his hand on Tess's arm as if to draw her away.

She shrugged him off. "I don't understand."

"You have no moral compass. You make poor choices. If you will not protect yourself from those choices, protect your child, someone has to."

"Mama."

"Going to that clinic. A woman alone."

"I told you."

"I know. You told me. You had taken the drugs, your…eggs were ready. But you had an out, Theresa. You could have walked away. Worked on your life. Instead, you impregnate yourself by a stranger. A single mother. No way to make it work."

"People make it work." Tess put her hands to her temples, her throat afire. "They get pregnant all the time. I would have made it work. I *will* make it work."

Jasia looked to the sky. "I hope so. I hope you figure out your life,

Theresa." She leveled her gaze. "But maybe you should do that before you take on another life to care for."

Tess stepped back, the ground unsteady beneath her feet. "Why do you hate me?"

"I do not hate you." Her mother stood taller, held her purse tighter, as Aleksy tutted. "I am disappointed in you." She paused, her eyes filling. "I know about the late nights. The drinking. The men."

Tess stepped back.

"Jasia, this is enou—"

"Mrs. Dulski," said Jasia, ignoring her husband. "Her son is a bartender. He has seen you. A different man every time. Like a—"

"Jasia!" Aleksy moved his hand to Jasia's arm now, tried to direct her to the car.

"I don't do that anymore." A thick heat rose in Tess's chest as she imagined the word her mother was about to use. "I haven't in months."

"Because things are good? Because you are trying?" Now it was Jasia's turn to shrug off Aleksy's grasp. "Well, things are not so good anymore, are they? If you mess up again at work, and they fire you. If this trial does not go the way you want, or if it does, but in time things go bad again, as they will. Then what?"

"I...I wouldn't—"

"You have done much wrong, Theresa, and I would rather miss out on knowing my granddaughter than have her in an unsafe situation."

The blood drained from Tess's face. "And you say you don't hate me."

"I spoke the truth, Theresa." Jasia turned and stepped into the car before looking back. "Something I tried to teach you to do." She closed the door with a bang.

Tess looked at her father.

"Your mother, she shouldn't have... It's not right that..." He sighed, glanced at the car, then back at Tess. "It's not over, mój kwiatuszek." He put his hand on her cheek. "You are a good girl. The judge will see that. Just hold on. Have faith."

"Faith?" Tess scoffed. "In what?"

Aleksy half smiled, his eyes wet, his shoulders bowed. "Life, mój kwiatuszek."

56

KATHERINE

THE FOLLOWING MORNING, AS KATHERINE WAS PREPPING BREAK-fast, she reached for her buzzing phone.

"Are you sitting?"

"Tracey? Hello?" Katherine held the phone between her ear and shoulder as she secured Rose into her clamp-on high chair, the scent of yesterday's takeout still heavy in the air.

"Yes. Are you sitting?"

"No."

Tracey's voice sounded clipped, thinner than usual. "Log in to Halifax Vibes, then sit."

"I'm a little bus—"

"It's Tess." A loud sigh carried over the line. "She gave an interview. The legit news sites are already picking it up."

Katherine thanked Tracey, a cold sensation settling through her. She gave Rose her plate, reached for her laptop, searched for the podcast, and then clicked play.

"'Ess!" Rose exclaimed from her high chair. "Dat 'Ess?"

Katherine swallowed. "Yes, sweetie."

"See 'Ess?"

"Not right now," said Katherine. "Eat."

Hands shaking, Katherine grabbed her earbuds, opened the case, and popped one in.

"You think you're okay. Then a word, a look, a thought, and the pain rushes over you, erupts from somewhere deep within, and you're shattered, you're struggling just to breathe." Tess inhaled. She sounded broken, but in a sweet way, a way that garnered sympathy, her voice breathy and clear all at once. "And all around you, life goes on as if nothing has happened. One day you're carrying this little soul inside you, your body devoted to giving it life, and the next it's gone."

"Does it ever get easier?" the other voice asked. "Recovering from miscarriage?"

Tess paused, contemplating. "In a sense. I don't still cry every day. I can handle the sight of a baby or a rounded belly without shaking or needing to get away. But I'll always love them, always feel the loss." Another pause. "It's such an odd type of loss. Rather than missing all you've had with a person, it's missing and mourning all the dreams you had for the future—for them, and for your life with them."

Silence. Then the podcaster's voice. "I can't imagine. And so you thought, after losing Hanna, the baby from your final IVF treatment, your chances of being a mother were gone for good."

Katherine tensed.

"How did you feel when you learned your child, your true child, was still alive, being raised by another woman?"

Silence.

"Tess?"

"Hanna was my child, too. My true child."

"Of course, but—"

"I couldn't believe it." From the change in tone, Katherine could almost see Tess's expression shift, head raised and eyes shining. "Joy doesn't even begin to describe it. I had a daughter. A living, breathing daughter. I have one."

"And you knew the couple?"

More silence. Katherine's phone buzzed. She swiped the call away.

Tess, now hesitant. "Well, I mean—"

"I do my research."

"I, uh, I'd met them, yes." Tess was probably feeling the fear now. Wondering exactly how much the woman had researched, what she knew. Katherine's phone buzzed again. She dismissed the call and set it on Do Not Disturb.

"Mama? Mowr!"

Katherine stood and crossed the kitchen.

"I was hopeful," said Tess, her voice as tentative as she must have been. "Hopeful that would make it easier. That they'd be reasonable."

Katherine sliced up strawberries, plopped a pile on Rose's plate.

"And they weren't? I'm guessing not, seeing as I found you outside the courtroom for a custody case." Katherine set the food in front of Rose, sat again.

Tess's voice shook. "They're lovely people. I want to make that clear. And they've given my daughter a beautiful life. But she's *my* daughter." Her voice strengthened. "I tried to be reasonable. I suggested shared custody from the start, even said we could ease into it. But they wouldn't listen. They wanted her and they wanted me to have nothing to do with her. They offered me photos and letters a few times a year. That was it."

"Wow." The podcaster's voice dripped disbelief. "And they thought you'd stand for that?"

"I..."

Rose bawled, drowning out Tess's words. She'd been asking for something as Katherine listened to the podcast, and now, her patience gone, she banged her fist, knocking half the strawberries to the floor. Without a word, still trying to focus on the interview, Katherine scooped Rose out of the chair, not bothering to wipe her strawberry-covered hands and face, turned on the living room TV, and sat her in front of it.

"Don't you think it matters," the podcaster asked, "for your daughter to be raised by a woman who looks like her, a woman she can see herself in?" A pause. "The birth mother, she's a Black woman, isn't that correct?"

Tess faltered. "It matters that she's raised by me because I'm her mother. Katherine being Black has nothing to do with it. That's not what this is about."

She'd said her name. Katherine's skin tightened. She returned to the computer and clicked off the link. She couldn't listen anymore. Tess had said Katherine's name, though not her own. *IVF SWITCH MOM, WHO CHOOSES TO REMAIN NAMELESS, TELLS ALL IN THIS EXCLUSIVE INTERVIEW*, the post's subheading read. It was a mistake, Katherine knew, Tess saying her name. A bad one.

But it was a bad mistake for Tess. For their anonymity. Yet for the trial, it may be incredibly good.

Knowing she shouldn't, knowing it was unlikely any good could come from it, Katherine returned to her laptop after putting Rose down for her nap. Tracey wasn't kidding: CBC had picked up the story, CTV, Global News. Twitter was exploding. She saw her own face on the thread; scrolling down she saw Patrick's, Tess's. She navigated to Facebook and deactivated her account, where her picture had been stolen from. She returned to Twitter, scanned the thread. Some were sympathetic—to Tess, to Katherine and Patrick, to all of them. Most weren't.

50/50 split. Is that so hard! Save us our tax dollars. Stop the trial.

Kick the birth mother out of the picture. The biological parents should get together. Wouldn't that be destiny?

Katherine froze.

Maybe they are already! I'm sure I saw them chatting it up, all friendly, at the high school reunion gala a couple years ago. What was THAT about?

Katherine closed her eyes and breathed. It was speculation, only speculation.

They know each other? What?!? Are you sure the bitch didn't organize the switch herself?

Serves them right. Taking life into their own hands. That baby is a freak of nature.

Katherine shook, a cold chill settling over her.

Amen, sister. If a person can't conceive, it's probably because they shouldn't!

Of course that child should go with her biological mother. Save her from being raised by a—

Katherine slammed the screen shut, her breath shaky, her shoulders tensed. After a few minutes, she reopened the computer, reread the comment. She relaxed her shoulders, sat straighter, ignored the tremor shuddering through her. It wasn't the first time she'd heard that word directed at her; it wouldn't be the last. And she'd known it was coming, or would be if their identities became known. She kept reading the comments beneath the comment. Some censured. Some agreed in less hateful language, talking about culture, heritage, identity, self-representation. Others agreed straight out, no qualifications needed.

Katherine wasn't surprised. But she was afraid, a fear she'd tried to push aside from the moment she learned the biological truth. If these people, so many people, thought this way, the judge could, too. Perhaps on a level he couldn't even pinpoint.

Of course, genetically, Rose's complexion was perfectly possible. Katherine had seen mixed-race families with each child a different hue, but when she'd first looked at Rose, stared into the face of the child she'd so longed for, the fear had been there.

Katherine rubbed her hand on her forehead. She looked at the screen and kept reading, hoping for kindness, support, acknowledgment that what she was doing was right, that she deserved Rose exclusively. Those voices were few and far between.

57

TESS

TESS PACED HER KITCHEN FLOOR. SHE LET OUT A GUTTURAL YELL. She wanted to hit something, curl up in a ball, and sob. She returned to her computer, heard her own words sounding back to her.

She should have stayed silent.

The legit news sites had picked up the story, and social media was exploding. She drew her gaze back to the Twitter thread embedded on the main page, then scrolled as she took in more of it, hating herself for putting this out there, for being the one to reveal Katherine's name to the public when, all these months, who knew how many people had known and not let it slip. Someone must have tipped the reporter, but it was Tess who had just confirmed it publicly.

In the courtroom, as her mother spoke, disdain pouring out of her, Tess had held it together. Her palms became slick as she rubbed them beneath the shelter of the courtroom table. But she had sat listening, watching, a placid look on her face. Taking it.

And then, as she stood in the parking lot, watching her parents drive away, a woman had stepped forward, no camera, no mic held out, her voice kind, full of empathy…and Tess hadn't been ready. "I hear it got pretty rough in there," the reporter said. "Sounds like others are trying to tell your story." She paused, her head tilted, her smile genuine. "Would you like a chance?"

She had asked all the right questions, framing them with sympathy and understanding. No names, she assured, but it didn't matter; before the interview was even over, Tess knew it was stupid, throwing fuel on the bonfire of evidence questioning whether she was a fit parent. As the questions dug deeper, Tess was saying more than she meant, things she didn't believe. She heard her own voice, at times timid and sad, at times kind and composed, morphing to righteous and indignant. And underneath it all, pathetic.

Then that slip of the tongue.

She told the reporter she'd changed her mind, that she didn't want the interview aired, but with that same smile she'd worn in the parking lot, the woman, who Tess now realized was merely a podcaster, shook her head, told Tess it was too late.

Tess's screen lit up. Messineo. She swiped it away, continued to swipe as he called two, three, four more times. The supervised access worker's number flashed across her screen, then Mikolai's. She powered down her phone and looked back at her laptop.

She was selfish, stupid. Now, more than ever, she feared she was in danger of losing Rose. She read the comments again, those hateful, hateful words—she shook her head, tears building—*that* word. About Katherine.

Tess slammed the laptop closed. Her chest shook, her stomach knotted. She sobbed.

The next day, Tess rose early, taking the time to do her makeup perfectly, hoping to mask the sunken dark circles from her night of sobbing. She still hadn't turned on her phone, not wanting to see the inevitable texts and messages of shock and chastisement, though she could imagine much of what they said. When she got off the bus and approached the courthouse, her stomach twisted and she resisted the urge to turn back. Knowing the custody trial was now public, she'd expected the media to show up, but not like this. Crowds covered the sidewalk. News vans lined the street, and reporters flooded the parking lot, microphones up.

Tess noted the Mathesons' lawyer exiting her vehicle from across the lot. Kerra Campbell spoke to a group of reporters, and from the look on her face, Tess could imagine the sharpness in her tone. When Katherine and Patrick exited their car, the reporters turned on them. Kerra dashed over, trying to shield them with her body, barking at the story-hungry mass as the trio plunged through. With the media's attention distracted, Tess raced across the lot, then pushed through the doors, breathless. Inside, the comparable silence was deafening.

Tess escaped to the restroom and stood in a stall, waiting for her breath to settle, for the time to run out, so Messineo wouldn't have a chance to lecture her. When at last she stepped through the courtroom doors with two minutes to the trial's start, whispers erupted.

Tess walked to her seat, and as heads turned, she kept her gaze to the floor. The gallery was less crowded than it'd been a couple of days ago. Her parents were missing, as well as several people she'd assumed were Patrick and Katherine's friends or family.

As Tess approached the front, she kept her eyes downcast, fearful of Katherine's gaze. She slipped past Messineo, not looking at him, either, then waited with her hands clasped. With one minute to go, Judge Cormier entered. The room filled with the shuffling of chairs, feet, and clothing as everyone stood, then sat back down after the judge. The hush felt heavy. Cormier organized his papers, adjusted his seat, then looked upon the room.

"I would like to proceed as normal, but with the events of the last two days, I don't see how that's possible. It's been years since I've had to fight through hordes when coming into court. I am not a fan of it." He paused. "Even more, I am not a fan of a parent making a public record of matters that should be private." He turned his gaze on Tess. "Ms. Sokolowski, would you please stand?"

Tess obeyed; her legs trembled.

"As I am sure you know, one of the key factors I consider when deciding custody is maintaining stability in a child's life. Another is avoiding conflict. Although you are not legally prohibited from speaking to the press, I cannot see any way in which you thought parading your life, the life of the Mathesons, and most importantly, your daughter's would be beneficial to these proceedings. If you hoped to get sympathy for your plight, congratulations, you got it. Though not from me. To my thinking, a mother would want to save her child, her child's life and digital footprint from as much scrutiny as possible."

Tess swallowed, the urge to vomit rising as an even deeper shame settled in.

"Although this action of yours will not determine my decision, I want you to know it will certainly weigh on my considerations."

"Your honor—" Her voice squeaked.

"You will have a chance to speak during your testimony."

Tess stared at her hands.

"Anything you wish to say, you can say then. Please be seated."

Tess sat. A collective intake of breath seemed to suck the air from the room.

"Counselor."

They exhaled, and the trial proceeded. Patrick and Katherine's witnesses and character references appeared energized by the tension. Katherine seemed to keep their gaze when they looked her way, smiling as they spoke about Patrick and Katherine's years of trying, their strength as a couple, as individuals, the exceptional job they were doing raising Rose, a job they should be able to continue without having to figure out the complexities and stress of divided parental time.

Katherine must have chosen their witnesses carefully or kept her marital problems as secret as Tess had kept her own dark truths.

The witnesses who spoke for Tess had less to say. Mikolai spoke of her kindness, her tender heart, the love shining from his sister at the biweekly visitations. How it would be a sin to separate mother and daughter now that they'd formed a bond. Rose, he said, loved Tess.

He talked of her mistakes, which must have been a challenge after yesterday's huge one. "But we all make mistakes." His voice was calm, without the rambunctious energy it normally held. Tess imagined the disappointment coursing through him. "I know if I were on trial, there would be moments in my life, both before I became a parent and after, I wouldn't want scrutinized, used to judge my fitness." He paused. "My sister's not perfect. But she is Rose's mother." He looked at Katherine, smiled. "One of her mothers. And she should be in her life."

Carl spoke of her reliability, her attention to detail. Traits he imagined could translate to her role as a parent. "She made a mistake," he said, "and bad luck made it a disaster. Another day, another batch of samples, and it would have been nothing more than a reprimand." He shrugged. "It's due to the exceptional quality of work she displayed before this mistake that we didn't let her go. And to be honest, it would have only been a reprimand, not suspension, if the choice had been mine alone. Tess is smart and diligent, and before the stress of this coming trial started to affect her focus, she was one of my best workers."

Tess held her head to the side, hardly hearing, hardly registering, thinking, *Will any of this matter?*

When he stepped down from the stand, Carl looked at Tess, his smile sheepish, his shoulders slumped. *Forgive me*, his eyes seemed to say. Tess forced a smile, her mind telling her lips to rise, but the movement felt rigid, awkward, and grotesque. She was still reeling from her mother's words. Reeling from her own stupidity, from the rows and rows of comments she'd stayed up late reading, and from imagining all the words still to come.

What if she didn't deserve Rose? Even her mother thought she'd fuck it up if the judge was stupid enough to give her sole custody, which he never would, not now. She'd fuck it up, just like she fucked up her own life.

58

KATHERINE

FOLLOWING THE TESTIMONY BY TESS'S MANAGER, EACH LAWYER asked questions of the psychologist, seeking pointless explanations and expansions on what had already been a thorough report. The minutes ticked by, and yet a glance at the clock revealed they still had an hour before lunch. Katherine readied herself, knowing that after the character testimonies, she'd be called next.

Kerra had warned that Mr. Messineo would do all he could to make her look incompetent, press her buttons, present her as irrational or selfish, as the lesser choice. If he brought up the affair, she was ready. She'd decided she wouldn't out-and-out lie, but she'd get as close as she could.

As Katherine was preparing for her name to be called, the judge announced that a letter from one Saadia Medina—who was unable to be present but had been called as a witness by Ms. Sokolowski—would be read for the court record. Katherine sat back. She hadn't even realized Saadia and Tess knew each other beyond a patient-practitioner relationship. As Saadia spoke of Tess's qualities—the effort she'd made to ready her life, the joy and excitement she'd shown after learning Rose was her biological daughter, and then the way Tess talked about her time with Rose during their visits, how her eyes lit up with love—an odd discomfort settled in Katherine's gut. Saadia's treatments, maybe more than the team of doctors and nurses, had been the reason Katherine finally became pregnant, and here she was, stating she believed that Katherine's child should share a life with Tess...though not exclusively. She mentioned she knew Katherine, too, knew of the years she'd tried for a child, what joy Katherine experienced when that dream came true, and what a devoted mother she was, but that Katherine and Tess both deserved to be Rose's mother.

After finishing the letter, the judge looked at the clock. "Counsel, I believe this is a good time to pause. We will reconvene for the parents' testimony Friday." He nodded to the registrar.

"All rise while the Honorable Judge—"

Katherine leaned past Patrick toward Kerra as they stood. "What's going on?"

Kerra sighed. "Sometimes they do this, draw it out. It's a way of punishing the parents, upping their legal fees for not being able to figure things out on their own." She paused, neatly putting her tablet, papers, and pens into her briefcase. "I wouldn't have expected it with this case. Punishing Tess, perhaps, making her succumb to more of the media frenzy before her testimony."

"And us, too," said Patrick. "Ending it today would have been nice."

"You're slated for morning sessions." Kerra zipped her briefcase and stood. "You wouldn't have finished, anyway. That could be it, too, wanting to give everyone an even playing field. Wanting to make sure vigorous questioning didn't take us past lunch." She let out a laugh and shrugged. "Could be he needs to use the facilities."

As they made their way home, then picked up Rose, Katherine replayed Saadia's words in her mind. She hadn't spoken to Saadia once since the party at the center. Theirs was a professional relationship, sometimes they went years without communicating, but whenever Katherine thought of Saadia, it was with fondness. She was intelligent, kind, discerning, a good judge of character…and she thought Tess should be allowed in Rose's life.

Would Luela have recorded the love Saadia and Mikolai both saw? Each week, Katherine had accepted the visitation records, then filed them in her home office, not wanting to know what they held. After settling Rose down for her nap, Katherine stepped into her office. If she was ever going to read those records, now was the time.

Hands shaking, Katherine opened the cabinet, then set the file on her desk. They were just words, but words that would reveal a window into Rose's life that Katherine, until today, had known nothing about. Katherine read Luela's account of the first visit, the way Tess had seemed uncertain at first, but how she'd worked to relate to Rose, finding things to engage her, clearly working to play at Rose's level. *She's tender and patient,* wrote Luela, *and Rose, though somewhat hesitant at first, warmed to her surprisingly fast.* As the weeks went on, Luela talked about Tess's creativity, her obvious love and affection for Rose, the way she picked Rose up when she fell, comforted her when she cried. *She's one of the most attentive mothers I have ever seen,* wrote Luela, *never checking her phone, never seeming bored or distracted. She delights in Rose's accomplishments and takes obvious joy in making her smile, while allowing ample opportunity for Rose to display her independence.*

She wrote of Rose's increasing excitement for the visits, which Katherine had seen herself, of the obvious pain Tess felt whenever the visits ended. *However, Ms. Sokolowski hides it well, always working to assuage Rose's disappointment that the visit is at an end, reminding Rose she'll get to see her mommy (Mrs. Matheson) soon, and how fun that will be.*

Katherine looked up from the pages, a tremor in her throat, her eyes burning. After a deep breath, she returned to the pages. By the time the reports ended, before the visits fell to Mikolai's care, Rose was running toward Tess, leaping into her arms, overjoyed, and Luela was giving her opinion that a solid and important bond had been formed. One that should not be broken.

In the living room that night, Rose asleep in her arms because, knowing what she was about to do, she couldn't bear to let go of her, Katherine lifted her gaze to Patrick as he flipped through *The Hockey News*. "What if we're making a mistake?" she whispered. "What if it isn't the right thing, trying to cut Tess out of Rose's life?"

Patrick glanced up from the pages. "It's the right thing, Katherine. Based on how things are going, we may win sole custody. We're doing great."

But what were they doing, exactly? Tess had poor witnesses, made bad choices. And she and Patrick were letting all their loved ones unknowingly lie. The words from the visitation record kept floating through Katherine's head. All this time, Katherine had feared missing the moments—first step, first time riding a bike, first day at school. But they weren't for her, shouldn't be about her. No matter who witnessed them, Rose would have someone to cheer. Tess loved Rose. She'd witness, she'd cheer.

And Rose loved Tess.

"Tess is Rose's mother, too," said Katherine, the words still difficult to form, "whether we like it or not, and the past days haven't gone well for her."

"Because of the choices she's made."

"We all make bad choices," said Katherine, not speaking the one at the forefront of both of their minds. "It doesn't mean...doesn't mean..."

"Leave it to the judge." Patrick returned his gaze to the magazine, his jaw tense and twitching. "I don't even understand why you're talking about this."

Why was she? Because she was planning to go up on that stand tomorrow and confirm a lie. Because if she lied, and if Tess couldn't defend her actions, the judge might side with them. Because Katherine was realizing that if she did that, kept Tess out of Rose's life, she'd be keeping something else out of it, too: Tess's love.

"Isn't more love a good thing?"

Patrick raised his head from the magazine, set it in his lap. "What?"

"More love. For Rose. Wouldn't that be a good thing? The most important thing?"

Patrick sighed. "She has all the love she needs."

Katherine looked back to their girl. "But what if—"

"What are you even talking about?" asked Patrick.

In addition to the affair, Katherine thought of the intel Adee had gathered on Tess—the drinking, the multiple one-night stands that, based on the timeline, started with Patrick. Tess wasn't perfect, but Katherine and Patrick weren't, either. Katherine had been guilty of giving in to drink, too, in the months before IVF, when she'd hit rock bottom. There'd been nights Patrick had to guide her out of a pub or a house after what should have been a relaxing dinner with friends—friends who managed to pop babies out like Pez from a dispenser. Nights when he'd carried her up the stairs, pulled off her shoes, laid her on her side, and pulled up the sheets.

After all Tess had been through—the loss, the abandonment, the heartache—she must have felt that. At the bottom.

"I'm talking about stopping the lies, letting the judge know we have problems, too." Katherine's voice faltered as she gazed at their girl. "She's not ours, you know. Not mine. Not yours." She looked at Patrick. "We just get this short time to believe it, but she's not ours, no matter what the judge decides. Not Tess's, either. She never has been and never will be." Katherine pressed on, ignoring the voice within urging her to take back the words.

"It's more like she's on loan. No." Katherine shook her head, offered a slight smile. "Not loan. We get this gift of watching over her, guiding, molding, but she's her own person. And our job, our responsibility, is to do what's best." She hesitated. "I'm not sure that if we go up on that stand pretending everything's perfect, we'll be doing what's best."

Patrick shifted to sit beside her. "As I already said, we actually have a chance at sole custody. If you do this, we may lose that. Eventually, we could lose her."

"We could." Katherine's breath quickened, her conviction wavering at the fear behind those brilliant-blue irises. "One day. Maybe. Or this could be the thing that helps us keep her, prevents her from resenting—"

Patrick stood, threw his hands in the air, the patience he'd clearly been cultivating run out. "This is ridiculous. She's ours, damn it. Rose is ours. You're the one who's fought all this time, not willing to budge an inch, you're the one who's worked so hard on cultivating the perfect life, and now you want to air our dirty laundry? Now you want to let Tess in?" He paused, eyes narrowed at her. "Maybe this is just vengeance."

Rose shifted in Katherine's arms, whimpered as Katherine shushed, rocking her. Patrick stepped away from them, then turned back, his voice tight and low. "We may have a shot at keeping Tess out of our lives, or at least barely having to see her, and you want to risk throwing that away?"

Katherine swallowed.

"If this makes the judge more likely to go with shared custody, how are we going to deal with it? How are *you* going to deal with it? Seeing Tess at events, holidays, knowing, knowing…"

Katherine held Rose tighter as she felt the truth of Patrick's words, how horrible it would be. "We'd make it work. We'd be amicable."

Patrick stood rigid, his jaw tensed and trembling. He spoke quietly, but with just as much intensity. "This is crazy. *You're* crazy."

Emotion built in Katherine like steam rising to the surface. Her cheeks warmed with the hot tension bursting to escape. "I just… I'm just finally realizing, Tess *is* Rose's mother, too."

Patrick sat again, his shoulders slumped, his head in his hands. He looked up, his eyes moist.

"And yet all this time…" Katherine paused. "I've been thinking more about me, what I wanted, what would make me whole, when I should have taken myself out of the equation. Focused on Rose."

Patrick extended his hands as if in prayer. "We're what's best for Rose."

"But maybe—"

"I don't understand"—Patrick stopped, his voice hoarse—"how you could want Tess in our lives after—"

"I don't." Katherine looked again at Rose, then back at Patrick. "I want to make sure we're giving Rose the opportunity for all the love she deserves. Tess loves her, and she wants to be a part of Rose's life. That means something."

Katherine paused, her heart pounding, so much of her resisting. "I can't stand up there and lie in an effort to have Rose miss out on knowing her biological mother just because it'll be hard for me, for us." She squeezed her eyes, her smile wavering, her breath pinched. "As much as I'd like to, I can't."

Patrick rubbed the heel of his palm against his chest. He looked past Katherine, his gaze vacant, his voice flat. "If you do this, there may be no going back." He stood, placed a hand on Rose's head, staring at it, then turned away. "It may be the end."

59

TESS

TESS HAD DASHED OUT OF THE COURTROOM THE MOMENT THEY were dismissed, not wanting to hear Messineo's reprimands or Mikolai's worthless encouragements. In her haste, she'd forgotten the media, stepped into an onslaught as they barraged her with questions and accusations, snapped their pictures, and filmed her shame. They'd asked everything the commenters had about her divorce, the drunken club-hopping, leaving with a different man every night, her friendship with Irene, the fact she'd been seen talking and laughing with Patrick. They wanted to know what she thought of her daughter being raised by a Black woman. Beads of sweat popped along Tess's spine as she crouched to the ground, wanting to drown out their voices as they asked whether she'd get her daughter, whether she should.

A security guard had come to her rescue, helping her rise and then push through the swarming mass. At home, Tess spent the rest of the day into the next watching the news, reading the articles and comments underneath, a bottle of Soplica by her side. She turned off her phone. She kept her lights low. The story, just like the switch, wasn't merely local news. It was national. International.

Tess's name and face would appear whenever people searched cases like theirs—forever. Katherine's, too. She hadn't seen any photos of Rose, thankfully, and though several social media comments had used her name, the media hadn't.

But the story was there. In articles and newsclips, in social media posts and comments, in the memories of everyone they knew. The word that should never be used but had been a dozen times or more—that horrible word labeling Rose's birth mother—was there. Because of Tess. And it would resurface. All of it.

It was unconscionable. *She* was unconscionable; the judge had practically said it. Any chance Tess had of sole custody had vanished days ago, but still she held on to hope for shared.

If only the judge could look past her idiocy, see how much she wanted Rose, loved Rose.

Tess tipped the bottle of Soplica up once again, then brought it to eye level. Empty. It hadn't been full when she'd arrived home yesterday, but it'd been close. She stumbled to the couch, curled up.

Hours later, with the sun setting, her stomach clenching, her head pounding, Tess awoke. She searched her cupboards, her freezer, the hall closet, looking for more drink to numb the pain. She took two ibuprofen and an acetaminophen, then lay back down on the couch. Waited. The pain eased, but not enough.

After another hour, Tess stood, her head still throbbing, her steps unsteady. She needed out of this apartment, somewhere loud, to drown out the thoughts that beat upon her skull like a drum. *You're stupid and care- less. You're a failure. Your mother was right.* Somewhere she could numb herself just a while longer, forget, for just a few minutes. She pulled on an old T-shirt and jeans, slipped her feet into a pair of sneakers, and made her way to the door.

The sun had barely started to set. Children walked the streets, hand in hand with their laughing parents. Even if it'd been late enough, Tess wouldn't have hit any of her usual spots. She wasn't looking for a man. She just needed a place with no TVs, no well-informed people. A place to disappear. Walking along the harbor, she avoided the smiling faces of families in love, couples in lust, and paid her fee to take a ferry to the dark side.

The shiny new terminal shocked her with its gleam. She remembered a dingy port, homeless people and drug addicts congregating by the tracks. Just like the North End of Halifax, downtown Dartmouth had gotten a face lift.

Once outside, she saw young families and sharp-looking business people pass by but hoped she'd still find the sort of place she was looking for. She shouldn't, of course; she should go home. Shower. Spend the night racking her brain, trying to find a way to spin all of this, convince the judge she was worthy. But first she needed to numb the voice that told her she wasn't. She needed just one more drink, maybe two, to quiet her mind for sleep. Then she'd wake early, figure out how to script her defense, return to the courthouse with a prayer on her lips that all would be well, that the judge would have leniency.

She headed up the hill to a dive she'd only been to once, sat as the drink worked its wonders, quieting the voice, settling her limbs. It felt so good, one turned into two, then three, then she wasn't sure how many.

Tess raised a hand to the bartender.

He sidled over, a middle-aged man with a lean torso and muscular arms. He had a lilt to his voice. Irish. Or Scottish, perhaps? She didn't know. Didn't care. "Think maybe you've had enough, lass?"

Tess shook her head.

"Have some water."

"Just get me another." She paused at his raised brow. "Please."

He loomed above her. "Nope."

Tess pushed herself to standing. "Fine." She pressed a hand against his chest as she moved past him. "No more tips for you."

She tripped into the night, swayed past all the young shiny people, wearing clothes their parents wouldn't have been caught dead in. And the older ones, trying to remember their youth. When had Dartmouth become so…hip? She laughed, weaved her way back down the hill. The ferry terminal sat across the street, a boat just coming into port, but in front of her sat a cab, a passenger exiting. Tess leaned over, smiling. "Free for passengers?"

The man nodded.

Tess slid into the back seat and gave her destination. No sense waiting to get booted from another bar. While they crossed the bridge to Halifax, she gazed out the window. Mist hovered over the surface of the harbor as the city's lights cast long colorful streams of refraction, as inviting as a dream. Tess leaned back, aching for the taxi to arrive, for the moment she'd hold a bottle of vodka in her hand. Minutes later she paid the cabbie, then stepped out in front of her favorite liquor store, the rows of Soplica a straight shot from the door—meaning she didn't have to control her speech—or her sway—for long.

The five-block walk home, on the other hand, made the sway harder to mask. Tess cut through Gorsebrook Park, gripping the paper bag. She leaned against a tree as she watched teens in the dark—swinging, playing, soaring down the slides in their socked feet, surf-style, the shadows hiding their supposed shame at enjoying this thing society said they shouldn't.

Tess let the paper fall, opened the bottle without thinking, took a long swig. Would that be Rose one day? Afraid to stay a child, to let the world see she wanted to be young and free and careless. Would Tess miss it? Not be there to tell her to stay a child as long as possible, no matter what anyone thought? Tess couldn't remember that feeling of freedom. Fun, without the burden of responsibility, the world on your shoulders.

A girl with long blond hair and awkwardly thin limbs whooped as she flipped from the monkey bars, posing in an Olympic-style landing. Tess smiled. Drank. A boy who was so close to being a man pumped his legs until the swing buckled and jerked. He leapt into the air, landed in a mimic of the girl's stance, then lost his footing, rolled, and collapsed not twenty feet from Tess. Their eyes met.

"Hey, what're you doing?"

Tess straightened.

"Guys, there's some drunk over there. Staring at us."

Tess looked at the bottle, nearly half-empty. She shook her head. "No. I…"

The teens gathered around the boy, who, up close, looked more like a man than she'd realized. The blond-haired girl's face contorted in distaste.

Tess fled, not knowing what they'd do, say, not wanting to know. She cursed herself as she stumbled through the night, imagining one of those bright-faced youths recognizing her, snapping a picture. The Soplica slipped from her fingers, the glass shattering on the concrete, as she envisioned a picture of her, like this, plastered all over tomorrow's news.

She tackled the stairs to her apartment, pushed through the door. *Some drunk*, he'd said. She stared at her vodka-soaked shoes. She should have headed home after one drink, like she'd intended. She should have taken that water.

She'd told herself that the night after Rose's party was the last time.

She'd promised herself. Yet here she was, the night before her testimony, "some drunk" watching unsuspecting youth in the night. She'd do better. Be better. Maybe she *was* a drunk. Maybe she needed help. Alcoholics Anonymous or therapy. Tess collapsed onto her couch, the room spinning. She wanted to sleep, to fall over and never wake up. But more, she wanted Rose. Wanted to do whatever she could to ensure she got Rose...in some way, at least, for some of the time. She pulled out her phone, powered it on, and waited for the screen to light up. She ignored the missed calls and messages, struggled with navigating to the correct number.

It rang and rang. At last the automated voice, followed by a piercing beep. "Messineo." Her tongue wobbled over the word, so Tess spoke slower, enunciating carefully. "I'm just a tad inebriated." Her stomach lurched. She held the phone away; a false alarm, nothing but a trickle of bile. She drew the phone back. "So my apologies if I slur." She paused, determined to get the words out, speak them clearly. "I messed up. I get that. But I think we can reframe it, don't you?" Her head spun, her eyes watered, she fought to focus. "I can't think quite how yet. Perhaps I'll have a revelation in the morning. But if not, maybe you can? Lawyers are good at that, I hear." A tiny sob erupted. "I'm sure you can find some way to make it okay."

She hesitated, fear pushing through the drunken blur. "And if not, visits. Regular visits. Okay? Weekends. A few weeks on summer vacation. I want shared custody, fifty-fifty, but...there's probably no chance of that now, huh?" She held a hand to her head, willed herself to stay focused, awake. "So, if there isn't, the judge'll go for regular access, won't he? I'm not too far gone for that?"

The hot pain of resistance welled within her and streamed down her cheeks. Was she admitting defeat, to even put these words out there? To say she'd take anything less than the shared custody she deserved? Her voice broke, wavering as she pushed out each word. "Fight for me, okay...?"

She stared in front of her, the empty bottle from that afternoon fallen haphazardly to the floor. The tears coming harder now, faster. "Because right now, I have no idea what I'm supposed to say to fight for myself." A horrible sound burst from her throat. She ended the call, slumped to the cushions, the phone falling from her hand as her head landed on that undeserved softness. She sobbed into the pillows, hating herself, her failures, her weakness, until all that existed was the spinning, that horrible, sickening spinning.

60

KATHERINE

KATHERINE DRESSED IN AN ELEGANT BLOUSE, SKIRT, AND LOW heels. She styled her hair in a chic high bun. Her hands shook.

After a hug she let linger, her heart swelling at the solidness of her girl, the smell of her—honey and vanilla—she kissed Rose's cheek, her neck, then blew a raspberry. She thanked Tracey for babysitting, then returned to her car.

Rose's giggles still echoed in Katherine's mind as they walked into the courtroom. Patrick laid no hand on her shoulder or on the small of her back. He barely looked at her.

"You might not hear the decision today," said Kerra, "but it's the last day the judge will take evidence. Don't worry." She grinned at them. "Even if you botch the testimony, this trial's in the bag. Tess has done the work for you. Most she'll get is partial custody. Weekends. Maybe some summer vacation."

Katherine sat, her hands folded, her face forward, silent as she took in the muffled chatter from the gallery. She looked at Mr. Messineo. He sat rigid. He looked tired. Every minute or two, he turned his head toward the door. Each time, when he turned back, his anxiety seemed heightened. He rubbed a hand along the back of his neck. He checked his watch. Checked again.

Two minutes to start, and Tess's chair sat empty. The judge entered the room. All stood.

Judge Cormier sat, gave the word, and the courtroom filled with the various sounds of people taking their seats. He looked at Mr. Messineo. "Counselor, your client?"

"She should be here soon." Mr. Messineo seemed to fight the urge to look at the door once more, his body tensing.

"Should?"

"I...I'm not sure when. I have full ability to speak for her, to hear—"

"You do not have the ability to give her testimony, which is on the schedule for the day's proceedings."

"I know." Sweat beaded at Messineo's temple.

"Where is she?"

"She's uh...I think, well...indisposed."

"Indi—" The judge threw up his hands. "A medical issue? Is she in the hospital?" He paused. "Or the facilities?"

"Well, uh..."

"Is she in the building?"

Mr. Messineo stepped around the table. "May I approach the bench?"

Katherine leaned forward. Patrick leaned forward. The judge nodded.

Messineo approached slowly, then leaned in toward the judge as they conferred in whispers, the judge moving his arms in frustration and Messineo shaking his head, rubbing a hand through his hair. Less than a minute of discussion and Messineo retreated to his seat. The judge addressed the court, an expression of distaste altering his features. "Ms. Sokolowski might not be joining us this morning. Apparently, she was, by her own admission, in a state last night. Inebriated..." The judge paused, for effect or out of disbelief, Katherine couldn't tell. "And despite Mr. Messineo's efforts to contact her this morning, he's heard nothing."

A wave of nauseous disbelief passed through Katherine. She looked at Patrick. He rubbed his jaw and stared at her, presumably at a loss for words. Murmurs erupted behind them.

Judge Cormier cleared his throat. "Although we do not know the details of Ms. Sokolowski's absence this morning, she is absent, and there were inevitably poor choices made that led to this absence. Choices that, in light of the current circumstances and the other choices she has made, are very concerning regarding her interest in and ability to care for Rose." He looked first at Kerra and then Mr. Messineo. "We will forgo questioning of the parents. I feel there is little more their testimony could reveal to help me make my decision. However"—he turned his attention to Katherine and Patrick—"Mr. and Mrs. Matheson, as Ms. Sokolowski may petition for an appeal, I think it fair I give you each the opportunity to address the court for the record. Is there anything you'd like to say?"

Patrick shook his head, then spoke. "No, Your Honor."

Katherine opened her mouth, no sound emerging. Should she count herself lucky, continue with the deceit? No. Tess's actions, no matter how horrible, didn't make her own lies okay. She started to stand. Patrick laid his hand on hers, squeezed as he held it down.

"Mrs. Matheson?"

Katherine looked at Patrick. At Kerra. Straight ahead. She saw Tess's face in the photo album, gazing upon Hanna.

"Mrs. Matheson?"

She saw the words in the visitation records, felt again what she'd felt reading them. A mother's love.

"Yes." The word squeaked out. Katherine cleared her throat and stood. Patrick groaned. "Yes, I'd like to speak," she said, more clearly.

"By all means." The judge waved her to the stand.

"Katherine," Patrick pleaded as she stepped around him. "Don't."

Katherine hesitated, hearing the terror in his voice. The anger. The words he'd spoken last night: that this could be the end. But they had no idea what the future held. Eight months ago, Katherine may have feared a mistake at the lab, but she never would have imagined what had actually happened: a woman intentionally deciding to upend all of their lives. She had wondered if the reason would come out on the stand as Tess was questioned, but now she'd probably never know why Irene had done it, or if Tess played some role. And it didn't matter. What mattered was that Rose was here now, that, whether Katherine liked it or not, her daughter had two mothers who loved her. If Katherine wanted to be the mother Rose deserved, she needed to do what she believed was right. Avoiding Patrick's pleading gaze, she sat on the stand.

"I want what's best for Rose. We all do." Katherine turned to the judge. "I'll always be Rose's mother. But I think I've been afraid that Tess being in Rose's life, in any capacity, would steal that from me. Tess has made mistakes. Big ones." Katherine resisted the urge to look at Patrick, see his pleading, his fury. "We all have. I think you should know, when making your decision, Patrick and I aren't as perfect as our friends and family have made us out to be. Our marriage isn't. We have struggles. Big and small." She hesitated, then continued. "Rose and I recently moved out. We're back home now, for convenience, and if I'm to speak honestly, for appearances. But I…" She stared at her hands to avoid looking at the judge, at Patrick, at all the faces of the people who must be wondering what the hell she was doing. "I'm not sure how long we'll stay."

Judge Cormier leaned back, his expression registering surprise and something Katherine couldn't quite decipher.

"I'm not sure if we'll be able to work out our issues," said Katherine.

"We want to try. I want to try. But right now, trying for me means having time alone to think things through. To figure out who I am and what I want outside of being a wife, a mother." Katherine heard the words, and it stoked something inside of her, the act of speaking these thoughts aloud.

"Whether or not Patrick and I repair our marriage, whether we live together or apart, our love for Rose and our commitment to seeing she has the best life possible is solid—if that life is with us together, us apart, or shared with Tess."

Katherine looked at Patrick, the small shake of his head, the disappointment brewing. She looked at their parents. Hers had at least suspected they had problems, maybe even suspected the infidelity. His parents, though…she looked away. "We don't know what's best for Rose. I guess we can't know. Maybe no one can. But you're the one to decide." She swallowed, returned her gaze to the judge. "I wouldn't want to be in your shoes. None of us should have had to decide this, but here we are." She looked once again at her hands before focusing on Judge Cormier's eyes. "The important thing is Rose. Forget about me, what I've been through or will go through, forget about Patrick, forget about Tess. It's not about us. It's about Rose." Katherine sighed, her shoulders shrugging. "You know that. I know you know that." The tension in her chest faded, the tremor in her legs melted away. "I guess I'm just reminding myself."

61

TESS

TESS OPENED HER EYES, HER HEAD THE VICTIM OF A JACKHAMMER, her mouth dry as cotton, her bones battered by a deep ache. She pushed to sitting, her other hand pressing against her brow, wishing she could push the pain away.

Light filtered through the window, making the ache all the worse. She looked around and it all came back, the stupidity of going out the night before, thinking she could just stop at one drink or maybe two. She never stopped. She drank to oblivion. Always. She needed help. Professional help, most likely. Fully upright now, she let her elbows fall to her knees, her head to her hands. At least she'd woken early. She'd need a long shower this morning—to let the heat pound at her aching bones, then a switch to cold, to jolt her into alertness. She moaned, then reached for her phone to cancel the alarm. She clicked the power button once, twice.

"Damn it!" She stood, the jackhammer digging in, then ran to the kitchen, took in the time on the stove. "Shit!" Nine thirty-two, and she was due in court at nine thirty. She ran to her bedroom, then back to the living room, searched beside the couch and the chair, then back to her bedroom, where she found her charger beside the bed. She plugged her phone in, then flew to her closet, pulled out clothes—that she'd meant to iron, but couldn't now. She dressed in a frenzy, dashed to the bathroom. Her hair was a mess. Her mascara had made raccoon eyes around her own. She wiped and wiped, then pulled her hair up in what was a more-than-messy bun.

She ran to the phone, turned it on, waiting, waiting—three percent—enough to make a call to Messineo, tell him she was on her way. She pulled it away from the charger and raced to the door.

Tess stepped into the glaring sun. Shielding her eyes to adjust to the light, she hesitated as she looked up the road. A taxi was too unreliable; they could tell you five minutes and not arrive for twenty. She ran in the direction of the courthouse, feeling the strands of her hair flying free as she dialed Messineo's number, which rang and rang, and then cut off. She looked at the phone—dead again. She turned her gaze back repeatedly, hoping for a bus. Then, as she approached the IWK Health Centre, she realized there'd be taxis waiting to cart women and children recovering from surgeries and parents with their new bundles of joy to their desired destination. She changed her course and whooped with relief as she saw one idling. Sitting in the back, her knee bounced as she urged each light to change faster, inwardly cursing every time a yellow turned to red.

She closed her eyes, cursing, too, her own foolishness for heading out last night, for not stopping after one or two drinks, like she promised herself she would, for being the screwup she clearly was. She did have a problem. She must, to have done something so foolish. Her lip trembled, thinking of the trial going on without her, thinking how she would possibly explain this. But she wouldn't turn back now, despite what she'd done. She was going to that courthouse, wrinkled clothing, messy hair, and all.

Tess lifted her phone. Right, dead. But she could see herself clearly enough in the screen's glass. She tamed her hair as much as possible, then squinted at her reflection. It was too late to do anything about the bags under her eyes, the pallor of her skin. She set the phone in her lap as they approached the courthouse, all her focus on Rose, on saying whatever she had to say to convince the judge she wasn't as horrible as she seemed, that she still deserved her daughter; she loved her daughter, and love was what mattered most.

When the cab driver pulled to a stop, Tess didn't even glance at the reporters. She ran, keeping her gaze ahead, her focus narrowed.

62

KATHERINE

THE DOOR TO THE COURTROOM BURST OPEN. TESS RUSHED DOWN the aisle, her hair disheveled, a corner of her blouse untucked from her pants. "I'm here." She shuffled past Mr. Messineo and into her seat. "I'm sorry. I'm here now."

Judge Cormier narrowed his gaze. "Ms. Sokolowski, I'm afraid you're too late. I've decided to forgo testimony."

Tess's face fell. She looked crazed, on the verge of Katherine didn't know what. "Did you tell them?" She turned to Mr. Messineo. "Is that—" He shook his head, a somber expression on his face.

The judge turned his cutting gaze back to Katherine. "Mrs. Matheson, anything more?"

Katherine pulled her gaze from Tess, revulsion and sympathy at war within her. "No, Your Honor."

"Please take your seat."

Katherine walked to her seat, avoiding Patrick's stare.

"Mrs. Matheson," said Judge Cormier. "Thank you for your words. Your candor." He addressed the gallery. "I began this trial in distress, uncertain how I could make a decision in what seemed an impossible case, frustrated"—he turned to Katherine, Patrick, and Tess—"by your inability to show consideration for each other, but also understanding that you couldn't figure out this tragedy on your own. As the trial wore on, I saw more clearly the Mathesons' request, which I first viewed as unreasonable. My job, my role, as you stated, Mrs. Matheson, is to look out for Rose, to have her best interests in mind, always.

"Originally, I will admit, the possibility of cutting Rose off from one of her biological parents seemed unthinkable. However, with the events of the past days, the testimony I've heard, and the actions of Ms. Sokolowski—her failure to show up on time this morning, the decisions that led to this tardiness, and the choice to share her story with the media…not even the media, a glorified blogger." He paused. "With all of that, the judgment that best takes into consideration the interests of the child is no longer a difficult one."

Katherine's heart pounded.

Judge Cormier turned to Tess. "Ms. Sokolowski, please be aware you have a right to appeal this decision. If you make that choice, I don't recommend you waste either your own time or the court's until you have made substantial changes to your life." He addressed Patrick and Katherine. "Mr. and Mrs. Matheson, I grant your request in full. Sole custody of the child in question, Rose Matheson, is given to her biological father, Patrick Matheson, and her birth mother, Katherine Matheson."

Katherine blinked, unsure she was hearing the words.

"You are obligated," said Cormier, "to provide Ms. Sokolowski updates on Rose's life and development, letters and pictures at least twice a year, until Rose turns eighteen."

Katherine stared, dumbstruck, frightened that at any moment she'd wake and realize this was all a dream.

"I recommend," said Cormier, "for Rose's mental well-being, as soon as you deem her mature enough to understand, you tell her about Ms. Sokolowski. As it is beneficial for all people to understand where they come from, once Rose is eighteen, you are required to inform your daughter of her biological mother. The choice will be up to Rose whether she initiates contact."

Katherine had imagined, hoped, and yet this was no dream.

"If," continued the judge, "as time goes on, you choose to involve Ms. Sokolowski in some stronger way—invite her into Rose's life—that decision is yours. You have no obligation. You do not need to contact Family Services for guidance, although you may if you wish. There are many resources available." The judge cleared his throat. "Court is adjourned."

63

TESS

THIS COULDN'T BE HAPPENING. IT HAD TO BE A MISTAKE. TESS HAD sat, listening to the judge's words but not understanding. She had to be dreaming. At any moment she'd wake, hear words that made sense. But this was no dream. Tess had lost her daughter. She looked at Katherine, an amazed, almost dumb look on her face, then at Patrick, where relief and happiness radiated.

She turned to Messineo, pulled on his shirtsleeve. "Please. Tell him. Visits. I'll take visits." Messineo shook his head, removed her hands, started to speak. Tess pushed past him toward the judge. A muscular arm reached out, blocked her. Tess wanted to scream, to reverse time, to do everything differently. "Please. I can do better. I will do better. The visits. Just let me keep the visits. I'll be happy with the visits."

Judge Cormier looked down at her, staring at her as if she were trash. "My decision's been delivered, the registry will have the orders sealed, and—"

Tess looked around, stepped back from the guard who still clenched her arm. Her gaze latched onto Katherine's. "Don't do it!" she pleaded.

"Counsel! Your client—"

She could hear the ugliness in her voice, the desperation, but she couldn't stop. "You're stealing my child. She'll hate you for it. Please!"

Hands grabbed her, pulled her toward the door as she fought and moaned. She didn't even recognize the sounds coming out of her. In the hall she shook the hands off, saw herself the way these people in uniform saw her: disheveled, desperate, pathetic. She stood tall, looked to the courtroom doors.

Then Mikolai's arms were around her, telling her it was okay, they'd figure it out, but she pushed him off.

Messineo stepped toward her. "We can appeal."

She read the words on his lips rather than heard them, the world suddenly in slow motion. She turned, walked toward the exit, feeling as if she were walking out of her own body, leaving behind the person who, for months now, she'd believed she was. The person she'd hoped to be. At the courthouse doors, she wiped her hands under her eyes, down her cheeks, and pushed through. What a sight she'd been for the reporters as she ran in. What a sight she'd be now.

64

KATHERINE

A S SHE STOOD IN THE COURTROOM, A TREMOR SURGED THROUGH Katherine, followed by tingling pins and needles piercing her skin. Tess ran past them—yelling, pleading—then turned on Katherine, desperate, like an animal. It took two security guards to usher her out as Katherine stood, paralyzed with shock.

"Katherine!" Patrick threw his arms around her. "We won. She's ours. Rose is all ours."

Their parents moved toward them; Kerra clapped a hand on her shoulder. Patrick embraced her once more, then turned to his parents, to hers. Myriad arms wrapped around her. Rose was theirs. And they'd done it without the PI, without lying about their marriage, without doing anything at all to rub Tess's name in the dirt.

"She's ours!" Katherine laughed, jumped, hugged her parents back.

They left the building, walked through the crowd of reporters. "We couldn't be happier," said Patrick, his arm across Katherine's shoulder, smiling for the cameras.

"We'll have our life back." Katherine looked at Patrick, grinned. "So we'd very much like it if you left us alone. Let us live that life in peace."

Once away from the swarm, they stood in the parking lot, deciding where to go to brunch, laughing about how none of them had eaten well that morning—the nerves!

Less than an hour later, as Katherine sat, her family and Patrick's around her, her daughter beside her, the reality sank in deeper. They had won.

Katherine rubbed a hand along Rose's hair. She leaned down and breathed in the sweet scent of her girl. Up until last night, Katherine had stuck to her belief that she was the best choice, the only choice, despite everyone, even Patrick at times, thinking she was unreasonable—and she had won. She'd have to think about what she was going to do now that Tess had shown herself so damaged, so unreliable. If it would be the right thing to let Tess in—the right choice for Rose, not Katherine—and how she'd make it work, to keep her daughter loved *and* safe. She could take it slow, determine ground rules, figure out what she'd be comfortable with.

She looked at Patrick. Pure contentment beamed from him. She thought of his expression the night before, and then again in the courtroom, pain and anger and grief swimming across his features, tightening his voice. If she still went through with it, especially now, after what Tess had done, after the judge's decision, it could destroy what little hope they had left.

She could lose Rose, too, when she was old enough to decide who she wanted to live with, which mother to turn to with her fears, her trials, her joys. But she could lose Rose either way, because if she kept Rose from Tess, one day the pretending would have to stop. Rose would know Tess was out there, know she had another mother Katherine had kept secret.

But she didn't need to decide right now. Katherine leaned back in her chair, her family around her. Thanks to the judge's verdict, she had time.

65

TESS

TESS SAT IN HER APARTMENT, THE WEIGHT OF THE PAST HOURS clinging to her like oppositely charged ions. She winced, remembering the reporters' seeming glee at her appearance as they held out their microphones and cameras, asking for the verdict, asking why she'd come running into the trial almost a half hour late.

Her brother had saved her, his arm around her shoulder, whisking her away from where she'd stood frozen. Now he and her father sat on either side of her, each with a hand on her shoulder. Tess collapsed forward, in almost the exact position she'd been in this morning, but this time, her body racked with sobs.

Mikolai leaned forward, picked up the empty bottle of Soplica, held it in his hands. She didn't know whether he was staring at it or her and couldn't bring herself to look. "So it's true," he said, his voice barely above a whisper. "This is why you were late?"

Her eyelids clenched, her mouth hanging open in a silent cry.

"Mój kwiatuszek." Her father's voice now. "Why?"

Tess's cheeks quivered. Her lips. So many times in her life she'd thought she hit bottom, but this was it. The lowest she could go. She looked at her father, his moist eyes, then turned her face away.

Why? Because she was lost, broken in ways she'd never fully realized. She had to be. How else could she have done what she'd done? She was "some drunk," just like that kid said. And she'd lost her daughter because of it. The sobs returned and Mikolai pulled her to him, the bottle falling to the floor once more. He wrapped his arms around her, held her tight. "It doesn't matter why." His voice was loud, yet it wavered. "We're going to figure it out. We're going to help *you* figure it out. You're going to get through this."

Tess clung to him, wanting to believe it. Daring to hope. Promising herself that any time she was tempted to drown her sorrows again, to numb her pain, she'd think of this day, this moment, of how, through her own foolish actions, she'd lost her daughter.

A month later, Tess took in the well-adorned walls of her apartment, which seemed like the home of some other, better woman—a woman who'd thought her life was on track, that she had it all together. Tess hadn't… didn't. Not even close. But she was trying, and unlike before, she wasn't doing it alone. She'd seen a counselor three times now, and while sitting in that chair still made her writhe, she was learning things about her choices, her fears and hurts—where they stemmed from, how they influenced the choices she made each day. She knew she had a lot more to learn, that she hadn't even scratched the surface. She was thinking of going to Alcoholics Anonymous, on her counselor's recommendation, and had learned that an alcoholic wasn't necessarily someone who drank constantly, that, whether she associated herself with the term or not, she undoubtedly had an alcohol use problem.

And while something in her wanted to fight back, to say it wasn't true and she could have just one if she wanted—when she did have one, she knew from experience, she never stopped there. She likely had a sex use problem, too, said the counselor. It wasn't the sex, exactly, but the reason behind pursuing it when she did, in the way she did.

She still wanted Rose. That hadn't changed, and it wouldn't. But she also realized she had a lot of work to do in order to become the person, the mother she wanted to be for her. And, said the counselor, it started with little steps every day—some that were habit-building, some that required inside work. The habits were easier. The inside work…well, it was called *work* for a reason.

She'd been introduced to cognitive behavioral theory, had identified several of her "cues" for destructive behavior, was working on the motivation to change her reactions to those cues, learning that Rose, alone, likely wouldn't be enough.

Tess turned back to the table, a smile on her face, and lifted the paper that was the reason for tonight's festivities. Her acceptance had come. She would return to school in the fall, finish her degree, then get another, one that would ensure employment after graduation, a salary that would provide not only for herself, but for Rose, too.

When she felt ready, strong, and confident in herself, certain that if life got too difficult, she would have healthy ways of coping, she would appeal Judge Cormier's decision. She'd do it as many times as the courts allowed, being reasonable this time, not letting anger and vengeance get in the way, but sticking to her original plan—easing into shared custody—the plan she knew in her heart would be best for Rose. If they denied Tess, not allowing any access, at least if Rose came looking for her one day, she would know Tess had fought for a better life, fought for *her*.

The wait would be hard—the desire to see Rose a constant ache—but tonight would bring a healthy distraction. Mikolai and Karina with Aleksy and the kids. A barbecue in the backyard, with lettuce and tomatoes the children could harvest from her garden and berries for dessert. A celebration of Tess finally taking the step she'd been too scared to take for years.

Tess lifted her head to the sound of her doorbell. She set down the letter, then looked at the clock. Three hours early? She tightened her ponytail, dashed down the steps to the door, and yanked it open. She stepped back as if she'd been slapped.

Her mouth hung open. She closed it, painfully aware of her old T-shirt, her cut-off jeans. "Katherine. Can I, uh, help you?"

"Well." Katherine's voice shook; her smile trembled. She stepped aside, gestured to Rose, asleep in the stroller behind her. Tess lunged forward, drawn to her girl, then stepped back, hardly daring to hope, to dream. "We're on our way to the park," continued Katherine. "I thought you might like to come."

Tess stared, her breath coming quick, her chest a balloon, filling, filling, threatening to burst.

"You could push Rose on the swing." Katherine's voice cracked. "She likes that."

Tess's chin quivered. She nodded, her gaze on Rose. "Yes. Absolutely, yes." Tess stepped onto the path, stood beside Katherine, who moved back from the stroller to allow Tess to grasp the handles. They walked down the street, Tess's knuckles tight, her focus on breathing calmly, on the fact that her daughter was less than two feet from her. She glanced at Katherine, who offered the slightest smile.

"You're looking good," said Katherine. "Better."

"I'm doing better."

Katherine nodded. "Mikolai told us."

"Mikolai?"

"That you've been working on yourself."

"Is that why—"

"No." Katherine answered before Tess could finish the question. "No, it's not."

They walked on, Tess's gaze ahead, her chest tight with wonder—fear, too. "Has your lawyer been pushing you—about the lawsuit?"

Katherine nodded. "Not pushing, but it is something we should talk about at some point. Not today."

"Uh-huh." They crossed Robie Street, down to Gorsebrook Park, where Tess had stood before those young people, drink in hand, as low as she could get. She turned again to Katherine.

"You can wake her," said Katherine before Tess could speak. She gestured to Rose. "Put her in the swing."

Tess's face quivered. She locked the stroller, circled around, rubbed the back of her finger against Rose's cheek. "Wake up, sweetie," she whispered. "Time to get up." Rose shifted, still half asleep, her lids fluttering, her cheeks rising in a pressed-lip smile. "Wake up." Tess jiggled Rose's hand.

Rose's eyes opened; she focused on Tess, confusion and then recognition shifting her features. A smile spread across her face as a laugh burst out. She stretched her arms. "Tess!"

Tess lifted Rose out of the stroller. With eyes shut, she hugged her close, breathed her in, her body so full she could hardly contain the emotion. Tears slid down her cheeks as she reveled in the feeling of those tiny hands around her neck. Tess opened her eyes and looked at Katherine. "I don't understand." She exhaled through the tears. "I thought you hated me."

Katherine's lips formed a soft smile as her eyes grew moist. She shrugged. "Rose doesn't."

AUTHOR'S NOTE

Dear Reader,

In Canada, where I live and where this book is set, infertility affects one in six couples, and the stats are similar in other countries. Yet so many of us find it hard to talk about. We're ashamed or embarrassed or simply feel broken. We do all we can, trying to take control of our fertility, but so often, there's very little we can do.

If this is you, please remember you're not alone. For too long, I felt like I was the only one going through this. For too long, my infertility and losses were something I couldn't talk about. However, once I did start opening up, I was able to find so much more strength. I connected with people who were going through similar experiences, which helped, as we were able to go through this struggle together.

If this is you, I hope this story has helped you feel seen. And please remember, there's support out there, whether it's through an organization such as Fertility Matters Canada or online support groups, or simply through talking with the people in your life.

If infertility or pregnancy loss is not one of your struggles, I hope this story will help you see and support the people in your life who've experienced this unique pain.

Either way, I hope you've enjoyed this book. If you did, it would mean so much if you took the time to leave a rating and review on Goodreads or your favorite online retailer. It may not seem like a lot, but reviews are SO important to the success of an author. They help us find new readers and ensure we're able to continue writing books for you to enjoy for years to come. Even more important, your words could be the ones to help readers discover a story that could lift them from their struggles for a few hours or potentially transform their lives.

I love building relationships with my readers, so if you'd like to keep in touch, please sign up for my newsletter at charlenecarr.com/HMG. When you do, you'll receive a free e-novella that will give you some backstory to one of the characters in *Hold My Girl*. After that, you'll receive (mostly) infrequent updates about my upcoming books, sales, and general writing life.

If social media is more your thing, you can find me on Facebook, Twitter, and Instagram—but Instagram is where I spend most of my time.

Read on, my friend.

Charlene Carr

READING GROUP GUIDE

1. Although the switch at the clinic would have greatly affected Patrick—just as the years of infertility did—we see very little consideration throughout the novel of how he's handling everything. Do you feel Katherine was selfish in carrying this as her burden and tragedy rather than truly seeing it as Patrick's too?

2. Patrick's infidelity was a huge shock to Katherine; that Tess was the person he was unfaithful with, an even greater one. What role, if any, do you feel Katherine played in Patrick's betrayal? Is there room for forgiveness and moving on together, or was the betrayal too deep? The book's ending doesn't indicate whether Katherine and Patrick will try to "make it work." Do you think they should? Why or why not?

3. As a result of the story's setting (and Katherine's socioeconomic status), the fact that Katherine is a Black woman who gave birth to a white child who is not biologically hers played a fairly minor role in the novel. This would not have been the case in many other parts of the world. How do you feel the same story would have played out where you live, and why?

4. Tess has had incredible pain and trauma in her life, which has led to poor decisions and a reliance on alcohol to dull her pain. Do you feel confident she's had the breakthrough she needs to become the type of mother who can keep Rose loved and safe, or do you hope that (in the imagined future) Katherine is extremely cautious about the boundaries she places around allowing Tess into Rose's life?

5. Both Tess and Katherine experienced feelings of brokenness during their years of infertility and felt like they were disappointing not only themselves but also the people in their lives. How common do you think it is for women to feel like this, and what can (or should) society do to support women through this very unique pain? What do you think—for the most part—society gets wrong in this area?

6. Tess hypothesizes that if she'd just been honest about being raped, so much of her life might have turned out differently. Despite the #MeToo movement and the conversation about sexual assault transforming over the past few years, do you think that many women still keep silent about sexual harassment and assault? Why? And what do you believe needs to change for more women to speak up?

7. At its core, *Hold My Girl* is a novel about motherhood. What, to you, makes a mother? And what should determine whether a person is entitled to raise a child, be it their biological offspring or not?

8. Did you find yourself relating to either Katherine or Tess throughout the story? Did you hope one woman would "win" sole custody of Rose?

9. When you learned that Patrick's infidelity was with Tess, what was

your reaction? How did you think the story would play out after that reveal, and how did it color the previous interactions among the three characters for you?

10. *Hold My Girl* has been optioned to be adapted for TV. Who would you like to see play Tess, Katherine, and Patrick? Why?

11. At the beginning of the novel, Tess seems to be a bit in awe of Katherine. How do you think that affects Tess's initial decisions? At what point do you feel that shifts for Tess, and how does that affect the power dynamic between the women?

12. Katherine is presented as a hard-core perfectionist, but there is certainly a lot in her life that's far from perfect. How do you feel the image she tries to portray to the world conflicts with reality, and how might her life have been easier if she hadn't tried to portray the image she did?

13. Would you want to be friends with either Katherine or Tess? Why or why not?

14. The book ends with Katherine inviting Tess to spend some time with her and Rose, but she offers no promises about how much time or whether a visit will happen again. What do you think of this ending? Do you hope Katherine lets Tess have a regular role in Rose's life—maybe even shared custody?

15. After you finished the book, what struck you the most about the story, and how did you feel?

ACKNOWLEDGMENTS

There are SO many people who played a role not only in the writing of this book, but in getting it into your hands. So, in no particular order…

To my dear readers, thank you so much for your emails and reviews and for supporting my writing. When the days pursuing this dream felt too hard, it was your words that gave me the motivation to keep going, to stick with this goal of not only being a writer, but of finding a way to make a living from it. My stories are for you.

To my amazing agent, Hayley Steed: Your belief in this book and your commitment to not only making it the best it can be but getting it into the most hands possible has been the greatest gift. You have very literally changed my life and the life of my family, and I couldn't be happier that we found each other. To the incredible team at Madeleine Milburn Literary, TV & Film Agency, you have been a wonder. Particular thanks to Hannah Ladds (dramatic rights agent extraordinaire!), Elinor Davies, Giles Milburn, Valentina Paulmichl, and Georgia McVeigh.

To my editors, Iris Tupholme, Rachel Hart, and Kate Roddy: I'm so glad each of you fell in love with this story, and I can't thank you enough for all your work in helping to make it what it is today. A huge thanks, also, to the teams at HarperCollins Canada, Welbeck Publishing, and Sourcebooks Landmark.

To authors Julianne MacLean and Shauntay Grant, thank you for opening my eyes to the possibilities in store for a fellow Nova Scotian author. You expanded my view, providing inspiration, advice, and answers to probably far too many questions! I appreciate you so much.

To Lawrence Hill, thank you for your guidance and for always being so gracious and generous with your time and advice. From our first meeting over a decade ago, you've been a source of inspiration for this fellow mixed-race Toronto kid.

To Heather Marshall, my agent-sister, thank you for all the emails and Instagram chats, and for guiding me through this journey to traditional publication.

Thanks, also, to the many wonderful authors from the Women's Fiction Writers Association and Write Around the Block who've offered support, encouragement, advice, and inspiration.

To my mother, the first reader of all my books, thank you for reading and giving feedback on five iterations of this novel! And for the time you've given me to write—the hours and hours telling stories and playing games with my daughter through video calls, so I could write and revise without feeling that I was neglecting my girl—no thanks would ever be enough.

To my beta readers, Dawn McCrea, Nancy Grist, Vanessa Dugas, Clare Hawksworth, Tanya Slessor, Sharde Davis, Victoria Fernandez Suratos, Lydia Collins, Marsea Nelson, and Kay Petrini: Thank you for your time, your insights, and your excitement for this story, even in its earliest (much longer!) form.

To the kind volunteers who assisted with my research: biologist, former lab tech, and dear friend Laura King; embryologist and laboratory director Megan Dufton; lawyers John MacMillan and Deanna Huclack; and Vicki Cobb, a foster parent who shared her knowledge of social services and supervised access in custody cases. I hope I got things right! Any mistakes, inaccuracies, or changes related to artistic license are mine alone.

To Jeanna Cammarano and Barbara Kluge-Rodgers, thank you for the hours and hours you spent listening as I talked about this story (through writing and revising), searched for an agent, and went through the submission and publication process. Your friendship and enthusiasm have meant the world.

To Peter, my husband, my partner, my friend: Thank you for such unwavering support as I've written my stories these past seven years. Thanks to you, I never had to be a literal "starving artist." You've given me time, encouragement, a roof over my head, and food in my belly. I know I've given you so much, too, but I am super glad your "investment" in me is finally paying off. 😉

To my girl: This story never could have existed without you. You're my joy, my inspiration, my reason for getting out of bed each time I had to say goodbye to the siblings you'll never meet. Thank you for defying incredible odds and being the only one of my many children I've been able to hold in my arms. Thank you, also, for being one of the coolest, funniest, and kindest people I know. I love you.

ABOUT THE AUTHOR

 CHARLENE CARR spent much of her childhood creating elaborate, multifaceted storylines for her dolls and reading under the blankets with a flashlight when she was supposed to be asleep. After traveling the globe working an array of mostly writing-related jobs, she decided the time had come to focus exclusively on her true love—novel writing. *Hold My Girl* is her tenth. She lives in Nova Scotia, Canada, with her husband and young daughter, and loves connecting with readers. If you'd like to see if Charlene can join your book club for a virtual visit, please reach out at contact@charlenecarr.com with the subject: BOOK CLUB REQUEST.